HALE

HALE
THE RISE OF THE GRIFFINS
A NOVEL

JK NOBLE

NEW YORK

LONDON • NASHVILLE • MELBOURNE • VANCOUVER

HALE
THE RISE OF THE GRIFFINS
A NOVEL

Published in New York, New York, by Morgan James Publishing. Morgan James is a trademark of Morgan James, LLC. www.MorganJamesPublishing.com

Publisher's Note: This novel is a work of fiction. Names, characters, places, and incidents are either products of the author's imagination or used fictitiously. All characters are fictional, and any similarity to people living or dead is purely coincidental.

Morgan James
BOGO™

A **FREE** ebook edition is available for you
or a friend with the purchase of this print book.

_____

CLEARLY SIGN YOUR NAME ABOVE

Instructions to claim your free ebook edition:
1. Visit MorganJamesBOGO.com
2. Sign your name CLEARLY in the space above
3. Complete the form and submit a photo
   of this entire page
4. You or your friend can download the ebook
   to your preferred device

ISBN 978-1-63195-555-6 paperback
ISBN 978-1-63195-556-3 ebook
Library of Congress Control Number:
2021904060

Cover Design by:
JK Noble and
Chris Treccani
www.3dogcreative.net

Morgan James is a proud partner of Habitat for Humanity Peninsula
and Greater Williamsburg. Partners in building since 2006.

Get involved today! Visit
MorganJamesPublishing.com/giving-back

Thank you, G-d, my mother, uncle, my grandparents. I am so grateful for your boundless, unconditional love and support. I wouldn't be where I am now without you.

ACKNOWLEDGMENTS

Thank you to my wonderful editor, Kevin Anderson. And thank you, David Hancock, for your enthusiasm, support of my vision, and your publishing team.

Thank you to my grandpa in heaven, Amnun, and my beautiful grandma, Roza—the two people I ran home to every day. You taught me right from wrong, the meaning of family, and true love. And thank you to my uncle, Rubin, who I always looked up to for your righteous character and good heart. You spoiled me rotten, and it is because of you that I love everything I love.

Huge thanks to my gorgeous, genius, wonder-mom, Rina. You have supported each of my creative outlets since I was three and pushed me to become the best version of myself.

Thank you, G-d, who made sure to give me his undivided attention, for surrounding me with the best people who mold me into the greatest version of myself. I hope I make you proud and do what you put me on this earth to do.

DARK SHIELDING PROPHEC[Y]

BLAND'S SECRET PLACE

TRUE DOME

BANSHEE FOREST

ELDER'S DOME

THE STAGE

THE GRIFFIN CLAN

PRIESTESS SANCTUARY

N
W E
S

ARKETCHA TRIBE

THE EXTRODINARY DIVISION OF MALPHORA

LIGHT

ARDOR

ENDURANCE

MARCUS'S COTTAGE

KINGDOM OF BIMMORUS

OBSERVATORY

ACADEMY

ROYAL PALACE

EMSEQUET

BREATHING BAY

ISLES OF NEPENTH

GORGES OF NAVMALA

TEMPLE AND CEMETERY

PROLOGUE

January 5, 1720

Flickering torches line the hall, illuminating the three shadows that creep through. A midnight-black sky camouflages the snowfall behind the paneled windows. Felix, Bayo, and Greon pass the hall in great haste, unseen by all. The gift of illusion is Greon's. As a master of this power, Greon can will all eyes before him to see whatever he dares to imagine. In this case, he has made himself and his companions invisible. But he has overlooked one minor detail . . . their shadows.

Greon's forehead wrinkles, his eyes shifting while his body shakes. Felix looks down at the pendant in his hand, which he'd enchanted to beam an amber blaze as it got closer to their treasure. There is no change in his contraption, and the veins in Felix's neck throb with frustration.

The windows rattle from the storm, and Greon springs up at the sound. At once, his eyes fly to Bayo to see if he noticed his embarrassing moment, but Bayo is preoccupied.

Bayo examines the pendant from the corner of his hungry eyes for it is *his* treasure the three are after. In pursuit of this treasure for nearly a century, Bayo found that it had been hiding here in a neighboring kingdom. The moment he knew where it was, there was no time wasted in retrieving it.

"We're nearly there," whispers Felix.

"Hush now," says Greon. "I cannot conceal sounds."

"Hush thyself. I hear you quivering from over here," Felix says.

Greon glares at Felix. "I would not be so distressed if *your* wretched footsteps were not booming in these halls!"

Felix turns to Bayo. "Isn't it astonishing that the person whining about the noise is making all the racket?"

Greon's enraged interjection cuts off as his face gives a great twist. A mighty wail, desperate to escape, is released in a mutter past his clenched jaw. Beside him, Felix fares the same. This is Bayo's gift, the gift of anguish. He can will any victim to experience immense physical torment. *Endurance*, his people call it. This gift is superior to all, and Bayo, the master of this power, is also the master of his people.

Bayo stands before them and watches with heavy eyes as his companions are forced to their knees in the physical agony that he inflicts on them. With Felix's loosening grip, the pendant falls with a clank. Bayo snags it from the sparkling stone floor.

"Are you children finished? Or shall Greon conjure the image of both your mothers?" Bayo says, leering toward the pair.

At that moment, a group of men approach the entrance behind them. On the other side of the door, a man stutters in hysteria, "Sh—shadows, sir! Walking about. I've never s—seen such a sight! Spirits walkin' among us, sir!"

At once, Bayo stops using his power on his companions to listen in, and Greon and Felix slowly pull themselves to their feet.

"How many were there? What did they look like?" asks another man, his voice steady.

"There were three, sir," the first voice says.

Bayo's eyes widen in horror. "You imbecile!" he whispers, cursing Greon. Greon hastens to fix his mistake, but it is far too late for that. The three begin to run.

The guard then asks, "Which way did they go?"

"Through these doors!"

They freeze once more.

"Through the window!" Felix says frantically, recalling the swords that disable magic in this nation.

Bayo snaps his head to meet Felix's eyes. "I'm not leaving without it!" he hisses with rage. He worked too hard to find it; the one weapon that could be used to invade their nation . . . and conquer the worlds.

The double door behind them crashes open with a bang. In the doorway stand five armed guards, peering through the hallway. But they see nothing. The guards walk through the corridor with waiting swords that ring in the proximity of any magic. Bayo, Greon, and Felix back away quietly until their backs are pressed against the white stone walls. The guards' swords begin to buzz.

The cold of the stone sends shivers up their spines. Yet, Bayo's hand grows warm. He looks down at the amulet in his palm; his face is illuminated with an amber glow. His heart skips a beat. *It's close!* Bayo walks on despite the approaching guards, searching for a door, anything besides these endless halls. However, even around the bend, no exits appear.

Greon presses his back against the ice-cold window, his brow slick with sweat as he struggles to keep up his illusions while managing his panic. A guard passes by him, only an inch away, yet he notices nothing.

The guards then pass Felix, who stands across from Greon. He clutches the stone, trying to keep still and out of their way.

"What's that ringing? There is nothing here," says a guard, staring at his pulsating sword.

The superior of the royal guards answers, "Ah, it's The Eyes."

Bayo's lips curl into a smirk as he begins to pat the wall silently. *It's here . . . somewhere.* The swords are nearly brushing against his back. If they were to touch him, he would be temporarily cleaned of all magic, including his power of Endurance. Long enough to be killed. But Bayo keeps on. He knows there is something here, a trick to the wall that hides his prize behind the stone. He continues down the hall silently, all the while patting the shimmering stone with the warm pendant in his hand. Finally, at the end of the corridor, his hand falls through the wall.

"Calling five guards on Lorain's Day!" scoffs the superior of the royal guards. "As a witness to shadows in the night! Go home, men. There is nothing here." With that command, the guards exit with a slight murmur.

Felix and Greon peer around the bend in search of Bayo, but he is nowhere in sight. They come to a dead-end, utterly dumbfounded.

"What on Malphora?" mutters Felix as he holds out his arm to touch the wall at the end of the corridor. His arm passes through it completely and without feeling. He and Greon share an astonished look. Neither has experienced such magic before. They both walk through.

The air beyond the corridor is warm and inviting, unlike the brisk winter they left behind. They stand on black earth lined with magnificent rock structures below a brilliant sky with stars and constellations they have never seen before. In the distance are strange planets so large they seem to be a short flight away. At the horizon, a blazing orange sky fades into pink, then blues and purples. There are no clouds, and the air is entirely still. A gentle hum echoes through this strange world. Although Felix and Greon stand here for only a moment, it is evident this mystical place is alive.

In the distance, they see Bayo's figure approaching a great white light in the center of this strange world. Once Bayo is close, the objects emitting the dazzling light emerge. They are three glassy orbs, each the size of a palm, floating several feet from the ground. They spin slowly and continuously, as if they were in one another's orbit. Each orb represents an existing world. Through their glass-like forms, one can make out the world within.

The Mythical Three Eyes.

Bayo beholds the orbs in their beauty, his arms extending out to touch what he has so long searched for. *This* is Bayo's treasure.

Felix and Greon stand behind him. The strange world echoes with Bayo's chuckle. Sound moves differently here—more slowly and in clear waves.

"I've crossed the ends of the earth, and finally, I've found you," he whispers, a rapturous grin on his face. Bayo touches one with the palm of his hand, and it feels as though the world stops.

The magnificent starry sky turns black. The orbs' light lessens altogether, and their rotations pause. All is still for a moment until the rocky earth beneath them begins to tremble.

Felix shouts to Bayo, "We must leave!" He and Greon turn around, but the expanse of land looks all the same, obscuring the way from which they had come.

"Do not fear, friends," Bayo calls. "Come closer. These orbs are our salvation. See here, Malphora, our world, bountiful and beautiful in every way."

Malphora is most commonly known as the realm of the humans, though it is also home to the extraordinary, as they call themselves. Although both humans and the extraordinary share Malphora, the ancients of all the extraordinary nations created a divide between the two regions of the world to protect their people. To accomplish such a feat, they used the oldest magic in existence: The Three Eyes and the oldest Tree in Malphora. Thousands of years passed, and neither humans nor the extraordinary could pass through the divide between worlds unless they had the orbs or the location of the oldest tree.

Bayo touches the orb of Malphora and chortles as the air before them rips open in a long gash. A portal. Through the gash is an image of a pristine beach with waters so clear the sand beneath is visible. Rays of sunlight pour through it and into the now black world Bayo stands in. Cooing birds and crashing waves seem only a step away.

"The human divide," Bayo mumbles.

Without a moment's hesitation or fear, Bayo stuffs the orbs into a large sack and throws it over his shoulder. The earth begins to quake beneath their feet. And yet the portal remains open.

Greon and Felix jump through the gash, and Bayo follows before the portal closes. As soon as they've gone, the earth they had stood on but a moment ago falls into oblivion.

CHAPTER 1

July 1, 2020

The only way to tell time inside the cellar is by studying the sunlight, which pours through a large crevice in the brick wall. Two ragged bodies sprawled across the cement floor watch as the light fades. They share a troubled look, knowing what horrors the evening will bring. One of the bodies is Hale, a young man, sixteen years of age. He extends a heavy arm to his older sister, Carly, and the shackles that bind him rattle. His cuff digs further into his skin, and he bites his lip. Carly reaches out for him as well, wrapping her arm around his shoulders. He can feel her shivering.

Carly must sense his worry. "Hale, I'm fine. Just a little cold."

Carly's once plump, berry-colored lips are now a sickly shade of purple, and her cheeks have lost their fullness and color. Under her eyes are heavy, dark circles. It is hard for Hale to look at his older sister this way, recalling the beauty she once possessed.

Grabbing the blanket that they share, Hale throws it over himself and his sister. He pulls himself closer until his head rests on her bony chest. As he moves, his left arm dangles above his head; the three-foot chain connecting him to the stone wall is not long enough. His iron shackles press deeper into his open skin, but Hale tolerates the pain as warmth finally radiates between them.

To their left, the door above the stairs opens with a light screech, and candlelight from the floor above pours through, illuminating the dark cellar. The cellar is bare except for two large buckets, one in the far corner for defecating, and the other beside Carly, filled with water for drinking and bathing. The shelf to Carly's left holds two bathing rags, two glasses for drinking, and a few candles—which were lit and replaced at sunset.

A man walks through the door and locks it behind him, descending with slow, lumpish steps. Hale knows this man only as his abductor. Carly, on the other hand, would have dared to call him family in another life. His somber eyes, the color of deep waters, droop with lack of sleep. His lips quiver as he lights the candles on the shelf.

Carly takes a deep breath and removes her arm from around Hale's body. The abductor halts before her, and they lock eyes for a long moment.

Watching the two staring at one another is off-putting for Hale, but he is clueless about the fact the two are engaged in a telepathic conversation.

Carly senses the lack of the man's mental barrier. He has not taken the potion he regularly uses to keep her telepathic gifts at bay. She understands this as an invitation to enter his mind, that he has something to say to her and only her.

We've wasted enough time, Carly. Bayo needs him to come back home, says the man.

If you were in my place, would you give him to Bayo? she counters.

His life is not your concern. Bayo is his rightful guardian, he declares.

I will not destroy his life for that reason.

At least tell him. Give him a choice, he pleads.

The less he knows of our true identities, Greon, the better. He still has a chance to live a good life.

Your stubbornness will only bring you strife. Greon sighs and kneels down to unshackle Carly from the wall.

Hale's stomach turns as the man touches his sister's wrist, and he lashes out, kicking him in the leg. "Don't touch her!"

Greon ignores Hale's blow and gazes at the fearful young man.

Those eyes puzzle Hale ever more, for Hale could never understand how a person with such kind eyes could act so maliciously. Hale watches in horror as Carly is pulled from the ground with a tight grip on her forearm. Her legs falter beneath her, the cement scrapes her knees.

As Hale's rage intensifies, he recalls Carly's words just a few hours prior. "When he comes for me today, do nothing. Stop fighting, Hale."

Dumbfounded, Hale had retorted, "Do nothing? He wants to kill you!"

She had shaken her head. "No, he doesn't. He would have done it already. Hale, listen to me. Don't push him to hurt you. Close your eyes and do nothing until it's over."

"If we don't fight, we will never escape."

"Fighting won't do us any good. We are too weak to fight. We need to be smarter than that."

Ignoring his sister's words, Hale had continued to try to slip through his cuff like he was able to do a few evenings ago. However valiantly Hale thought he fought against his kidnapper those nights prior, his efforts were futile, and as punishment, his arm was burned with a hot piece of metal.

Now Hale watches his sister kneel before this man as she is struck down with a heavy hand across her face. Her hair goes flying in front of her. Hale shakes and pulls at his shackles, fresh blood trickling from his wrists. It is no use. They are tighter than they used to be. Tears overwhelm his eyes with every passing bang and moan. He tries with all his might to heed Carly's words and not look. For a long moment, there is no noise, and Hale opens his eyes, assuming it is over for the day. Instead, he sees his sister on the ground, the man crouching over her with his hands at her throat. Carly kicks her legs and tries to pry his fingers from her neck. The sound of her gasps fills the cellar, and suddenly her arms fall to her sides. Hale screams.

Greon releases his hold on her neck. The marks of his hands are on her throat. Tears pour from his eyes, but he is quick to wipe them so Hale will not see. He stands up as Hale screams, turning his back to the boy completely. He can't face him now after what he's done.

Hale's sobs echo throughout the cellar, and he scrambles to his knees, trying to reach out to his sister.

"Carly! Wake up! Wake up!" His heart pounds from his chest as he shouts her name. He pulls on his chains, but she is too far. Through his flowing tears, he cannot tell if she is breathing. He wails at the man, "What do you want from us?"

Greon simply stands, his expression melancholy. Hale looks up at him, waiting for something, anything. But Greon gives no answer.

"What do you want from us?" Hale asks again.

Greon doesn't respond.

"Why won't you kill us?" Hale whimpers. "End it already!"

Greon lifts Carly into his arms and carries her back to her place to the left of Hale. He gently lays her down and begins to shackle her wrists. Hale quickly takes her unshackled wrist in his sooty hands and checks for her pulse.

"She's alive," Greon says. It is the first time he has ever spoken to Hale. Hale is shocked. Greon's voice is soft and quiet. "I need something from her, and, therefore, I cannot kill either of you."

"What do you need?" Hale asks. "I'll give you whatever you need. Just *please* let us go."

The man kneels down to unlock Hale's cuffs, and Hale's heart leaps with hope. As Greon pulls at the metal, Hale's skin tears from the places it's bonded it. Hale whimpers, and Greon continues on with a gentler hand.

Then Greon gravely responds, "You cannot give me what I need." He pulls Hale up and pushes him toward the large tin bucket to the right.

Hale screams, "No! No! Stop—please!" He tries to fight his way free, but Greon overpowers him. Hale is forced to his knees, and his head is pushed into the bucket.

Hale fights the grip at his crown, straining his neck. He begs in panic, "We'll give you anything you want. Please! You're not an evil man!"

Greon hesitates before he flatly says, "You know not what you say." He pushes Hale's head down.

Hale's arm thrashes, and he hits the brim of the bucket in panic. But Greon pins Hale's hands behind his back. For a brief moment, Hale's head rises from the water. He inhales deeply and gasps, "Please! Stop!" But Greon pushes him under once more. Hale's gurgling rings in his ears.

"Do you see what you have forced upon me?" Greon shouts. "I've waited patiently for you. I shall wait no longer!"

"Stop!" Carly manages with a hoarse voice. "You cannot kill him."

"No. That I cannot do. But how long are you both to suffer from this pain? Shall I keep you for an eternity?"

Hale feels his head becoming light. Unable to hold his breath anymore, he exhales. Hale frantically scrabbles at the bucket, and in his fit, he manages to wiggle his left arm free, snagging the pocket of his assailant. Out from this pocket, something falls with a slight clank. Greon tries to regain control of Hale's arm, and Hale's vision dims to black.

The water stills, and Hale's body is limp. Greon pulls Hale from the water and rests him on his back. He turns Hale's head to the side and presses on his chest until water spews from his mouth. Calmly, Greon places Hale back beside Carly and shackles his wrists once more.

He turns to her. "Give me what I need. I will no longer hold back. You both cannot take much more of this. If not for your life, do it for his."

She pulls Hale into her arms and checks his burning forehead. "Then you will have condemned us either way."

He sighs while climbing the stairs. "You are giving me no choice."

She looks at him with disgust, her voice weak and frail. "You've told yourself that for hundreds of years. Do you truly believe you are not a monster?"

There is click as the door locks, then all is silent.

CHAPTER 2

Greon obsessively works over a large wooden desk. He writes as fast as his mind works, all the while mumbling bits of incantations he ought to use. The room is lit by candlelight, some on nearby candelabras, others scattered across the room. The cabin is lined with oak from ceiling to floor. Beside the living room is a bedroom in the corner, the shadow of a small cot visible from Greon's seat.

Greon's hands grasp the roots of his hair as he looks over his notes. "No. No. It can't be this. I'd have to remove the Nymph's Dew for it to . . ." He crosses his writings.

⁕ ● ● ● ● ⁕

Down below in the cellar, Hale wakes. Carly is lying over him to warm his cold, wet body, and he squeezes her tightly.

She smiles. "Guess what?" Before Hale can respond, she whips out a set of keys. Her wrists are unshackled.

Hale gasps.

"They fell from his pocket," she explains. "We're getting out of here. Tonight."

After she unshackles her brother, they creep up the stairs and crouch beside the door. Hale holds his hand out for the keys, but Carly places a finger to her lips. Voices sound in the room beyond.

∘ ● ● ● ● ∘

Right above Greon's desk comes a voice, startling him half to death. "What progress have you made?" He jumps and his pen flies behind him. The voice chuckles, "Honestly, Greon, you should be used to my visits by now."

Greon sits back in his chair and looks up at the levitating window above the desk, its oval rim clouded with smoke. In it is Bayo.

∘ ● ● ● ● ∘

Hale presses his ear against the door and whispers, "That other person's voice . . ."

Goosebumps rise on Carly's forearms before he'd even finished his sentence.

"It's so familiar, isn't it?" Hale continues.

"No," Carly says at once. "I've never heard it before."

The sound of the voice replays in Hale's mind, calling him to find a memory lost in the void.

Carly eases Hale away. "Let's wait until he falls asleep."

∘ ● ● ● ● ∘

Greon rests his arm on his chair and covers his mouth. "She is reluctant, Bayo," he says. Bayo's cheerful expression turns ferocious. His eyes narrow dangerously.

"But I've made progress on my own," Greon adds hastily. "I shall try this cure tonight."

"You mean the paper whose contents you just crossed out?" Bayo asks sarcastically. Greon looks up into the window.

"Yes, I believe I'm getting closer to the answer," he assures Bayo. Fierce pain courses through his body, and he gasps, grasping the back of his chair. Greon's knees buckle, and slowly, he sinks to the floor, holding in his screams.

Bayo fumes, "Ah, but you see, that is what you've said to me for the last three months since you've captured them. And what you said to me since before then as well."

Gritting his teeth, Greon manages, "Yes, but remember it is I who found them, not only once but twice since the incident. And I've captured them on my own. I have done well by you, Bayo. I suspect in no time at all I will have ready what you require."

"You are too soft on her. I should have sent Rioma to do the job."

"Soft! I have done everything you asked me and more to try to persuade her, going against my every instinct to do your bidding!"

"What is your instinct?" Bayo asks with a biting tone. "Setting them both free to make a muck of my plans?"

"She is Felix's daughter!" Greon counters. "This isn't *easy* for me . . . nonetheless, she won't be able to go on for much longer." Suddenly, a sense of relief washes over Greon's body. He rises to his feet.

"May your words hold value, Greon," Bayo responds coolly. "I have been gracious to you with my time. Think of your Mary and Ianna."

Greon replies in a whisper. "Yes, they are the reason I do your bidding."

Bayo laughs. "There will never be an escape from me, old friend. I will always find a way to get what I desire."

Greon purses his lips. "And once you achieve even that, you will desire more."

"I always did appreciate your honesty," Bayo says with a smirk.

"Carly refuses to tell him the truth. Why don't I do it?"

"No, Greon. It is not your place. Leave such matters to me." Then the portal vanishes.

• ● ● ● ●

Hale and Carly keep watch for nearly an hour, waiting until the candlelight fades from the crack beneath the door. Then a set of footsteps shuffling above their heads makes its way to the end of the house. A plop sounds on a spring mattress, then all is silent.

"A little longer," Carly says in a rough whisper. "Don't fall asleep."

Hale nods, his heart beating feverishly. He notices Carly's bruised neck and shaking hands, marks of her bravery.

A half hour passes, and Carly signals Hale to make their way up the steps. He creeps behind her. At the top, she turns the key in the door as carefully as possible. It opens. Hale is suddenly lightheaded as Carly scans the room. Finally, she signals him to follow her.

The cabin is old-fashioned. There is no electricity. The only light comes from the moon peering through the window and shining on a desk stacked with leather-bound books and loose papers. On the way to the door, Hale glances over the papers written in purple ink. They are written in a strange language—and yet, miraculously, he is able to read it.

He mumbles the words written at the top, "Antidote for Blood Protection against Magic." Carly grabs his hands and pulls him along. Atop a counter is a dagger, and Hale snatches it impulsively before they leave.

They run. They are finally free.

Carly darts for the woods several yards away with Hale right behind her. A light gust of wind washes through the clearing, and a sharp squeak sounds from behind them. The front door! They hadn't closed it when they left. Carly rushes back to the cabin, attempting to prevent it from shutting with a bang.

But it's too late.

Carly locks eyes with her panicked brother. "Run," she mouths, dashing to the trees. She sprints with a limp, clutching her bruised rib cage. They just make it to the trees when the door reopens, and Greon storms out from the cabin clutching a dagger. He spots them in the distance and bolts after them.

Panting heavily, Carly commands, "Hide behind the trees." Carly and Hale sink into the darkness of the woods as cautiously as possible. Hale peers over to his sister several trees away, and swallows. She brings a finger to her lips. He nods. There is a rustling.

Greon enters the thicket. "Come back, and no harm will come to either of you!" he shouts. Then internally, *Carly, don't do this.*

She responds in his mind. *Please let us go.*

But he could not let them go. An image of Mary and Ianna floats through his mind, and Carly understands.

Hale's blood pounds in his ears, and he takes in deep breaths to keep calm. He hears Greon breaking twigs nearby, getting closer and closer to his hiding place. Hale focuses on his breathing. In and out. In and out. His palms feel sweaty on his dagger, and he tries not to think of all that is at stake.

Suddenly, a cool blade is pressed against Hale's throat, and a strong hand grabs his upper arm.

Hale spins around and kicks Greon in the stomach. Greon releases him, clutching his beaten torso. Hale's kick carries him off balance, and he falls. As Greon advances once more, he can see the fear in Hale's eyes and the dagger shaking in Hale's hands. Greon slows his approach. "Come now, we both know you won't hurt me," he says.

Hale spots his sister's silhouette behind Greon and throws his dagger to her without a thought. She catches it. As Greon turns, Carly attacks.

She slashes her knife downward, but he backs away just in time. Their knives clash. Hale rises to his feet, bewildered by his sister. He watches in shock as Carly and Greon dance around the woods, skillfully dodging one another's blows.

Carly moves to stab Greon, but he catches her arm and twists it, forcing her back to him. As she struggles to break free, she falls into his dagger that he had pointed toward her with his free hand. The knife enters the left side of her lower back, and she falls to her knees, crying out in pain. Greon's hand still clasps the dagger. Carly's back is stained red with blood.

Hale rushes to his sister and screams her name in horror. Before he makes it to Carly's side, Greon grabs the hysterical boy. He wraps his arms around Hale's torso, pulling him back toward the cabin.

Hale's body shakes with adrenaline. His eyes blur at the sight of Carly's lips slick with blood. A wave of fierce anger pulses through him, and Hale's vision turns black. Suddenly, Greon wails in great agony and drops Hale.

Carly.

Hale jolts to his feet and runs back to her. He finds her resting against the base of a tree trunk. She holds her back, trying to contain the flow of blood, tearing through the pain.

"Hale," she manages. "I don't have a lot of time . . . don't be afraid."

His eyes well up as he moves her to look at the injury. "It's not that bad. We can go get help."

"Listen to me," Carly says urgently. "Your amulet. Do you still have it?"

He nods, his tears flowing freely.

"Good," she coughs. "Never take it off. It is the only thing protecting you now. Do you understand?"

He nods again. She smiles and holds his hand with both of hers, and Hale is disturbed by the lack of strength in her grip. "Promise me you will live a good life." Her wet blood smears his palms.

His body heaves, the forest echoing with his sobs.

"Promise me," she says again weakly. Unable to breathe, she wheezes.

"I pro—I . . . I . . . I promise," he stammers. Her hand slips from his, and her body slides down the trunk. Her head falls to the side. "N—no. Carly! Don't leave me!"

His sobs grow heavier with each breath. He buries his head into her chest, rocking back and forth in an endless motion.

"Please."

CHAPTER 3

Bayo stands over an oak table with his palms pressed against its surface. He watches with intensity through a window that levitates over the Three Eyes, observing the events taking place in the Human Division of Malphora. There are no images shown in the orbs of Carly and Hale. They are invisible, protected by an unknown magic he had ordered Greon to destroy.

He stares as Greon lifts a dagger to the void and slashes at the air repeatedly, as if he is fighting himself. If it were any other match, Bayo would have found the scene comical. But not now. Now there is too much at stake for humor.

Bayo's pale skin grows paler as his brown eyes pierce into the orbs. "Deor!"

A moment later, the door behind him opens, and a tall man enters.

"Come quickly!" Bayo commands. With steady steps, Deor comes to stand beside Bayo. "Tell me what you hear."

Deor is of the power of the Dark, like Carly, and he is the strongest of his kind. Using his gift, he can read minds as well as manipulate them. Although Deor can read thoughts through the orbs, as much as he tried, he has never been able to manipulate a person through their image in the orb.

"Greon is fighting the girl," Deor says, rubbing his long jaw. "She and the boy escaped while Greon slept."

Bayo's face reddens.

"Greon has injured her . . . there is another person; I assume the boy. Greon has him in his grasp."

They stare into the window, and at that moment, Greon's thoughts go blank. Then an expression of great pain comes across his face.

Bayo's eyes widen in shock. "His powers are active!"

They watch as Greon falls to the ground. A moment passes, and Bayo roars, "Deor!"

"There is a faint consciousness. He is reviving. He is thinking, but no thoughts are clear enough to understand." They wait a moment longer. Greon's arm jerks, then he is completely still.

Deor steps closer, and Bayo turns to him, fuming.

"That's impossible," Deor says coldly.

"No, no, NOO!" Bayo screams.

However, Deor is certain. "He is dead."

Bayo howls in anger, and his power surges through his body like electricity. Deor falls to the floor in agony until Bayo's rage ebbs.

* ● ● ● ● *

Greon had forgotten he'd been holding the dagger until Carly shrieked in pain. *What have I done?* He couldn't let her die, not if blood magic bound her life to Hale's.

As if in slow motion, Hale rushes toward Carly. This is Greon's chance to pull Hale back into the cellar and take Carly right after. He needs to make haste so he will have time to save her life and Hale's.

A mighty surge courses through Greon's body as he pulls Hale from Carly. Hale had stopped fighting his way free and stands frozen. His eyes glow a blazing white. Greon's pain is so electrifying that he falls on his face, paralyzed in agony. The shock would have killed him if it weren't for the potion Greon drank earlier that day. It was the same potion he drank every day for quite some time, dulling the effects of the power of Endurance. A power Hale and Bayo shared.

The light from Hale's eyes dims, and he runs back to his sister.

Greon has never experienced such strength from an Endurance Griffin, not even from the great Bayo. It takes several moments for Greon's pain to subside. It is clear to Greon that though Hale's powers were unknown to Hale himself, they are stronger than the High Elder of Endurance. But more erratic.

I have a great opportunity here. He removes a small vial from his breast pocket and drinks its contents. This particular potion is able to prevent those who wield the powers of the Dark to enter his mind. *I could create the illusion of my body staying lifeless on the ground while I make myself unseen. Then I can catch them off guard and bring them back to the cabin.* As Greon rises from the ground, a perfect likeness of his still body remains where he lay.

Greon approaches Hale and his sister and catches the sight of blood. His stomach sinks. *Is it too late?*

"Listen to me," Carly was saying. "Your amulet, do you still have it?"

"Yes."

"Good. Never take it off. It is the only thing protecting you now. Do you understand?"

Greon's eyes widen. *Felix, you genius!* Hale's life was never bound to Carly's. Months of trial-and-error spells were, evidently, time wasted.

Greon watches as Felix's daughter dies. He stares as Hale clings onto the girl he believed to be his blood sister.

"N—no. Carly! Don't leave me!" Hale cries, burying his head into her lifeless chest. His sobs are heartbreaking.

Greon could take Hale this very second. This was his chance to finally bring him back to Bayo. All he has to do is rip off Hale's necklace to remove his protection against magic.

Instead, Greon stands there, thinking of Felix, his old friend, and how he and his daughter sacrificed their lives to keep Hale from Bayo. Greon looks at the illusion of his own dead body, and his mind begins to spin. *I could be free from Bayo—if I can recreate the pendant.*

Once Hale falls asleep, Greon creeps back to his cabin.

⚬●●●●⚬

Hale wakes up at dawn. At first, he doesn't remember a thing until he opens his eyes and sees Carly's flat, white body. He screams and runs from the woods, sobbing. Reeling through the trees, he trips. He stays on the ground shaking until his crying subsides. After pulling himself to his feet, he walks back to the cabin.

Greon notices Hale through the cabin window and immediately makes himself invisible. Hale takes the shovel resting against the cabin and returns to the woods. Greon is in awe of this young man. He watches as Hale picks a spot in the field and digs.

In the late afternoon, Hale walks back to Carly. When Hale passes the illusion of Greon's dead body, he clenches his fists and forces his eyes away. He tries to lift her, but he is too weak. Fresh tears stream along his face. He drags her by her hands instead. He pulls her out from the trees and across the field. Her body leaves a trail of blood.

He lays his sister beside the hole he prepared, positions her hands gently on her sides, and lies beside her. *She looks like she's sleeping.* He stays with her for some time, memorizing her face, the color of her hair, and the small birthmarks on her arms.

Finally, he sits up and bursts out, "I don't want you to go!"

But despite this, he steps into the hole, takes her in his arms, and pulls her down in it. He climbs out and pushes his bare hands in the shoveled dirt. He hesitates.

Burying his face in his knees, he whispers, "I can't do it. I can't do it." But he pushes the soil into the grave, and it falls over her. His heart breaks with every push.

When Hale finishes, he runs away from Carly's gravesite, through the woods and farther. He stops at the sound of rushing water and stumbles upon a pristine stream. He sticks his head in and swallows his fill. Afterward, he let his body fall in, and he stays there, letting the water lap over his skin.

●●●●●●

It is midafternoon that same day when Greon lifts a black pendant in his hands. He ties a wire around it and forms a necklace, placing it around his neck.

He yanks a strand of his hair to try a locator spell to check if the pendant works. The locator spell gives no trace of himself at all. "It works!" Greon hisses.

He lets the illusion of his dead body evaporate.

"A thousand years! I'm free!"

CHAPTER 4

A thick fog descends from the sky five mornings later. Beside the stream is a dewy triangular shelter made with sturdy branches, leaves, and mud. Inside it, sticking his feet out to warm up beside a smoldering fire, is Hale, drifting in and out of sleep. He is shivering despite the hot air. Beneath his wet, matted hair, his eyes shift as he sleeps fitfully.

In his mind, he relives that night over again. Images of a knife in Carly's body jolt him awake. Half-dazed with exhaustion, he hopes it was just a dream. When he looks up to see his shelter, he remembers it wasn't.

He rolls onto his side, his arms wrapping around his chest as he cries. *We should have never left that cellar. I should have made sure the door was closed. It was my fault.* He wonders what their kidnapper could have possibly wanted from Carly. More so, he wondered why she refused to give it to him. Was it worth the sacrifice? *It must have been worth it.* But it seems he will never find out.

How did his kidnapper die? Had Carly done it while Hale blacked out? She must have. She must have saved his life.

He wonders whether he should stay here beside the stream. He's free now to leave, to go anywhere. *But where would I go?* He begins to convince himself that the cabin is a better option than staying out here in the mud. But he shuts down the idea almost immediately. *I'm never going there again.* Tears pour down his face. *Never, ever.*

•••••••

Greon makes notes as he hunches over a large hand-drawn map that takes up the whole surface of his desk. His shoulder-length blond hair falls over his face while he ponders the limited possibilities he has to reenter the Extraordinary Division of Malphora. Creating a portal without the Three Eyes between the Extraordinary Division to the Human Division of Malphora is futile as long as the division remains. Even so, creating a successful portal would take ingredients that are not found in this part of the world.

I only have one option. Greon rolls up the map and places it under his arm. There is no time to dally. The longer he waits, the greater the chance that Mary and Ianna might become victims of Bayo's wrath—unless they proved themselves useful.

He stuffs all necessary contents inside a leather bag: a flask filled with water, a loaf of bread wrapped in cloth, fresh meat of the deer he had recently hunted and wrapped, and then throws his bag over his shoulder. He also packs two more pendants similar to his own and Hale's that he hides within his breast pocket. They are too valuable to keep anywhere else. He is about to lock the door, but thinking of the boy, he leaves it open.

The sun is setting, the sky painted in colors of vivid oranges and reds. The grass is alive in a vibrant shade of green. Greon walks deep into a secluded part of the woods. The trees are so hefty and plentiful that the sky above cannot be seen.

Everything is still and silent; not even the birds chirp. Greon understands this silence all too well. *They* were watching him.

Out into the void, Greon shouts, "I am Greon, Elder of the Light of the Griffin Clan. I am in need of your assistance." There is no response. "Please," he pleads, "I know you can hear me. You are my only chance of returning home."

He looks around in search of a sign and waits. "We share a common interest. I assume you would not like to live under the tyranny of Bayo, leader of the Griffin Clan." A moment of silence passes. "You are expendable as long as the Three Eyes are in his palm! Do you think you will survive much longer?"

The wind had not passed through the woods, yet the trees start to sway and there is a great chatter above where the leaves brush together. Hundreds of murmuring childlike voices sound throughout the forest, growing louder and louder.

The voices whisper from all directions of the woods. "Greon."

"Greon."

"Greon."

Greon looks around, but he sees no one.

"You wish to return to your home?" they ask.

"Yes," he answers. "Bayo holds two people very dear to me as hostages. He uses their great powers to fortify his own. Once removed from him, he will be too weak to complete his mission."

The trees whirl violently, and the voices whisper to one another. "Why should we help you?" they say. "You could be lying to return to your master."

"I have freed myself from his rule. He thinks I am dead. A thousand years I have given in service to him. No longer will he be my puppeteer."

One voice exclaims from among the soft chattering, "You are *bad*, Greon, Elder of the Griffin Clan! You have hurt people in the shrine built from our kin!"

Greon's body stiffens.

"We've been watching you, Elder Greon of the Griffin Clan. Your spirit is as corrupt as your master. You dare come to nymphs spitting cheap lies?"

The existence of the nymphs surpasses any magic. Their spirits have existed on Malphora since the dawn of time. They are all connected to one another. Thus, they are connected to all places in the world, including the Extraordinary Division of Malphora.

"Yes." Greon hangs his head. "Everything you say is true. I have hurt innocent people on behalf of my master. But as soon as I found a way to free myself from him, I did. I have no proof or evidence of my words. But I will do anything to free my family. Anything." There is a long pause as the trees continue swaying. "He will begin his plan at the next full moon. He has already lost his most valued weapon. And me. If he loses my wife and her child, who are necessary to achieve his goal of conquering all of Malphora, he will self-destruct. He will be ruined forever."

An airy, childlike voice speaks out, and the trees stop swaying. "Even if we were to help you, only a spirit can travel to and from the bounded destinations of Malphora. A spirit," the nymph says, "not with its body."

Greon's heart sinks, "Do you mean—"

The nymph answers before Greon could finish. "You must die."

• ● ● ● ● •

Hale sits on a large rock in the center of the stream with his bare feet in the cool water. He fiddles with the net he is making, lost in the memory of the first time his father taught him to make one.

Often, his family would go camping, and his parents loved to be outdoors. Hale remembered his father was handy. As a child, Hale would often watch him build a tent, make a fire, even fashion a fishing rod. The first time Hale watched his father make a net, he was about five years old. He didn't remember much before that. Hale had sat across from his father and stared. His father stared back. He had an angular face, with full lips that always curled to a smile. He often had a light stubble, the way Hale's mother, Naomi, liked it. His short blond hair was kept a bit longer on top to show off his curls, also the way Naomi liked it.

"Let me show you how to do it," he said. Hale walked over to him and watched closely. "Look. You put this through here, and pull this end like that. And it becomes a knot. Do you want to try?"

Hale nodded and sat in front of his dad. His father placed both pieces of twine in his hands, and, holding Hale's hands, they made the knot together.

"There. Good job," he said. "Now try it on your own."

Hale did, and though he remembered each step, he wasn't strong enough when pulling the knot tight, so his dad pulled it for him. "Perfect. Look at that! You're a natural!"

Hale beamed.

Now looking down on his own net eleven years later, Hale knew that the knots still weren't tight enough. As tight as he pulled, he couldn't get it to look exactly like his dad's.

Distracted by his thoughts, Hale doesn't spot the grizzly bear emerging from the woods. Both take no notice of one another until the bear looks up after drinking from the stream. At the sight of Hale three yards away, it bares its teeth and growls.

Hale stands up slowly, and the bear growls again. Hale backs away from the stream altogether, keeping his eyes on the bear. But, the bear strides toward him. Hale picks up speed, and the bear pursues. Hale's heart pounds as he turns and runs full out through the stream, but the bear gains on him with every step.

Hale's foot catches on the stones in the water, and he trips, hitting his head hard. His vision goes black.

As the bear approaches Hale with a fierce snarl, a smoky apparition in the form of a girl appears between the bear and Hale. Frightened by this spirit, the bear jumps back and bolts.

Hale wakes up that afternoon still in the stream, baffled about how he is still alive.

●●●●●●

While strolling through the trees, Hale gathers his fallen branches, recalling Carly's solemn voice in a dream. "It's just you and me now." However, Hale knows it was more than a dream. He can't shake her words from his head—and the day she said it.

Two years earlier, Hale was fourteen years old, and his family had gone out camping to their usual place, an hour's drive from their home. It was a sunny Sunday afternoon. There was a light breeze and not a cloud in sight. Hale and Carly had been packing up the campsite while their parents went fishing.

Suddenly Carly paused and turns deathly white. A pendant in her hands. "Hale, you dropped your—"

"Oh, thanks," he says, throwing his amulet over his neck. "Are you all right?" he had asked Carly. She was shaking while she looked around and did not respond.

"Carly?" Hale asked, becoming worried.

"Yes, I'm fine," she said, though she seemed distracted. "Let's go for a walk." Hastily, she took Hale's arm, and they walked deep into the park. "When was the last time you climbed a tree?" she said with a slight smile. "Come on, let's see who can climb the fastest." She grabbed hold of the tree closest to her and climbed it.

Hale beamed, and he began to climb the tree next to hers. They climbed and climbed and didn't stop until the leaves hid them both. Peeping through the leaves, Hale saw Carly get there after him. He mocked, "Guess I won."

"Yup, you did," she said, rather sweetly but seriously. That struck Hale as strange. Normally, Carly never would have let him win.

"Let's stay here for a little while. It's so nice here," she said. They sat in the branches across from one another playing quiet games like rock-paper-scissors. Hale knew something was very off by the way Carly was behaving. But he soaked in their time together. It wasn't every day his older sister wanted to hang out with him.

"Carly," Hale said later on. "We probably have to get back now. Mom and Dad might be looking for us."

Carly paused for a moment before saying, "It's all right. Dad told me we are staying for the night and leaving in the morning. I told him I wanted to go tree climbing with you. Plus, they're fishing—you know they take forever."

Hale nodded and dozed off on the tree branch. When he woke up, the sun had already set, and Carly was gone.

Minutes later, she returned and urged Hale to descend. "Hale, we have to be fast. I need you not to be afraid. We have to go to the car," she said. Staggering behind his sister, Hale wondered what went wrong. *We were just playing a minute ago.* They ran together as fast as they could. She told Hale to sit in the front.

"What's going on?" Hale asked as he got in. That was when he saw their mom lying in the back seat, badly burned from head to toe.

"MOM!" She was breathing but unconscious.

Carly got in the front seat and sped out of the park.

"Where's Dad?"

Carly's knuckles were white on the steering wheel. She didn't respond right away. "I don't know."

"Is he okay?" Hale asked.

"Yes."

Carly drove them to a hospital, and a group of people came to take their mother from the car. Hale followed them to the waiting room. Carly was right behind him. She grabbed hold of his arm and whispered in his ear, "I need you to wait here for a little while, okay? I'll be right back."

He nodded.

"Don't speak to anybody. If anybody asks, your name is Joe or something—got it? And you're waiting for your . . . sister to give birth. Make something up. Do you have your phone?" she asked, pulling on the collar of his shirt, her fingers brushing along his pendant. "I'll come back. Wait for me here."

Hale distracted himself with the small television in the corner of the waiting room. A kind nurse brought him a snack from the vending machine, but he could not eat. His body wouldn't stop shaking. Where could Carly have gone? What happened to his mom? Where was Dad? What's happening? Is Mom okay? There were so many questions, but he found himself unable to talk or move.

Carly came back a few hours later. She looked at Hale with tear-stained eyes, then went to speak to the doctor. It took all of Hale's courage to stand up and walk over to his sister. It seemed like an eternity getting there.

Hale watched numbly as Carly covered her mouth with her hands and cried, doubling over as her sobs overtook her.

Shaken, he dared to ask, "Is Dad all right?"

Carly didn't answer.

Tears welled in his eyes. "Is Mom . . ." He couldn't bring himself to ask the question.

Carly wrapped her arms around him and said, "It's just you and me now."

◦●●●●◦

In his parlor, Bayo watches the orbs obsessively with bloodshot eyes. Since the day he saw Greon die, he never parted from the orbs in case there was any indication that Hale was still alive.

Just then, from his left comes a noise like something being dragged across a surface. On the table behind him is a dust-covered map Bayo had placed there eleven years ago. On top of it is a pendant enchanted with a locating spell with a strand of Hale's hair embedded in its crystal. Shocked, Bayo turns to see the pendant rise from its resting place and drag itself across the map, landing along the East Coast of the Americas.

Bayo rises so abruptly that his chair topples over behind him. He lifts the pendant from the map and slides it directly under the hovering orbs. Immediately the orbs stop their orbit. "Show me Hale!"

A portal emerges above them in the shape of a pyramid. His heart pounds in excitement. As clear as day, there is Hale in front of him, collecting wood in the middle of a forest.

This boy is older than Bayo remembers him, but there is no mistaking it—they have the same eyes. Bayo eagerly places his hand on the orb of Malphora, closes his eyes, and recites an incantation in a dead tongue. When he finishes, he watches Hale's surroundings dim. The orb representing Malphora glows with a bright light. The portal closes, and the orbs resume their rotations. As they spin around, Bayo peers into the orb of Malphora. In it is Hale, right where Bayo wants him—in the Land of the Griffins.

Admirably, he notes how mature Hale has become since their last encounter. With a gleam in his eyes and a wide grin, he whispers to himself, "Welcome home, brother."

CHAPTER 5

Stuffing fallen branches under his arm, Hale doesn't notice the string holding the pendant around his neck has loosened. As he bends over, the pendant falls to the ground. Oblivious, he continues collecting firewood, too lost in his daydream to hear the sound of the stream fading in the distance or note the sudden change from day to night.

But then, the ground begins to thud. Hale snaps out of his daydream and curiously follows the sound. He looks over his shoulder and jumps backward. His firewood flies from his arms. He is not in the same place he was a moment ago.

Under a starry sky, Hale is hidden in the shadow of a tree and several shrubs. Beyond the shrubs are hundreds of people making their way to an enormous platform, surrounded by blazing torches. They scream in exuberance, stomping to create a constant, even boom that pulsates the ground. Behind them all are several people shape-shifting into large winged beasts, clawing at one another in their beastly forms. Before Hale's eyes are real, live Griffins!

Two adolescent girls stand on the platform, one on either side, circling one another as a wildcat would its prey. One girl, a dirty blonde, tries to jump off the stage, but the crowd simply pushes her back on top. While she is turned, the other girl dashes toward her and tackles her. The attacker lands on top of the blonde, her legs crushing her victim's ribs, her hands wrapped around her neck. The blonde's face reddens, and still, her attacker holds on, suffocating her. Groups of people charge onto the stage then. Hale, on the other hand, retreats to the shrubs.

Just then, a tall, beefy young man cuffs his arm. "Where are you going, newbie? The party's just getting started."

A group of guys stands behind him. "Haha, told you! Evan's a pro at sighting them out," one says as Hale struggles.

The big one, Evan, smiles as he drags Hale across the open field through the crowd and throws him on top of the platform. "Get off of me!" Hale screams. The crowd hollers below him.

To his left is the girl who had lost the match, lying on the stage. Her eyes are open and unblinking, and her arms are outstretched in defeat. Red handprints line her neck, just like Carly. A petite, doe-eyed girl with auburn colored hair jumps onto the platform. She wears a leather crop top and jeans. Her long hair blocks her view of the crowd as she presses her palms over the blonde girl's chest. The crowd roars.

Evan stands in the first row, pulling the auburn colored hair girl away. "Grace, give it up. She's gone!"

Grace thrusts her foot backward at Evan to keep him at bay. To keep up appearances to his buddies, he laughs at the boot mark on his forehead. Then he jumps on the stage and grabs Grace by the waist. Her petite body only reaches his chest. While she kicks and screams, he says in a low voice that Hale barely hears, "You have to stop, Grace, before you attract attention." He carries her off so the next match can start. Hale swallows. *What did he mean by that?*

Hale jumps off the stage but is dragged back to face a boy just as scrawny as he is, covered in filth, with matted brown hair and freckles. They look at one another, at the fear in each other's eyes.

"I don't want to fight you," Hale calls to him, still distracted by the Griffins fighting in the distance. Their wings spread so magnificently, their claws whoosh in the air and land painfully on one another's bodies. Otherworldly shrieks that Hale's never heard before ring in his ears.

Hale's focus returns as the boy asserts, "Neither do I." However, he positions himself with his fists above his head.

Hale puts his hands out in front of him. "Wait," he objects. But it is too late—the boy throws the first punch. Hale dodges. The punch itself is weak and silly. The boy staggers closer to him, already nervously jumping to and fro as he notices the crowd laughing at his weak thrust.

"Come on!" someone shouts.

"Loser!" yells a stranger.

The boy looks back to Hale, who meets his eyes with kindness. "Whatever you're afraid of, don't be. You shouldn't do something you don't want to do," Hale says.

"I guess you haven't been here long," the boy says with a cracked voice, throwing another punch. Hale dodges again, catches the boy's arm, and twists it. He seizes the boy's other arm and pins them both behind his back.

The crowd roars, "Finish him!"

Hale's eyes widen, and the boy whimpers, "You have to do it. Or they'll end us both."

River is a seventeen-year-old boy who stands apart from the crowd. Unlike the rest, he does not applaud. Instead, he stares up at Hale with curiosity. The people surrounding him violently push and rage. As River tries to keep his balance in the commotion, he knows it won't be long before somebody jumps up and finishes both Hale and his opponent. He pushes his way through the mob and jumps on the stage, cuffing both their arms. "Don't make eye contact," he warns. The three walk off in a huddle, past Evan and his friends, and the crowd boos.

Once the three escape the crowd, River whispers, "We aren't through the fire yet." Just as Hale's opponent is about to make a break for it, River warns, "Don't run." Then he turns to Hale. "You got a lot of fight in you—you're going to need it."

Hale's body shakes as he processes his surroundings. Evan and his two friends emerge.

"Hey!" Evan shouts. "You can't interfere in a match!"

But River ignores them. "I'm River, by the way," he says to Hale and the other boy.

"Hey!" Evan roars, coming one step closer. "I'm talking to you." As Evan barks, "Hand them over!" Grace appears fuming with rage.

River locks eyes with Grace, and he smiles. "Grace, it's fine," he calls out. "Your brother just impressing his friends again."

That is enough to get Evan roaring. He runs to River with his fists balled.

River deflects Evan's fist with his arm and kicks him in the ribs. His black hair flies in his face. Evan grunts through the pain. Despite River's warning, Hale's opponent bolts, and Evan's backup runs after him. Distracted, River turns his back to Evan, and taking advantage, Evan prepares to tackle River from behind when Grace steps between them and kicks him in the stomach. Evan stumbles.

"Enough!" she demands. Evan looks down at her in shock and storms back to the stage.

River walks calmly toward the runner and the two boys clutching his arms. "Hey, let him go," River says.

"You know the rules. The ones picked have to fight to the death," declares the one on the left, Logan. His hair is tied, exposing his rough face, which is marked with fresh bruises.

"Forget the rules," River begs.

Logan shouts, "Shut up, you gorrum!"

Gorrum, the trending curse word among the young Griffins, means Griffin scum. River scoffs in response to the pathetic name-calling.

Mark, the boy on the right, says, "We'll give you the scrub for the newbie!"

"What are you doing?" asks Logan.

River's eyes are fixated on the hostage boy. Sweat beads the kid's forehead, and he is pale and shaking. "Hey, what's your name?" River asks him with a calm voice.

"N—Norton," he stutters.

"You're going to be all right, Norton. Don't worry," River says.

"Do we have a deal?" Mark asks. "You have ten seconds, or we gut him." He whips out a knife from his pocket. It glistens with the light from the torches.

Hale's stomach drops, and he takes a step back unconsciously.

Logan and Mark begin their countdown, "Ten! Nine! Eight!"

River winks at Hale. Hale swallows hard and takes a step toward them. "Seven! Six!"

Hale looks at the two boys in front of him, and he sees the emptiness in their eyes.

River shouts, "Let him go. We made the trade."

With that, Norton is released from their grasp. He stumbles across the field until he is behind River.

Logan and Mark advance toward Hale. But Hale is not coming quietly. He throws himself at Mark, and they tussle on the ground for the knife. Hale manages to snatch it, and he stands above the boy with the blade pointed at his attacker. Mark stays on the ground.

River aims a punch at Logan, but Logan grabs River's arm and with a sickening crunch, dislocates it. River yelps and jumps away. He locks his shoulder blade back in place, stretches, and then focuses back on his opponent. Finding an opening, River knees Logan in the ribs until he falls.

River and Hale lock eyes. The fighting is done. They walk away from the pair of boys gasping for breath on the moist ground. Holding on to his sore torso, Logan threatens, "This isn't over!"

As they leave, Hale notices Norton is long gone. Hale doesn't know whether to think of him as a coward or an opportunist. Though it doesn't matter much, Hale supposes.

"You never told me your name," River says.

"Oh. I'm Hale."

"You're very lucky," he says. "Most newbies die their first day. Especially when they come during a bonfire."

Puzzled, Hale looks around. "There is no bonfire."

"In about an hour, when the fighting is over, they'll make one. That's how they get rid of the bodies," River explains.

What in the world? "Where are we?" Hale asks slowly.

River raises his eyebrows. "Where do you think you are?"

"I have no clue. I've just seen kids turn into monsters and kids killing each other on stage. What is this place?"

"This is where Griffins live," River explains.

"Griffins?"

"Mhm."

"Gr-ee-fons?"

"Yeah. That's right."

"I'm leaving. I must have been picking wood in a twilight-zone section of the world that somehow warped me here." Hale turns.

"Where are you going?" River calls.

"Back," Hale answers over his shoulder.

"To where?"

"My camp."

River's chin lifts. "It's not there."

"What do you mean? That's the direction I came from."

"You won't get back to it."

"What?"

River sighs. "Well, it's like this, see. You, like the rest of us, got picked out of the blue sky and got dropped off here."

"And there's no going back?"

River shakes his head solemnly. "There's no going back."

"There has to be some way."

River chuckles. "You're telling me. I've searched up and down this awful place. We all have. But we're not calling the shots. We're stuck."

Hale's brows furrow. "Then who's calling the shots?"

Shoving his hands in his pockets, River answers, "The Elders, the leaders of the Griffins."

"Why?"

"Because we are Griffins, plain and simple. And if you're here, that means you're one of us."

"But I grew up in Colorado. You're telling me I'm somehow part lion-eagle?"

"It's pretty cool once you get used to it," River says.

Thoughts of Carly rush through Hale's mind. *Stuck here forever.*

* * * * * *

In a dark room with dim lights, Bayo huddles beside Rioma, a fiery-red-haired woman. Rioma is the Griffin Elder of Ardor. As a Griffin of Ardor, she can produce fire from her body on a whim and control it.

Rioma and Bayo overlook a table lined with a velvet midnight-blue tablecloth, the Three Eyes hovering over it. Rioma's thick, wavy red locks glisten in the light of the orbs.

While gazing into the orb of Malphora, they can see all the commotion happening a few miles away from where they stand.

She grimaces as she watches an image of Hale through the orb. "Seems as though your rival has arrived just in time."

"Yes, it seems that he has. However, I'm quite certain we can change the folds of destiny if we play our cards right," says Bayo coldly.

"You are hopeful you will make him see reason," she says.

He smirks. "Yes, I am, my dear. And I am quite aware you are not. How is it that you can doubt me so when I always get my way?"

In an airy tone, she declares, "I do not doubt *you*, Bayo. It is he whom I am doubtful of."

Chapter 6

River leads Hale to a long table filled with food. When the aroma reaches Hale, he salivates, remembering how very hungry he is. The table is guarded by "Hogs," as River calls them. "Hogs" are anybody who fights over the right of the table each night and wins. Whatever food they don't eat they trade for something valuable, and the currency in the Griffin Clan is the golden chips given to the victors of every duel.

"They'll only give you food if you have those chips," River explains, pointing to a girl as she trades a golden chip for access to the table. She hides her second chip in her sleeve.

"What are they for?" Hale asks.

"From what I've heard, the Elders are going to collect them on the next full moon and reward the victors." He looks at Hale. "Long story short, we don't have those chips—unless you want to go kill somebody at the moment. And considering the weakest people are probably all dead by now—or in hiding—and with your current . . . physique, I don't think you'd make it. So we gotta steal. You know, ethically speaking." He nods his head while waiting for Hale's reaction.

"Okay, how are we going to do this?" Hale asks.

River points his finger at Hale. "You hide," he says. Then he points at himself. "I get."

"I hide? You get?" Hale repeats, with the same finger action. "Are you sure this is a good idea?"

"You have a better idea?" asks River.

"Not at all."

"Then let's do this!"

River and Hale hide by the trees directly behind the table. There are two Hogs, one on either side of the table. Hale whispers, "What happens if you get caught?"

"Well," River says, "then it was nice knowing ya." He winks and jumps out from the shrubs.

Hale watches as River sneaks under the table and lifts his arm over the side to grab food from the top. River peeps his head out watching for Hale's signal that it is clear to leave. But the girl now approaching the Hogs' table distracts Hale. It's the girl from the stadium, with the auburn hair. River attempts to flee from under the table the very moment the second Hog turns to face the shrubs. Hale tries to signal him to go back, but River does not see. *Oh no!*

Grace recognizes River immediately. She calls the name of the second Hog, who turns to her attention.

With a flirtatious tone, she asks, "Wow, you're guarding the table tonight? That's so impressive." She comes closer. This captures the attention of the first Hog as well.

The second Hog flashes a smug smile. "Yeah, wasn't so hard."

"I bet," she affirms, "especially with those *muscles*."

"Oh, these things." He smirks, and the first Hog rolls his eyes.

River makes it back to Hale's side safely and turns to watch the strange interaction going on between Grace and the Hog.

Grace stacks food on her plate and walks away, the second Hog drawls, "Wow."

The first Hog looks at him and scoffs. The same moment River says, "He's got no chance," the first Hog proclaims, "You've got no chance." Hale and River look at one another and chuckle.

Hale and River take their leave, munching on their stolen goods.

"I see why you call them Hogs now," Hale jokes.

"Yup, they're porky in more ways than one."

Hale chuckles at the joke and says, "I like her."

"Then you better get in line."

Hale only meant he liked her as a person, and now he felt it was very important to make that distinction, "No. I mean—I'm not going in the line." Hale casts a sideways glance at River and asks cautiously, "Are *you* in that line?"

River considers Hale's forwardness and says lightly, "I would, but I have enough problems with her brother as it is. You know, the blond one that tried to kill the both of us tonight? But we owe Grace big time."

◦ ● ● ● ◦

While strolling through the woods, River explains everything he has learned about this mysterious place.

"It's just like you said. I was walking through the street one day, blinked, and was suddenly here," he says. They come to the edge of the woods. "There is a camp where most of the kids stay, but I like my place. Keeps me out of trouble. Do you want me to take you where the others are?"

Hale thinks for a moment and says, "If you don't mind, I would rather go with you."

"I don't mind."

Hale stumbles as they walk through the trees. "Aren't there any animals here in the woods?" he asks. "You know, wolves, bears, mountain lions?"

"Not one. We're the only creatures in these woods to be afraid of."

That strikes Hale as was very, very odd.

"Today was the last day newbies were supposed to arrive," River explains. "Seems just like bad luck on your end."

"What if I'm not like you? I mean, you can shape-shift into a Griffin," Hale says.

"Well, try not to think about it too much. You'll see tomorrow."

"Where do you get everything you need?"

"The Elders give it to us, strange as it sounds. We're here," River says, coming to a stop. "Look up."

In the tree beside them is a glass dome above their heads, shining in the moonlight of the half-moon. Hale is awestruck by its beauty. River climbs the wooden ladder attached to the tree, using his teeth to hold the cloth filled with their food, and Hale follows.

Once inside, River lights the lamp nailed to a large tree branch that enters through the center of the floor and exits through the ceiling. There is no furniture, only a pile of blankets on the floor.

"You can't tell anybody about this place," River cautions. "Nobody knows about it. You got it?"

Hale nods. "I won't tell."

"I'm trusting you," River says seriously. "Don't make me regret it." He tosses Hale a blanket. "I only have two. If you're uncomfortable, we can get another tomorrow."

Hale lies down on the floor, and River blows out the torch. Hale looks through the glass dome and up at the sky. "I've never seen stars this bright in my life," he says. "I pretty sure I'm going to wake up back where I was, but right now, I think this dream just might be real."

River smiles. "So, when you wake up, what's gonna happen to me?"

Amusing him, Hale says, "Where do you want to go?"

River doesn't answer for a moment. "I've always wanted to go somewhere tropical. But I think I'd rather go home, honestly."

"Done!" Hale says, crossing his arms and bowing his head quickly like a genie.

River laughs. "Good night."

"Good night."

But try as he might, Hale is not able to fall asleep. He is afraid and mystified all at once. He relives this night in his head repeatedly, and so much baffles him. He is suddenly in a place where dangerous people turn into Griffins and where people are accustomed to hurting one another for rewards. And Hale just so happened to meet one of the few who isn't like any of them, who has risked his life twice in one night for him. A place where the night sky is so alive it feels like floating in the middle of space. For once, he doesn't think about Carly or how he has spent his last several months locked away in torment. He has never felt more at peace than inside this indefinite distraction.

* * * * * *

River dreams of a girl's voice, so close it's as if she is talking in his ear. "River," she whispers. "River, it's me."

He wakes up, though he is not startled. This isn't the first time he has heard this voice. "What do you want?" he groans silently into the void.

The voice snickers. "I thought we could finally meet."

"Where are you?" he asks.

"Look straight ahead."

He squints, straining to see through the darkness, but he sees nothing but trees through the dome. A moment later, a silhouette of a girl becomes visible as it climbs down a tree. *Finally.* He has waited so long to put a face to the voice that echoes in his mind.

"Meet me at the edge of the cliff," she says, showing him an image of the setting in his mind.

He leaves without another thought and arrives in a clearing beside a cliff. River slows his pace cautiously when he spots her in the distance.

"Come closer," she says in his head. Warily, he approaches. When their eyes meet, he feels he has known her all his life, though he is sure they have never met. She is stunning, with pale skin, dark hair, and full lips.

She smiles. "Finally, we meet." He doesn't respond.

If Hale were there, he would have recognized this girl—she is the same girl who killed the blonde the moment he arrived.

But River had not seen that match.

"My name is Mary."

"Obviously, you know me already," he blurts.

"I do. I'm sorry I didn't let us meet earlier. I was . . . scared," she explains.

"Scared?" he questions. "How about having a voice in your head that's not yours? *That's* scary."

"It's like I told you before. It's my power. I can read minds. I can see your whole life. I spoke to the Elders about it, and it's a rare case. They say I got my powers early—we aren't supposed to get them until the next full moon, just before the celebration."

River sighs, holding back so many questions.

"No, not everybody will be like me," she answers. "There are different kinds of abilities. And I wanted to meet you because you're so unlike everybody here. You're kind. I saw what you did today for that newbie. It was very brave. What reason did you have to help him?" Mary asks.

He shrugs. "I guess I saw that he was different from everybody else, too."

Mary stares into his eyes and admires their green color in the moonlight while learning all she wants to know about Hale through River's mind. "I agree. He does seem quite special. He wouldn't have lived through this night if it weren't for you." She pauses for a moment. "You know, I can feel emotions, too. You have *so* much pain. I can take it away if you want me to."

She places her hand gently on his heart, and before he can object, he suddenly feels like a weight has lifted from his body. No thoughts cloud his mind. There are no deep memories to keep him down. He breathes in the fresh air, as if for the very first time.

"You should probably go to bed now."

As River nears his dome, the weight that Mary lifted from him returns, hitting him hard as if he were drowning in his own sudden sorrow all at once.

He stares through the glass in his dome to the place Mary stood before, partially hoping she's there. She didn't tell him that this terrible feeling would return once they were apart. *I shouldn't have let her touch me.* As he drifts off into sleep, aching from the gloom inside him, he thinks, *I need to see her again.*

CHAPTER 7

"H ey, Hale. Sorry, but you're still here," River says, standing up to stretch the next morning. "Oh, forgot to tell you, there's a bathroom in here, too. Well, not what you're probably used to, but it's the closest thing to a bathroom in this horrific place." He walks around the tree dome to the torch and pulls it like a lever. At once, the trunk opens like a door. "Cool, right?" River says.

Hale peeps inside. "Very."

Inside the hollow of the trunk is a floor that extends only halfway through the trunk. Hale can see the depths of the hollow inside the trunk where the floor does not reach. Above this, over the gap in the floor, a wooden doughnut-shaped seat is attached to the wall of the hollow.

"You stand on this, here," River explains, pointing to the shelf by their feet, "Then, sit on that part there," he said, pointing to the circular shelf above it. "Tell me that's not awesome."

"But wait, there's more!" River exclaims, sounding like a carnival barker. "There's a window here." He points to the rectangular hole covered with glass. "And now you're probably thinking, 'Why is the window covered with glass?'

Well, that's so the tree dome won't get wet. And why would it get wet, you might ask? Well, during your shower of course! Behold!" River turns a switch inside the hollow, water flows through the ceiling in a light pressure like a mist.

Hale's eyes widen. "This is amazing! How does it work?"

"This funnel was built into the tree to collect rainwater. All the water it has collected is right above our heads. There is even a strainer that works as a filter. Also, there's a latch outside the bathroom on the trunk—when you turn it, a stream of clean water comes out of a small pipe for drinking. Whoever invented the tree dome is a genius. Since I found it, I had one less thing to steal or beg for from the Elders and those kids." River hands Hale a bar of soap and a clean rag. "Go on, try it out."

Hale is ecstatic. He takes the soap from River's hands and heads inside the tree-hollow bathroom.

The sight of himself in the full-length mirror on the door makes him jump back. This was the first time since the kidnapping that he has seen his reflection. He has dark circles under his eyes, and his cheekbones are more defined than ever. His skin is a sickly shade of white. Then there are his clothes, the same clothes he wore that awful day he and Carly were abducted. What used to look brand-new is now ripped and greying, stained from months of grime and sweat and heartache. Navy blue capris he loves, and his favorite t-shirt that reads, I'D FLEX BUT I LIKE THIS SHIRT.

Now, as he looked at himself, he realizes the irony of the shirt, hanging on his thin body. Hale remembers how Carly used to make fun of him every time he wore it. She would say, "Come on, show me those muscles!" And he laughs ever so lightly as he recalls flexing for his sister's amusement and her saying, "You don't do the shirt justice."

Her face. He can see her face so vividly in his mind. Grey eyes that were a replica of their mother's, her rosy cheeks, the playful disgust as she watched her brother flexing his thigh muscles.

"Those don't count, Hale." Her voice was so delicate and soft. If only he could hear her voice again, just so he could truly remember what it sounded like. Tears silently pour from his eyes.

He takes off his clothes and turns the switch River had shown him. Water drizzles from above. It feels refreshingly cold. Months of grime gently melt away, and he feels with his own hands what months of malnourishment has done to him. He is skin on bones.

However, that doesn't cause as much surprise as recognizing his bare neck. He looks down just to make sure. The amulet! The amulet his father gave him is gone. His heart pounds in his chest. All he can picture is his sister's last moments. "Your amulet, do you still have it?" Her voice repeats in his mind. Hale abruptly turns off the streaming water, dresses himself, then scours the tree dome floor.

"My necklace," Hale explains to River. "I can't find it."

"It's okay. It's just a necklace," River says.

"It's the last thing I have from my father. The only thing I have . . ." Tears again stream from Hale's eyes. "My sister told me to always keep it on."

River tries to comfort him. "I'm sure we'll find it. Let's check outside."

• • ● ● ● • •

The search is futile, and somehow River convinces Hale—in hopes of distracting him—to accompany him to a remote clearing just above the ocean. The waves push up violently against the rocky edge of the cliff, creating a cooling breeze through the summer heat.

"So, you're going to change into a Griffin?" Hale queries.

"Well, that's the plan. Everybody calls it transforming though. You should probably step back."

River smirks, then crosses his arms so that each fist nearly touches the opposite shoulder. His legs are comfortably apart, and he releases his arms quickly. Suddenly, a bright white light illuminates him. Then River is replaced by a white essence morphing into a Griffin.

Hale watches in wonder as River the Griffin materializes. He is magnificent, huge. His black hair catches the sunlight, tints of various colors gleaming over his silken coat. River spreads his wings and flashes his feathers. Hale's jaw drops. He really did it! He turned into a Griffin! *This is crazy!*

River turns to the ocean and leaps without a thought. He spreads his wings, flapping them until he flies above Hale and motions him to follow. Hale shakes his head. River shrugs his beastly shoulders and swoops into the sky. Hale watches until River is just a speck in the distance.

Neither knew that hiding in the trees near the clearing were Evan and his friends. Evan rests his back against the trunk of a tree, one leg hanging off the branch. With a knife in hand, he hacks away at a block of wood. His friends rest on branches beside him.

"What are we waiting for? They're right there," says Logan.

Evan watches as Hale heads back into the woods. "Follow the newbie back to their hideout. I'll get the gorrum and meet you there."

Evan slides down the tree as soon as Hale heads to the clearing. He spots River in the distance, then transforms and begins his chase.

• ● ● ● ● •

River hears Mary's voice in his head, calling his name. *River?*

Where are you? he says, desperate to see her.

Just beside the waterfall, she answers.

He is almost there when he spots her. Her expression is solemn. *There is somebody behind you, following you.*

River turns his head around and catches a glimpse of Evan on his tail. River picks up speed.

Calm down. He is too close and will catch you at that speed. Dive into the water and transform just before you hit it, Mary says.

River does as she says, but Evan follows River into the rough water.

Hide in the water and swim to the clearing next to you, Mary commands.

Evan is gaining on him. River swims and swims, but he is no match for Evan's build. *He will catch you. You will not outswim him. Acquiesce to his commands, and he won't hurt you,* says Mary. Evan snags River's leg. River manages to kick Evan with his free leg and swims farther. Just when he can't hold his breath much longer, Mary says, *don't be scared.*

Something heavy hits River in the head, and his eyes roll back. Before he sinks into the ocean, Evan wraps his arms around his chest, transforms, and skyrockets into the air, clutching River's body.

• ● ● ● ● •

Hale is only a few trees away from the tree dome when someone cuffs his arm.

"Nice to see ya, newbie!" Logan seethes.

Mark seizes Hale's other arm and flashes a slimy grin. They both pull Hale to the ladder of the tree dome. As Hale struggles his way free, memories of the cellar reappear in his mind, and the boys' grips on Hale's arms tighten. *Not again.* Hale fights his anxiety, his forehead slick with sweat, and his vision blurs. They force him to climb up into the tree dome.

A new voice comes from inside. "Where is the other?"

Hale's heart jumps. *They want River, too. This whole thing was planned.*

"Evan is working on it," says Mark while Logan ties Hale's hands behind his back and pushes him against the glass wall. "He doesn't know you're here."

Hale looks up at the stranger while picking at the rope around his wrists. The young man standing before him is tall, gazing out the window to scout for Evan. There is no emotion in his expression. He stands there, waiting.

A rustling comes from below, and someone is climbing the ladder. River enters the tree dome, completely soaked and pale. As River sees everybody inside, his face drops. His eyes meet Hale's, and Hale's stomach turns with guilt. River stands idly as Logan and Mark pull his arms back and tie his wrists. All the while, the stranger says nothing.

Hale says, "River, I'm so sorry. I didn't mean for this—"

"What, you surprised?" says Logan to River with a chuckle. "We told you it wasn't over, gorrum." Logan pushes River against the glass beside Hale and punches him in the stomach. River keels over and grunts breathlessly.

Mark snoops through the tree dome. "Didn't he used to carry a guitar around?" he says, rummaging through the blankets.

"That's right," Logan says. "It's probably here somewhere."

Evan enters the tree dome and his jaw drops at the sight of the stranger. "Leon," he says in an icy whisper. "What are you doing here?"

Leon looms large over Evan.

"I'm taking over," he answers flatly.

Evan broadens his shoulders. "What's that supposed to mean?"

"It means, this place is mine, and *they* answer to me," he says, pointing to Logan and Mark.

Evan clenches his fists while the vein in his neck pulses angrily. "Oh, really?" He looks to Logan and Mark in astonishment, then back at Leon. "You think you can come here out of the blue and take what I worked for?"

Leon smirks. "We all knew this would happen eventually. So, let's make it fair then." With a glint in his eyes, he says, "Let the best man win."

Evan punches Leon across the face, but Leon is unfazed. Without warning, he grabs Evan's collarbone and hits him in the stomach. After the third blow, Evan deflects Leon's arm and kicks him to the floor.

Leon pounces once more, and they grapple until Leon pins him down. He beats Evan's face until Evan's arms fall limply to his sides, and then once more, for kicks. Leon rises and smiles down at his beaten opponent while wiping away a trickle of blood from his upper lip. It is over so fast. Evan is motionless, his face bloody and swollen.

River turns to Hale and mouths, "We need Grace."

Mark finds a latch on the floor, opens it, and pulls out River's guitar. "Ha! Here it is!"

"Wow, what a good spot—kept it in real good condition," Logan exclaims, grabbing it from Mark. Without warning, he swings it over his head and smashes it against the trunk of the tree until the neck of the guitar is the only thing left in his hands. He looks to River for a reaction, but River makes no sign of emotion. Not even when Mark laughs in River's face.

Logan pins River against the wall, his hands around his neck. River keeps his eyes closed through the pain, and Hale wonders why he doesn't fight back. He can't stand it. Shocking both assailants, Hale jumps to his feet and kicks Logan in his side with all his might.

Logan sneers. "You wanna fight, newbie? Let's see how long you last today."

Hale pushes River toward the exit. But it's too soon, considering his recent beating and short breath, and River nearly plummets to his death but manages to grab the ladder just in time.

Logan swings his fist at Hale but misses, and Mark approaches the two while screaming, "End him, Logan!" But Logan is too slow, and Hale escapes down the ladder. His hands slide down the rope, and he tightens his grip, the rope cutting his palms.

On the ground, Hale pulls River's arm around his shoulder, and they make a run for it. Mark and Logan are on their way down when Leon stops them. "Leave them, and get this one out of here," he says, pointing to Evan.

●●●●●●

"I can't run anymore," River gasps.

The clearing is just in front of them. "We're almost there," Hale urges, looking behind him.

River grunts and trips. Hale helps him sit up. "They're not coming after us. They would have been here by now." With hazy eyes, he says, "Find Grace. Tell her that Evan is in trouble. Now!"

Hale immediately runs off in search of Grace. Griffins fly over the field, while some rest on the ground. Hale pushes past groups of people and keeps his eyes peeled for the petite girl with long auburn hair. He finally spots her and shouts her name. "Grace! Grace! Evan and River are hurt!"

"Where are they?" she asks at once.

He points behind him.

"James, can you come with me?" Grace asks the boy beside her.

James nods, and he and Grace follow Hale into the woods.

"Did they do this to each other?" Grace asks.

"No. Evan was in a fight with someone else. I think his name was Leon."

Grace nearly stops in her tracks at the sound of the name. A short moment later, they find River lying still on the ground, his eyes closed. Grace rushes to him, placing her head on his chest and taking his wrist in her hand.

"He's fine. James—" Grace begins, but James has already hoisted River in his arms. "Take him to my tent."

With that, Grace takes off with Hale to the tree dome.

Above their heads, peeping out from the tree dome are Mark and Logan snickering. "Look at that, his little sister coming to his rescue."

"Here, little sister, catch!" shouts Mark.

They toss Evan from the entrance, and he falls through the air. Grace transforms and catches his body with her claws just before it hits the ground.

* * * * *

River is sound asleep in a tent. Someone enters, kneels beside him, and combs the shoulder-length hair from his face. He opens his eyes and sees Mary looking down at him.

"I got here as soon as I could," she says. "You need to know that it wasn't Hale's fault. They were planning this attack for days."

River nods, yet even that subtle movement makes him cringe in pain.

She places her hand softly on his heart. "It won't hurt in a moment." Immediately, River's face calms. "See, it's better already. There's only a matter of days until the full moon. Everything will change when you get your powers. You'll see. They won't be able to hurt you anymore." She creeps into his mind and sees a woman that once took care of River. "Is that your mother? She seems lovely. I see why you miss her." Mary asks.

"Can you please not read my mind? No, she's not my mom. My mom left when I was small. I was fifteen when I ran away from my foster parents. They weren't good to me. And she found me on the street and took me in. She was a single mother of four kids, then five, including me."

Mary is quiet for a moment. "I was also raised by a different woman after my mother didn't want me," Mary confesses. "Strange coincidence."

River asks, "Did you like her? The woman who raised you?"

"Not really, no. It was better than nothing, I guess. I can feel your love for this woman. I'm sorry—sometimes I can't control it."

He believes her.

CHAPTER 8

The next evening, some of the young Griffins build a bonfire before the fighting commences. Grace watches the rising flame, its color matching the setting sun. She stands beside her chattering friends, not paying attention to a thing they say as she wraps her knuckles. Right on cue, she spots Evan, who attempts to conceal a limp as he makes his way toward her. She looks away in fury.

"Hey," he says.

She doesn't answer him.

"What's wrong?" Evan asks. But she continues to ignore him. "What, you can't hear me now or something? I'm talking to you," Evan says, stepping in front of her. But she doesn't give in. "I wanted to tell you that the Elders are deciding between me and Leon to be their guard. They want me to meet with them." He kneels in front of her.

She finally meets his eyes. "I don't care."

"What's up with you?"

"What's up with me?" she spits back. Her friends turn toward them. "What's up with you? The guys you call friends just turned on you and handed you over to Leon. You're lucky you're still alive! And you got everything you deserved by the way. I know what you did to River." Grace stands to her feet. "Just because half the people here think it's cool to hurt people doesn't mean it's okay. Are you *that* desperate for attention? They threw you out of the tree dome! If I didn't catch you in time, you would have died! Do you even know how I knew to come get you? Who do you think told me? Take a wild guess!"

Evan stays quiet as Grace waits for an answer. "Yeah, the boy you tormented went out of his way to make sure you are all right, even after he was beaten up by you. And now you want to go to the Elders? We haven't even met the Elders yet! How do you know that information is accurate? Go. You want to go, go!"

* ● ● ● ● *

Evan doesn't know where he should go. He is expected to arrive at the Elders' Dome alongside Leon. Yet, Grace's words stick in his mind, and now he can't help being cautious. So he walks to the tree dome to Mark and Logan. The place is clouded in herb smoke and scoundrels.

Evan takes a seat beside them against the windowpane.

"What's the matter?" Logan says.

Mark adds, "His sister's meddling into our business."

"Aww, is little Gracey tellin' you to be a good boy again?" Logan mocks.

Without warning, Evan punches Logan in the mouth. Logan falls to the floor and the tree dome echoes with laughter. Becoming red at the sight of onlookers, Logan shouts, "You better pray that I can't find you. Say goodbye to our connection with the Elders."

Evan leaves and decides it is best if he never comes back.

* ● ● ● ● *

Leon approaches the large golden dome where the Elders reside. Just before he knocks on the door, it opens.

A tall woman bows her head respectfully. "Welcome, Leon. My name is Ianna. Bayo is eager to meet with you." She is beautiful, with innocent features and a soft voice. Leon steps inside. The hallway is dim, lit only by torches on either side.

Ianna escorts him to a closed room at the end of the hall, her long black hair whooshing behind her as she walked. She opens the door for him.

In the center of the room is a circular, in-ground seating area with white semicircle couches. At the center is a fire pit, the crackling fire bringing a smoky aroma to the room. On the couch sit two men. One sips a hot beverage while the other stares at Leon. Their expressions remain stony as Leon enters, and Leon has the impression that they knew he was coming.

The first man puts his beverage down and smiles. "Welcome, Leon. I am Bayo."

Leon grunts. Now he could truly put a face to the name he had heard so many rumors about.

"It seems as though your rival has decided not to join us this evening. That makes this brief meeting something of a formality."

"To be your guard?" Leon questions.

"More along the lines of my apprentice. I see great potential in you. Apart from Evan and yourself, I've also been watching another potential pupil. However, he has only just arrived here, so I've decided to give him some time."

"We have to compete for this decision?"

"That depends on whether he is worthy of your competition."

Leon nods. "When do I begin?"

"I will find you when I need you," says Bayo. That is Ianna's cue to escort Leon back out the door.

Mary waits in the hallway for her cue to enter. Once Leon passes her, she can't help but shiver. There is something off-putting about his energy. Mary watches Ianna escort Leon from the dome. *His dark aura is so strong. I wonder what he's thinking . . .*

As Ianna returns to the lounge area, Rioma emerges. Her serious expression fades once she sees Mary.

"How have you been, Mary?" she asks.

Mary does not reciprocate her smile. "Well, Mother, and you?"

"Well, thank you. Don't keep them waiting, Ianna. Go on and open the door," says Rioma.

Ianna does as she is told, and the women enter. Ianna and Rioma take their places on either side of the door.

With a wide grin, Bayo exclaims, "Mary! How is my best girl?"

Mary is taken aback. Bayo isn't always this exuberant. She knows that hiding anything is a fool's game with Deor present. Nobody can conceal anything from him. "I'm well, Bayo. Thank you."

He gestures for her to take a seat beside him. "How are you liking the new generation?" he asks.

Tactfully choosing her words, Mary responds, "They are as brutal and ignorant as you wished, Bayo."

Bayo smiles. "Yes, they are, aren't they? Finally, all our preparation is coming along."

"Yes, finally." At that moment, Mary loses her composure for a split second and thinks back to River. Deor locks eyes with her.

"Can we get you anything?" Bayo asks Mary, taking a sip of a creamy, white drink.

"No, thank you." She knows the aroma well, Bayo's favorite drink. The white flower that is brewed to make it is a rare find in the Extraordinary Division. She remembers traveling far away nearly a century ago, just to find the flower for him, and how relieved she felt when he smiled at the sight of the gift.

"Very well," Bayo says. Then his expression suddenly turns serious and grave. "Do you know this girl?" Deor invades Mary's mind to show her an image of Grace.

Mary nods. "Yes. I know of her."

"Good," says Bayo. "I need you to keep an eye on her. Nothing too obvious, of course. To put it plainly, she is a nuisance, sticking her nose in all the wrong places."

"Yes, Bayo," Mary says.

"With that said, feel free to stay at your leisure. You are always welcome here."

"Thank you. But I think I should go. There is a bonfire tonight, and I have built myself a reputation with the young Griffins."

Bayo smiles proudly. "Yes, we've noticed. Well done, Mary. Continue the good work."

She bites her lip. "May I ask . . . how is Greon?"

Bayo looks at her with a solemn expression, and Mary immediately feels as though she had stepped out of line. She quickly adds, "It's just that . . . I haven't seen him."

"He is well," Bayo answers slowly. "I will tell him you asked for him."

Deor stops Mary on her way out. "This boy clouding your mind. What is he to you?" His cold black eyes pierce through her.

She swallows. "He is a trinket." Looking him in the eye, she says, "I plan to make him my pet."

Bayo interrupts. "Do with whomever what you will—as long as it does not get in the way of the plan."

"Yes, Bayo." She walks out.

As she passes Rioma and Ianna standing beside the door, Rioma says, "Good night, Mary. Be well."

"You as well, Mother. Good night."

Ianna follows Mary through the hallway, taking in her every step, and slowly closes the door behind her.

CHAPTER 9

Young Griffins covered in soot tend to the bonfire with driftwood. Hale watches the flames rise higher in the sky.

He turns to Grace. "Is it true they throw the bodies into the fire?"

Her eyes are fixed on the many people congregating in front of the platform. Distractedly, she answers, "Yes."

"Why are they making it now? Isn't it early?" Hale asks.

Grace sighs, annoyed. "I don't know." Then a moment later, "Don't worry, Hale. You're going to be fine. I told my friends to look after you."

Hale finds it hard to believe the people in front of them are true friends to Grace. They only seem to care to help once she throws them a coin.

She turns to him. "You should probably check on River. But come back soon, before the match starts."

Hale leaves for Grace's tent. When he passes the fire, he wonders how the ritual ever began. He watches the boys feeding the flames and wonders whether they would still build it if today would be the day their bodies were laid to rest on it, if their ashes would be the ones falling over the crowd, blowing across the field. Distracted, Hale bumps into Norton, who is staring down at his feet. His hands are stuffed into his pockets, and sweat drips down his forehead.

51

"Hi," Hale says awkwardly.

Norton looks up. "Hi."

"Are you all right?" Hale asks.

Norton doesn't answer.

"My friends are sitting together next to the fire. You can sit with us if you want."

Norton shakes his head firmly. "No. No, I'm good . . . thank you." He rushes away past Hale.

Hale watches him leave and sympathizes with his lack of trust.

●●●●●

The torches around the stage are lit and blazing a fierce orange as heavy clouds start rolling in. The air has become cooler, but Grace hasn't noticed. She is scanning the crowd for a particular face.

She spots her target. There is no doubt that this person would be the main attraction of tonight's event. As he pushes through the young Griffins, they cheer for him. He makes his way to the stage, and she rushes to challenge him before anybody else can. Leon rises to the platform with a smug smile. He raises his arms in the air, welcoming any volunteers.

"Over here!" Grace calls from behind him.

He turns and laughs. "You can't be serious."

She moves to the center of the stage and motions him forward. "Come on," she says.

He sneers, "Tired of living?"

"No. You?" Grace replies smoothly. Suddenly, without warning, Leon dashes toward her. But Grace is prepared, and she roundhouse kicks him in the head. Hard. Leon turns forcefully from the impact, and he cups his face. He reveals a blood-gushing nose a moment later and spits whatever blood was in his mouth on the stage floor. While wiping the outpour with the back of his hand, he glares at his opponent, prepared to take her on.

They jump back and forth for a while, each waiting for the other to drop their guard. Leon finds an opening, and in the blink of an eye, he tackles her to the ground. She falls with a thump, and he stands over her body, aiming a punch. With a thundering heart, she manages to kick him in the knee. Leon falls, leaving him open to be elbowed in the face.

Leon laughs through the blood dripping down his chin while Grace rises to her feet. Her lips curl in disgust. She raises her knee and kicks him in the jaw with all her might. A pop sounds from Leon's jaw at the impact. She aims another strike, but Leon catches her leg. She flips over and falls, hitting the base of her neck against the stage.

He looks down at her and spits. He kneels down and aims a ground-breaking jab at her head, but she moves just in time. His fist rams into the stage floor with a loud thud.

● ● ● ● ● ● ●

River and Hale enter the crowd. Like a child striding toward the smell of sweets, River is subconsciously moving closer and closer to Mary. Though they cannot see one another, Mary senses River's pain, and she lessens it.

The crowd thrashes and shouts. Following everyone's gazes, Hale and River turn to the stage and see Leon lifting Grace above his head and throwing her onto the stone pavement with belligerent force. They gasp.

"We need to get her out of there!" River shouts as he and Hale push through the audience.

● ● ● ● ● ● ●

The skies grow dark as heavy clouds roll in. It starts drizzling as Evan emerges from the woods. He squints, trying to make out the match only yards away from him, and his heart nearly stops at the sight. Without a second thought, he speeds toward the crowd, transforming as he runs, his claws digging into the wet soil. He stretches his wings and rises into the air. His beastly body skims the heads of the audience below. They duck and topple over one another to get out of the way.

A Griffin is storming its way toward the stage!

Evan soars to within inches of Leon's head and rakes his shoulder with his claws, rocketing upward in the sky with Leon dangling from his paw. The rain pours, soaking his fur and feathers. He looks down, anticipating fear in Leon's eyes. But Leon is expressionless. This infuriates Evan, and in his rage, he drops Leon midair just as Leon dropped Grace a moment earlier.

Leon transforms and spreads his wings before he hits the ground. The crowd shouts in exuberance for their thriving victor.

* * * * *

Grace struggles to open her eyes and tries to stand. Leon is nowhere to be found—she doesn't think to look up. In the front row is Mary, who has found a key opportunity to please Bayo.

Grace rises to her feet while Mary climbs the platform behind her. Catching Grace off guard, Mary kicks her in the back, and Grace falls back to the ground. Mary had assumed taking down Grace would be simple. She reaches out toward Grace.

But Grace is quick. She rolls and trips Mary before she can grab her.

* * * * *

In his Griffin form, Leon shoots into the air with extended claws. With a colossal bang, Leon and Evan clash into one other. Leon bites into Evan's neck, and Evan shrieks with pain. In retaliation, he wraps his hind legs around Leon's torso and squeezes with all his might. Leon unhinges himself from Evan's neck, his beak bloody. Evan uses the moment to his advantage and bangs his head against Leon's, then belts him over and over.

Leon strikes him and then takes to the stage, returning to his human form just before he lands. He looks up to Evan and calls, "Come and fight me like a man!"

Like a moth to a flame, Evan sees nothing but Leon. Following Leon's gaze, Grace looks up and sees her brother descending from the clouds and starts to put together what happened after she fell. Her body tenses in frustration as she returns her gaze to her opponent.

Mary and Grace stand in front of one another, arms extended in fighting position, each anticipating an attack. They hop around the stage, dodging one another's blows. Mary lands several blows to Grace's torso. Grace blocks her arm and side-kicks Mary in the chest, then immediately in the face. Wasting no time, she aims a jab at Mary, but Mary seizes her arm and twists it. But Grace won't allow herself to be taken so easily. She grabs hold of Mary's shoulder and flips her over. Mary lands with a *thump* and groans.

• ● ● ● ● •

Hale looks to the stage and recognizes Grace's second opponent from the first night he arrived. Evan and Leon's brawl is a terrifying sight. Both Evan and Leon move quickly. Hale watches in horror as Leon does whatever it takes to win.

Evan falls to his knees, blood gushing from his nose and his arm is bent unnaturally. Leon kicks Evan in the spine, and Evan falls facedown onto the stage.

Grace is pinned down on her stomach. Mary sits on top of her, pulling her arms back.

But suddenly, Mary feels emotions that are out of place in her mind. She feels Grace's intense helplessness and anxiety as if it were her own. But her helplessness and anxiety aren't for herself. Mary's eyes glisten with tears. She has never experienced such intense love before. She hesitates.

On the other side of the stage, Leon jumps on top of Evan's unmoving body and pulls the roots of Evan's hair, exposing his neck.

"Let go of him!" screams Grace while struggling in Mary's grasp. "Let go of him!" Tears pour from her eyes.

Mary looks into Evan's swollen eyes as he stares at his sister. She feels his terror—not fear for himself but fear for Grace. Evan's overwhelming emotions cloud Mary's mind, and she finds herself at a loss of what to do. That brief moment of hesitation knocks her off guard. The strength of her arms lessens, and suddenly Grace is free.

It would be simple for Mary to save this boy from Leon. But she could not—and would not—impede Bayo's new pupil. Whoever Leon was going to destroy, she would not stop him, no matter what she felt. But she also would not stop whoever else were to get in Leon's way.

Hale climbs onto the stage, tackling Leon from behind and throwing Leon off Evan's body.

Although Mary could have stopped Grace, she doesn't. The crowd boos with disappointment, but Mary doesn't care. She will regain her reputation in another match. But it wouldn't be Grace. Grace grabs her brother and jumps off the stage, safeguarded between friends, and escapes the wrath of the crowd. Mary takes off in the opposite direction.

Leon slams his back onto the stage, and Hale hits his head against the concrete. A blurry vision, a raised fist swims before Hale's eyes.

Right on cue, someone pulls Hale by the arm away from Leon. Hale turns and meets Grace's eyes. Stepping in front of Hale, she punches Leon in the face. Grace's friends jump the stage and join the brawl. Leon is overwhelmed and has no choice but to flee.

Suddenly, River grabs hold of Hale's shirt and pulls him off the stage. Slapping him on the back, River exclaims, "You're crazy!"

* ● ● ● ● *

Sitting in a comfortable upholstered chair, Bayo stares at the Three Eyes, watching Grace and Evan rejoice while Leon flees. He tightens his grip on the table's edge and digs his nails into the oak as he rises. Bayo's face reddens as he lifts the chair above his head and screams, throwing the chair to the other side of the room. It crashes against the wall and breaks. He stares at the wall for a moment.

With a deep growl, he mutters her name. "Mary."

* ● ● ● ● *

Hale and River sit with Grace's friends away from the crowd. Another match is beginning now, and Leon is long gone.

Evan limps up to Hale. "Thank you. Why did you help me?"

Hale pauses for a moment—thinking to himself that Grace's relationship with Evan reminded him of his relationship with Carly.

River interrupts, "Since you're in the sudden mood for politeness, I don't suppose you could apologize for being so horrible all the time?"

Evan hardly acknowledges River before walking away from them.

Hale's brows rise.

But River isn't surprised. "Yeah, didn't think so."

CHAPTER 10

In the middle of the night, a barefooted girl stands in a clearing somewhere deep in a jungle. The rain has ebbed, and she is soaking wet, her dark curls clinging to her back. Her hands are chained behind her, and she wears a white nightgown. Her heart and head are pounding, and she can't control her shaking body.

The surrounding jungle is alive. Fireflies and chirping crickets fill the landscape. Something wet slithers slowly over her foot, but she is too afraid to care. Two women stand behind her. As the law states, behind the accused will stand one friend and one foe as escorts to the trial. She can feel both pairs of eyes on her. The girl looks over her right shoulder to her grandmother. But the woman on her left is a new enemy who was currently whispering a dark incantation under her breath. The grass explodes beneath Ellionna's feet until they are long enough to encompass her body, burning her back and torso in a matter of seconds.

Ellionna holds in a shriek. She tries to move away, but they are too tight and dig into her skin until blood stains her nightgown.

When Ellionna looks back pleadingly, her assailant shouts, "Keep your head forward, demon!"

Ellionna cries silently as Livia, her grandmother, demands, "Release her at once!"

"She must obey the law!" replies the woman.

"Ellionna! Do not be afraid, you understand? Everything will be fine—"

"You will do well to keep your mouth sealed, Livia! I'm not above hurting the elderly!"

"*You* will do well to calm yourself, Nella. The trial has yet to begin."

"I have the right. It is the law! She *murdered* my two sons!"

"I . . . I didn't mean to. It was a mistake—AHH!" Ellionna screams from the pain as razor-sharp grass pushes further into her skin. She falls to her knees, feeling the skin at her back and torso separate. With her forehead on the wet ground, she sobs hysterically.

"You wicked woman!" Livia hollers as she rushes to her granddaughter. No matter Nella's steady incantation, the grass retreats as Livia approaches. Livia lifts Ellionna from the ground and whispers a spell in Ellionna's ear before she returns to her position. Ellionna inhales with the strength from her grandmother's spell and stands silently while her back bleeds through her nightgown.

They wait in silence for several minutes more until the clearing rumbles. Ellionna feels the trembling beneath her feet, and her heart skips a beat. Assella—the guardian angel of judgment—must be coming. Ellionna's only heard of such beings but never experienced them firsthand. Assella emerges from the woods as a grand, white spirit, towering above their heads. Ellionna trembles in her presence. Would Assella punish her for her crimes? She stares at the ethereal being in horror, though Assella does not acknowledge the humans present until hooded figures emerge from the darkness. It is then her glowing eyes meet Ellionna's.

Ellionna gasps.

Each carries a small lantern to guide their way through the dark. Facing her are thirty of the most prestigious people in her tribe, most of whom Ellionna knows very well. Usually friendly and familiar faces now look upon her in disgust and judgment.

Coming forward from the darkness of the jungle is their chief, Naloo, and beside him, his son, Prince Sokos. Ellionna feels a surge of relief. Surely, he will argue on her behalf since she was promised to Prince Sokos.

Chief Naloo removes his hood. "Name yourself!" he shouts at Ellionna.

She takes a deep breath. "I am Ellionna, Siren of the Arketcha tribe." Though Naloo and the rest of the people standing know this already.

"Who among you is the victim?" Chief Naloo asks.

Nella proclaims to the crowd, "I am! Nella, the descendant of Franto the Warrior!"

Naloo continues, "Explain the circumstances which have brought us here on this night."

Nella does not hesitate. "This demon has killed both of my sons this night."

Tears pour from Ellionna's eyes in a mix of regret and fear. "I did not mean to. I—" The grass consumes her once more. She falls over at the impact, gripping the soil in her agony while the sharp blades of grass enter her skin.

"Let the girl speak," says a woman among the crowd. Ellionna recognizes the voice immediately. It is Palla, the spirit guide of the tribe. The great power that Palla possesses is well known by all those present. Palla knows more about this world and the next than anyone can fathom, but she has never told a single soul what she has learned from the spirits. Though nobody knows her age, Palla always appears young and beautiful, her grey eyes bright and her hair thick and shiny. Palla had never wed or conceived a child. Ellionna's grandmother once said it is her purity that allows her to see through the veil. Palla greets Assella with a nod, and to Ellionna's surprise, the angel returns the greeting.

The crowd remains silent, waiting for Ellionna to speak. The grass shrinks back into the ground once more and with a heavy breath, Ellionna explains all that's happened. "As the siren, I must expel my voice once a day; otherwise, it will explode from me at random. This evening, I went to the lake and checked, as I always do, that it was empty before singing. But I was mistaken. Nella's youngest son, Kai, had followed me. I—I did not know he was there." Ellionna swallows thickly. "Then I was woken up in the middle of the night with a blade at my throat. It was Nella's oldest son, Lias. He said that I had killed his brother at the lake, and he would do the same to me. I was frightened. I could not contain it, I swear!"

"You lying demon!" Nella screams, about to spew her venomous spell yet again.

Ellionna braces for pain when Palla interjects. "Enough!"

"It is not a lie!" Livia proclaims. "Instead of fleeing the tribe, Ellionna confessed everything to Nella. It was Nella who brought us to this trial."

A voice Ellionna doesn't recognize shouts, "If the grandmother was not there while the eldest son was murdered, how could she have possibly known it was an accident?"

Livia exclaims, "Because I know my granddaughter!"

Another voice proclaims, "She still murdered two men!"

Then another, "The siren has been housed in an Arketchian vessel long enough! It is about time we free ourselves from its harm!"

"Yes. The siren has caused enough damage! We should kill it!"

Livia's steps forward with a finger extended, "Might I remind you, as the previous vessel of the siren, I know better than any that the siren cannot be killed. Killing its vessel will not kill its spirit. The spirit is everlasting and erratic if uncontained. You will have a mightier death toll than you know."

"She is right," Palla says seriously.

"What should we do then?" someone asks.

"She is a menace to the tribe. We should imprison her if she cannot be killed."

The chief finally speaks up. "This has to end. We were lenient when she killed her father. Now, two more men have died. This is enough. She has proven incapable of containing the siren."

Ellionna looks up at the chief in shock. Even Sokos looks stern.

Palla speaks up. "This girl did not murder these boys. She was unaware she was being followed, and the second death was a consequence of self-defense."

"There is no witness to either of these accounts besides the girl. We do not know whether that information is true."

"Yes, we do!" Palla proclaims loudly, walking to the center of the clearing beside Ellionna. "I have the witnesses with me. Both the boys, Lias and Kai, are with me now."

Everyone begins to murmur at once.

Nella yells, "She's lying! Do not believe her!"

"It is well known that Palla is able to communicate with the spirits. I do not doubt her abilities." It is the first time Sokos had spoken. "Are you able to show us these spirits?" he asks.

"I am." With that, Palla blows out her lantern and places it beside her feet. She closes her eyes, bows her head, and mumbles an incantation the rest do not understand. She lifts her head, and with her arms outstretched, her incantation rises. Her eyes open and are afire with a bright green light. On either side of her appear two transparent and floating spheres. One burns a bright blue, the other an immense purple. It looks as though these orbs are on fire, each with its own flame, though no heat radiates from them.

The crowd gasps.

"Lias and Kai," Palla says. "Thank you for agreeing to this. Don't be afraid— show them your true form."

Both spheres glow white and a bright flash lights up the jungle. Everyone but Palla turns away from the blinding light. The apparitions of two young men float an inch or two above the ground. They look beautiful and magical, unharmed in any way. They look to their mother.

Nella rushes toward her sons, trying to hold them, touch them, but she cannot. "My boys!" she cries.

Lias looks at her solemnly. "Mama, don't cry. We're okay."

Kai then says, "There is a place, Mama. This magnificent place that explains all."

Lias continues, "Yes, I was shown that my actions were wrong. Vengeance cost me my life and deprived you of your sons."

"I was foolish, Mama. I doubted the curse of the siren and followed Ellionna, knowing the intent of her voyage to the lake," Kai explains. "Please do not continue this line of wrongdoing, Mama."

Nella stares up at her sons in shock. With overflowing tears, she tells them she loves them both.

Lias says to Palla, "We are ready now."

Palla nods and closes her eyes. There is another flash of bright light, and the boys are gone.

The crowd is silent for a long moment as Palla looks to her tribe. "This is the first time I have shared my gift with the tribe. I did so because I was told to save this girl's fate. The siren is an asset to our people, not an enemy. As you know, we need her now more than ever."

Someone interrupts. "She is not an asset if our warriors are needlessly dying. How many more will die if we choose to be merciful?"

"He is right," the chief proclaims gravely. "I have decided."

The forest goes quiet except for the beating of Ellionna's heart. Tears stream down her face. *Please say I'm innocent. Please.*

The chief says, "I choose to pardon Ellionna from execution. Furthermore, because Ellionna was not at fault in either death, I will not condemn her to prison." Ellionna sags in relief. "However," Chief Naloo continues, "I do not take lightly the damage caused today and the damage that could be caused in the future. We have housed the siren long enough! Because of that, I am left with no other option. Ellionna," he says, looking gravely into her eyes, "I hereby banish you from the Arketcha tribe."

CHAPTER 11

S leeping high in the treetop, Mary awakens at the sound of Deor's voice in her mind. *Bayo is expecting you.* If Bayo was calling her in the middle of the night, it wasn't good.

Behind the waterfall, Deor directs. Mary knows the place all too well. It is Bayo's favorite place on the island. Mary walks to the cliffs and spots the waterfall rushing to the ocean. She transforms and jumps, flapping her magnificent wings in the air. The sea spray is cold and refreshing against the humidity. Mary flies around the massive waterfall and into the cave behind it.

On the other side of the cave, small waterfalls flow down a rocky, moss-covered mountainside. At the base of each waterfall, a light mist clouds over the calm bay. The water glows against the light of the moon, which would be full at its next phase.

Mary transforms back into her human self, and she sits by the shore, waiting patiently. Staring into the water, she loses herself in memories of her travels at sea centuries ago.

Suddenly rising from the bay is Bayo in his massive Griffin form. His sleek coat shimmers with the blue light reflecting off the water. Bayo hovers above Mary's head and returns to his human form, landing on his feet beside her.

Mary starts to explain. "Bayo, I apologize for disobeying your command. Leon and I were outnumbered."

"You need not explain to me what happened. I saw it all," Bayo says casually. "I asked you to keep an eye on that girl. And the moment you had her in your grasp, you let her go. Tell me, Mary, what did she project in that pretty little head of yours?" He looks down at her. "Did you see her love for her brother? Was it love that melted your cold heart?" he taunts.

Mary cannot meet Bayo's eyes. "Yes," she says, shaken. Mary was startled by the thoughts of Leon's opponent. Evan did not think of losing his sister, nor about his own life. But instead, the thought that terrified him was that his sister had to watch him die. He couldn't bear to see her go through such pain. But Mary cannot disclose this.

Can she conceal the truth as long as Deor is Bayo's confidante? Mary takes a deep breath as she risks her life, "The accumulated thoughts of all those at the arena were so overwhelming, I couldn't bear it."

Bayo cocks his head to the side. "Stop lying." Mary's heart drops as Bayo continues, "I know the thoughts of the subject's brother caused you to feel pity, and that is why you destroyed your chance to remove that girl from *my* brother."

"I—" Mary begins. "Please, Bayo. I made a mistake—" but she cannot finish her sentence while the mighty surge of his power courses through her. She cringes in pain while trying to fight his hold over her.

"I have been lost to my brother for eleven long years!" Bayo growls. "He was stolen from me by my most trusted friend! And finally, he's returned to us. All on his own, without my interference. As if fate has aligned the stars! And I ask you to keep a potential enemy from him. That same night, not only do you allow that enemy to live but also allow her to grow closer to Hale and embarrass my heir! You then have the nerve to come face me and lie—"

His power intensifies, and Mary lets out a scream. Finally, he loosens his grip, and she falls to the floor, pleading for her life while gasping for air. "I—I'm sorry, Bayo."

This calms his temper. "This girl . . . Grace . . . is dangerous. She corrupts the minds of the young Griffins, pushing them to act apart from the norm. She does not participate in their games but makes a mockery of them instead. If she has such a following now, imagine what will happen once I make an army of the young Griffins? And coercing her brother with power as a means to manipulate her had not worked . . ." he trails off. "Leon is a prize for the crowd. He will not let this night become him. Once his powers are revealed to him, he will stop at nothing to end the life of Evan and Grace to prove himself worthy. Though I wouldn't mind ending her life, this cannot happen since I plan to make Leon my heir. If he ends their lives, Hale will turn on him and, therefore, turn on me."

He looks at Mary closely. "It must be you. No one knows of our ties. You have less than three days before the Welcoming Moon to complete the task. End their lives before Leon has the opportunity. This is your last chance, Mary."

"Yes, Bayo."

CHAPTER 12

G reon works over a mirror on the hardwood floor back in his old cabin, trying to find a way around the nymph's offer. He pours a liquid concoction over the mirror and chants a spell. The purple mixture spreads evenly throughout the mirror and turns transparent. The spell is working. As he chants, he feels the ancient magic pouring through him. His eyes sparkle with hope, and he dares not stop. He places an object from the Extraordinary Division on the mirror, his own Griffin feather tied to an Arketchian spear. Then he places his bare hand against the mirror pane.

He closes his eyes, concentrating hard, and falls into a meditative state. The power flows through him.

Greon continues on like this for hours. The magic flow increases, and a strong, magnetic surge flows through his body. He feels the mirror warm beneath his hand, and he quickens his chanting. Just when he feels the power at its peak, there is a loud *crack*. Beneath his hand, the mirror has broken into hundreds of shards.

He opens his eyes in horror.

"No, no, no, no. NO!" he screams. He dashes to his small supply cupboard and digs through vials and jars, shaking them, inspecting how much is left in each. They are all empty. There is nothing.

Greon stares at the cupboard for a long time, slipping into despair. Tears pour from his eyes as he remembers the nymph's words.

He takes in a deep breath. Try as he may, there isn't another way.

Greon walks out the door and straight into the forest. "I've lived a long time," Greon says aloud. "I always said I should have died nine hundred years ago. Not a big deal at all."

Greon stops in the middle of the forest and calls out, "I'm ready."

After a long moment of waiting, he sits down and leans against the trunk of a tree. Will they pop out beside him and snap his neck? Or a tree limb falling on his head might do the deed. Greon looks around anxiously, and the forest starts to chuckle.

"Are you afraid of dying, Greon?" asks a voice.

"It's something I've never done before. Who wouldn't be frightened?"

"Maybe we can make it easier for you."

Suddenly, a voice shouts right in Greon's ear, "Maybe we can pop out and GET YOU!" Just then, Greon is pushed from behind.

He jumps and screams. He spins around, but there is nothing.

Then the nymphs appear before him. They emerge from the trees and other flora. They are transparent, different shades of green, and all different sizes. All their bodies are genderless, their limbs are long and limber. Greon is in awe of how many there are. There are hundreds.

"We weren't planning on *stabbing* you!" says another. The nymphs laugh. "Just a simple poison will do the trick."

Greon raises his brows. "Very reassuring."

"We will guide you through the spirit realm and continue to be your guide until you complete your task."

With a fast, unthinking breath, Greon says, "I am ready. Which poison will I be given?"

A youthful voice comes up from the crowd. "Mine! Mine! Have mine!" It pushes through its kin and makes its way toward Greon, taking his hand. "Come. I'm this way." Its hand is soft and lush and moist. It leads Greon to a bush a few yards away. "That's me." The nymph points to the bush. "I killed a deer last year. He was very dumb . . ."

More nymphs crowd around it. "That's all right," says another nymph. "But I'm much, much stronger. You should have me!"

"No. You are not stronger. You've never killed anything."

"Yes, I have!"

"The worst thing you've done is make a wolf vomit!"

"Yes, and I'm very good at it. I can make a wolf vomit so fast it vomits before it—"

Greon interrupts them. "Which will give me the most peaceful death?"

Silence.

"Mmm—none of us. What do you think? Dying is easy?" exclaims a nymph.

Then another pipes up. "I have an idea. We give him all of us. That will be one deadly concoction."

"Yes. Grind it up, down the hatch, and he'll be as good as gone!" another nymph agrees.

The nymphs vanish into thin air, leaving behind a giggling echo, and Greon is left alone in the woods yet again.

He slumps down against the trunk of a tree once more and closes his eyes. He wonders if this is the last time that he will feel the warmth of the sun against his skin. He thinks of the golden vision of Ianna. She emerges from the sunlight and comes to rest her head on Greon's shoulder, and Greon soaks in the comfort of his soulmate. Just when Greon thought he'd fallen asleep, something is placed on his lap. It is a cup made of large leaves, and in it is a watery blend of poison.

He looks down at it and nearly whimpers. "This is to be my downfall." He lifts the cup to his lips, Ianna and Mary his last thoughts. He parts his lips to swallow the mixture. Then the cup is thrust from his hands and spills into the soil beside him.

A voice whispers urgently, "Don't drink that!"

The voice sounds older than the nymph children. It whispers again, "They want you dead. One less Elder in the world and all that."

"But it's the only way to get back," Greon counters.

There is a pause, and then the voice confesses, "It's not."

"Why should I trust you?" he asks. "Who are you?"

"I am one of them. I am a nymph. I have put my family under a sleeping curse. It will last only moments. There is no reason for you to trust me besides the fact I have gone against my own kind for your life. Run to the nearest clearing. We must go!"

Perplexed, Greon obeys and hurries through the woods. All is quiet until the trees begin to sway violently.

"Keep running!" the nymph orders.

The ground begins to rumble furiously. Large branches crash down beside Greon as he sprints into the clearing. The nymph that had saved his life shouts, "Transform!"

"Are you insane? This is the Human Division of Malphora!" Greon argues.

The nymph becomes visible and stands in front of Greon. "Anything I touch can remain unseen. And you have the power to do likewise." Startled by the nymph's knowledge, Greon is speechless. The nymph repeats, "Transform!"

Greon crosses his arms over his chest and releases them. His human form disperses into light, which fades to reveal Greon in his Griffin form. His blond fur shines in the pristine sunlight.

An army of angry nymphs emerges from the woods. Greon runs across the clearing, spreading his wings wide. The helpful nymph grows a long vine from its hand and throws it around Greon's neck. Greon rises into the air as the nymphs below throw long spears at them.

The nymph climbs up the vine around Greon's neck and onto Greon's back. The other nymphs' spears cut through the sky, and Greon dodges hastily, making himself invisible in the sky. But several shards scrape Greon's thigh. He shrieks in pain and shudders. The nymph pulls on the reins around his neck and forces him to fly higher.

"West!" the nymph shouts. "We must travel west!"

Greon struggles for breath and flaps his wings in the sun's warmth. Though his leg throbs painfully, Greon can't help but wonder why he hadn't transformed in so long. *There's nothing like it*, he thinks, *the pure indescribable feeling of soaring through the sky.*

CHAPTER 13

"I hereby banish you from the Arketcha tribe!"

Ellionna turns white. She sits in the mud, motionless, as the elites around her shout in rage.

"How could you allow her life to be spared?"

"She is a murderer!"

"She should be executed!"

Filled with fury, which her sons warned her not to act out, Nella is dissatisfied with Ellionna's sentence and spits, "Good riddance."

Palla's voice cuts through the crowd. "Chief Naloo, you are making a grave mistake."

But Chief Naloo has had enough. "Silence!" he shouts, and the crowd quiets. "Ellionna," the chief calls, but she cannot meet eyes with him. "You have until sundown."

The chief and Sokos leave without another word, their lanterns in hand and hoods over their heads. Everybody disperses along with them. Among them, Assella is the last to depart, her every step shaking the earth.

Livia approaches her granddaughter, placing a steady hand on her shoulder. Ellionna bursts into tears, and Livia embraces her. "Come on now," Livia says. "Let's go home."

She pulls Ellionna from the ground, and they leave the jungle together. Dawn has come, and the sunlight grows brighter by the moment.

Two cloaked women in grey robes, which Livia and Ellionna had not noticed, stand in the clearing. One calls out to them, "I will go with you, Ellionna."

Livia and Ellionna look back. The girl removes her hood. She is about the same age as Ellionna. Her black straight hair ends at her shoulders. She wears a thin gold band around her forehead. The gold band is symbolic of female warriors who train at the temple of Chiba.

Ellionna runs to embrace her cousin. "Robin! What are you doing here?"

"The Warriors of Chiba attend every trial," Robin says. "Pity this time it was yours. Ellionna, as the born guardian of the siren, it is time I take up my duty to protect you."

Livia nods. "Your family would have been proud of you, Robin."

•●●●●•

Livia and Ellionna walk silently from the jungle and onto a dirt path. In a matter of moments, the sun would peek through the mountains along the horizon. Seagulls and other birds flock toward the port. The shoreline swarms with people, some arriving from their travels and others setting out to the sea or setting up by the docks to sell their fresh catches.

They enter the city square, which is still closed for the night. The white sand buildings in the square are so different from those in the tribe's dried mud villages. Piled atop each building are awnings made of wood and woven hay.

The square continues up the hill. Livia and Ellionna turn to a beaten path that leads to their village. The early morning chirping of birds surrounds them, and the air is suddenly humid near the waterfalls that cascade over the sides of the mountains. They pass wooden homes built on boulders and stilts. Each connected to one another with staircases and wooden bridges.

They arrive at a wooden bridge built across the bay when Ellionna feels faint. The lightness of her head causes her to stumble, and she catches herself on Livia's arm.

Livia holds Ellionna steadfast and says, "We're almost there. Hold on a bit longer." She takes Ellionna's hand. "I'll get you healed, and we will eat. Everything will be okay."

The bridge shakes and rattles along the way, but this bridge is the only way to and from their home. The green jungle lessens, and there, visible in the morning's cloudy sky, stands a single mud hut.

They enter the home, which is furnished with a short glass table and embroidered pillows in the center of the room. Against the wall is a long wooden dresser, and above it hangs a mirror. Each piece of furniture is carved with intricate designs representing famous Arketchian stories.

Livia takes Ellionna to her room where there is a single window, a wooden bed, and a trunk filled with her belongings. Though this might seem simple, a bed and a trunk full of belongings are more than what most girls or boys had at Ellionna's age in the Arketcha tribe.

Ellionna collapses on the bed, her skin pale and sweaty. Livia lifts her nightgown and Ellionna gasps in pain as the dry blood glued to the fabric opens her skin. Upon Ellionna's torso are long slashes, red and swollen, covered in sticky blood. Ellionna cries once more, clutching the sheets beneath her.

Livia shakes her head. It amazes her that anybody can be exiled in such a condition. Livia gathers a bucket of water and a clean rag. Her hands shake as she washes away the blood. She wraps her granddaughter's upper body and instructs Ellionna to repeat a numbing incantation. Ellionna repeats after her grandmother.

While Ellionna rests, Livia prepares a meal for two. The savory smell of meat drifts to Ellionna. She sits up in her bed and, for a split second, thinks the previous day was only a dream. But then the wrappings around her upper body remind her she is a murderer. And this is her last day in her own home.

Ellionna meets her grandmother in the kitchen. Every step, she feels as if it is her last, and she bitterly savors every second of what she sees, smells, and feels.

Livia says cheerfully, "You're up."

Startled by her optimism, Ellionna stays silent for a few moments until she is able to express a portion of her many thoughts. "Grandmother, what should I do? What should I take?"

"We have all day, Ellionna. We will figure it out after we eat."

They eat together in the main room on the floor, as they always do, beside their low table. Livia has prepared Ellionna's favorite meal: rice dumplings stuffed with tender meat and vegetables. Ellionna eats slowly, making sure to remember the taste, holding the welling tears in her eyes. Neither speaks.

At the end of their meal, Livia looks to her granddaughter. "There is no land suitable for you and Robin. It's too dangerous. There is only one place you could go and live peacefully." She looks meaningfully at her granddaughter. "Bimmorus. You must understand, Ellionna, traveling to Bimmorus will be difficult, but it is necessary for your survival. It will take you nearly two years to walk by foot. Never stay in one place too long. Trust nobody. Make sure no one in the outside world knows who you are."

Livia hands her two pens and a pocket-sized book with empty pages. "Take this pen with you. I have its twin. Whatever you write with yours will reach me here. I will be able to write back to you. Keep in touch with me, so I may know you are safe."

Ellionna nods.

Livia then brings out an armor vest that ends mid-thigh. From afar, it looks like glistening fabric, but up close, the woven metal is visible. "It's made from titanium. Nothing will be able to touch you."

"Thank you, Grandmother," Ellionna says, feeling the armor in her hands. It was very light.

"Ellionna, use your voice at anybody who wishes you harm," Livia commands. "Your safety comes first."

Though Ellionna does not agree, she knows it would be best for her to heed her grandmother's words. She nods. "I will."

She touches her granddaughter's shoulder and smiles. "We will see each other again. Give it a while until they forget. Sokos needs to get married eventually. You are still his betrothed."

Ellionna inhales deeply and nods.

●●●●●

Robin walks alone through the jungle and comes to the temple on a plateau. In front of the temple is an overflowing pool. Small waterfalls create a mist in the air, and a stone bridge—carved out of the mountain itself—leads to the entrance of the temple.

It has been several years since Robin has visited this temple, and she notes how decayed it has become. She steps out from the shrubs and to the bridge. Only halfway to the temple, she hears a rustling coming from behind. She pulls out her sword from inside her cloak and spins around.

But there is nothing there.

She waits for several moments, but nothing approaches. Must have been a small animal. Robin moves forward to cross the bridge but holds her sword ready.

As she enters through the open archway, sunlight pours in from the open ceiling overhead. The space is shaped like a large circle and rises nearly fifty feet high. The floor is made of smooth, sandy stone, and monuments of the famous fathers of the Arketcha tribe stand twenty feet tall, all with their own stories of heroism. In the center of the temple is a well filled with holy water.

Drinking from the well after losing a loved one or visiting a gravesite was a means for cleansing and keeping death from spreading. Beyond the well is another archway leading to the gravesites. Robin walks around the well and then through the archway, her footsteps echoing in the chamber. Looking out into the grassy scape, she cannot see its end. The most prestigious of families are buried near this archway. Poorer families must travel farther into the graveyard to visit their loved ones.

Robin continues through the plateau, passing hundreds of monuments. Finally, she reaches what she came for. She kneels. In the Arketchian language, the names read: Benya Nerezza, Mother, 28. Laila Nerezza, Daughter, 5. Damin Nerezza, Son, 3. It is one gravesite with three names on its monument, all buried together.

From within her cloak, she pulls out three flowers that grow only on the outskirts of the tribe's land. They are bright red with several thick petals and give off a sweet aroma. This was her mother's favorite flower. She places one by each name.

A deep voice comes from behind, "You still remember."

She whips around, her sword extended. She has been anticipating this moment. Robin stands and does not lower her sword. The man facing her is tall, with dark skin, thick eyebrows, and light brown eyes. He is clean-shaven, and his straight black hair is tied low behind his back.

"Stop following me," she demands simply, turning to leave.

"Don't go," he pleads, and she pauses.

"What is it you want?"

She notes the vulnerability in his eyes as he reaches out for her and says, "Just a few minutes of your time. I've missed you."

Her eyes pierce through his soul. "I haven't missed you."

"Robin, please." He comes closer.

She brings the tip of her sword to his neck.

"Let me explain," he says, raising his arms in surrender. This is an odd position for an Arketchian man, who would never bring himself to a standard below or equal to that of a woman.

Though Robin is taken aback by his eagerness to talk, she snaps, "No. You're lucky I've left you alive for so long."

"I know. I know. But I've learned to control it now."

"Hear me carefully," she says. "I wish to be away from you. Indefinitely!" She walks away.

"I will never be apart from you. Not so long as you are my daughter," he calls to her.

"I am not your daughter, Atomi! All your children died the day you killed them!"

As she passes through the archway, Atomi suddenly appears in front of her. Robin jumps back and extends her sword once more.

"Robin, I know you're angry. Please, will you listen? It didn't happen the way you think." Robin storms around him toward the temple's entrance. At the well, a blur passes her, so quickly her hair flies. Atomi stands before her once more.

She cuts through the air in a downward slash with her sword, and he blocks the blow with his bare forearm.

"Robin! Stop!"

She stares at his unmarked skin. He takes a step closer, and again, she slashes her sword. Atomi blocks each attack with his forearm, still unscathed. But Robin's anger is unending. She screams and rages and, eventually, grows tired. He appears unbreakable.

There are no other options. She must flee. She lowers her sword, her chest heaving with adrenaline. Atomi approaches her and places his hands on her shoulders as if to embrace her. She kicks him in the legs and runs. While running as fast as she can, she looks back to see if he is running after her.

The same blur passes her again, and she feels her sword push through something. She skids to a halt. Turning her head, she meets eyes with her father once more, her sword impaled in his midsection and sticking out his back.

She holds her breath in shock. Blood pours out where the sword entered him, and his mouth is slick from it.

"Robin. I did not kill them," Atomi says. "I swear to you. It wasn't me."

"I saw you do it. In your beast form."

He pulls the sword from his body, his hand directly on the blade. His eyes roll back, and he falls backward onto the ground. He mumbles, "It wasn't me."

Despite herself, Robin shakes him, but he does not stir. Suddenly, his spilled blood recedes. She lifts his shirt and finds Atomi's wound healing. Soon, the only remainder of the incident is the blood on his clothes and the tear in his shirt. His eyes snap open, and he gasps for breath.

"Seems you're still alive," Robin sneers, getting back on to her feet. "Guess you should explain yourself then . . . since you won't leave me alone until you do."

Atomi stands up and starts walking back toward the temple. "Come. You didn't drink the water before you left."

By the edge of the well, Atomi watches his daughter take the water into her hands and drink.

"You haven't aged," she says.

"It is part of the curse."

"You didn't kill them?"

"No."

"And I should believe you?"

"It's the truth," he says.

"Go on then," she urges. "What do you say happened that night?"

He takes in a deep breath. "Your mother laid you down to sleep. You remember?"

Robin remembers very well. She and her siblings shared one room, and their mother put them to bed every night. They had one large cot on the floor. Their parents had one identical to it in their room. Her mother, Benya, was a beautiful woman. She always wore her hair in a braid. It was so long; it reached the end of her back. Her eyes were like Robin's, her eyelashes thick and long, her skin fair.

"I came in shortly after work. I was late, and it was the first night of the cycle," her father says softly.

"Yes. You came in, and you were unwell," Robin adds.

She got up when she heard her father come home. She wanted to say goodnight to him, but she saw him stumble through the open door and fall. Benya ran to him and lifted him from the floor before noticing Robin in the doorway.

"Robin. Go back to bed," she said.

Robin quickly turned and jumped in bed. Shortly after, she saw her mother guide her father down the steps to the floor below. Robin knew her father was cursed. It wasn't a secret, though she was still too young to understand the extent of it.

Her mother returned and locked the door behind her. She walked past the kids' room and noticed Robin was still awake.

"Go to bed," she whispered, closing their door.

Robin called out, "I love you."

"I love you, too." The door shut, then Robin heard the rattle as her mother locked it.

Her father continues. "Your mother took me to the room below and locked me in, as she always did at such times."

"Do you remember what happened when you changed?" Robin asks.

He says, "At that time, I seldom remembered. But, that night, I remember some of what happened."

"How can you possibly know if it was you or not? You escaped your cage—I remember the doors were ripped apart," Robin says, taking a step back.

"Robin," he says, frustrated. "Yes, I escaped. Because while you were sleeping, someone was walking above. Their scent was unlike yours or the children's or your mother's."

This seems vaguely familiar to Robin. "Our door rattled. Somebody was trying to open it from the outside, but it was locked. They began to bang it in," Robin recalls slowly.

"That was when I began my escape," he says. "The house was dark, of course, so you were not able to see all of what had happened. By the time I reached you, you were hidden under the cot, and the intruder was nowhere to be found."

"I . . . I tried to wake them up . . . They didn't want to be moved," Robin says.

"I know you did. You saw me from under the cot. Then I ran off . . ." he trails off. "I caught his scent—the taste of his blood. Then nothing. I woke up the next morning in my human form. There was a severed arm beside me. I didn't know who it belonged to.

"After they were buried, after my cycle ended, was the night of my judgment. I left you that night with your grandmother."

He tells Robin about the trial, standing in the center as the elites of the tribe looked down on him. "I caught the scent of the killer during my trial. The wolf is a part of me even when the cycle is finished."

* * * * * *

"Why have we come?" asks an elite. "We know all too well what this man has done to his family. There should be no trial. He is a killer!"

"I did not kill my family!" shouts Atomi. "I would never do such a thing!" He is whipped for speaking out of line by Chief Tati's command. But Atomi continues anyway. "There was an intruder in my home! I buried my family with my own hands. They were not slashed by teeth or paw but by a dagger!"

"Strike him!" bellows Chief Tati.

"Stop!" cries Amoz. "He speaks the truth. I was there the day they were buried."
Amoz is Ellionna's father and the tribe's medicine man. As such, he was regarded as
the most trusted member of the tribe.

"Who would kill your family?" asks another.

"I have evidence!" shouts Atomi in rage. He kneels and unwraps the severed arm
and lifts it above his head. "The left arm of the man that did it."

"He could have gotten that arm from anyone!"

Atomi retaliates, "I chased him that night, the first night of my cycle. I remember
catching him and ripping his arm out. If that is not sufficient, I have found one
more thing that belonged to the murderer." He reveals a blood-crusted dagger and
continues, "This weapon not only matches the wounds of my two children and wife,
but the injury inflicted on my living child across her midsection!"

"I checked her myself. It is a true match," vouches Amoz.

"Assuming what you are saying is true," says a voice, "that would explain why the
person whose arm this belongs to did not come forward."

"Do not be naïve," says Chief Tati. "Atomi could have killed his family and
framed a man to make it seem as if he isn't the murderer!" He moves awkwardly as
he speaks.

Atomi snarls. He has caught the scent.

The crowd shouts, "The chief is right!"

"Atomi is the killer!"

"You cannot mask yourself, monster!"

"The person is not dead. He is very much alive. And I can prove it to you. I know
exactly who it is. The arm belongs to somebody here!" Atomi steps out from the center
of the clearing.

There is a great uproar throughout the circle. Palla's voice shouts above the rest.
"Please! For the sake of his argument, let us amuse his theory. Lower your whip!" she
demands. "Let us for the sake of the argument, each show both our arms."

Palla reveals her arms from within her cloak. Amoz follows. Slowly, the rest
follow. The chief's face is stony when it is finally his turn to reveal his arms. When
he exposes his arms, his left forearm is missing. The crowd gasps. In a blaze of anger,
Atomi vanishes and reappears in front of Tati.

Atomi lifts the chief by his throat and shouts, "Why did you kill them? Why?"

The chief gurgles and chokes, his face turning purple.

Amoz approaches his friend. "Atomi!" he yells. "Drop him! You are above this!"

Tears pour from Atomi's eyes. "Tell me! Why them? Why?" His cries echo throughout the forest, and all the people stand in heartbroken silence.

Amoz speaks calmly. "Do what you will with him, Atomi. But remember Benya when you do it. Would she be proud of a man who would fall into vengeance?"

Robin asks, "Why did he do it?"

"He never had the opportunity to answer that question," Atomi says.

"Did you kill him?" she asks.

"No. As the chief attempted to sneak away, Assella, the angel of judgment dematerialized into smoke, reaching out for the chief who ran away deeper into the wilderness. There was a loud scream in the distance, and shortly after, Assella returned empty-handed, only to look me in the eye before she vanished. I would never forget it . . ." he trails off. "The elites found his body afterward.

"The treachery of the chief is not discussed among the commoners of the Arketcha tribe," Atomi finishes. "It is the wish of the current chief, Naloo, that his brother's madness would not disgrace the family name. That is why all of the commoners believe he died suddenly from illness. You were too angry, Robin, to let me tell you when you were younger."

•••••••

The evening has come for Ellionna to leave the Arketcha tribe.

"Take these weapons, just in case. You probably won't need them—Robin will take good care of you," Livia says.

Ellionna hides the various small knives on her person.

Livia holds out a cloak to her. "For the chilly nights," she offers. Ellionna throws the cloak over her armor.

There is a knock on the door. Before Livia answers it, she hands her granddaughter a large sack of food and says, "Ellionna, do not be afraid. Do not show fear or shame. Walk out with your pride and your dignity."

She takes the sack in her hands and bows her head. "Yes, Grandmother."

The door opens. It is Sokos. "Good evening," he says coldly.

He is pale for an Arketchian, with small, slanted eyes and long dark hair that he styles half down. He wears a silk navy blue shirt. Such expensive clothing is rare to come by in the tribe. Over his extravagant shirt is his cloak, tied around his neck with black crystal pendants connected elegantly with chains.

Ellionna hasn't expected Sokos to come. At the sight of him, she finds that she cannot move.

"I have permission from my father to escort Ellionna from the Arketcha tribe," he says.

Livia nods. "Come now, Ellionna. It's time."

Ellionna throws her arms around her grandmother, and they embrace for much too short a time. Sokos is impatient. He grabs hold of Ellionna's arm and pulls her away.

"You are strong and fierce, child. You will be okay," Livia calls. She looks at her granddaughter one final time.

Sokos's hand is firm on Ellionna's arm, leading her away. A sickening thought enters Ellionna's mind. Will this be the last time she sees her grandmother? Hastily, she turns back to shout, "Grandmother! I love you!"

"I love you, too!"

When they are far from Livia's home, he suddenly grabs the roots of Ellionna's hair and pulls with great force. She winces in pain. "You will never be free from me, Ellionna. Not even in exile. Remember that, will you?"

She grabs the back of her hair to lessen the pain in her scalp. But he pulls harder.

"This exile was written in the stars, Sokos," she manages. "And fate will continue pushing me away from you."

Suddenly, it struck Ellionna that she did not have to be afraid of him anymore. The endless hidden beatings were at their end. There is a gleam in her eyes as she kicks him in the shin. Ellionna then elbows Sokos in the stomach and runs as fast as she can from him. It is the first time she has ever fought back. What an empowering feeling!

"Remember that, will you?" she calls back from afar.

She stops running once she reaches the square. Sokos is a ways behind her. Waiting for her at the entrance to the square are several warriors, Chief Naloo, and several elites. They allow her to pass, and the warriors group behind her. As she walks, everyone stares. The adults heckle her, and the children laugh as they throw stones at her.

"Murderer!" shouts a woman. "They should have killed you!"

"You wretched witch!" exclaims another.

Ellionna feels weak upon hearing them all. People she once knew so well turn their backs to her. Harsh stones land on her, one after the other. But she keeps walking and quickens her stride away from them all.

"That's right! Go!" they shout, and they cheer as she leaves.

"Finally! We are rid of the siren!"

"May the High Being be pleased with us!"

Ellionna's throat throbs. The voice is trying to emerge. It feels so dry, so painful. She swallows hard and forces herself to hold it in just a bit longer. Finally, Ellionna arrives at the edge of the Arketcha tribe. She has never ventured into this jungle before. Waiting for her is Robin. At the sight of her, Ellionna's throat soothes itself.

A warrior from behind calls to Robin, "If you leave with her now, you will never be allowed to return."

"I am aware," Robin says firmly. "There is nothing left for me here."

And Ellionna and Robin enter the wilderness.

CHAPTER 14

T he air is as brisk as it is humid, but Marcus doesn't mind it one bit. He loves sleeping outside, even during the hot summer rain. If his mother hadn't forced him otherwise, he would have stayed outside in the rain the night before. Resting on his belly, peering through the magnificently tall grass, Marcus makes out a single road swooping, disappearing, and appearing again through the trees. This road is forgotten, cracked with age and neglect, muddy, and covered in weeds. But following this path, he can see the peaks of the capital of Bimmorus. Its towers sparkle like a pearl resting in crystal clear water.

Marcus scratches his muddy ash-blond hair and wonders what it must be like to live in the capital. Would someone like him be welcome? He rolls onto his back and faces the swaying trees and open sky. He is wet and covered in dirt, lying on the muddy ground.

The sun is almost a quarter-way in the sky in the east. He closes his eyes and counts to twenty. He does this a few more times before he gets up. Taking a basket of freshly picked vegetables and fruits, he walks up the cobbled dirt path leading to the blistered and humble wooden door of his cottage.

The cottage is hidden behind moist, green shrubs and trees. Long vines growing on the cottage reach from one side to the next.

The light shines through the house as he steps in. He looks around as if for the first time, as if this weren't actually his home, as if everything surrounding him had never been there before. He cocks his head when he notices a long scratch on the door, wondering if that had been there before.

He rests the basket beside his mother, Ariah, who is kneading dough in the kitchen. Her hair is tucked away in a scarf, her light and greying brown hair peeping through at her forehead. Though her hair is greying, her face is moist and plump. Strangely enough, none of her features belonged to Marcus.

Flour dust glitters the air around her hands. Ariah takes one look at him and exclaims, "Marcus! You're filthy!"

He looks down at himself and then up at her. "It's not that bad," he begins.

"Not *that* bad? You're caked in mud! Lying in the wet ground again! Even after I asked you last night to do no such thing!" she declares. He tries to explain his side further but is interrupted, probably for the best. "How do you expect to go to the capital in such a state? You best be quick. It's getting very late."

Marcus parts his lips again in protest, but before words can emerge, his mother shoos him away.

He lingers at the door.

"You're stalling, aren't you?" she calls out to him.

He turns around, his expression like a thief who has been caught in the act.

"I won't make you go if you don't want to. I've told you that already. But this will be an amazing opportunity for you. You have always wanted to see the capital."

"It's not that," he explains. "It's just . . . just, I'm afraid it will be very different there. And there's nobody like me."

"It is very different there than it is here," Ariah agrees. "But it is also just as beautiful. And yes, there is nobody like you in Bimmorus. But that does not mean you can't find similarities with others." She searches his eyes. "Nerves are normal. Once you get there, you'll see there is nothing to be nervous about."

He nods.

"And if you don't like it," she continues, "you can always come back home. Though I imagine the king will eventually see your power as a great asset to the kingdom. And you will live in the palace in a life of luxury. You'll have servants to help you wash up and pick your food for you." She chuckles lightly.

Marcus smiles. "Of course, you and Pa would come live with me if that should happen."

"And leave *this* palace of my own to rot? What a notion!" They laugh. "Now go get yourself ready."

Marcus departs as his mother places her dough in a metal pan and covers it with a lid. She holds the pan from the bottom, and the dough begins to cook at her touch. The ability to produce fire or heat from one's body is a rare gift. Such Griffins with this talent are known as the Griffins of Ardor.

Marcus heads to the outdoor shower beside the cottage and quickly bathes himself.

Meanwhile, his father, Eliath, tends to the cattle nearby. Marcus hears the folk tune Eliath sings when he is in high spirits. As Marcus scrubs away the mud, he daydreams how quickly his mother would leave this place for a life in the capital—even though she wouldn't admit to it. *One day, I will make it so.*

The rooster crows, and that is when Marcus realizes he is very late. As he rushes inside, he tracks in mud. Ariah spots him and says, "Wear your holiday clothes for the journey!" She peeps her head out and sees the mess. "You couldn't have taken your shoes off at the door?"

"I'm sorry!" he calls back from his room. After a series of clanks and banging, Marcus comes out, his wet hair combed back, wearing a royal blue robe with silver embellishments and matching slacks. The robe ends at his upper thigh. The holiday shoes he always detested are pointed and silver flats. It is the nicest pair he owns. He carries his father's old case filled with clothes and some small possessions, and he places it beside his feet.

Ariah beams and exclaims, "You are so handsome!"

Marcus pulls her in an embrace. She holds him tightly, pulling away to dab her eyes with a handkerchief. She hands him the bread, wrapped in white cloth, warm to the touch.

"You've got everything?" she asks.

"Yes."

"You're sure?"

"Yes."

"Then go on. Pa's waiting outside."

Marcus looks back to Ariah and smiles as he leaves.

Once Marcus and Eliath are atop the horse-drawn carriage, Eliath says, "If we were allowed to *fly* to the capital, it would be a *much* faster commute."

Marcus has heard this complaint hundreds of times. Eliath commands the horse forward.

"But Griffins aren' allowed to fly in Bimmorus. 'Em blue-blooders will squirt their pants if they see the likes of us flappin' about." He chuckles. Eliath has a particular way of speaking, a dialect of the old Griffin generation that once lived at the cusp of the Griffin Clan. A friendly, hardworking village, while it still stood. . .

Eliath is a large man but as peaceful as they come. His ash-blond hair, flinted with streaks of silver, is kept long on top and short on the sides. But his real trademark is his beard. Although it is on the short side, it gives him a distinguished appearance. It brings out his wise eyes and serious demeanor. However, his wife would argue that his tongue contradicts any wisdom in him. He likes to wear loose-fitting, long-sleeved shirts, which he always rolls up below his elbow. He could never roll them up any higher because his forearms are so large. His shirts are always sooted because he cannot go a minute without getting his hands dirty. If he isn't working, he isn't happy. This is a trait his wife learned to love, along with dirty shirts.

Marcus doesn't respond. His father's little reminders only make him more nervous to go to the capital. "Why should I go at all, Pa, if they are so against us?"

Eliath looks at him with wide eyes. "Are ya serious, boy? It only takes one person to show the rest our kind ain' so bad. Don't go hiding who you are. Never be ashamed! Be proud! Now, they'll not understand at first—they're likely to call you Flying Vermin and all that in the beginning. But they will see."

Marcus's father throws his arm over him. "Ahh, Marcus, my son! You don't know how important ya are! You're going to align the stars, ya know! Now hand over that delicious bread your mother made, will ya? I smell it from all the way over here!"

CHAPTER 15

"You have nearly three days before the Welcoming Moon to complete the task. End their lives before Leon has the opportunity. This is your last chance, Mary," Bayo says.

"Yes, Bayo."

Mary transforms and flies from the shore, back through the glowing cave, and past the waterfall. The moon continues to glow above her; stars twinkle through the clouds. She peers into the minds of the Griffins she flies past, looking for one in particular.

She feels a burst of darkness course through her body and takes that as her cue to descend. Mary transforms and lands on her feet atop a large tree branch. The emotion she felt grows stronger, and now the person's thoughts become clearer. The hairs on her skin stand on edge. As much as Mary wants to turn and leave, she pushes herself to move closer.

Leon is sleeping inside the glass tree dome that he had stolen from River. He lies on a small bed given to him by the Elders. She comes closer to the windowpane, all the while scoping the area for any other wandering minds. There are none. Leon is alone. She sits down on a large branch next to the glass of the dome. The range is perfect. Now all she has to do is listen.

She knows entering his mind will be as equally eerie as listening to his thoughts. But if she is going to manipulate his intentions, she has no other choice.

Mary closes her eyes and stills her thoughts. On the tenth breath, she falls into a trance. When she opens her eyes, she is no longer in the woods. In this strange, dark place, Leon stands with his back toward her.

A gloaming darkness creeps over to him. Its lengthy limbs grow longer as it reaches out to grab him. It towers over Leon's frail internal body, and Mary can sense its hunger. With fingers of vine-like branches, the black ooze engulfs Leon, entering every crevice, blackening his soul until he is consumed. Mary's heart skips a beat. A ghostly cackle of the shadow, morphed with Leon's own voice, echoes the space, rushing like wind past her ears, causing her hair to fly. The shadow and Leon are one, and Leon is the perfect host for this demonic creature.

It is coming for her. There is no place to hide from this monster in a sea of empty. A jolting fear of losing herself to Leon's consuming darkness has her rushing to retreat when, suddenly, the barren scape develops.

Mary stands on the stage of the Griffins. In slow motion, the events of the fight between Grace and Leon repeat. Mary experiences this situation as if she were Leon herself.

Consumed by Leon's mind, she finds herself tugging at the cuff of Grace's shirt.

She deserves this for what she did to me.

Grace cries, and this satisfies him all the more. His anger festers as he thrashes his large hand across her face, and he feels a surge of gratification.

While belligerently wrestling for dominance over Leon's subconscious, the looming presence of the malicious shadow reemerges. With every minor success of control, the terrifying gloom festers up Mary's existence as it notices her gain power. She desperately holds in a gut-wrenching scream while its icy touch seeps through to her core. With her power of the Dark, bursts of waves emit from her being as a last resort to fight off the black ooze. Finally, the coursing vines seem to recede, returning her lost warmth. But Mary's relief is short-lived, for the shadow's clutch returns with a vengeance, clawing its way further and deeper than before. Her excruciating yelp only entices the beast.

Leon resumes his malevolent actions while Mary grapples for her life from the inside. His large hands yank at the roots of Grace's hair. *She deserves this for what she did to me.* He covers her mouth and nose with one hand, then strangles her with the other. While the shadow conquers her, Mary's last heartbreaking thoughts are of never making it out alive, never seeing River again, and becoming one with this unholy being for all of eternity.

Suddenly Mary is hurtling hundreds of feet down through a black hole. She crash lands in a cold and wet hallway. After a long recovery period, she finds the strength to stand. Taking note of a noise, she walks toward it. A woman shouts beyond a closed door in this hallway. Mary takes the knob in her hand, daring to enter.

The woman is frightening, and something in her eyes resembles Leon. Is it his mother? Her shouting is unworldly. She steps closer to the child beside her, leaning crookedly into his ear, and screams at the top of her lungs. "How dare you use that tone with me? I've had enough of you!" She lifts him by the collar of his shirt. "It's your fault I'm fired! It's your fault I'm alone!"

The child holds his ears to protect himself from the crazed shouting.

In her rage, she drops the child on the floor, and he falls on his head. She picks up the broom, and with its hard end, she bashes him again and again. The child tries to hide under the table, but she flips it over.

Mary attempts to stop the woman by wrestling the broom from her hands. "Leon. She can't hurt you anymore. Tell her to go away."

The boy runs into the cabinet and peeps his head out to look at Mary. "I can't. She never leaves me alone!"

"She will. I promise. Tell her to leave."

The woman searches for the boy in the room as if Mary does not exist. She threatens, "When I find you, I'm going to kill you!"

"I'm afraid!" the kid says as he closes the cabinet door.

Mary walks over to the cabinet and opens it just a bit. "Try it. Maybe it will work. All you have to say is 'Go away. You can't bother me anymore.'"

Leon peers out of the kitchen cabinet and whispers, "She won't listen to me."

"She will. I promise," she urges. "You just have to believe. Come on, scream it at the top of your lungs. You can do it."

Little Leon takes a deep breath. Just then his mother discovers his hiding place. He shouts, "Go away!"

The woman's face turns white. "What did you say to me?"

He continues, "Go away! You can't bother me anymore!"

The woman vanishes, and sunlight shines through the room. The kitchen melts away and becomes a bright green field.

Mary pities the child and tries to reach out to him. "That should never have happened to you. I'm so sorry. But you are free from her now. Hurting people is wrong. You will be much happier if you forgive."

The boy smiles and says, "You know that memory we were in—it doesn't scare me."

"That's good," Mary assures.

"It doesn't scare me. It makes me happy. Do you want to know why? If you would have stayed a bit longer, you would've seen."

"Seen what?"

He smiles. "You would have seen me kill her."

The child points, and there is his mother, dead on the grass. She is bloody and impaled with the broom she once beat him with.

Mary freezes.

"She deserved it." The boy grins just like the monster grinned, and his eyes blaze a fierce red. He runs through the field in complete freedom and turns into a black shadow. The sunlight peels away like old paint. All that remains is the woman's corpse and the sound of the chuckling monster.

Mary wakes from her trance and is back on a branch beside the glass dome in the woods. She has no idea how she escaped. So shaken, she feels sick. All of Leon's feelings cling to her like a rotten stench. Holding on to the branch for dear life, she kneels over and hurls.

But his dark thoughts and emotions are still so loud and overwhelming, even now that she is not in his mind. She struggles down the tree and runs through the woods until she makes her way into River's tent.

He groggily looks up. "Mary?"

At the sound of his voice and the sight of his face, she lets herself fall. She collapses and cries hysterically.

He rushes to her, wraps his arms around her. Earnestly he asks, "Are you all right? Are you hurt?"

"I'm fine," she stutters between sobs, clinging to his body.

"Did someone hurt you?" he asks.

"I had nowhere else." She continues to weep, clutching his shirt tightly.

"Shh. Don't be sorry. Everything's okay now." He holds her until she falls asleep in his arms.

CHAPTER 16

Hale watches Grace's friends transform and rocket upward in the sky in awe. They are racing to the cliff on the mountainside.

Grace approaches Hale. "Why aren't you going with them?"

Hale shrugs. "I don't want to."

"You've never transformed, have you?" she asks, and Hale blushes.

"Whatcha talkin' about?" River says, stretching massively.

Grace purses her lips and answers, "Hale's never transformed."

"Come on, Hale," River urges. "It's simple. All you have to do is—"

Hale interrupts. "I know. You showed me a bunch of times. It's just . . . I'm not like you. I'm telling you, it's impossible for me."

Grace says, "Try it once, at least. Prove to yourself that you're not like us."

Hale grits his teeth. He doesn't want to try it because he fears it is true. But he supposes that it is time to find out for certain.

"Fine," he mumbles. "But I'm telling you, it won't work."

River smirks. "Let's make a bet. Loser steals the winner some food."

"Deal!" Hale agrees, and they shake on it. Hale walks away from them and closes his eyes. He crosses his arms over his chest and releases them just as he'd seen River do. Then he feels something he has never felt before. He feels . . . free.

He opens his eyes, and suddenly, his friends are smaller than they were a moment ago. He towers over them and looks down at himself in astonishment. His eyes widen in horror when he sees his new form. When he opens his mouth to speak, all that escape are high-pitched shrieks. He jumps, and he spreads his wings wide.

"Hale, it's all right!" calls Grace. She places her hand on him. "You need to calm yourself to turn back. Deep breaths."

Hale manages to regain his human form, stunned at everything that has just happened.

"You finally did it!" Grace congratulates him.

River smiles and slaps him on the back. "Wow, look at you! Part human, part fictional creature, part loser of a bet!"

• ● ● ● ● •

While River attempts to convince Hale to transform one more time and try to fly, Mary's voice interrupts in his head.

River? she calls. *I need to tell you. . . I read Leon's thoughts last night. He's planning something terrible for your friends. We don't have a lot of time.* In a flash, a vision comes hurtling into River's mind. River nearly topples over as he is overwhelmed with this terrible daydream.

Beside him, Hale cheers for the racers returning from the sky. River turns to see Grace and Evan talking.

"Hey," River calls out to Evan and Grace. "I need to talk to you two. It's important." Hale automatically follows. River swallows as he explains, "It's about Leon. He's planning to attack."

Evan's fists clench tightly. "How do you know this?"

"I know a girl who runs in the same circle. She warned me."

Grace asks, "You trust this girl?"

River nods.

"We have to think of a plan," Grace says when she spots Logan and Mark dashing their way. "Quickly, they found us!"

With that, Grace and Evan transform. River commands Hale, "Transform!" Hale tries several times, but he remains resolutely human.

Thinking fast, River says, "Okay, never mind. Get on my back!" River transforms, and Hale clumsily climbs on.

The three of them run through the field, spread their wings, and rise into the sky. River shoots up so fast that Hale's legs dangle in the air. His tight grip on River's fur is the only thing that keeps him from falling to his death. The Griffins level, yet Hale continues to grip River as tightly as he can.

They fly above woods to the green hills in the distance. There are caves in these hills for them to hide and come up with a plan.

Below them leap several Griffins from the trees, their claws extended to attack.

They catch everybody off guard, and Evan is suddenly battling three Griffins, while Grace is nowhere to be found. Claws dig into River's torso, pulling him down. Hale holds on for dear life while River spins out of control. A Griffin slashes at River's wings.

In the dizzying confusion, Hale cannot keep his eyes open. Another Griffin appears behind River and digs its claws into Hale's shoulder. Hale screams. They press deeper and deeper into his skin, and Hale is unable to hold on to River a moment longer. The Griffin whisks Hale away. River turns as soon as he feels Hale is gone, but that is a mistake. Another Griffin kicks him in the head, and he plummets toward the trees.

Hale pulls but cannot get free. He catches sight of River falling. "No!" he shouts. And without realizing it, Hale is crossing his arms and releasing them. There is a blinding flash of light, and Hale transforms. His attacker reels back in shock. But Hale doesn't know how to fly yet.

Just before he hits the trees, Hale spreads his wings and rockets upward. He is flying! River is just a few yards away, over his head. Hale pulls his wings back to pick up speed to cushion River's fall.

Hale's aim is true, and River's unconscious beastly body falls on top of Hale's. Both crash into the woods below, breaking several branches on the way down. Hale loses consciousness for a moment and awakens on the grassy ground in his human form, scratched and bruised and aching all over. He wills himself to stand, but his legs do not listen. River is a few feet away, still in Griffin form, wings outstretched and eyes closed. A large branch has toppled over his midsection. Several shadows approach between the trees.

Hale blinks, trying to focus his sight. The shadows are, in fact, several boys. Hale crawls toward River.

"River!" he cries weakly. "Wake up!" Hale looks around. They are surrounded. The boys grab Hale by the arms. "Let go of me!"

The boys pull on the branch that was crushing River's body, and River transforms back into a human. While doing so, one boy says, "We could have left him. He would have died."

"Leon's orders. He wants them finished his own way."

Hale's heart thumps. His nostrils sting with the stench of smoke, and he takes account of his surroundings. On the outskirts of the woods is a blazing bonfire. At its base are large smoldering branches. They bind Hale's hands behind him and then bind his feet together. A rag is wrapped around his mouth. River is done up exactly the same way and remains unconscious. The boys do not linger.

Hale squirms until the rag around his mouth falls to his chin. "River," he whispers. He nudges him again. "River!"

River's eyes finally flutter open, his body jolting at the sight before him. He wiggles his body around until he faces Hale and then squirms more to free his mouth.

They look at each other for a moment with wide eyes. Then River whispers, "So. How's it going?"

"Well, fine, considering we're gonna die."

"We're not gonna die, Hale."

Hale huffs, "Okay, what do we do then? Do you have a plan?"

"Uhhh." River looks around for ideas. "I sort of just woke up."

"Turn back around," Hale offers. "Let's try to untie each other."

Keeping an eye on the boys from afar, both shimmy until their hands meet.

Hale eventually unties River's hands, and River turns around to untie Hale's. They start to unbind their feet when the boys who had bound them return, giddy with laughter.

"Well, lookee what we have here," says one. "They're trying to escape."

"Let them. It's more fun this way," says another.

Hale and River stand up to face the five young men.

Hale dares to blurt out to his opponents, "There were more of you before."

With glints in their eyes, they come forward slowly. River's stomach whirls with Grace in mind. "We don't have time for this," he says, snatching a blade from one opponent's hand, spinning the boy around until the blade rests on his neck. They back away slowly, and once River is ready to make a run for it, he pushes the boy, who then falls on his face. He and Hale make a run for it.

Pushing Hale down into the tall grass, River hands Hale the blade. Hale pauses. "Take it!" River urges. "Go for their arms and legs so they can't come for you anymore." Hale takes the knife warily and creeps silently away from River.

Alone in the field, Hale waits for someone to approach him. Sweat beads his forehead. Suddenly, a sharp wail of pain comes from the direction River had been. Hale jumps at the sound but continues to wait, taking in shallow breaths.

Something approaches from the right. Hale turns to meet it. Then another rustle comes from the left. Holding in a deep breath, Hale backs away slowly and sinks down.

The two boys must have met, thinking it was either Hale or River. There is a blistering scream as a boy cries, "You stabbed me!"

Taking advantage of the distraction, Hale creeps farther away, but the boy hears his rustling.

"Who's there?" The uninjured boy turns to follow the sound. His bloody knife is ready. This is Hale's chance.

Hale springs at him and uses the back of his knife against the boy's head. The boy stumbles. Hale runs.

Someone is gaining on him. Hale picks up speed while looking behind anxiously. He zigzags in the field, but his hunter runs around and bumps straight into him. It is River. They waste no time. Both transform, Hale with ease this time.

Mary reenters River's mind. *Turn around. Leon is in the tree dome. It's time.*

CHAPTER 17

A single torch is lit on the wall of the tree dome. The sunlight has faded, leaving a royal blue sky swirling with roaming clouds. Grace is alone. The knots that bind her tighten with every pull. She shouts, but her screams are muffled by the rag around her mouth. She tries anyway, despite the rag, aiming her shouts out the window, where Evan stands on a branch with a noose around his neck and a faulty platform below his feet. His arms and mouth are also bound. He balances precariously on top of the platform.

When he spots his sister inside, he screams her name and immediately loses balance. The platform slips. His feet swing wildly, and the rope around his neck chokes him. Thankfully, he lands on the branch below and steadies himself, balancing on the tips of his toes.

Grace is so shaken at the sight that bile rises in her throat. She swallows it back to keep it from choking her.

Leon walks toward the tree dome from below. Leon calls out, "You enjoying the view, Evan?"

Evan continues trying to work his way free.

Then he hears a voice above him. "Psst."

Evan looks up and recognizes the black-haired girl who had fought his sister last night on the stage. She cuts him down from the noose, and he is left on the branch confused as to why she helped at all.

Down below, Leon enters the tree dome and approaches Grace smugly. Grace can hardly breathe but holds her own so as not to give him the satisfaction.

· ● ● ● ● ·

"Turn around," Mary whispers to Evan.

Three boys are climbing up the side of his tree. The boys mount Evan's branch, which is too thin for their added weight. There is an unsettling movement beneath him followed by a loud crack. Evan springs into the air in the nick of time and catches a branch above.

Mary pulls out a small blade from her breast pocket and throws it. The blade shoots through the air and lands in the head of one of Leon's nearest goons. With a grunt, he falls from the tree.

· ● ● ● ● ·

Leon's smile would have been rather charismatic if he weren't completely insane.

Without warning, he lifts his large hand in the air and smashes down across her face. Her face stings painfully from its new red hand mark. She lets her tears pour out silently, but her daggering expression has not changed.

Outside, Mary jumps inconspicuously from tree to tree to the entrance of the tree dome. But the entrance is guarded. She has to find another way.

Mary sinks in the leaves of the trees to conceal herself and connects to River's mind. The connection is stronger now that he is closer. *How far are you?*

Almost there, he responds.

Mary feels his beating heart and his tired wings. Despite herself, Mary digs through River's mind. Her heart sinks as she realizes his immense worry should Leon attack Grace. As her sadness deepens, Mary digs deeper to learn more. And when she finds what she was searching for, tears well in her eyes. River needs to protect Grace . . . because he loves her.

But it matters not. Shaking away her emotions, she recalls the mission forced upon her. She must stop Leon from killing Grace and Evan, just as Bayo commanded, for the ultimate future Bayo has in store for Hale. Eying the tree dome, she wonders if she can get onto its roof without being seen. Mary jumps to the next tree, then to the next branch and the next, until she is directly over the roof. She has to get closer. As Mary climbs down, she feels River's presence, and immediately, her stomach turns. She tries with all her might to ignore his thoughts.

•●●●●•

Leon pauses his brutal beating. The rag has loosened from her mouth in the commotion.

Outside, Mary has finally reached the roof. *Listen carefully to me, River,* she says. *I'm going to smoke bomb the tree dome. Land somewhere they won't hear you, and on my signal come to the roof. We have only a minute to do this.*

Mary creeps to the edge of the roof beside the entrance. In her satchel, she carries four smoke bombs. Mary lights the first bomb and throws it inside. She hears the shouting and panicking begin. *Yes, it's working. Just a few more.* She throws in the other smoke bombs, one after the other, until the tree dome is silent. She calls for River to come down and hands him a wet cloth when he arrives.

"Tie it around your nose and mouth," she directs

Without another word, he climbs into the smoke-filled dome.

Go straight, Mary directs him from outside. *Then turn left.*

River follows her orders and finds the bed. Leon is stretched out beside Grace. He takes out his knife and feels around for Grace's limbs. His head starts to feel light as he saws frantically at the ropes binding her. He pulls her into his arms. The smoke inside the dome is fading by the moment. River doesn't have much time left. He runs to the entrance with Grace, who is out cold in his arms.

Above the entrance on the roof are four waiting hands. Hale and Evan. "Lift her up," Mary urges, and they pull her up.

River feels faint and his vision clouds. His arms give out, and his eyes roll back. Before anyone can do anything, he tips over and falls out of the tree dome.

Mary jumps, transforms, and catches him by the tip of her claw only a few feet above the ground. She sets River down gently, transforms back, then pulls the wet cloth from his face and checks his breathing. It is faint but steady.

She shakes him. "River," she calls anxiously. "River. Wake up."

River's eyes work their way open.

From the rooftop, Evan says, "We need to go." He transforms and takes off with Grace on his back. Hale follows. Mary and River come shortly after.

They fly to a secluded beach. The sky is a deep blue, and the high tide rolls in. There is not a cloud in sight, and the horizon glitters with thousands of stars. The moon is small in the distance behind them, hidden behind the trees.

River makes his way over to Grace when Mary stops him.

"Just so you know, this isn't the end," Mary says, "Leon is going to try again tomorrow—and every day—until you're both dead. We have to come up with a plan."

CHAPTER 18

While the group is asleep on the beach, Mary is again called in to see Bayo. Exhausted, she walks far from the beach before transforming and flies to the Elders' Dome.

Ianna opens the door before Mary knocks, as usual, on Deor's command. She notices Mary's slumped posture, baggy eyes, and the scuff marks on her skin. "You look exhausted, Mary."

Mary wearily raises her head. "I need to speak with Bayo. Do you know where he is?"

"He's upstairs in his study."

Mary climbs up the mahogany stairs. Bayo's study is at the end of the hall. Bayo grunts at the sight of her. "My, my. You look terrible. Trying day?"

"Yes. I have news, though."

Bayo gestures to the sitting room beside his desk. "Yes, I imagine you have much to tell me."

Mary slumps in the seat. Bayo's eyes are fixed on her as he impatiently says, "Are you going to explain why you're aiding the enemy?"

"Yes. I've aided them today, and I have gained their trust. I've kept Leon from harming them for now. However, Leon will continue this hunt tomorrow."

Bayo stares at her.

"I have a plan," Mary continues.

Bayo leans back in his seat with raised brows, waiting. "Do tell," he says.

"When Leon learns that I killed them, he will be out of the way, and Hale will be yours."

Bayo's eyes narrow dangerously, "Wasn't that the plan all along?"

Mary's head sinks, "Yes, Bayo."

As she leaves, Mary feels a cool hand on her shoulder. It is Ianna, who places her index finger against her lips. From the pocket of her robe, she reveals two small vials containing illuminated potions, one sapphire-blue and the other ruby-red. She slips them into Mary's satchel.

Mary looks at Ianna with wide eyes, understanding the risk Ianna is taking. Ianna gently pushes Mary out the door and closes it behind her.

After locking the door behind Mary, Ianna turns around and jumps in shock. Rioma stands on the stairs watching her, her shining eyes piercing through the darkness. Ianna walks through the corridor with her head bent as though nothing has happened.

"All these years," Rioma calls down to Ianna from the stairs, "and you still haven't learned your lesson."

Mary is a few yards away from the Elders' Dome when she hears Ianna's bloodcurdling cries coming from inside. Mary stops in her tracks for a brief moment. Through the closed curtains, she sees sudden bright flashes of light. Mary recognizes Rioma's infamous power. She is a Griffin of Ardor, with the power to produce fire from her own flesh and bend it to her will. Mary takes a deep breath, grips tightly to her satchel, and runs into the night.

CHAPTER 19

Perched along a desolate mountainside is Greon in his Griffin form. Nestled in his fur, the little nymph who saved him clings on for dear life. "We must rest Greon, Elder of the Griffin Clan," the nymph says. "Look, the sun is descending. You cannot go on much longer without proper . . ." It tries to think of the word a flesh creature would use. "Sustenance. Yes, sustenance. You must nourish yourself. I feel your body growing frail, your energy diminishing like a wilting blossom."

Greon scowls. But the nymph is right; they have been flying nonstop for two days, and they need rest. Greon stretches his enormous wings and realizes he cannot fly another moment. He digs his claws into the mountainside and climbs upward until they reach a flat surface. A quaint little place, with no growth of any kind—which means no nymphs.

The nymph hops off Greon's body and takes a look around. Greon transforms into his human form.

"There's nothing here. Nothing!"

"What's wrong?" Greon asks.

"I need water for nourishment. I need vegetation! I've never been separated from a vessel this long. I can't stay here. Take me from this place!" The nymph begins to panic.

"I cannot. Where there is vegetation, there are nymphs. You betrayed your own people to help me. You are unwelcome everywhere."

"Then what should I do? I'll die!"

Greon thinks for a moment. "Perhaps the nymphs in a different place will not know of you."

"No, nymphs don't travel from their birthplace. I've made a mistake coming here, a mistake helping you." The nymph plops on the ground and looks across the horizon, its color fading from a vibrant, glowing green to a pale green. It takes in a dry breath. "There is nothing here. I can feel it. Nothing for miles."

Greon expels a long breath. "Well, come on, then," he huffs.

The nymph jumps up again. "I suppose it is better this way. Where there is vegetation, there is nourishment for flesh creatures, such as yourself, unlike here in this desolate land. Transform into your beastly form, Greon, Elder of the Griffin Clan."

"Do you ever stop talking?" Greon hisses.

The nymph pauses for a second. "I suppose not. Nymphs don't sleep as flesh creatures do, and therefore, we do not stop talking, unless we are ill, of course. By ill, I mean lacking in nutrients needed for our vessels and spirits to survive. Even then, we move along to another vessel to keep ourselves alive."

The nymph continues on like this, and Greon considers leaving it there on the platform along the desolate mountainside. But he transforms and invites the little creature to climb on nonetheless.

• ●●●● •

After what seemed like an eternity of flying and listening to endless jabbering, Greon spots greenery down below. He swoops down, leaving the nymph on his back speechless with fright. They head for a large lake that glimmers in the moonlight.

"Greon!" the nymph cries. "Ahhhhh!" is all it manages to say before they crash with a loud splash into the lake. Greon's aching body suddenly eases with the caress of the cool water surrounding him. Light radiates from the pool as he transforms and emerges as a man. A tired, wet man.

The nymph makes its way to shore and hugs the nearest tree.

"This tree is uninhabited," it says, astonished. "I wonder why that is. That is very, very peculiar." It enters the tree and stays there, though its voice is still very clear. "Why is such a lovely tree uninhabited? I think I just might want to stay here, though this is very, very odd."

Greon drinks from a small stream feeding the lake, paying no mind to the nymph's muffled blabbing.

"I've never seen an uninhabited growth before!"

Greon wipes the water from his chin. "That's marvelous. Means no confrontation. Any fruit trees?"

The nymph sticks its head out. "Greon, Elder of the Griffin Clan—"

"For the last time, just call me Greon!" he calls from inside the woods.

"Greon, Eld—Greon, you should not go in there. This is very, very irregular. Not a good place. We should go."

"Don't be silly. This is a blessing. We are alone in peace. Ahh, a fruit tree! The air around it is so sweet."

The nymph steps out of its trunk and quivers as it moves toward the shore. "Greon. I think you should not take that fruit to your mouth. Fruit should not grow without the spirit of the tree. It's unnatural."

Greon emerges from the woods with the fruit in hand. "It's just a peach. We flew all this way, and not only are we safe, but we have food, water, and millions of empty vessels for you."

"We *aren't* safe here. Don't—" the nymph pleads, reaching out for Greon. But it is too late.

Greon takes a bite of the fruit. He salivates at the taste of its sweetness. Juice drips down from the corner of his mouth. With his mouth full, Greon says, "I've never had fruit so good." He takes another bite. Then another and another. "More!" he demands. "I need more!"

A thought strikes the nymph. There was no pit in Greon's peach.

"A peach without a pit?" it mumbles. "A fruit with no intention of growth? Why would a fruit tree not want to spread its seed into the earth? Oh, this is a bad place. A very, very bad place!" It wraps its arms around its torso and roots its feet into the soil.

At that moment, the ground rumbles with an eerie, cold vibration. The nymph sprints to the edge of the woods and sees Greon's shadow reaching for his next fruit. The nymph pushes the fruit from Greon's hands, and it falls to the cool ground with a thump.

Greon shouts, "What have you done?"

The nymph pulls at Greon's arm. "You are being enchanted. We must go."

Greon strikes the nymph and continues his panicked search. "I need to find it!" he rages. As he pats the ground, he feels an unmoving furry figure. A dead wolf. The body is deflated; its stench masked by the flowery smell of the tree. Greon continues searching the ground for the fallen fruit, unaffected.

An unnerving breeze passes through the trees, and the vibrations of the earth beneath them accelerate. Greon finds his fruit, and he gobbles it down furiously, licking his hands and lips, not leaving a single drop behind.

The nymph notices the carcasses of various beasts scattered all around and shakes uncontrollably. *I must think of something, quickly.* It springs up to catch Greon's attention. "There is a fruit tree beyond the woods! With a fruit savorier than this!"

Greon's eyes widen in excitement. "There is?" he asks in a childlike whisper.

"Yes, yes. Come, let me show it to you. With sweeter-smelling fruit than this, with juices sweeter than these."

Greon climbs to his feet.

"Come, come." The nymph motions as another breeze passes. "We should hurry before the other flesh creatures leave none for you." Greon follows, though his footsteps are short and slow. He examines the hasty nymph.

When they are near the shore, Greon stops in his tracks. The nymph presses, "Come, it's this way."

With a dazed look, Greon says, "There is no greater, sweeter fruit than these! No better place to live and stay!" He turns back, and the fruit tree gives off an appetizing glow. Its peaches sparkle like crystals in the night. Even the nymph can smell its sweetness, and it watches as fruit materializes right before its eyes.

It jumps in front of Greon once more. Light from the tree reflects on Greon's bewildered and hungry face.

"No, you are mistaken!" cries the nymph. "Do you not see the dead all around?"

Greon ignores it. The nymph stands motionless. It has run out of all ideas to keep Greon at bay.

The tree glows brighter as Greon approaches. He is so dazzled by its beauty that his eyes dare not part from it. The potent scent causes him to drool. He reaches his arm out to pluck another fruit, and the tree moves! The tree contorts and distorts itself. Its roots spring out from the ground ferociously.

The tree is not a tree at all. It is a glowing figure, possessing the curves of a woman. It has a head with no face and a crown of intimidating horns from which its fruit hang. With long arms and elongated, skeletal fingers. It is a woodland demon.

The demon extends its long fingers out to Greon and presses them against his chest. Heat courses through Greon's body at its touch, and he feels a painful pull from within. Through Greon's clothes glows a red light. Greon screams and tries to move away, but the demon wraps its hand erratically around his body.

"In exchange for my fruit, I will have your soul," the demon says.

The nymph circles the woods, sneaking through each uninhabited tree until it nears the demon and Greon. Though the nymph is frightened, it musters up the courage to shout, "Leave Greon, Elder of the Griffon Clan, alone!" And with all its power, the nymph possesses the lifeless tree and hits the demon with its branches.

The demon stands unaffected, snaps its head toward the tree, and reveals its mouth. A black, gooey smile spreads across its faceless head.

"A nymph! How delightful. I haven't encountered such a creature since I've devoured all those that lived here."

The little nymph tries its best to hit the demon again. The demon drops Greon in a rage and whips the tree the nymph possesses. Greon hits his head and falls unconscious. The impact of the demon's blow is so powerful that the nymph's tree separates completely in half, the top half crashing down. The nymph quickly jumps into another to lure the demon away from Greon.

"How lonely it's been in these woods without such entertaining souls. The average beast is a short-term enjoyment. Their souls are not as delicious as a more intelligent soul."

The demon turns to Greon's unconscious body. Black ooze seeps from the corner of its gaping mouth as it approaches him.

The nymph possesses another tree and swings its branches at the demon. They graze its bony spine. The demon snaps its head back and hisses, "You ought to do better than that, nymph!"

The demon digs its skeletal fingers into the dirt, and long vines grow from the earth, wrapping Greon's body. The demon hovers above him and inhales deeply, sucking the air from Greon's lungs. Greon's chest burns a bright red.

The nymph emerges from its tree and stands behind the demon. It extends its arms and calls forth all the power it possesses. All of the trees in the woods sway, and the nymph wills them to grow.

The branches reach out for the woodland demon, grab hold of it, and trap it. The nymph commands the branches to pull the demon away, but the demon roots itself into the ground, continuing to suck the life from Greon's body.

The nymph pulls and pulls but to no avail. It tries pulling the vines that bind Greon, but they are too strong to break. Then the nymph has another idea.

It plucks the fruit from the demon's horns and allows the demon to inhale them all, one at a time. Unaware of what is happening, the demon consumes its own fruit, and after a moment, it begins choking.

The vines that spewed from its fingers slowly retract from Greon's torso. The demon hacks and coughs. It shouts, "What have you done to me?" It tries to grab the nymph but cannot reach it.

The nymph runs over to Greon and slaps him on the face. "Greon, Elder of the Griffin Clan! Wake up!"

The woodland demon falls to its knees, and though it gasps for air, it chuckles. "Elder of the Griffin Clan, you say? How *mighty* are the legends of the Griffin Elders! And this insignificant creature I nearly killed is one of them?" Its dark, eerie laugh echoes. "Oh, nymph, you are a fool! You saved the life of one who has taken more lives than I. Beware a Griffin, nymph. You will soon be as dead . . . as I."

With that, the woodland demon's ivory white exterior turns black and hardens to stone before crumbling to ash.

The nymph takes a step away from Greon, holding its emerald limbs to its torso nervously.

"What have I done?" it whispers and makes itself unseen.

A moment later, Greon's eyes flutter open. He sits up and holds his aching head.

I should have let the demon get him. I betrayed my own people for the likes of him. I should have let them get him!

Greon walks toward the shore. "Nymph? Why do you not show yourself?"

"I saved your life this night. I have saved your life twice now," hisses the nymph.

"I do not have time for this, nymph. Are you coming with me or not?"

"I will never travel with the likes of you again. I will never travel with the likes of you again," he repeats.

"Nymph. I need you to lead me to the tree!" Greon pleads.

Silence.

Enraged, Greon transforms at the edge of the shore and rises into the air.

CHAPTER 20

Many potions share the sapphire color of the potions Ianna had given her. Though Ianna put herself on the line for Mary to receive these vials, Mary still has no reason to trust her. Mary smacks herself on the cheek to keep herself awake. She kneels over a single flower in the field, pulls at the cork of the vial, and lets a single drop fall upon it. The potion is viscous and odorless. As soon as the droplet falls upon the flower, its sapphire color turns clear.

Mary continues to observe the flower, waiting for any change at all. Nothing happens. Growing impatient, she grunts in frustration. "Why would she risk her life to give these useless potions to me? Bringing the open vial to her lips. She swallows half its contents.

It burns down her throat like strong alcohol. Within a moment, she watches as the veins down her forearms glow a vivid red. The color cascades down her body. Her veins burn from within, and she cringes. A moment later the color and pain fade, and her arms return to normal. *Strange.*

Just then, she falls over with a thud. She urges herself to get up, to open her eyes, to move at all. But she continues to lie there. The blackness behind her eyes turns into distinct images. She sees River's unmistakable smile. *He looks so much like him*, Mary thinks, the boy she fell in love with hundreds of years ago. *He looks most like him when he smiles.*

The River she sees now looks different. His hair is a bit longer, finally out of his face. He has light stubble. But it is his eyes, eyes that have lived, that convince Mary that this River is older. Mary looks down and sees she is not in her own body. Thick auburn hair hangs down from her shoulders. She is shorter, smaller than she usually is. It is then she understands. In this strange dream, she is Grace. River leans in for a passionate, heartwarming kiss. She melts into him with no control of her own.

The scene changes. She is herself again, standing in an empty field. River is beside her. Mary reaches out for him, pleadingly. Desperately hoping he'd take her into his arms and want her instead of Grace. Yet when their eyes meet, she can tell his expression isn't as loving as it was with Grace, as warm or as happy. Mary's heart breaks. He looks so sad. Placing her hand on his chest, she lets her power wash over him to take his sadness away.

Though she masks his emotion with warmth and love, River is in pain. He takes her hands gently and whispers, "Stop."

She lets the power fade from his body. "What's wrong?" she asks him, but his eyes drop to his feet. "Why are you sad?"

There is a blade hidden behind River's back that Mary hadn't noticed. He meets her eyes, whips it into her midsection. As though this vision was real, Mary feels the cool blade force its way through her body.

Tears pour down her face. "Why?" She feels herself fading. River catches her as her knees buckle.

"Because I know who you are. Who you really are." And though he holds her, his eyes do not meet hers again. Hale stands nearby with Grace and Evan, all with blank faces.

The blood gushes from her body. And she is frightened. River continues to hold her as the cold rushes through her body, and she begins to feel numb. She is slipping away, and she manages as best she can, "I love you." She struggles for breath but cannot draw another. Then darkness.

Mary wakes with a gasp. Hysterically, she clutches at her torso, making sure it isn't impaled. She takes in deep breaths, trying to calm herself, but tears spill from her eyes.

The vial she drinks from is empty on the ground next to her, the remainder of its contents spilled into the grass. She knows exactly what this potion is, and hate grows in her heart toward Ianna for giving it to her. Bayo had forbidden such magic. To know one's future is a curse worse than death.

Mary's anger grows within her, but all that comes from her body are bursts of tears. She can't unsee the way River looked at her right before he struck her.

That look was more painful than the blade.

CHAPTER 21

There is a subtle rustling of the shrubs to the left—a wildcat unlike those native to the Human Division of Malphora. Among the Arketchians, it is known as the Kali. Their eyes, the color of emeralds, matching the greenery of the jungle, are believed to enchant prey before they strike. Stumbling upon a Kali is a bad omen to the Arketchians as it is similar to the Griffin in one particular way. The Kali's ears are long and elegant, like that of a Griffin. Anyone who's crossed paths with a Kali and lives is met with tragedy in their lives shortly after.

The Arketchians teach that the Griffins had once been only one form. They were envious of humanity's wisdom and asked the Higher Being for that which they lacked as beasts. Their wish was granted, and the whole nation of Griffins permanently turned human. And yet, even though these people had wisdom that they did not have before, they were wicked and returned to the acts of beasts. The other human nations did not accept them, respect them, or do business with them. Half of the Griffins acted civil while the other half behaved wildly. And so, the Griffins were deemed unworthy, and they were cursed with two forms, human and beast.

A wild gazelle grazes nearby, the sunlight glittering in its antlers. The Kali behind the shrubs meets its eyes, and for a second, the gazelle is dazed rather than frightened. The Kali sprints forward, its muscles rippling with each elegant pull over the ground. It pounces.

The pointed nails of the Kali dig into the gazelle. Swiftly, the Kali twists its neck, and it dies. The Kali sinks its teeth into the belly of its prize, staining its pearly mane with blood.

Robin and Ellionna approach—shuffling their way through the jungle, tired and weary. Robin hacks at the vegetation with a sword while her cousin walks behind, rubbing her irritated throat.

∘ • ● ● ● •∘

Robin places her sword back in its scabbard, her arms tired from slashing their way through the jungle. She notices Ellionna rubbing her throat but says nothing. It has been three days since Ellionna last sang. She claimed to be on a mission to suppress the voice, trying to train herself away from the need to sing. But Robin knows better: Ellionna is punishing herself.

They come across the dead gazelle. Its eyes are open, and its neck twisted. Feasting on the gazelle's body is a bloodstained Kali.

The Kali lifts its head and bares its teeth, prepared to defend its prize. Robin steps backward, hoping the Kali will let them be. Ellionna follows. The Kali growls again; then, it suddenly cocks its ears and looks up before sprinting away.

"Do you feel that?" Ellionna asks, looking around. It sounds like hundreds of running feet. Shrubs shake violently beside them, and one by one, beasts leap from the greenery and gallop fiercely toward the girls. These lanky animals are as black as night and stand on all fours. Their menacing grey eyes have no irises. With elongated tails, they whip through the air trying to strike down their prey, snapping their razor-sharp fangs at the girls.

Robin recognizes these animals. They are Shigbis. Their venom kills their victims within minutes, and, should someone ever catch a Shigbi, they would find out their meat is just as poisonous.

One of the creatures pounces on Robin. She whips her sword in the nick of time and strikes the beast.

Meanwhile, Ellionna feels the voice of the siren welling up in her throat.

"Sing!" Robin screams at her.

"It won't work on animals!" Ellionna cries.

The Shigbis are gaining on them, and both girls are losing speed. Robin slashes at as many as she can, but the more she kills, the angrier the pack becomes.

"Quick, into the shrubs!" she says. Part of the pack follows them. There are ten of the beasts against two girls. Ellionna and Robin are surrounded. The Shigbis approach them slowly, snarling. One runs forward and jumps several feet into the air, and something springs out from the bushes to meet it.

A massive black wolf with sleek fur has the Shigbi by the throat. *Snap*! The Shigbi dies as the wolf breaks its neck. All at once, the remaining Shigbis attack the wolf. The wolf yelps as a Shigbi bites into its arm, tearing at its living flesh. And yet. . .

One at a time, the Shigbis die before their eyes. Their poisonous bites do not affect the wolf. When the fight is over, the wolf stands before the petrified girls. Its eyes are hazy brown. Robin knows these eyes well.

Ellionna pulls at her cousin's forearm. "Let's go before it hurts us."

Robin pulls back. "He won't hurt us. He's my father."

CHAPTER 22

May 5, 1965

The sun had just risen when a few gentle thumps sound against Mary's bedroom door. She opens it, and there stands Ianna with a tray of food and clothes hanging over her arm. The intricate embroidery is the latest in Arketchian fashion. Considering the Elders never leave their dome these days, Mary is fairly certain Bayo had used the orbs to steal this ensemble.

She moves aside to let Ianna in while she packs a bag for her journey. Ianna places the tray on the polished mahogany desk. The room fills with the delicious smells of Mary's favorite breakfast. A fresh cup of coffee and eggs Benedict with fresh salmon caviar and a platter of fruit on the side. Mary glances at the tray and salivates, though she knows this might be her last meal.

Ianna gently places the clothes down and wishes Mary luck before exiting the room.

She gazes out her window to the grey sky. Great winds push against the glass and make whistling noises. Mary wonders if she will have to fly through this weather to get to the Arketcha tribe.

Mary finishes packing quickly and takes a look at the clothes Ianna left behind. It is a red silk Arketchian robe with dazzling embellishments, a matching shirt that reaches mid-belly, matching pants, and flat, pointed gold shoes. Perfect for her disguise as an Arketchian.

In his study, Bayo shuffles through papers dedicatedly as Mary enters. His eyes are tired and it looks as though he hadn't slept the previous night. He looks at her for a second and returns to his work.

Bayo holds out a piece of paper. "This is the treasure you will retrieve for me. Come to the location specified at the time written. There will be a portal awaiting your return. The portal will remain open for only thirty seconds, so I suggest you make it on time."

Mary's eyes light up. "I will travel by orb today?"

Bayo peers at her through his glasses. "Yes. Are you ready?" Bayo asks.

She nods.

He motions to the room inside his study, pulls a key from his breast pocket, and unlocks the door.

He gestures. "Go in." She opens the door, and the room is illuminated with white light. Floating several inches above a round table, in a horizontal orbit, are the three orbs. Their mesmerizing beauty stuns Mary.

Bayo waves his hand in front of the orbs, and they cease their rotations. Mary recognizes the orb that represents Malphora but is clueless about the other two. She peers into them curiously.

"The one you're looking at is Thurana," Bayo explains. "Thuranians are gruesome people. They resemble the serpents of this world and will make fine allies in the near future."

"And this one?" Mary asks.

"Orcura, their people call it. They are intelligent, organized, and at peace in their world. They have some extraordinary powers to manipulate the elements. Their world is truly a treasure to behold. After I've conquered Malphora, their world will be mine."

Bayo makes a small circular motion over the orb of Malphora, then he strokes the air in front of Mary. The air splits open in an oval.

With the paper in hand and her satchel against her waist, Mary steps in.

●●●●●

Through the lush greenery of the Arketcha tribe, Mary can see the seaport in the distance. Magnificent ships sail to and from the shore. Men bustle along, carrying off crates.

She makes her way down into the square and looks around. Hundreds of people crowd the outdoor market. Potent spices are stacked high in handwoven baskets. Mary spots a basket of lychees in a cart of fresh fruit—her favorite. She hasn't eaten lychee in years. They don't grow in the Griffin Clan. She takes five and pays the old woman who is selling them.

After peeling the fruit, she takes a bite of its white flesh, its juice dripping down her hand. The taste of it reminds her of the freedom she had decades ago to roam the Human Division of Malphora. Free to take anything she never had in the Griffin Clan, including endless exotic fruits. She was once powerful and in love. She spits out a shiny pit. *I will try to grow these.*

As she eats the second lychee, the face of the boy she once loved floods her mind. The soft flesh of the fruit reminds her of his gentle lips. But he is long dead, and these thoughts should have died with him.

A swarm of people shoves past, and Mary decides it is time to leave the square in search of Bayo's treasure. Looking up, she immediately meets eyes with a beautiful woman. Her hazel eyes pierce into Mary so intensely.

Why is this woman staring at me? she wonders.

As people walk down the hill and pass this mysterious woman, they bow to her and greet her, young and old alike. It baffles Mary why the old would greet this young woman in such a manner and why young men walk past her beauty. Mimicking the gestures of the others who pass, she bows her head, then casually walks away.

The mysterious woman calls out to her. "Mary."

Mary tries to keep calm. *How does she know me?* Mary continues walking as though she heard nothing and peers into this woman's mind.

I suggest you stop walking, says the woman from within her mind.

Mary stills.

I know who you are and why you're here, she continues. *Turn around and follow me, or I will tell the chief what I know.*

Mary turns, but the woman is not there. Finally, she catches sight of her brown robe in the distance entering a small shop. Mary pushes people out of her way to catch up. She enters the shop and shuts the door.

Somewhere in the center of the dark room, the woman speaks. "Have a seat."

Mary asks, "How do you know who I am?"

"My name is Palla, Spirit Guide of the Arketcha tribe. I'm sure you've heard of me. After all, we are the same age."

Mary tries with all her might to see into this woman's head, yet she cannot make out a single thought. Her head starts to spin, and she almost loses her footing. "No, in fact, I do not know who you are."

"Seems fitting. I only heard about you yesterday. I was unaware any Griffins existed besides the Six Elders and Bayo's comatose brother."

Mary's eyebrows furrow. *Bayo's been keeping Hale a secret for centuries; how does she know about him?*

"Your power won't work on me," Palla says. "I have taken a potion in anticipation of your coming here on this day. Have a seat, Mary. We have much to discuss."

•●●●●●•

Sitting across from Palla in silence while she sips her tea aggravates Mary. Her mission is ruined, and Bayo will surely punish her. She wonders whether she should kill this woman. Her dagger is in its halter against her calf. But she stops herself from reaching for it. This woman is very important to the Arketcha tribe. Her death would cause a lot of attention.

"Are you going to kill me?" Mary asks.

"No," says Palla.

"What do you want from me then?"

"Only to talk."

Mary fumes. "I will not be giving you any information you do not know already."

Palla smiles. "It is I who will give you information."

"Why?"

"I was told to tell you, that is why. It is my obligation to do as I am told, similar to your obligations to Bayo."

"Whose orders do you follow?" Mary asks.

"I follow the orders of a higher being. I was chosen seven hundred years ago to guide this tribe. Like you, I do not age but that is because I communicate with the spirits." She stops to pour herself more tea. "Would you like some?"

"No."

Palla takes a sip. "The object you seek is not in the location Bayo has given you. It is in my custody, and I swore to guard it with my eternal life. However, now I must break this promise I've made to my people and give it to you."

"Why would you do such a thing?"

"These are my orders." She moves to a wooden chest hidden in the corner of the room and unlocks it. She pulls out a rectangular crystal box and brings it to Mary. "There you are. Half of the spirit of the siren. This essence is powerful. It longs to reconnect with its other half, but if that should happen, it would be a tragic fate. It will never satisfy its bloodlust. However, this essence can be tamed and manipulated to terminate the spirit of the siren completely. It could create the ultimate weapon—or the antidote to the bloodshed."

This confuses Mary. "Why haven't your people killed the siren?"

"The siren is the greatest weapon we have. We need her voice to protect our people."

"Then why give this to me?"

"It is fated for Bayo to have this in his possession."

Mary purses her lips. *There is no such thing as fate.*

"The spirit cannot be transferred to any other container. This container was forged in the fire by the last Dragon of Malphora, made from the crystal of the lands of Orcura. It is the strongest vessel in this world. If someone opens this box, the spirit will enter the nearest person. Here, take it," Palla says, handing it over.

Mary takes it into her hands.

Palla pulls a chain from around her neck. "And this, the key." She places it in Mary's palms. Palla's hand continues to linger on Mary's skin, and her eyes blaze neon green.

"I see a spirit connected to you. The spirit of a man you've loved . . . Jacob . . ."

At the sound of his name, Mary jumps and removes her hand.

But Palla continues. "He shows me the fierce motions of the sea. Fierce and wild like your love for one another . . . He wishes to tell you he is at peace."

"Is he here?" Mary dares to ask.

"He is in another world, where the spirits go. But he looks through the veil occasionally to see if you're all right."

Tears pour from Mary's eyes.

Palla laughs.

"What? What's so funny?"

Palla continues to chuckle. "He is. He is very funny!"

Mary wipes at her eyes. "Yes. He was. What is he saying?"

"Jokes, about you. He says if I tell you, you'd be mad."

Mary smiles.

Palla says, "He shows me a symbol. The symbol of the spirits when they decide to return to this world."

Mary's eyes light up.

"He shows this to me to let you know. At the time of Bayo's plan, he will return with a new name, a name of water. He tells you this as a sign so you will know it's him. He leaves you for now with a smile. You will meet again."

Mary lets her tears flow freely.

Palla leans in and whispers, "You are very lucky—such a soul has kept himself from ultimate peace to return to you. The spirits whisper about you. They know your destiny. It is split, like a fork in the road. I am not allowed to speak too much of the future to the living, and yet, I think you should know. For you, there will be two paths. The first with Bayo. Its end is your death. The second is against him. Its end is unclear. It is up to you which path you follow."

Palla's words stun Mary. Palla hands her a vial. Inside is a vivid, metallic lavender liquid.

"Drink this," she advises. "It will keep the events of this day masked from the power of your father, Elder Deor."

Mary hesitates. Palla extends the vial once more. Before Mary pours its contents into her mouth, she asks, "You've been too kind to me. Why?"

Palla says, "I see myself in you."

●●●●●●

July 13, 2020

Mary stretches out her black wings as she rides the wind like a wave. Soaring like this reminds her of the ocean. How desperate she is to enjoy a boat ride, feeling the tides under the soles of her human feet, River by her side.

She swoops down, and the wind whooshes against her long ears. She spots specks on the shore of the beach—Grace, Evan, River, and Hale—all still sound asleep.

She lands on the beach silently and settles against the trunk of a tree. River sleeps deeply several feet away. Though unable to forget the blade he pushed into her torso in her vivid dream, she gazes at him tenderly. *I have waited so long for you to come back to me,* she thinks, sighing at the sight of peaceful waves in the distance. She drifts off into sleep and thinks back to the day she met the Spirit Guide of the Arketcha Tribe all those many years ago. Her words have haunted her to this day, and yet, she has been unable to part from Bayo's rule.

I've risked my life every day since I've returned to Bayo. And I can't run, not with the invisible barrier around the Griffin Clan. Whether or not that existed, he'd still find me with his orbs. And now Jacob has returned to me, only to love another girl. A lump rises in her throat. *I can mold him in minutes to love only me. It would be so simple. I could kill Grace and her brother just as Bayo commands, live to fight another day with River by my side . . .*

Suddenly, she can hear Palla's words as clear as day: *For you, there will be two paths. The first with Bayo. Its end is your death.*

Knots form in Mary's stomach, and she has a great urge to run into River's arms. Moving to lie next to him, she stares at his sleeping body, desperate to look into his perfect green eyes while she can. She strokes the side of his face ever so gently. "I missed you so much," she whispers looking over his shoulder to a sleeping Grace. "Maybe we were just never meant to be. And I can't force you to be mine."

River's eyes flutter open and meet hers. Watching his pupils dilate in the sun makes her heart melt. He reaches out for her hand and smiles, "Hey."

There is great grief behind Mary's returned smile. "Hey."

Suddenly, it feels that eternity was worth the wait for this one moment. She squeezes his hand as she gazes into his eyes hypnotically. "I need your help today. Take Hale and fly to the cliffside where the waterfall flows."

He nods without question. Mary kisses his cheek while internally swearing this will be the last time she'll ever use her power on him.

◦●●●●◦

River and Hale leave shortly thereafter with Mary's promise to help Grace and Evan on her own. The three remain on the beach in silence until River's and Hale's Griffin bodies are specks in the sky. Mary cannot hold her gaze with Grace for too long. This girl is better than her in every way—brave, strong, fearless, and good. She has River's heart in ways Mary never could.

Opening her satchel, Mary pulls out the ruby-red potion Ianna has given her. On it is a small tab, which she unrolls. The word "Protection" appears and disappears in a flash. With a gleam in her eyes, Mary finally knows what to do. After popping the cork, she takes the vial to her lips but only drinks a third of its contents before making her way to Grace and Evan.

"I need to show you guys something, but this stays between the two of us," Mary says.

With one glance at her hypnotic gaze, they share the potion without hesitation.

CHAPTER 23

Bayo hunches over his desk studiously, reading from an ancient book and scribbling his notes. To his left, the door to his most prized possession is left open. The light of the three orbs illuminates the study.

He peers over, taking notice of Mary's image alongside her charges. Was this to be the defining moment of her allegiance to him? Would she do as she is told? Too intrigued to continue his work, he makes his way over to the orbs to watch the events unfold.

⁘●●●●●⁘

Without warning, Mary tackles Grace, and the two wrestle on the sand. Grace screams in pain, and Evan does not hesitate to pull Mary off. But Mary has Evan struggling for breath under the pressure of her arm, which is wrapped around his neck in a moment. Evan tries to pry her arm away from his airway, but she presses harder, using her legs to squeeze his torso.

Dizzy with the pain of several blows to the torso and head, Grace struggles to rise to her feet. Hazily, she sees Evan in front of her and Mary on top of him. She bites her lip and pulls the blade from her body. She whimpers and stabs Mary's leg with it while holding her own pouring wound.

Mary slides off Evan with a blistering scream. Taking initiative, Evan kicks Mary in the head, and she slumps to the ground.

Mary wakes up sometime later with a searing headache. After pulling herself up, she follows a faint trail of blood.

Mary quietly climbs a tree, positioning herself close to where Evan and Grace's inner chatter comes from. With precision, she springs from branch to branch and spots them past the leaves. She pounces.

Evan acts quickly and shoves his foot into Mary's abdomen. She loses her balance and falls but catches another branch. Grace and Evan jump down from the trees and run to a dead-end at the cliffside. Mary speeds toward them, and Evan rushes to take her down. She knees him in the groin then kicks him in the knee. While he bends over in pain, she raises the knife over his head, prepared to shove it into his spine.

Grace hastens to wrestle the knife out of Mary's hand with her good arm. Losing her strength, Mary presses her fingers into Grace's wound, and fresh blood oozes out. Grace shrieks, and her grip on the knife weakens.

Evan aims a punch at Mary's head, but she grabs his arm and flips him over her head. She races back to Grace with the knife extended, but Grace catches her arm and pulls it up while Mary pulls down. They fight over the knife at the edge of the cliff. Mary presses harder, and Grace tries with all her might to counteract her strength, sinking to her knees, her head over the edge of the cliff.

Grace gives a giant shove and squirms her body free from Mary's weight. She pulls her knees to her chest and kicks Mary with both legs. Mary flips over and plummets off the cliff. But as she falls, she grabs Grace's arm, and the weight is too much. Grace tumbles with her.

Instinctively, Evan dives over the edge.

Grace and Mary plunge into the water. As Grace tries to pull herself to the surface, Mary takes a fistful of her hair and pulls her down. The potion's potency is dulling, Mary can feel it. Mary strains mentally to use her powers to block Doer from entering her mind. The block would only last a moment, but a moment is all she needs. She enters Grace's mind.

I am hundreds of years old and have worked under Bayo for most of that time. It is you, Grace, that is corrupting all that he's trying to build through your rebellious actions in the Clan. He asked me to kill you and your brother, and I've resisted as best I could until now. I won't do as he asked me, but I do need your help so we can survive this.

Their blood turns the clear water red, fogging their vision. Mary wraps her legs around Grace's body, causing them to sink. But then, Mary lets go and swims to the surface while Grace descends into the depths of the ocean.

"Grace!" Evan screams frantically from a distance.

A figure catches his eye. He can make out long black hair. Evan holds his breath and slips under the water, swimming as fast as he can toward her. He explodes to the surface and grabs Mary around the torso. She pounds on his back, trying to force him to let her go, but he is relentless.

"Where is she?" he screams. "Where is my sister?"

Mary wraps her arms around his neck. "Where do you think?" she growls.

Evan thrashes, but Mary does not let go. Struggling for air, he releases Mary and pries at her hands around his neck. Mary rams her elbow down onto his head. Once. Twice. Three times.

A wave washes over Evan's motionless body.

You can hold your breath for thirty minutes, Mary says in the void of Evan's mind, as if it were true. This is how her power usually works; her influence is all she needs to make anybody less powerful do as they are commanded. *After that time, you will find one another, stay hidden, and be safe.*

⁕⁕⁕⁕⁕⁕⁕

Rioma enters Bayo's study and watches Mary alongside him, smiling smugly. "It seems *my* Mary has come through after all," she says.

A sense of relief washes over Bayo. Finally, it seems his plans are coming together, and soon enough, Hale would be by his side . . .

Rioma continues, "She's a wonderful soldier. I've taught her well."

Bayo closes the window above the orbs showcasing Mary's victory and pulls Rioma from the room with a tight grip on her forearm. "I would choose your words wisely if I were you. Though you stole that girl from Ianna at infancy, Mary was never yours. You have never taught her a single thing in her entire existence, besides how to call you mother and stay silent in your presence. It was me who created a soldier."

Rioma's beautiful face morphs into a scowl.

Bayo continues, "Your face is turning as red as your fiery hair, my darling. A thousand years of ever-changing fashion, and this is not your best look." Bayo stands from his seat and places his hand against her burning cheek. "If your life was in danger, she'd never come for you."

CHAPTER 24

The cobblestone path causes the rickety cart to bounce at every corner. It is an uncomfortable ride as the green terrain slopes and rises often. Marcus pities their steed for her slow pace and heavy breathing. Bree is a Cremello, a white horse with a glistening metallic sheen. She was a "beaut," as Marcus's father would say. A beaut—in her earlier years. Now, her shoulders slump, her eyes are heavy, and she is a bit too thin, though Marcus's father made sure to give her more than her portion. Even her shining coat now dulls with age. Flies circle Bree's head constantly, tiny nuisances, poking into her caramel eyes. Marcus sighs and jumps off the carriage.

Eliath bellows, "Marcus, son! What on Malphora are ya doing?"

"I'm stretching my legs," Marcus responds.

Eliath groans. "You're pitying that ol' horse again, aren't ya?" He shakes his head. "What do you think horses are for? Standin' around and lookin' pretty? This is good exercise for 'er. Good for 'er heart."

"I know, Pa."

Eliath groans once more. "Ahh! Good boy my wife raised!" If this was a snide comment or a compliment to his mother, Marcus was unsure. Eliath stretches his arms wide and pats the seat beside him. "Come back up, son."

Marcus always listened to his parents, no matter if he agreed with them or not. True to his character, he climbs back in to sit beside his father. Marcus watches as Eliath stands up, then climbs off the barely moving carriage.

"Pa!" Marcus exclaims.

"Ah, better me off the carriage than you. I'm heavier," he says with a smile, slamming his strong palms onto his large belly. The slap makes a hollow sound, like tapping a perfect watermelon. "And besides, I'd like to send my son off on a horse-drawn carriage, if ya don't mind." He gives Marcus a stern expression.

A half-hour later, Marcus's head aches from the constant bobbling of the cart. He watches his father walk beside Bree and thinks of how tired he must be.

"We're goin' to stop 'ere for a bit, son," Eliath says, breaking the silence. "I'm deliverin' that Hall Tree I built."

Marcus nods and asks his father to climb in once more. "I promise I won't get out."

Eliath gleams and jumps in with a grunt. "Finally seein' reason, my boy!" He puts his arm around his son and squeezes. Marcus could tell Eliath had been working on that Hall Tree for weeks on end. It was truly the best craftsmanship Eliath had ever completed. And yet, Eliath never looked more worried when delivering his work, evident in the deep wrinkles in his forehead and eyes.

A stone bridge emerges ahead of them, leading to the town. Beneath it is a flowing stream. Marcus peeps over the side to look at the rushing water running under them, and as he admires the sun-kissed beauty of the river view, the cart nearly tips over from the displaced weight. Eliath grabs the back of Marcus's shirt and pulls. The cart plops with a bang back on the ground. The simple touch of Eliath's hand on Marcus's shoulder has his vision blurring to a time in the recent past . . .

Though Marcus's body remains in the cart, he could swear that he is suddenly in front of a shining full moon. It shrinks hastily until it is a waxing crescent. This wasn't the first time Marcus was here. It was how his gift of premonition expressed the time passed. Marcus makes sure to count the days he is traveling backward. Three weeks. Suddenly, his vision drops from the moon, through the tops of the trees, and stops at his own front door. It is left open for him to enter.

His Pa had fallen asleep in his seat beside the crackling fire. While Eliath stirs and mutters, Marcus feels a strange pull to draw nearer. After reaching out to his father, the scenery quickly develops to one of chaos and flame.

Behind a barricade fights a young version of his father, flames escaping from every crevice, smoke filling the room. "MA! PA!" Eliath shouts. His power of Shielding dwindles with his lost strength, and his protective bubble fades. Suffocating for breath, Eliath has no choice but to escape the terrifying space, crawling through any openings, dodging the collapsing pieces of his parent's home.

Eliath makes it out. Grasping the hot grass, he desperately takes in the free air. After rubbing his smoke-filled eyes, Eliath dares to gaze up. Before him is a world of fire. Epic screaming fills the village, screams of his people as they burn. Eliath pulls himself to his feet and tries to reenter the blazing home. Marcus is at his side, prepared to dive in with him when it suddenly collapses.

The vision jumps forward. Marcus and Eliath are somewhere in the middle of the fiery village when they spot a flaming orange star hovering only hundreds of feet above the ground. It shoots balls of fire out in every direction. They duck for cover. Marcus peers closer. It is not a star at all but a Griffin of Ardor engulfed in flames. *The Phoenix effect. Only one Griffin in all of history is known to have such immense power*, Marcus recalls his mother's teachings.

"Elder Rioma," Eliath mutters in disbelief.

The vision jumps once more. Marcus's soot-covered parents are leading the survivors out through underground caves. His mother holds her pregnant belly. Marcus knows each person here very well. They are his neighbors in his village in Bimmorus.

Like a wave pulling from the shore, Marcus is sucked out of Eliath's dream. The moon lessens once more until it is black. Night turns to day, and Eliath enters his empty cottage after plowing the field. Galloping sounds from around the bend of the beaten path. Five horses come to a halt. Their riders, Bimmorian guards.

They enter Eliath's cottage.

"Lord Genrik has assigned you a task." Eliath is handed a scroll, and Marcus dares to gaze over his father's shoulder. They were blueprints for a mechanical mechanism disguised inside a Hall Tree.

He is handed a sack of coins. "You will receive the other half when the job is complete. You have three weeks."

The Lord's men mount their horses and dash from sight. Eliath slumps in his seat and looks over the blueprints with wide eyes. "What in Malphora?" He shakes his head. "In time for the full moon . . ."

Marcus returns to the present, his aching head in his hands. He is back on the bobbling cart, and his Pa is staring at him wildly. "Dreamin' again?" Eliath asks softly.

The sudden unbearable path is no match for their old cart, and just as Marcus had expected, there is a loud bang, followed by a jolt. A wheel is stuck between rocks, forcing Eliath out to remove them. Wasting no time, Marcus jumps to the back of the cart and unmasks the dazzling craftsmanship. Eliath is too slow to stop him.

"No, Marcus!" But it is too late. Marcus's consciousness has already fled, and he passes out a second time. Seizures course through Marcus's frail body, his eyes half-open. Eliath takes him into his arms, though no matter how much Eliath shakes him or calls his name, he does not wake.

The blackened moon in front of Marcus now grows until it is full. Marcus counts the days . . . *But today is the full moon*, he thinks. Suddenly, Marcus sees himself. His squirming arms and legs are chained, and there is a rope tied around his mouth. He is wearing the same holiday clothes he wears now, confirming the time this will take place. But he is not alone. Beside him is Eliath and their Griffin neighbor, Francis, bound in the same fashion.

Marcus gasps at the sight when a Bimmorian man dressed in elaborate green robes works his way toward the Hall Tree at the center of the room. Judging from his clothes, Marcus believes this to be Lord Genrik. After fiddling with its disguised knobs, a deep rumbling quakes the dark space. Every crevice within the Hall Tree glows with an intense red light. Bimmorian guards emerge from the shadows.

The guards unchain Francis and pull him to the contraption. Eliath shouts through his gagged mouth while Marcus rushes to stop the guards, until he realizes they are intangible. Francis is shoved into an open compartment of the Hall Tree, then in goes Lord Genrik at the other end. A window in the ceiling is opened overhead, showcasing the brilliant full moon. The contraption shakes, twists, and makes strenuous sounds. Its blood-red light floods the room and, suddenly, Marcus's ears are overwhelmed with Francis's painful screams. The light fades, and the doors to the contraption open. Francis falls out on his face—pale and weakened—while Lord Genrik takes in his newfound strength.

Lord Genrik's laughter fills the room. "I can read your thoughts!" he boasts to his nearest guard. "You have done well, Eliath . . ."

Marcus gasps. This contraption transfers magical energy. Francis's power of Dark now belongs to Lord Genrik.

Marcus's eyes come wide as he returns to the present, and his fist tightens on Eliath's shirt. "Please, Pa. Don't deliver this."

Eliath's worried expression intensifies with deep wrinkles etching into his forehead. There is a long pause until Eliath pats his son on the shoulder and assures, "Don't worry, son. I have a plan."

● ● ● ● ● ●

The cart turns onto a street lined with leaning, disheveled homes that seem to be corroding before their eyes. The vivid, beautiful scenery they had just passed is gone. Everything is brown and dark. Even the vibrant grass has faded to brown. Bimmorians walk past, their appearance in the same distress as their surroundings. A woman and her child pass the cart, their skin the natural Bimmorian shade of azure, dirtied with the earth.

The woman holds a large bucket of water over her head, and her daughter clutches tightly to her dress. She catches sight of Marcus's and Eliath's white skin color, with not even a freckle of blue, and the woman's hateful glare digs into Marcus's very core. Meanwhile, Eliath rides on unaffected.

Eliath brings Bree to a halt in front of a molding tavern. It smells of putrid rot and decaying wood. "We're going to stop in here for a bit, Marcus."

Marcus had never been to a tavern, and he isn't the least bit curious, especially with the previous premonition consuming his sanity. Despite the time of day, the pub booms with song, swarming with Bimmorian guards cheering, raging, drinking, and feasting. Sweat beads down Marcus's temple as he hangs onto the glimmer of hope his Pa has a good plan. Eliath moves inconspicuously through the crowd.

Just then, Marcus hears a strange buzzing from behind.

Off in the dimly lit corner of the room, a cloaked man sits. Marcus can hardly make out his face as his hood casts a dark shadow over it. But there is something this man hides under his cloak. An object calling to Marcus with this buzzing sound. Peering closer, he swears he can see a blue glow emitting briefly from within the man's cloak . . . illuminating the chain around his leg, binding him to the wall. The cloaked man, who sits so still, suddenly whips his arm over to shut the small gap of his cloak. He had spotted Marcus looking.

There at the bar stands a man in uniform, just as in Marcus's vision. It is Lord Genrik, addressing the crowd. His long, sleek black hair is combed back, and he flashes a terrifyingly outdated Bimmorian sword. Marcus's poor heart begins to pound right out of his chest. His panic heightens to a point where he starts tugging on his Pa's shirt to urge him out of the tavern. Genrik pauses as he notices the flash of color on his sword, which grows brighter as Eliath and Marcus draw nearer.

Genrik meets Eliath's eyes with a wide grin. "Well, look who's here!"

The music suddenly clips as everyone focuses their attention on Eliath and his son—two Griffins in a strictly Bimmorian town.

"Men! Arrest these Flying Vermin at once!"

The guards rise abruptly and close in. Marcus is forced forward to keep his distance, but their strong hands reach out and pull him and Eliath from the pub. Marcus and his Pa are pushed into the dirt. Bree neighs violently from afar. The guards approach with growling noises, shouting despicable things at them. The sting of pain from the fall has Marcus paralyzed for far too long. All at once, they pull him and his father away from the tavern.

"Don't touch my son!" shouts Eliath from beneath the hovering men. They throw their fists at him and kick him with force. Bystanders in the street flee the scene. Eliath brings his hands over his head to protect himself from the countless blows. Lord Genrik comes forward, "Where is my contraption?"

"In the cart," says Eliath desperately.

"Pa!" Marcus shouts. Like a tiger surrounded by circus folk, Eliath, who could have taken everyone down with one pulse of his Shielding Energy, remains submissive.

Suddenly, a great black shadow explodes out from the pub as quickly as a puff of smoke. It is the cloaked man, wielding a massive crescent-shaped blade. With one flick of the wrist, the blade flies out from his hands and cuts through the air like a boomerang! Every one of Eliath's assailants is knocked down. Everyone except Lord Genrik. The boomerang blade returns to the cloaked man's waiting hand while his other pulls down his hood. His eyes are the shade of the thick clouds of a storm, his hair wavy and champagne blond, cut to his shoulders. His skin is a light Bimmorian shade of blue, dazzled with silver freckles. Only Bimmorian royals have such skin.

Lord Genrik stumbles back as if intimidated by the boomerang weapon. "Oh, Camden," he begins. "Your newfound treasure won't help you escape me."

Camden steps forward. "It's over, Genrik."

Genrik flashes his clenched teeth as he swings his glowing sword. Camden raises his weapon in defense, and the two blades crash. The relic sword shatters in Genrik's hands, as if it were made of pure glass. Wasting no time, Camden kicks Genrik in the stomach, knocking him down long enough for an escape. But the men holding Marcus quickly catch on and advance toward him, throwing Marcus into the dirt. The otherworldly boomerang flashes before their eyes, and in no time at all, there is no one left to challenge Camden.

Desperately searching for a means of escape, Camden spots Bree and the wagon. He jumps in and strikes her reins, just in time for Lord Genrik to regain consciousness and call his men after him.

Marcus rushes to his father, who is well enough to run. Soon enough, Lord Genrik's blistering scream sounds from a distance where Camden has escaped with Bree and the Hall Tree.

The sun begins its descent when Eliath and Marcus find their way back to the open road. "We need to get the Hall Tree back; it can't fall into the wrong hands," says Marcus.

Eliath places his hand on his shoulder, "Don't worry, son."

A neigh sounds from the distance. "Pa! Look. It's Bree!" says Marcus pointing beyond. Eliath and Marcus duck for cover. Lord Genrik is driving the wagon with the cloaked man bound in the back with the Hall Tree. It seems as though the cloaked man has lost his epic weapon.

Eliath whispers, "The man who saved us is King Owen's boy, Camden. Overthrown and exiled by his uncle for the crown after Owen's death. They're headin' for the capital. No doubt for the bounty on Camden's head. The king will surely kill him."

After a long pause, Eliath continues, "I owe his father a great debt for what he did for us Griffin refugees. We have to 'elp him, son."

CHAPTER 25

Though the city of Bimmorus looked pristine from afar, Marcus quickly understands the clouds that hide the glistening towers are not clouds at all but smog.

"We're goin' to meet someone 'ere who'd 'elp us. She used to work for King Owen. Always 'elped us Griffins a great deal," explains Eliath.

There is a strong smell of sulfur at the cusp of the city that has Marcus wheezing. "Bear with it. This is the fastest route," says Eliath wrapping a rag over the bottom half of Marcus's face. "There was never such pollution under King Owen's rule. Imagine livin' in such conditions." He shakes his head.

Eliath leads Marcus through the back alleyways. He stops in front of a humble door with a sign that reads, "Lady Thelmure's Gadgetry," and knocks six times rhythmically. The door opens immediately, and behind it is an older Bimmorian woman in casual Bimmorian attire.

"Eliath?" she says, her mouth stretching to a smile. She urges them inside.

"Lady Thelmure! It's good to see ya!" Eliath bellows.

"Eliath, how are you? Is this your Marcus I've heard so much about?" she says, gleaming at Marcus.

Marcus smiles.

"We need your 'elp, Lady Thelmure. Lord Genrik has Owen's boy in 'is possession, and he's on 'is way over to the palace."

Lady Thelmure takes a hand to her heart. "King William will be sure to kill him . . . what are you planning to do, Eliath? Don't tell me you're up to something foolish with your son at your side."

"Marcus was accepted to the Royal Academy, but at this point, the Bimmorian guards will be lookin' for us. We need to get to the palace safely. Can you 'elp us?"

Lady Thelmure remains stone-faced for a split moment before her eyes come alive. "I have just the thing!"

She goes to the back of the room and returns with a red box. Inside are two beautiful silver rings embedded with sapphire stones. "Lucky for you that I happened to make two," she shrugs, "Go on. Try them on."

Eliath and Marcus each take one ring and place them on their fingers. Lady Thelmure turns the tiny knob on their sides, and a projection appears right above the sapphires in the rings. They show three floating balls of light. Blue, white, and orange.

"Touch the blue one," she urges. Once Marcus grasps the blue ball of light, his hand adapts to its color, and that color spreads throughout his body. He rushes to look through the glass on the counter.

"Pa! I look Bimmorian!" He turns to his father whose skin has also transformed to indigo.

◦●◉◉●◦

The smog disappears as Marcus and Eliath reach the capital, showing off their new skin. The bright lavender and orange of the setting sun fill the sky. A wide stone street is before them, and on either side, are similarly-shaped buildings. Each roof is sloped in a triangle that extends several feet over the building itself.

Beautifully arched bridges stretch out above their heads, connecting buildings on either side of the street. Red lanterns hang everywhere, glowing orange, adding character to this enchanting place. Flying silver, hemisphere-shaped carriages zoom overhead. The street below is bustling with Bimmorians dressed in silken robes of every color imaginable. Their hems are embellished with jewels or fine stitching. There is a comfortable murmur all around. For the first time, Marcus doesn't feel out of place or afraid, but instead, a part of something special. Eliath, too, seems calmer.

In the distance are more stunning buildings, all built on top of one another on the side of a mountain. The light from each window shines from the towers, hundreds of feet above.

Music sounds over the crowds. It is an alluring folk tune played on a popular Bimmorian instrument called the sincerous. It is but a single bow, mechanically engineered so that when it cuts through the air, it not only emits a magnificent light of any color but creates a soft, stringlike sound.

It is most surprising to see the delicate notes played by a young Bimmorian girl. She looks to be ten years of age, but she plays with the precision of someone more than twice her years. Her bubbly dancing gains her a large audience.

Marcus wishes to stay to watch this captivating show. Sparks of light burst through the crowd like firecrackers, and the last he sees of that little girl is her black hair whirling in circles as she spins elegantly.

Further into the city are bustling marketplaces. The aroma of fresh spices fills the air. Marcus's eyes are wild with new sights. The spices are mounted in baskets in such a delicate formation, with spiral designs cascading downward. Stands are filled with fresh fruit, vibrant in color. Small dead creatures hanging upside down are pinned on a rope. On the tableside is a cheaper selection—squirming, slimy critters that are sold alive. Select cuts of animals are spread out, the purple, raw meat lying flat on display. And there are tons of vegetables—more than Eliath's farm and Marcus's hands could ever produce.

"How do they grow so much food?" Marcus asks.

Eliath shrugs. "Must be more 'elp on the farm, I suppose."

The murmur of the marketplace fades behind them. On either side of this passage are large, grassy fields scattered with evergreens and wonderful boulders. Magnificent birds roam the sky freely, one of which lands on Marcus's shoulder.

Winding down the sandy road, Marcus sees mountains lining the horizon. Straight ahead, a bridge comes into view. On either side of the walkway are statues like columns that hold up the bridge's domed archway.

"What are those statues?" Marcus asks.

"On the right are all the kings of Bimmorus. Across from them are their queens," answers Eliath.

They come to the edge of the bridge; the line of royal statues appears endless from here. Marcus looks at each face speculatively, as if trying to learn the past rulers of this kingdom from the way these people were portrayed—their stances, expressions, what they were holding. Some rulers hold books, some swords and shields. All of their expressions are humble and even happy. However, one pair of statues in the middle of the bridge perplexes Marcus as they are so different from the others.

This queen's face points away from the bridge. She gazes behind her, toward the east. With elegant features, big eyes and round lips, and her hair covered humbly with a scarf, Marcus thinks her to be beautiful. Though deep indentations, carved under her eyes, tell him she is weary. In her hands, she holds an open book, its stone pages carved with three orbs.

Her king stands across from her. He has a grave face, and his hair is combed behind his crownless head. His hands are held open in front of him, also holding two spheres. A third sphere, larger than the two he holds, is attached to his chest, right over his heart, to make it seem as if it is levitating.

Marcus can't help but exclaim, "These statues are so different from the rest! What are those spheres? And why are they not crowned like the others? Why is she looking away?" Marcus glances over at their plaques and tries to sound out the words while guiding his fingers over the lettering. Just then his eyes roll backward, and he is seizing on the ground.

"Not again! Marcus!" Eliath shouts.

Marcus is in an extravagant throne room where hundreds of people are cheering. "Long live King Loraine! Long Live Queen Norelle!" He gazes up at the two pleasant, crownless figures by their thrones. Three dazzling orbs fly in a circle above their heads.

King Loraine and Queen Norelle rise hand-in-hand. The king addresses the crowd, "Today we hold the greatest treasure in existence. The Three Eyes. Behold, each orb represents each world in existence! From this day on, the queen and I must share a great responsibility to you, our people, as we are the keepers of The Eyes. We vow never to abuse our power and leave the worlds free from any control except the whim of fate." With a wave of his hand, one orb floats down until it is near King Lorain's heart. "Here in Malphora, our magnificent and bountiful world. I vow to keep you, my people, safe. And we will proclaim this day a great holiday. Loraine's Day!"

Marcus's vision jumps to the oceanside, to the right of Queen Norelle who gazes at the rising sun. She titles her large book, *The Book of Peace*. King Loraine approaches from behind and takes a seat beside his wife.

"This will be the greatest book in all the worlds—a manual to The Eyes for our children, the future kings and queens of Bimmorus."

Suddenly the light of day fades, and Marcus is in a dimly lit room. He moves past the drapery to see a pale and bedridden King Loraine, clutching his wife's hand. His body is ridden with black sores. "I've failed you . . . our children . . . our kingdom," he says with a raspy voice, wheezing tremendously. "Bimmorus will enter a grand age of darkness."

Norelle shakes her head, "Don't you worry, my love. We will find The Eyes soon. Just hold on."

"*The Book of Peace* . . ." he inhales deeply. "Where is it?"

"It's hidden with cloaking magic. The thieves will never know the true secrets behind The Eyes."

"The fourth eye?" King Loraine asks earnestly.

"Hidden and embedded in the crescent-shaped blade you love so much." Tears flood down Norelle's face at the sight of Loraine's smile.

"Then I am at peace," he drawls, shutting his eyes one final time.

Norelle's sobs leave Marcus shaken. "From this day on, Loraine's Day will be a day of mourning."

Marcus wakes once more in his father's arms. "What on Malphora are ya doin' to my ol' 'eart!" Eliath exclaims.

"I'm sorry, Pa."

They resume their walk across the bridge, as Marcus explains his vision to his father.

Eliath nods understandingly, "That mus' be why the kings and queens after King Loraine look so distressed."

Pulling out from under the archway of the bridge, the palace of Bimmorus comes into view. Built on a plateau, waterfalls gush out from the mountainside on either side of the bridge of statues, creating a light mist in the air. Before Marcus's eyes stand individual buildings and towers, their windows aglow with an orange blazing light from within their walls. On either side of the main building, intertwining with the curvature of the mountainside, are elegant walkways held up by columns. From the ceilings within these walkways come lavender lights. The gate is arched, made of black iron, and detailed with plated gold. The metallic structure glistens from the light peering through its lace design. They see the entrance to the palace in the distance. A guard stands in the courtyard, inside the gate.

As Eliath and Marcus take one more step forward, it feels as if they are striding through a harsh wind that suddenly clips back to the normal weather. Eliath spots his son's blue skin reverting back to white. "Oh, no."

There is a protective shield around the palace, blocking all forms of magic, including Eliath's and Marcus's new disguising rings.

"Griffins!" Shouts the guard at the gate. Noisy bells ring immediately, and guards rush from every direction!

* * * * *

Two guards on either side pull Marcus and Eliath through the long, beaming white corridors of the palace. They are heading to the dungeon when Lord Genrik emerges up the steps.

"You've found my prisoners!" he says gleefully.

Soon enough, Marcus is reliving his premonition. The Hall Tree stands dramatically in the center of a large room where Francis, his neighbor, is held captive. Many Bimmorian guards arrive to watch Lord Genrik obtain his epic powers. "Have you turned off the palace's protective barrier switch?" Lord Genrik asks a guard.

"I will do that right away, sir."

At once, Eliath nudges his son and shows him that he is removing his ring. Marcus does the same, though his heart is beating out of his chest. He feels he might pass out at any moment. Didn't his father say he had a plan? *He doesn't even look worried,* Marcus thinks.

Francis is taken into the Hall Tree, and just as in Marcus's vision, Fancis's horrible screams quake the walls. Finally, the doors open, and Francis falls onto the cold floors while Lord Genrik laughs and points at the nearest guard, "I can read your thoughts! You have done well, Eliath . . ."

Marcus's heartbeat is ringing in his ears. He doesn't know what is to happen next. The guards come toward Eliath to put him inside the contraption, and Marcus screams through his rope. He spots his Pa wink.

Just then, Lord Genrik grabs his chest and groans, "Ugh." He fumbles to his knees. "Wh—what's wrong with me? My power. It's weakening."

Francis stands strongly.

"Command them!" Eliath says hastily.

"Release Eliath," Francis commands. At once, the guard does as he is told. "Unbind him," the lord points to Eliath.

Francis's eyes are wide. "My powers have never been this strong before!" he says in bewilderment. The other guards close in.

Francis glances their way, "Halt."

They pause in their tracks.

"All the Bimmorians here will forget this incident. You will forget us Griffins and your thirst for our power." Lord Genrik and the guards stare at Francis, as if mesmerized by his every word. "You will release us in peace."

Now that Eliath is unbound, he whispers in Francis's ear. Francis nods in understanding. "You will take us to King Owen's son, Camden."

CHAPTER 26

The guards barge through his door. "Your Majesty," says one, exasperated. "We need you now."

"What's happened?"

"It's the former general, sir. He's returned."

⁘⁙⁘

Eliath, Francis, and Marcus follow a lone guard down the dimly lit staircase. Water droplets sound from below, along with scurrying rats.

"This is where you lot belong—with the rest of the vermin!" spits the guard.

"Hush up," Francis commands, and at once, the guard's lips are unable to part. "You won't remember this in a moment."

As they pass the empty cells, Marcus notices the same buzzing sound he heard from within the pub. "Do you hear that?" he whispers to his father.

Eliath nods. At once, a bright blue light illuminates the dungeon, coming from inside a cell. "Woah! It's happened again!" says a man.

Marcus peers through the rails to see Camden, upright and majestically holding his epic crescent-shaped blade. In the blade's curvature floats a spectacular

143

orb, rotating on its own accord. Old Bimmorian markings engraved in the staff are illuminated in the same blinding blue light.

"Who goes there?" says Camden, quickly hiding the weapon beneath his cloak.

Eliath steps forward. "I am Eliath Theoden; this is my friend, Francis, and my son, Marcus."

Camden draws nearer. "You're Griffins!" he says in astonishment.

"Aye, we are," answers Eliath. "We've come to 'elp you, Camden Belflore. We owe your father a great debt for allowing us refugees into the kingdom."

Camden is thanking him when Marcus interrupts. "That buzzing sound, it's coming from your weapon."

"Yes," Camden says. "Oddly, this was never a weapon at all but an heirloom necklace handed down to the next in line of Bimmorus. My father gave it to me. It transformed for the first time in the pub—when you both arrived—and once more now."

"May I see it?" Eliath asks, holding his arm through the iron bars. Camden is hesitant to give it to him but obliges. Eliath inspects the weapon in awe. "This is a thin' of beauty! I suspect it's transformed into this weapon from the proximity of our magical energy."

Camden nods in agreement. "That makes sense, considering the kingdom was lost from such energy since The Eyes were stolen."

Eliath hands the weapon back and dares to ask, "Do ya know who's taken The Eyes?"

Camden looks sternly at Eliath, "No one knows . . ."

Eliath and Francis share a long glance before Francis nods in approval. Eliath then solemnly answers, "The Griffin Elders stole The Eyes from Bimmorus all those centuries ago. When I first came to Bimmorus, I asked for an audience with the king, your father, to warn 'im. But I was not allowed to meet with the king. Instead, I met with 'is brother, William Belflore. I told 'im everything. He told me to tell no one what I knew."

Camden glares. "So, my uncle has known this whole time? Sixteen years?"

Eliath assures, "I've suspected somethin' grave from the Elders since they nearly slaughtered our people. Perhaps the Elders won't attack Bimmorus. My son—he's the prophet of the current Griffin generation—he saw Queen Norelle tell 'er husband she hid *The Book of Peace* before 'is death. If the Elders don't have the book, they don't know how to use The Eyes."

Camden's eyes are wide with this new information. "So, *The Book of Peace* is truly still in Bimmorus!" He jumps joyfully. "I've known all along, but I could never find it!" Then his face turns grim. "The Eyes were stolen in 1720. If the Elders stole them, and you saw them sixteen years ago, that means they've had them for three hundred years. Queen Norelle wrote *The Book of Peace* in a span of two years. I fear our kingdom is not at any advantage."

"Aye," Eliath agrees. "Let's get you out of this cell."

Francis motions the guard forward with a set of keys to unlock Camden.

Camden emerges with his intimidating weapon gleaming in his hands. "After what you've told me, I have business with my uncle. Would you three be so kind as to help me gain an audience with him?"

"Aye."

●●●●●●

"I need to hide my weapon and retrieve my recording contraption that can prove my innocence. I hid it in the palace before I was exiled," Camden explains.

"Wonderful, let's go fetch it!" Francis exclaims.

"The guards will surely see us," frets Camden.

"I will protect us," Eliath says, extending his arms. At once, they are encompassed in an invisible and impenetrable bubble.

Camden reaches to stroke its smooth surface. "Amazing!"

The company moves through the long corridors of the palace inconspicuously, and then Camden hides his weapon in a secret compartment in his old bedroom chamber. Once leaving to retrieve his recording contraption, they attract the attention of many guards. Chaotic shouting comes from all sides as they are surrounded. But no matter how much the guards poke Eliath's barrier with their meager weapons, the bubble remains resilient.

"Your talent would be an immense asset in battle!" Camden exclaims. They jog past the swarming guards, knocking them out of their way as they reach the courtyards where a commemorative statue of Camden's father, King Owen stands. Loud bells signifying their intrusion jolt the ground.

"Quickly!" says Francis. "They are on their way to flip the switch that stops magic from entering the palace! We'd be defenseless!"

Camden sinks his fingers into the softened dirt and reveals his silver cubed recording device. "Follow me, I know how to get to the throne room undetected!"

Soon enough, Camden, Eliath, Marcus, and Francis walk through the arched double doors. By this time, Camden's staff has transformed to the crescent-shaped heirloom, and he wears it around his neck, signifying the magical barrier around the palace has once again been turned on. The room before them is rectangular, and down the center of the floor is a walkway made of shining aquamarine stone that makes the room inviting and peaceful. Above their heads, three large and elegant chandeliers float above the aquamarine walkway. They are not attached to the ceiling but levitating, lightly bouncing up and down in the air. Three long, arched windows rising to the twenty-foot ceiling stand in front of them. Before these windows, sitting atop a platform at the end of the walkway, is William upon his throne.

The throne is intriguing on its own. It is a short golden chair, its legs, arms, and back engraved with intricate designs. Beside the king are the Bimmorian elites who live in the palace.

Standing to William's right is a beautiful young girl. Her thick, blonde hair, parted down the middle, ends at her waist. There is a delicate vine band around her crown. Her big eyes, which match the color of the aquamarine walkway, look upon the two intruders passing through the halls. She is Evangeline, the princess of Bimmorus.

Camden waltzes up to the platform and bows before William. "Uncle." Then he looks to the young girl on his right. "Evangeline."

Evangeline purses her lips and does not return the greeting.

William asks, "Why have you come?"

"I've come to clear my name. Uncle—" Camden begins.

"You will address me as your king!"

Camden pauses in shock. William has never spoken to him like this before, but he accepts William's rule and corrects himself. "Your Majesty. While I was away, I learned who framed me. I am more an asset to you than an enemy. I have served you with love. Do you believe that I would stoop so low as to harm you? You banished me without trial."

"Rightfully so, for an act such as that. There were witnesses, Camden."

"Those witnesses were no allies to me. They planned the whole charade so they could stop my work here in the palace."

"You think your work was *that* important that the people who were closest to you throughout the years would betray your trust?" the king asks condescendingly. "Is that it, then? You're accusing the witnesses of the crime?"

"The witnesses were with me on that night, it is true. But their word was distorted. They were given an incentive. And I have evidence." Camden pulls out his recording contraption. When he presses this knob, a projection appears before the council and the king. He turns the knob to rewind the device, bringing it to the beginning of his first recording.

Within the projection is the image of a beautiful red-haired woman with pale blue skin. Her long hair is braided. She wears a silver dress, and the stars sparkle behind her through a window. At this very moment, this same woman stands to the king's left. Her stoic expression does not fool Camden, however.

"This is the day I proposed to my former fiancée, Annabelle, who currently stands beside you as your ambassador, Your Majesty.

"Here, once I've left, she moves, almost out of sight. But just—right there—she's taken something from the table into her hands. She opens it and reads it quickly. And here, I have returned with my gift—she was ecstatic, and I was over the moon with joy. But that paper she's taken is held right behind her . . . there. Do you see it? This paper was very important to begin building the barrier around the kingdom. That would not only ensure our safety against natural enemies but also whoever has stolen The Eyes. The technology my team created was meant to prevent even using The Eyes to trespass into the kingdom."

"We already have technology against magical energy," remarks the king, "which is why I was undecided on the project."

"I know, Your Majesty. That is why I set a prototype in motion to test whether or not this marvelous idea would work. It was the letter delivered to me that day by the inventors about their tests. The letter declared the experiment was a success."

Annabelle flushes. "This is absurd," she blurts. "I would never steal from you, Camden!"

"I thought that as well. I asked myself why Annabelle, the ambassador of Bimmorus, would not want the protective barrier. And for the life of me, I couldn't understand why . . . until I learned that you, Annabelle, have made a deal with the nation that has stolen The Eyes. The Griffins."

The elites gasp and whisper among themselves. William Belflore's voice sounds above the rest, "Camden! The Eyes were never proven to be stolen. You know this. They were probably hidden by King Lorain. I've explained this to you countless times. This obsession with The Eyes needs to end."

Annabelle steps up, "If I may, Your Majesty. How could I have possibly made a deal with the Griffins with the magical barrier around the palace?"

Unable to look her in the eyes, Camden presses a button on his recording device, and projected into the room is Annabelle, walking over to the massive switch that controls the magic barrier and flipping it. In that same moment, a long gash cuts through the air beside her, and out from it emerges a Griffin man.

"That's Griffin Elder Bayo!" exclaims Eliath from behind Camden.

The crowd gasps.

Camden continues through the uproar, "The Elders have created an army, and they are planning an attack. Annabelle made a deal with Bayo. And the deal was to let him into Bimmorus, which is why my barrier was a great inconvenience. In return, she and I were granted immunity, and with you out of the way, Uncle, she and I would be rulers of Bimmorus. As if Bayo would ever allow that to happen. She knew I would destroy her plans if I ever found out what she was up to."

"This just proves your hunger for the kingdom and drive to be rid of me," William declares.

Camden continues, "You know I would never harm you, Uncle. I've always thought of you like a second father. I have never done anything to betray your trust."

"This proves nothing—" King William begins. "Where is your proof against you trying to take my life."

In the projection, just when Annabelle and Bayo have finished their whispering, Bayo hands her a vial. Everyone, including Camden look on. Bayo departs, and the rift shuts. She takes the vial to her lips and suddenly, she begins to shake heavily.

Watching her projection in horror, Annabelle sinks back and away from the crowd, attempting to flee whilst everyone is distracted. The onlookers watch the recording and gasp as her body morphs into Camden's exact likeness. The projecting device follows her out the room silently, hovering several feet above the floor, undetected by its cloaking technology.

William's furious expression turns to one of astonishment, "It can't be!"

They watch as Annabelle pays the guards in front of the king's chambers to allow him to enter while he sleeps. Once at the foot of William's bed, she reveals a dagger, aimed and ready to plunge it through his body. But William's eyes open in the nick of time, grabbing what he thinks to be his nephew's hand, throwing the dagger across the room, leaving Annabelle free to escape through the window.

The recording stops, and the projecting device shuts down its display. The king rises, "Camden Belflore, you are cleansed of all charges. Arrest Annabelle at once!"

Guards in the room scurry past the elites to find where she's run off to, and though she gives a good fight, she is no match for their number. In their grasp, Annabelle cries for mercy, "Your Majesty, you know I would never do anything to harm the kingdom or you! My family has been in your loyal service for centuries! Please, Your Majesty!" The guards grab her arms. "Camden! Everything I did was to protect you! Camden!"

But Camden can't bring himself to look at her.

CHAPTER 27

All the young Griffins feel anxious the next morning, so much so that even the violent ones seem quiet. The fields and woods where they reside make no sound, and all is completely still. Everybody waits for the sun to set to see what will happen to the moon. Bayo has selected a random Griffin girl from the pack to spread the rumor, and soon enough, everybody knows where to be tonight.

⚫⚫⚫⚫⚫

Bayo sits in front of The Eyes, his head buried in a book. The small window above The Eyes is left open to spy on Hale.

"Everything is coming along according to plan." Bayo waves his hand over the window, and it fades from sight. He leaves the room and closes the door behind him with a wide grin. "Things are looking up!" he says to himself. "Ianna!"

As if she were standing right beside the door, waiting at Bayo's beck and call, Ianna enters and bows. "What can I do for you, Bayo?"

"Today is a wonderful day! It is a day of new beginnings!" He takes Ianna's hands and pulls her into the room, and she lets out a bit of a giggle. He dances with her in hand, spinning her whimsically. And she can't help but smile. "Let's celebrate!"

He spins her in the air, lifting her several feet above the floor then drops her suddenly. She falls on her bum. He turns toward the window, ignoring her completely, and starts to unclasp his collar. "Go fetch me a drink! And I want my clothes for tonight. Turn on the record player. I want this house booming with song again, like in the good old days!" he says with fiery eyes. "Time for seriousness is almost over! All our hard work is paying off."

Ianna pulls herself to her feet while recalling Bayo's kindness to her a thousand years ago. That single act of kindness had saved her from a lifetime of slavery, given her a home and possessions she never had, and awarded a mighty title to redeem her honor. *I will forever be indebted to him . . . and in fear of his power.* "Yes, Bayo."

Bayo gazes at her and adds, "Make yourself presentable for tonight, please. Can't have them see you looking as disheveled as you always do. Wear that red robe I gave you. It is my favorite."

Ianna bows her head. "But Bayo, Rioma was planning on wearing red this evening. She would be very, very cross with me if I wore the same color."

Bayo chuckles. "Remember the last time she burned you, and your whole face was covered in blisters? You looked absolutely horrendous. Then, as it healed, the pus continued oozing, and you were the laughingstock of the whole village. The power of Ardor will always best the power of Shielding." He lets out a long sigh.

He takes a moment to recount the marvelous memories he once had, then he notices Ianna still standing there. "Go, Ianna. I've given you instructions."

Ianna bows then leaves.

"And Ianna," Bayo adds, and she stops. "You can wear your blue evening gown rather than be scorched in front of the Griffins. We have an image to uphold. An image of strength and superiority!"

Ianna smiles. "Thank you, Bayo."

"*Enough*," he moans as he pushes her out of the door. He slams it shut and exclaims, "I want some *music*!"

•●●●●●•

When the sun sinks in the west, there are hundreds of Griffins spread out on the meadow, watching the sun slip from sight behind the trees. Finally, when the sky darkens, a spark flashes all around the field, and large torches light up on their own.

Hale stands at the edge of the field, all the way in the back. There is a vibration growing beneath him, a light buzz that tingles his legs. He finds he cannot lift his feet. He is stuck. But he is not alone. All of the young Griffins fare the same.

Auburn hair flows somewhere in the distance, and Hale perks up to get a better look. It is just as he suspected. Grace and Evan were here. A smile grows on his face.

The rumbling beneath their feet intensifies, and the vibrations ripple upward, making everybody tingle. People gasp and shout, "There it is! Look!" They point into the sky.

Hale gazes up at a moon, one unlike any moon he has seen before. It gradually rises to the center of the sky at a steady pace. It looks surreal. The Griffins are in shock, for the Malphoran moon they know never moves this quickly.

Hale suddenly recalls something his father told him once. "Do you know why the moon is so big right now?" It must have been years ago. Hale remembers being curled up next to his mom under a blanket on the patio in their backyard, looking up at the night sky. "Because the moon comes closer to Earth in the winter and travels further away in the summer." Hale loved it when Felix taught him about space. Remembering his father's words, he questions how this moon could be so big in July. *This place can't be Earth. And that's why nobody is able to get back home.*

Something forces its way through the crowd, and the Griffins quickly notice they are capable of moving once again, albeit clumsily. They knock one another over, left and right, yet amazingly, nobody starts a riot. Perhaps they are too curious to know who just pushed past them. In a whisper that spreads like wildfire, the young Griffins murmur, "The Elders."

⚬●●●●●⚬

The Elders enter the field, one directly behind the other. Bayo, Deor, Rioma, and, lastly, Ianna. Ianna has her palms out on either side. She creates a bubble around them so they can pass through untouched. All the Elders wear tinted circular spectacles and extravagant clothing. Bayo flashes a charismatic smirk as he looks up to the sky to see the moon almost exactly above their heads. From the inside of his vest, he pulls out a chain that hangs around his neck. On the chain is a pocket watch, which he checks with a gleam in his eye. He elbows Deor behind him.

Deor leans in, and Bayo whispers in his ear, "Are you ready?"

Deor nods. His expression is always serious and grim. "I've been ready for centuries, Bayo."

Bayo stops when they reach the center of the meadow. There are exactly six circles, each a point of a hexagon. Ianna clears the young Griffins from these six circles, and each Elder takes a position at separate points, facing out into the crowd.

Once the moon is directly above them, the great rumbling of the earth intensifies. And suddenly, the hexagon with the Elders standing on its points starts to rise above the field. Bayo grins, greeting this long-awaited moment.

"Griffins!" he bellows into the crowd. "The Elders welcome you all! Welcome to this wonderful land! Welcome to your true, magnificent forms! Welcome to the power you will gain from this all-powerful moon!"

The young Griffins cheer and roar with excitement. Bayo lifts his hand, and the crowd silences.

"There are five powers. Each individual will attain one," Bayo says. "The power of Shielding!"

At once, Ianna pulls down her hood.

Bayo continues, "The power of Ardor!"

Rioma pulls down her hood.

"The power of the Light!" Bayo gestures to the empty space beside him, where Greon was meant to be standing.

"The power of the Dark!"

Deor pulls down his hood.

"And I, the power of Endurance! There might be one of you who will receive the rarest gift of all—the power of Prophecy!" He gestures to the second empty circle. "The Elders will guide you and teach you to master your new powers.

From this day on, you will no longer be weak and meager. From this day on, you will be an image to the world of strength and supremacy!"

The crowd cheers, and Bayo looks up into the sky. The moon moves a degree more, and a light suddenly radiates from the ground, moving in waves. Different colors flow in random motions.

The vibration beneath their feet increases, and some of the Griffins gasp in shock. But the Elders stand still, looking up directly into the moon with their spectacles and their arms spread out wide, welcomingly. Around the moon appear the illusions of six moons, each smaller and in its own color.

"Woah," Hale mutters in disbelief.

There is a whirling at their feet, and the wheatgrass sways to and fro, as if a great wind blows through the air.

Bayo faces the East, and the eastern moon is a bloody maroon pigment, its craters as pitch black as the fur of a panther. Above Rioma, a moon blazes orange. The moon above Greon's place is a golden yellow. Directly beside the yellow, a moon blazes green, and beside that is a blue moon above Ianna. Above Deor hovers a deep, dark purple moon. And finally, between the purple and bloody red moons, above a vacant space, is the green moon for the lone prophet of the current generation.

At that moment, Hale notices a cool wave of air slowly floating down from above. It feels as though tiny particles of dust are pouring over his head. And yet, he sees there is nothing there at all. His feet feel an odd magnetic pull, connecting him to the earth. But once this wave rushes over him, his body lifts off the ground completely. A celestial and invigorating feeling courses through him. Under this inexplicable light, he feels a connection with the universe, and he can see everything—as if everything unexplainable suddenly makes perfect sense.

His eyes are wide as he looks up into the night sky. As he gazes up at the stars and the surreal moon, he swears he can see into their souls as an aura of energy in their physical image. Unlike anything anyone could ever imagine. Shapeless, massless, weightless, playful, powerful, epic.

Hale realizes that everything is alive, breathing, and speaking in its own soft hum. And he wonders why he has never realized it before because right at this moment, he knows for certain—as if he's always known—that it has always been this way. The world has always been alive and buzzing.

Hale is one with the heavens, and the warmth coursing through him satiates his inner being. It feels like his soul is distinct from his body, and he gradually forgets all ordinary urges. He feels as if he is capable of escaping this vessel and becoming one with the universe. Then, the pull from the ground—which is still constant underneath him—starts to tug at the soles of his feet, weighing him down. If that pull weren't there, he would float right up into the sky and leave this body behind. Instead, here he levitates, slightly above the wheat, balancing between the sky and the earth. The vibration beneath him subtly jolts the blood within his veins.

All at once, he understands this vibration is the earth's way of speaking to him. Though it says no words, Hale knows it's telling him not to break free from this vessel to become one with the heavens. He feels a calming wave course through him, starting at his feet, pulling through his legs, torso, arms, and, eventually, through his flowing hair, leaving every single strand with a gentle and solemn goodbye. As gracefully as he'd been lifted, Hale starts to descend. Knowing the earth would not dare let him fall with force, Hale feels at complete ease as he floats downward.

Once his body reconnects with the ground, the vibration in the soil fades away. The earth, too, seems to be bidding him farewell. Slowly, Hale's body settles back into its natural state, coming to terms with what just happened. He waits to feel like his old self again. The self that was ignorant of the magic all around and the magic within him.

After a long period of silence, he feels at home within this vessel once more, the way he assumes it should. But that heightened state doesn't part from him. Something from the pull of the moon stays behind, inside him. It has given him a gift.

Hale takes in a deep breath, feeling this inexplicable addition rush through his body. There is a glow from below.

Hale looks down. Faint light seeps from his skin. The red color, burning through his veins, matches exactly the color of his inner being. He takes in his surroundings and suddenly remembers he is not alone. The whole field is alight with hundreds of Griffins, each one glowing with one of five colors—a sixth color is rare and given to only one Griffin.

In the distance, atop the platform, which now gradually sinks back into the ground, the Elders stand in euphoria like the rest. The light within them—Bayo's red, Rioma's orange, Ianna's blue, and Deor's purple—fades away. He turns to look at Grace, who is engulfed in yellow, and Evan, in orange. Far away to Hale's right is River, glowing blue. As the light dims from each person's body, the additional moons disappear, leaving the young Griffins to wonder if they were but a figment of their imaginations. All that is left behind is the original moon, now shrinking in size, becoming more ordinary by the moment.

While the young Griffins point to the sky, Hale can't help but stare at Bayo. There is something about this man—something he can't place. Though Hale swears he has never experienced anything like this before, it all feels oddly familiar. On an impulse, Hale pushes through the crowd to approach this man to find out why.

Ianna makes another barrier to block the Elders from the young Griffins while they depart. The crowd cheers as they pass, and Hale shimmies his way through. He reaches out to touch Bayo's arm but feels only a cool surface, which blocks him, and Bayo passes. The last of all the Elders, Deor, locks eyes with Hale. Hale's brows furrow as he suddenly feels he has seen these eyes before. He pauses in shock while Deor turns back and continues to walk away.

With his power of the Dark, Deor sends a message into Bayo's mind. *Your brother recognizes us.*

Bayo smirks.

While all the young Griffins disperse, Hale stays for a while, trying to recall whether or not he knows these people.

He looks to where all three of them stood during the Welcoming Moon, but the field is empty. He kicks a rock beside his feet. It skips a few steps, landing close to the strange circles on which the Elders had stood. Hale moves closer, stopping in front of the one Bayo stood on, and stares at it.

"Have I been here before?" He bites his lip, trying to remember, and looks up with new intentions.

He decides he is going to the Elders' Dome.

●●●●●●

The night sky is scattered with Griffins flying blindly. River soars just below the clouds, his wings gliding through the air as he scours below for a good place to land.

Somebody pushes him, and he almost loses his balance. He assumes the push was just an accident until three Griffins surround him. One by one, they swerve into him with force. River is knocked twice before he realizes he is being ambushed. He descends lower into the sky to escape them, yet they follow.

He looks back and his stomach drops. Spreading his wings wide, he soars upward until he is above the clouds. The Griffins are slow to follow, and they squawk in anger. River hears them approach. He submerges into the clouds and hopes they can't find him. The moist air saturates his fur and feathers.

The Griffins skim the surface of the clouds above. If they moved a bit lower, they would graze his back. River wastes no time and descends with speed. As his heart pounds, all he thinks of is getting into the trees below . . . and to safety.

He is almost there—but he senses something near his tail. A Griffin is gaining on him, its eyes burning an unfathomable purple color when they meet his.

Its voice enters River's mind. *I can hear your thoughts, gorrum. You can't run.*

It is Logan's voice, one of Leon's goons. Understanding hits River then— Logan shares Mary's power, the power of the Dark. River can't even seem to recall the name of his own power, let alone project it from his body.

Logan digs into River's mind, flipping through his memories as if they are pages in a book. His claws graze River's back. Strangely, however, River hears Logan's thoughts, as well—something that never happened with Mary.

When River overhears Logan's plot to dig his beak into River's neck until it bleeds out, his heart thumps, and he is desperate to escape. Logan pokes and prods through River's mind and even dares to ask about the red-haired girl. "Where is she? Leon's been asking about her."

River shrieks from the thumping agony in his head. He feels himself losing control and collides with the top of a tree. *Get out of my head!*

But Logan persists.

GET OUT OF MY HEAD! He expels a ghastly shriek that nearly bursts Logan's eardrums.

River turns to confront Logan midair. Just before he is able to smash his enormous paw across Logan's beastly face, Logan is pushed out of the sky.

But nothing hit him. It is as though he were flying backward, then all at once, he is falling. River can't make sense of it. Logan crashes into the trees below. River hears the sound of branches breaking, then silence.

River is too confused to realize the other two Griffins are sneaking up on him from behind. They fly directly into him and hit their heads in midair so hard that they both fall down into the treetops as well.

River turns once hearing the crash, but again, he sees nothing in the black night.

River leaves as fast as he can and swoops for the empty clearing. He transforms back to his human form and collapses alongside the nearest tree trunk, trying to catch his breath. His heart is speeding uncontrollably, and he attempts to calm himself. Grace's beautiful smile hides behind his shut eyes.

Somebody approaches in the distance, and a figure walks through the tall grass. A girl. Her eyes shine purple. In a loving whisper, Mary speaks in his mind. *River, it's me.* And in a flood, she overwhelms his emotions with serenity. *You can relax; they're gone.*

Mary is close enough to use her own voice. Her glowing eyes return to normal. "I saw what you did to Leon's friends just now. I told you all it would take was you getting your powers. I knew you could do it." She can see Grace's image hovering in his mind, and her heart sinks, though she smiles.

CHAPTER 28

Greon sits in some repugnant pub he'd found across the Atlantic. It stands crookedly on a boarded shore that partially floods with the rising tide every evening and smells of rotting fish they dare to sell at decent prices. To his surprise, just a few tables away, two patrons are talking about a powerful witch. Greon assumes witches are uncommon in the Human Division of Malphora since modern society is always so repulsed by the taboo of bending nature at will. Still, when he hears this news, he can't help but lean an ear closer.

Sitting at a table, soaking wet with his collar up and an ale in his hands, a man leans in toward the table to whisper in an Irish accent, "So you've seen 'er den? Didn't I say she's—"

"Yes, yes," the other interrupts, looking around to make sure their conversation is unheard by the five other people in the pub. This man is on the thick side, his hair and clothes tidy. He seems like a kind man, though his brow quivers with worry. "She's legitimate, like you said."

"So, she ded what you wanted, den?" asks the first man, scratching his stubble.

The other removes his cap and nods. He raises his hand to get the bartender's attention and orders a drink. He confesses, "I've never seen anything like it."

His friend smirks. "I told you, she's class. Can make *anythin'* 'appen." He casually works his wavy dark locks away from his face.

The other nervously shakes his head and comes closer. Greon is unable to hear the following words, and he can't resist turning his head slightly toward the two gentlemen. The nervous fellow takes no notice, but the other has a cunning look in his brown eyes as they catch Greon's. Greon turns back around to mind his own business—or at least to pretend to.

The nervous fellow leans back into his seat, and his hands shake as he clutches his wet cap. "She's a demahn. I fear I've made a 'uge mistake."

His friend takes another chug from his hefty glass and puts it down with a loud tap. "You asked me to tell you where she was, mate. I tahld you everythin' you needed to know. I tahld you what would 'appen. These kinds o' things dahn't go without prahper payment."

"Dis was mahre dan I expected," frets the other.

The waitress brings over his drink. "Anythin' else, ahr is dat all?"

The nervous man looks up at her and stutters, "Th—dat's all. Danks." He proceeds to guzzle down his drink, at which his friend's brows raise higher on his forehead.

"Well, Lahrd, Bill! It ain't *dat* bad!" he exclaims. "You gaht exactly what you wanted!"

Bill nods. "Yeah, yeah. I'm naht mad, just dahn't know wit to do wit myself. You know? Wit de time I gaht left, I mean."

His friend shrugs. "Set it all straight. Get de paperwork done. 'ow's your wife? De keds?"

Bill smiles slightly. "She's 'ad a miraculous recovery. De doctors are all astonished. De kids are calm and happy and settled." He takes a long chug, finishing his drink. His ears and cheeks grow redder by the moment from the alcohol. "It's wahrth it." He pulls up his sleeve to scratch an itch, and all across his forearm are protruding black veins. Bill's eyes grow wide, and he quickly pulls down the sleeve, hoping nobody has seen. But Greon caught a glimpse.

"Is *dat* it?" his friend asks, questioning his arm.

Bill nods. "She said I've gaht 'til it reaches me chest."

"A life can't be saved without takin' another away."

Bill looks up at him and sucks his lips. "Ah, well. Best I get goin'." He pulls out money for the drink and places it on the table. Then he takes something else wrapped in a small bundle from his pocket and hands it over to his friend.

The friend takes the bundle from Bill's hands and nods farewell. Bill buttons his coat, puts his hat back atop his head, then walks out the door and into the pouring rain.

The nameless man who shared the table with Bill finishes his drink and drops some of his own money on the table.

Greon casually follows him out of the reeking bar, happy to be rid of it.

The rain is pouring. Greon sees the man's silhouette in the distance. He walks after it, but the rain gets in his eyes. Suddenly, the figure he's been following is gone.

After a few more steps, an arm squeezes around Greon's throat. Greon stumbles backward. Their strength is astounding, and Greon can tell whoever is behind him now has to be holding himself back.

The man bitingly whispers in Greon's ear as Greon struggles, "Gobshite! Dink you're sly?" The voice belongs to the nameless man Greon followed out of the pub. "Who are you and what do you want?"

Greon pulls at the man's arm to make room to breathe, and he explains weakly, "My name is Greon. I wanted to ask about your woman friend, the one who helped that man inside."

"You know it's rude to listen in on someone's conversation. What do you want wet 'er?"

"I need her help. I'm desperate."

To Greon's surprise, the man releases him at once. Greon spins around. "Greon, is it? That's gas. Poor choehmp, what kind o' name is dat? Call me Garet."

Greon shakes Garet's hand.

"So, what is it you need frahm me friend?" Garet asks.

Greon shakes his head. "That doesn't concern you. I need her help, that's all. But I'll pay you for your information."

"Well, if it doesn't concern me, den good loehck, choehmp." Garet turns to walk away, but Greon grabs his arm.

"I'm not from here. I'm just trying to find my way home. Where I'm from . . . you can't get there physically."

Garet cocks his brow again. "Humph. 'ow interestin'."

Greon looks into this man's eyes pleadingly. "Can you help me? I need to get back soon, or—"

"Ahr what?"

Greon says, "It's just very important that I get back home."

Garet looks him up and down, studying him with a quizzical expression. "Well, I don't dink you're lyin'. So, you want to see de wetch, hmm?"

"Yes, I need to see her. I have no other option," he confesses. "And not much time."

"I can see dat. You've gaht death 'anging over you like a shadow."

Greon's eyes widen. "I've got *what* hanging over me?"

"Death. Come. You want to see de wetch; I'll take you to 'er." He starts walking in the direction of the pub, but he turns around when he realizes Greon isn't following him. "Well, are you coming ahr naht?"

Greon stares at him for a long moment and then asks, "What did you mean just now by death is hanging over me?"

Garet rolls his eyes and mumbles to himself, "When'll I learn to keep me dang mouth shoeht?" Though he knows all too well his tongue often loosens after a little drink. "Well, comb ahn, I dahn't 'ave all night! It's a coehrse I've got. I can see a shadow when people are abooeht to die."

Greon goes white and sputters.

Garet slaps him on the back. "Well, good din you're meetin' de wetch. Dis is me job, so to speak. I bring 'er people who need 'er assistance. She gives me what I need, plain and semple."

Greon then asks, "And what's that?"

Garet shrugs. "Well, a cure, ahbviooehsly. I dahn't want to see dese 'ahrrid creatures 'til my dying day! It's an elixir she makes. She wahn't give me a permanent cure, ahbviooehsly. My talent gives 'er good business. But I'll take what I can get oehntil I fend anahther way."

"That man in the pub you sat with. Is he going to die?"

Garet nods. "Yeah. 'e sold 'is life to spare 'is dying wife. 'e knew what 'e was gettin into."

Greon looks at him horror-stricken and wonders what kind of witch this is.

Garet leads him through narrow streets covered in puddles in every direction. The buildings surrounding them look older, and the streets turn to cobblestone. They turn into a narrow alleyway. Small animals scurry past, creating a pitter-patter as they rush to safety. A stray cat shrieks nearby, and its eyes glow in the night. Finally, Garet stops at a door and knocks.

Greon suddenly blurts, "Can you see how much time I have left?"

Garet shrugs his shoulders. "No, mate. I ahnly see a shadow."

The door opens with a loud creak, and though Garet gestures Greon inside, he is leery of entering.

"Need sahme assestance?" he asks condescendingly, pushing him through the door. And as soon as Greon is inside, the door shuts. Greon jumps and turns, grabbing the doorknob, wondering why it doesn't turn.

There's no keyhole in the door at all, he thinks in panic. *Not a single lock.* And yet he cannot open it.

Garet's muffled voice sounds from the outside, "Make sure you tell 'er who sent you. Meet me in the pub when you're done! Don't forget me vial!"

Greon takes a deep breath and turns around to face an ordinary hallway with a staircase just ahead of him. He peers upward into the dark corridor and calls, "Hello? Anybody there?"

Greon begins to walk up the steps, each footstep making a creaking sound. The upstairs is not lit, and for all he knows nothing is here. So, he calls out again, "Is anybody there? Garet sent me."

At once, the upstairs lights turn on, and he can see a single door above. He approaches it noisily and extends his arm to knock. Just before his fist lands on the wood, it opens an inch. He pushes it further to see a small room. On the wall opposite him is a burning fireplace. In the center of the room is an ordinary round table with three seats.

He feels a wind behind him. This strange force pushes him inside the room and toward the table. The door swings shut with a bang. On the table is a single blank sheet of paper. When Greon looks at it, the letters *S – I – T* appear.

Everybody at home knows the Arketchians are capable of such magic, though he'd met none with this amount of flair. He doesn't know what to make of this person. All he knows is that he is frightened out of his mind. And for good reason.

He takes a seat in front of the paper and watches the fire burn while he waits. The paper moves slightly, and he looks down at it. The word *sit* is gone, as if it was never written there. Instead, the paper asks, *Why are you here?*

Greon looks around, waiting to see a person appear in this strange way, as well. But there is no one. He swallows and says aloud, "I'm trying to get back to my home. I can't get there by physical means. I was brought by a portal. I tried to re-create a portal to take me back, and I was almost successful. But I ran out of resources and time. I came to the nymphs as a last resort, and they said I must die to travel there. But I cannot die just yet. I have to save my family."

He looks down at the paper, waiting for something else to be written. Slowly the words *Why are you here?* disappear, but they are not replaced with a new sentence.

A moment later, more words appear on the paper. *I know you.* On the following line, *Elder Greon of the Griffin Clan.*

Greon's heart skips a beat. "How do you know me?"

But the paper does not answer him. Both lines erase on their own. *Whose lives do you wish to save?*

Greon answers, "Ianna, Elder of the Griffin Clan. And Mary, her daughter. I created amulets for them so Bayo cannot trace them. I need to give them to them so they can escape before Bayo begins his plan. But I cannot pass the divide into the Extraordinary Division."

Again, the question disappears and is replaced with, *You think, without them, Bayo's plan will be foiled?*

Greon nods, recalling Felix's prophecy. "Yes. What he wants will only cause chaos." Greon waits for an answer but does not get one. "Please. I don't have much time. Garet confirmed that I am dying. I know what he's saying is true.

The Welcoming Moon has preserved the age of each Elder each year. If I don't attend, I will die. There will be no one to stop Bayo's plan."

The blaze in the fireplace suddenly roars, and Greon jumps in his seat. The letters on the paper are written in capitals, as if the witch is angry with him. *YOU ARE WRONG. Your life does not matter. As long as Bayo's brother stands in his way.*

"I left his brother in the woods. He wears an amulet such as this one. Bayo will never find him."

The flames increase once more, the heat in the room becoming overwhelming. *WRONG! THE BOY IS IN BAYO'S CARE RIGHT THIS MOMENT.*

"How can that be?" he demands. "Unless he took the amulet off, but he wouldn't." Minutes pass, and there is no answer on the page. Greon stands up from the seat and asks, "Who are you? How do you know about us?"

The fire crackles and rattles, and the paper moves. In anger, Greon grabs the paper and tosses it into the flames. "Come out and face me. Enough parlor tricks!" This is the most courageous he's ever been, and he realizes that as soon as he discards the paper—and he deeply regrets it. The room echoes with laughter, traveling around like wind in a circle. It is an eerie laugh, with a voice that belongs to a woman.

In a puff of blue smoke, beside the chair Greon had been sitting in, a woman's figure forms. She sits with her long legs crossed. When Greon looks at the face of this woman, his eyes go wide, and his jaw drops.

The woman chuckles with a sinister smile. "Remember me?"

Greon is speechless and backs away until the heat of the fire nearly scorches him. "Kala? How? Bayo killed you himself. I watched you die."

Kala uncrosses her legs and stands from her seat. She strokes Greon's face with her long fingernails. "You're not the only one who can create illusions, Greon." Her emerald green eyes are just as dazzling as he remembered.

Greon pulls her arm from his face. "How did you escape?"

She explains casually, "If you must know, I left with Felix, his wife, little Carly, and the boy. Right after I found out what Bayo really wanted from me."

"It was you! You helped them escape with Hale!"

Kala rolls her eyes and turns from Greon. "Why are you so surprised?"

"Because you would have done anything for Bayo. You both were madly in love."

Kala's hair whips around her, and in a flash, she is in front of Greon once more, clutching his face, her nails digging deep into his jaw.

"Love? Yes. Love. Bayo seemed to neglect the fact that he was married to Rioma. Seemed to neglect the fact that he planned on killing the older Griffin generation, all as a means to create a moldable army of young Griffins to reign over all of Malphora!

"Whether he loved me or not did not matter to me once I learned everything. Like the lost Eyes he'd stolen from Bimmorus, collapsing their kingdom. Or keeping Mary hostage for his personal bidding. Or keeping Ianna a slave in the Elders' Dome because she is too afraid of him to leave. There are things he does that even Deor doesn't know. How many treasures he's kept hidden from you all. How many secrets he has for the sake of his ultimate plan."

"And you were one of them," states Greon flatly.

She looks up at him, her hair shimmering beside the fire. "Tell me, have you heard from my sister?"

Greon shakes his head. "I haven't seen Palla since she tried to stop you from leaving the Arketcha tribe with us. Why don't you go back?"

She sneers. "After what I've done to Bayo? Betrayed his trust, helped his best friend steal away his little brother. He'd torture me. I was living peacefully here away from him. But now, you've single-handedly ruined everything Felix and I have done to keep the boy safe! To keep Malphora safe!"

"I had no other option, Kala. I was bound to do as he said. The first chance I had I took."

Kala throws her head back and laughs. Her dark sleek hair falls behind her. "You're a coward, Greon. You have always been a coward. Hundreds of years have passed, and you and Ianna are still stuck under Bayo's rule. You've never stood up to him. You don't even agree with his logic the way Deor does, but you never did anything about it. You couldn't even walk up these steps without jumping from fright!" She laughs at him again, and he blushes.

"What can I say . . . better late than never. Will you help me?"

She walks over to him, her hips swaying. The light of the fire reflects on her tight silk dress, highlighting her every curve. It is the way she moves that first captivated Bayo. She presses her palms on his chest until she can feel his heartbeat. Greon holds his breath.

"You do know the Welcoming Moon is at sunrise in this part of Malphora, right? That is why the death shadow hangs over you. Your hair is already greying, Greon." She strokes a lock of his hair. "I have no reason to help you," she whispers seductively.

He chokes on air. "I'll give you anything you want."

She laughs. "You have nothing to offer."

"Think about it, Kala. Without Mary, Ianna, and myself by his side, he will lose. The boy will fulfill Felix's prophecy and turn on his brother."

Kala glares into Greon's eyes. "There were two prophecies, have you forgotten? The boy is an asset to Bayo as long as Bayo can successfully manipulate him. And Bayo is surely capable of that. Felix and his family have protected him, thus dulling Bayo's plan to begin with. Mary and Ianna are useless. Bayo would have no problem killing them both on a whim."

Greon boils at the truth in her words. "I'll give you my soul."

Kala's eyes light up.

"That's what you take from these people, isn't it? You feed off of their souls. It's the only thing keeping you alive, considering the guardian angels of the Arketcha tribe are not here."

Kala smiles. "You always did have your moments." She walks over to the table and leans against it, gazing at Greon beside the fire with a gleam in her eye. "You should have let the nymphs help you."

CHAPTER 29

H ale slowly flies until he catches sight of a golden dome glittering in the moonlight. It is alight in the dark, like an inviting beacon. He descends and shifts back to his human form. He wonders if it is appropriate to be here, if these mysterious Elders would even give him their time. Or if they would punish him for intruding instead. But he decides to take the chance. He has to know why their leader is so familiar to him.

He raises his fist to knock on the wooden double door. Before his hand lands, the door opens gently. Ianna stands in a blue dress, her hair in an intricate braid. Hale instantly feels that this woman is kind. Maybe it is in her smile.

"Hi" is all Hale manages to say.

"Hello. I am Ianna. Elder Deor sensed your presence. Would you like to come in?" She opens the door wide, and Hale sees a golden hallway lined with torches on the wall.

Hale steps inside. "I came because . . . well, now that I think about it—I just wanted to meet you all."

Ianna smiles because she knows Hale came only to see Bayo. Deor is quick to intrude minds subtly then spread the gossip. "Well, the other Elders have retired for the night. But I believe High Elder Bayo is still awake. I will call him down.

Come, wait in the sitting room," she suggests while walking through the hallway and opening the door to the parlor.

Hale awkwardly takes a seat as Ianna says, "I'll be a moment." Hale nods, and she departs.

Ianna returns with a tray in her hands. She places it in front of Hale on the table. A mouthwatering aroma fills the room at once, and Hale feels very uncomfortable.

"You must be hungry," she says.

"You didn't have to do all that. Really," he says.

"You are our guest. Enjoy," she says kindly and leaves once more.

Hale lifts the lid of the tray to reveal a steaming steak with buttery mashed potatoes and gravy on fine white china with gold trimmings. A glass goblet is filled to the brim with water. He hasn't had food like this since his parents died.

Just like that, Hale gives in. Comfortable or not, he is famished. He guzzles down the water at once, then wipes his mouth with his hand. Hale didn't notice the white handkerchief placed so elegantly beside his plate, but if he had, he wouldn't have used it anyway. Grabbing the fork and knife beside the plate, he hacks away at the steak, shoving a piece in his mouth and unconsciously moaning with satisfaction. The tender meat explodes with warm juice as he chews.

Once Hale has finished, Ianna returns with an elaborate serving cart filled with goodies from the Human Division. Hale's eyes are wide at the sight. There are piles of Chocolate Kisses, Twizzlers, Hershey bars of every kind, Jolly Ranchers, Reese's Peanut Butter Cups, and Kit Kat Wafer Bars. Steaming from a piping glass kettle on the top shelf is hot chocolate, filling the room with its creamy aroma. Hale's mouth salivates as his thoughts drift off to seldom memories of him sharing these sweets with those he loved.

Ianna pours Hale a cup of the hot drink and makes sure to top it with large marshmallows. After she departs, Hale suspects she'll return to share dessert with him. But then footsteps approach, heavier than Ianna's, and Hale turns to see Bayo walking toward the seat across from him. Hale quickly sets down his mug and looks up at this man, who extends his hand to him.

Though Bayo looks chipper, Hale can tell he is a serious person from his strict demeanor. He is well put together, even now, after dressing down from the Welcoming Moon celebration. He wears a red silk robe with a maroon satin collar and trimmings, along with matching slacks and reading glasses. There is a book in his hand. "Hello. I'm Bayo."

"I'm Hale." They shake hands.

"So I've heard. Pleased to meet you. Please, sit." They take their seats, and Bayo sets the book down beside him. "So, Hale, what brings you to the Elders' Dome this evening?"

Hale struggles to put his thoughts into words. "I wanted to meet you."

Bayo smiles. "And now we've met."

Hale nods, then his brows furrow as he asks bluntly, "Do I know you?"

Bayo raises an eyebrow.

Hale gazes intently at this person across from him. This man's mannerisms, his eyes, his hair—it all seems so familiar.

Bayo chuckles. "Not directly, no. Unless you've been hiding here for many a year—I haven't left the Griffin Clan for eleven years . . . except for one occasion. I do, however, know *you*, as well as most of the young Griffins. We've kept an eye on them throughout the years, until the Elders and I decided it was time they return home to us."

Hale asks, "What do you mean, return home?"

Bayo motions toward the serving cart. "Please."

Hale goes for a Hershey's chocolate bar. Carly would never fail to bring him his favorite treat on her way home from work after a good grade. He brings it to his lips with her in mind and thanks Bayo.

Bayo takes the same. "These are also my favorite," he adds. "The Griffins of the previous generation, meaning your parents, decided a long time ago they would like to venture off to the Human Division of Malphora. Malphora is what we call this world. I assume you've been taught its human name, Earth."

Hale nods.

"Yes. In this division of the world, we refer to Malphora as the earth and all that surrounds it. It is everything in *this* existence. But you cannot get to the Human Division of Malphora physically. It is enclosed. The technology required to move between the two divides was unknown to us until I discovered the technology and learned how to use it. It took me a while to come to terms with what our people wanted. It was a terrible feeling to know that the Griffin Clan was not good enough for them. Finally, when I agreed, I made them a deal. They were to live their lives happily in the Human Division of Malphora, but their children must return home so we could remain a nation."

Hale nods in partial understanding. "So, my family . . . they were Griffins like me? Why didn't they tell me?"

"Imagine if they exposed their true nature in that other world. The monstrosities the humans would have done to us! Even so, with our gifts hidden, the humans took a great toll on the previous generation. The Human Division is obsolete and ignorant."

Hale recalls the brutality of his kidnapping and the death of his parents. His eyes dart to the floor as he thinks about this question. "My father taught me there is a balance in everything. I think some people are more accepting than others." He looks up at Bayo once more.

Bayo's jaw tightens as he takes in Hale's words. "You are wise, like your father. Tell me, what was his name?"

"Felix," Hale answers.

"Ahh, Felix . . . there were many Felixes in the previous generation." Bayo takes a piece of cake. "Would you like some?" he asks.

"No, thank you," Hale says, feeling his swollen stomach.

"What is your father like?"

"Umm—" Hale begins.

"You have a mother, too, I'm sure," Bayo adds.

"Yes. I mean, I had . . . my parents died." Hale's cheeks and eyes redden immediately.

Bayo pauses. "I am truly sorry to hear that. You aren't the only one. Most of the parents of these young Griffins perished in The Human Division. Nearly all of them grew up on their own. It is a difficult place to get accustomed to. I never should have allowed them to leave here." Bayo looks off as if he is recalling a memory. "Do you know how they died?"

Hale answers solemnly, "They were killed. But we don't know by who."

"We?"

"My sister and me. She took care of me after they died."

"Oh, you have a sister! Is she here as well?"

Hale looks down at the table. "No," he says, almost in a whisper. "She also died."

"I should not have asked." He can see tears welling up in Hale's eyes even though Hale looks away, and he truly feels guilty for bringing it up. "Here." Bayo offers him a handkerchief.

Hale takes it but does not use it.

Bayo sighs. "No words can make up for someone's loss. No one should have to go through so much pain. But you are home now, and here in the Griffin Clan, you are safe. You are free to be in your natural state without fear of persecution. Free from any evil or harm."

Hale looks up at him quizzically. "We aren't free from evil or harm here. I was almost killed tons of times. I'm more afraid of this place than anywhere else I've ever been in my entire life."

Bayo attempts to contain his shock. "Ah, the Griffins are young! They will do as they please. Perhaps, I should have been more involved since their arrival, but I wanted to wait until the Welcoming Moon when they received their powers to mold them and teach them our ways."

Hale stays silent for a moment until he asks, "How were you able to find us and bring us here?"

"The Three Eyes. They are portals that allow one to travel to and from worlds. I assumed the young Griffins could coexist peacefully. I assumed they would have much in common and grow strong—as one nation."

Hale is confused. "So, you don't know that they fight on a stage to the death almost every night. The bodies are thrown into a fire. You don't know that the winner of every fight gets a gold coin so they are able to eat, and the only source of food is at the Hogs' table, which is rumored to come from you, the Elders."

Bayo is outraged. "What? The table of food was never supposed to be turned into a reward for victors. The coins we gave out, yes, but not for such means. We gave them out so the children could buy whatever they needed from us—new clothes or anything else they desired. It was meant to teach them responsibility. Never as permission to eat. I will see to this matter first thing in the morning. You have my word."

Hale feels sudden relief at Bayo's outrage.

"Where is it you stay during the night?"

"In the same field as the stage. All the Griffins sleep there."

"You sleep on the *ground*?" Bayo asks in horror.

"Yes."

"*Why?* There is another field filled with small domes, like my own, fully furnished with everyone's needs."

"I guess nobody knows where that field is. Otherwise, they would have used the domes by now."

Bayo's tone drops. He places a hand on Hale's shoulders. "We will correct this at once; otherwise, we will no longer have a nation to guide. I greatly appreciate your honesty. You are more than welcome to come visit me anytime. You are also welcome to stay here for the night if you like."

"That would be . . . very nice. Thank you," Hale says.

Bayo smiles then calls, "Ianna!"

She comes through the door immediately. "Yes, Bayo?"

"Hale is staying the night. Please prepare the spare room for him."

She gives a bow and departs.

Hale asks, "Are you the leader of the Elders?"

"Yes, I am. My power, Endurance, is the strongest of them all. I was once the strongest Griffin in all the Clan, and the other Elders were the strongest with their gifts, as well. In our youth, our nation was unwell. We took charge to create the nation anew. It was a time of great prosperity and rebirth. But that is a story for another day. Which gift were you blessed with on this night?"

"My skin was red, like yours."

"Well, congratulations! You are a Griffin of Endurance! It is a wonderful talent, though hard to master all its depths. But I see great promise in you, Hale. You have good character. I would like to train you to use your gift—if you would like, of course."

"That's very nice of you."

"I will train all the other Griffins of Endurance, as well. And the other Elders will train the young Griffins with their shared powers. But I should like to make you my apprentice. Would you like that?"

Hale nods.

"Good." Bayo beams. "Ianna is here to take you to your room. Goodnight, Hale. Pleasure meeting you."

"Goodnight."

Hale follows Ianna out of the room. She walks to the long staircase beside the front door, her dress shimmering in the light of the torches. As Hale climbs the stairs, he looks toward the room he has just come from. Inside, Bayo's head is lowered, reading the book he had brought with him. At that moment, Bayo looks up and smiles.

"This is my room," says Ianna to Hale, signaling to her right. "If you need anything, I will be here."

The paintings on the ceilings are directly in front of the doors to the rooms. Hale gazes at the one over Ianna's doorway. The painting depicts a fair woman with dark hair, her eyes closed, her hands extended on either side. She wears a long blue dress. Around her body is a bubble lined in blue. Outside the bubble, daggers and swords point toward her.

Ianna notices what he is looking at. "That painting depicts my talent and a battle I won. My power is Shielding. I can create barriers that cannot be passed. All the other Elders have such images as well. But best you see the rest in the morning, perhaps. I shall tell you all the glorious details of their battles then—if we can spare the time."

Hale follows along until she stops at the other side of the hallway beside a closed door with no painting above. She opens the door.

"Here you are," she says. Hale's jaw drops at the sight of the king-like room. "There is a washroom you can use behind this door here," Ianna says, pointing to the closed door beside the fireplace. "And there are fresh clothes on the bed."

"Thank you," Hale says again.

"Have a good night, Hale." She closes the door behind her and leaves him gazing in wonder.

He enters the bathroom. "Wow," he repeats gleefully. "They even have toilet paper!" Many awe-filled moments later, he decides to take a bath. Especially after he looks in the mirror. There are five different soaps on display, along with a razor and other essentials on the stone countertop. Excited, Hale turns the faucet and waits until the tub is full. Steam fills the room shortly after.

After jumping in the tub, Hale lets out a long breath and tries to think about the last time he'd been so pampered. He can't remember.

⚫●●●●⚫

Bayo hears the sound of the water running in Hale's bathroom and smiles. Deor then confirms telepathically, *Your brother is enjoying his stay.*

Who wouldn't enjoy their stay here, Deor? Bayo replies. A moment later, Bayo asks, *What has he thought about me?*

Bayo senses Deor's amusement. *He thinks you are a serious man. Noted by your movement and tone. He is aware of an unidentifiable connection between you two. And you confirmed that when he confronted you.*

That is all? Bayo says, disappointed.

You won his favor when you declared you would be more involved in the lives of the young Griffins.

Is that all? Bayo repeats.

He favors Ianna. He senses her kindness and sincerity. Such qualities are admirable to him.

Bayo huffs. *Even as a tiny thing, he always had a different perspective on life. All the same, I will appeal to him in due time.*

Indeed.

CHAPTER 30

"I hereby declare the Griffin refugees, Eliath Theoden and Francis Orden, will not be harmed for assisting Camden Belflore! Their company shall be escorted from the palace," King William bellows.

Before Eliath and Francis depart from the throne room with their assigned guards, Eliath tells the king, "My son was invited to the Royal Academy. Here are his papers." He pulls them from his pocket, unwrinkles them, and hands them to the closest guard, who checks for authentication before nodding certainly at the king.

"Your son may stay," William says.

"It will be my pleasure to take you, Marcus. I know the school well, and it is the least I could do," says Camden.

Marcus looks at his father, surrounded by royal guards and nearly pushed from the throne room. The moment he was dreading is now upon him. "You'll do great. Align 'em stars, boy!" Eliath calls before the double doors shut.

As Camden and Marcus walk side-by-side through the lonely corridors of the palace, Camden breaks the silence as he pauses abruptly. "I wish to tell you, Marcus, you need not be afraid here. I know it is daunting to be the only one of your kind, but I will be your ally. You have my personal protection always."

"Thank you," Marcus says in shock.

At the borders of the palace courtyard, Marcus feels as though he is passing through the same wind he felt when he first came. "We are outside the magical border," Camden explains.

Just in view, Marcus spots a row of dazzling chariots, which the upper class was using in the capital. He'd never seen such contraptions up close before, and nobody in his strictly Griffin village ever earned enough Zaire to purchase one.

"Have you ever ridden in one of these?" asks Camden, flashing a charming smile.

Marcus shakes his head rapidly, more than eager to experience such advanced technology.

The golden carriages are much more elaborate than the simple hemisphere-shaped carriages he'd spotted in the capital. It is evident these are exclusively used by the elites and made in the shape of the most popular bird in Bimmorus, a Femu, though a hundred times its size.

Marcus jumps in the red velvet cushioned two-seater beside Camden, prepared to witness wonders. Camden pulls a circular token from his person and presses it into an indent of the same size at the center of the dash. At once, the magnetic field beneath the contraption revives, and they are levitating off the ground. Indents all along the contraption become alight with a marvelous red glow, and the wings of the mechanical beast grow out from its body.

Marcus and Camden speed through the dim skies, shouting exuberantly, "Whooo!"

They glide over the ocean and toward a beautiful, three-story building on an island. Its first story has an open architectural design, supported by several columns. Behind the building are mountains and rushing waterfalls.

"This is what it must be like to fly in my Griffin form," says Marcus as they come to a halt on the island.

"You've never flown in your Griffin form?" Camden asks.

Marcus shakes his head. "I've never transformed. It's against Bimmorian law."

Camden is silent for a moment. "Well, that must be addressed," he says with a wink.

They enter the dim building. Along the edge of the first floor, white lounge chairs are positioned specifically for people to appreciate the view of gushing waterfalls and flora on all sides. The white stone floor is decorated with a long red carpet that leads up the stairs toward the end of the room. On either side of the luxurious carpet are tall, thin lampposts already lit with yellow flames. As Camden and Marcus walk through, the lampposts suddenly burst with color and change from yellow to green.

Camden notices Marcus's silent fascination with each lantern he passes. "They are enchanted to be a signaling device. They warn the head of the academy when a visitor arrives. It is she we need to meet with to get you settled. Come, we will find her on the second floor," Camden states, leading Marcus up the stairs.

Marcus turns around to peek at the enchanted lanterns once more, watching them turn back to their original color, one pair at a time.

Camden and Marcus approach the first room to their left on the second floor.

"This is the one," Camden says. He knocks three times.

At once, there is rattling and banging as objects crash on the floor within as the headmistress makes her way to answer her door. The door opens a crack, and a single eye peers through.

"Who is there?" Her voice is raspy. Perhaps she is old or has just woken up from a deep sleep.

"Good evening, Lady Meir. It is I, Camden Belflore."

"Camden!" the woman exclaims as she adjusts her glasses. However, she does not open the door any wider. "I thought you were exiled!"

"I cleared my name only this afternoon," he explains. "I'm escorting a friend of mine. He is to be attending your school here."

"Oh? Well, do come in then." She allows them inside. Lady Meir is an untidy woman. Camden remembers this quirk from when he was a student at this school and notes to himself that her habits never changed.

In her room are two square windows on the wall opposite the door. Between them, a large bookshelf completely filled with books. In front of the shelf is a long table covered with papers, along with vials and bottles, which are all filled with strange liquids. Lady Meir seems to be in the middle of concocting something in her study.

One of the windows is open, and a gust of wind causes her papers to fly around the room.

"Please excuse the mess," she says, placing the flying papers back on the table and shutting the window. To their right is her official desk, which is empty save for a few open books. She motions for both men to take a seat.

"I must congratulate you, Marcus Theoden. It is a difficult feat to be selected for this school. So how, then, do you possess a power of the Welcoming Moon, considering you were born in Bimmorus?" she asks.

"My parents immigrated here just before I was born, sixteen years ago. My mother was eighteen years old when she attended the Welcoming Moon. She was pregnant with me at the time," he explains.

Lady Meir's eyes glisten with interest, and she leans in closer. "Do you know what a fascinating find you are?" She stands up just then and walks over to the bookshelf, bringing a large book back to her desk.

"I've read much about the Griffins and their natural and given abilities. But never have I heard of a fetus receiving powers from the Welcoming Moon! Let alone the one power that is not shared among anyone else in a generation! Did you know that there is only one Griffin prophet per generation?"

Marcus stutters, "Y—yes."

She is so giddy with fascination that she nearly dances her way back to her seat. "It is a great honor to have you in our school. A very great honor. Please, would you explain your talents to me if you can?" She pulls a drawer from her desk and takes out a pad and pen.

Droplets of sweat bead down Marcus's forehead. His head suddenly feels light. "I have no control over it," he explains. "I fall to the ground. It feels as though my spirit escapes from my body momentarily."

Noticing Marcus's translucent skin, Camden interrupts, "Lady Meir, perhaps Marcus could go to his room now? He's had a long journey to get here."

"Yes, yes, of course. I just have a few more questions—"

Marcus feels his head spinning. Then his senses dull, and suddenly, he falls forward in his chair and onto the floor.

* ● ● ● ● *

The full moon rapidly recedes countless times, leaving Marcus's head whirling as he attempts to count the days he is traveling backward. It is no use, for as soon as the cycles cease, Marcus falls from the skies and finds himself in an extravagant bedroom chamber.

A wounded man lies in bed, his face deathly similar to that of the current king, William, though with some minor differences Marcus cannot put into words. He wears an open robe exposing his wrapped chest, which seeps with blood. There is a knock at the door.

"Your highness, Prince Camden has arrived as instructed."

The man hoists himself from the bed, hastily closing his robe, then rushes to place a crown on his head. His posture is slumped and with each move of his body, his face gives a great twist of pain.

"Your highness?" the guard asks once more.

"Let him enter," says the king with a voice so hoarse he has to repeat himself. As soon as the door bursts open, the king forces himself to stand upright. In comes a young Camden, no older than seventeen, rushing to embrace him.

"Father!"

"Oh!" the king groans as Camden squeezes his torso, though he manages to cover the pain with laughter. Camden is none the wiser. "How were your travels, my son?"

"Just wonderful! We've successfully made peace treaties with the Centaurs. Their young prince and princess should join the Royal Academy in a decade's time."

"Marvelous!" The king says as he gestures Camden to take a seat beside the small table. "I, too, have much to discuss with you."

"Father. The servant maids whisper about you. They say you seldom leave your chambers these days. Is all well?"

"Yes. All is well. But I have some very important business to discuss with you. Do not alarm yourself; this has to do with your succession." At the table rests a beautiful jewelry box that King Owen opens to reveal a silver necklace in the shape of a crescent. "This heirloom was passed down to all the future kings of Bimmorus. And now it is time it should belong to you."

Camden holds it in wonder, "Thank you, father!" His smile suddenly fades, and he cannot meet his father's gaze. "I know you are preparing me for my days as king, but I fear I am not fit to rule."

King Owen nods. "I know you never wanted the crown. You are young and full of folly, and I see the enjoyment of life in your eyes. My wish is that you continue to have this enjoyment for the rest of your days. It might seem like a long while before you will inherit the crown, but it is not a duty I am forcing upon you. I have noticed you have other passions, and William has had his eye on the crown since he and I were children."

"What are you saying, Father?" Camden inquires.

"You would make a great king, Camden, but sometimes, there lies a greater duty to family."

The bedroom chamber morphs into a grand courtroom where Owen sits upon his throne, with a large doctrine placed on the desk before him. William stands to his right, and Camden is on his left; an official courtier watches over them. Marcus peers closer. William kneels over the doctrine first and signs it enthusiastically. Just before Camden takes the pen to have his turn, Owen's shaking hands grab hold of his.

They share a brief glance. "It's okay, Father," Camden says, taking the pen and signing the doctrine.

The courtier then declares, "I hereby announce that Camden Belflore has abdicated his right to the throne, leaving the next in line for the crown to be William Belflore. Proceeding abdication, Camden will retain his authority over the military."

William interjects, "Owen, there is no reason for Camden to have power over the military. Bimmorus is at peace with all neighboring nations."

King Owen's voice booms loudly over his brothers', "The doctrine is signed, William. You will have your crown."

The moon appears once more, coming into a new cycle, signifying a month has passed, and Marcus stands beside a grieving Camden at Owen's freshly filled grave. "How could he have died so soon?" Camden mutters in disbelief.

Marcus struggles to open his eyes and wake from this sad dream, but before he does, he is pulled in another direction. Before him is Camden as the grown man he is now, entwined lovingly with a woman with vibrant red hair. She pulls away from Camden's embrace to look Marcus straight in the eyes while pressing her finger to her lips.

* ● ● ● ● *

Marcus screams as he returns to the real world. He's never made direct contact with anyone in a vision before. Lady Meir speeds to his side with an apple in hand. "Quick, eat. You will feel better."

"Are you all right?" Camden asks.

"Camden, the woman you once loved," he manages. "She's hiding many things you need to know. You need to go see her."

* ● ● ● ● *

Adrenaline shoots through Camden's veins. After what he learned about his ex-fiancé, he didn't wish to see her again. Camden continues down the steps. There are fewer imperial guards than usual positioned around the palace and in front of the gates to the dungeon.

He greets the lone guard at the gate and hands him a gold coin. "You may take your leave."

The guard bows and departs.

The dungeon is cold and wet. Prisoners don't stay here too long—they are generally executed quickly, no matter the severity of the crime. Fear had swelled throughout the kingdom at the unjust system. Still, Camden didn't think badly of William. He understands that William sincerely thinks he is doing what he believes best for the country.

Camden passes many cells and peers into each. "Annabelle?" he calls out, just above a hushed tone. "Annabelle?"

Her voice sounds a few steps away. "Camden?" He can hear her footsteps as she comes toward the iron bars.

As he faces her, his heart suddenly aches, and he doesn't know what to say or do. So, he just stands there, gazing into her blue eyes, and she gazes back. All is silent except for the dripping of water somewhere in this dark cold place. Though Camden wants so desperately to break her free from this cell and take her into his arms, he cannot move past her betrayal.

She slowly reaches out to him. When her fingertips touch his face, he wakes from his daze and removes her hand.

"You must be here for answers," she says.

"Do you have any?" he asks dryly.

She looks up at him, and his heart stops. "I have them all."

"Then tell me. What is going on? Why have you not told me prior to now? We could have solved these problems together. You threw away our future. You threw me away as if our relationship was dispensable. Was it real, or was it another ploy? I never expected such actions from you."

"Then this will be the moment I remedy my mistakes . . . if you'll allow it," she responds. She swallows, thinking of where to begin. "You were making moves to create a protective barrier with the new technology. What you did not know was every move you made, your uncle was strongly against, though he did not share these disagreements with you. He never meant to allow you to create the barrier, and I wondered why myself. When urged to pass the law, William agreed to it every time, but when the law was finalized and awaited his signature, he would not sign. At that time, you were still waiting on the papers that stated whether the technology worked in the experimentation phases, so no one thought anything of the topic since. I had also learned from the national treasurer that William withdrew great sums of money regularly.

"Then one evening, I entered the king's study while he was out. And it was plainly on his desk, open and exquisite, unlike anything I'd ever seen."

"What was?" Camden asks eagerly.

Annabelle grabs the railings with both hands and says, "*The Book of Peace.*"

Camden's eyes go wide. William had always countered Camden's belief that the artifact ever really existed.

"Where does he keep it?" Camden asks.

"He locks it away every evening before he retires, in his late wife's parlor room, where no one is bound to go looking. He takes it every morning and keeps it by his side throughout the day. I dared to look at the page it was opened to that evening. The book gives instructions to create portals to other realms without the Three Eyes. As we know, there are only two other worlds in existence—"

"Thurana and Orcura," say she and Camden, simultaneously.

"Yes," she continues, "so I flipped through his notes to see which of the two he was meaning to conspire with. Lo and behold, William has been conversing with the Empress of Orcura for many years. The book taught him to create small portals that can send objects to and from our world to theirs. But the portal he means to create now is of a larger scale. Large and durable enough to allow full-scale immigration to Bimmorus, thus explaining his disdain for—"

"My barrier," Camden finishes, understanding.

"Exactly."

"Why would he allow the people of Orcura safe passage to Bimmorus?"

"He is trying to form an alliance to help fight in the war Bayo is bringing to Malphora."

"Then his plan is quite smart. Why, then, did he hide it?" Camden asks.

"I wondered that myself. On his desk, on the scattered stacks of papers— directly on top—was a contract declaring an exchange of help for money and surrender of diplomacy to the Orcuran Empress, Talzra. It was signed," she says in dismay. "I knew if I told you, it would cause great trouble between you and your family. I did not want that—I know how important these ties are to you."

She drops her head from his gaze in shame. "I made a decision to protect you and the kingdom from William's deeds. I caused you to be away from the palace entirely while I made moves to ally with the Griffins against William and all of Orcura. The Griffins are already enemies of Orcura, and they have Thurana on their side. They've been in contact since the Griffins stole The Eyes on Lorain's Day. Bayo has told me himself."

Camden moves away from her in horror.

Annabelle reaches out for him. "Camden, please understand. I tried to save the kingdom." Her voice is just above a whisper, "Camden, please. I love you."

Camden swallows and asks, "How did you contact Bayo?"

Annabelle hesitates. "I used *The Book of Peace*," she admits.

"You knew I'd been looking for it, and you knew its location. You must have come across the book several more times, not just the one time you so briefly mention. Is that correct?"

"Yes."

"You are no better than him," he says. "You tried to prevent one superpower from corrupting the nation by allowing another to corrupt the nation in the same fashion. Not only has there been a bargain made between Bimmorus and Orcura, but there is also a second bargain made—by you—between Bimmorus and the Griffin Clan. Do you know what trouble you've caused the kingdom? Making deals with other nations when it is not your place to do so?" Camden pauses. "You were meant to be my *wife*," he says in disgust. "My life partner, meant to share everything with me. Stand by my side. Come to me in your times of trouble, as I have come to you. Why do you think the kingdom is resting atop your shoulders alone? Do you fancy yourself the queen?" He slams his hands on the railing in front of her.

Annabelle jumps in fright, but she answers. "No. I know what I did was wrong."

"Yes. I know for a fact that is exactly what you think. Otherwise, there wouldn't have been secrets between us. No need to destroy my name and reputation. You claim you protected me when, in fact, you put me in more danger. You claim you look out for my interests, but you sever ties between my family and me! You created a delusional fantasy in your head where William is out of the way, and you and I take the throne of Bimmorus—with Bayo's trusted help, hmm? Where in this convoluted fantasy was I still on good terms with my family after I overthrew my uncle? Where?" Camden shouts as he pulls his hands through the railing, grasping her arms. "You are no better than he is! You never *loved* me. You found a means to gain power. You found means to be the queen. You cover it up with pretentious, self-righteous acts of forming alliances with superpowers that have the means and capabilities to destroy us!"

He does not notice how strong his grip is on her arms until he sees the fear in her eyes. Tears overflow, and she quietly agrees. "You're right."

He lets her go at once and pants in anger.

"I wish I could have done it all differently, I swear," she says in a broken voice.

"I ought to leave you here to be executed."

Annabelle looks away from him and nods, gasping as the tears well in her eyes. "I deserve no less for what I've done. You are wrong in only one thing. My love for you is real."

Annabelle reaches for her neck and pulls at the silver chain around it. A pendant emerges from her breast. It was the gift Camden presented her the night he proposed. In the center of the locket is an inscription Annabelle now reads aloud: "The stars in heaven will envy the light of our love." She opens the locket, and the dungeon is alight with stars. Small white clouds drift through, and just behind Camden's head, a full moon glows. As the locket projects these surreal images, a soft melody plays. Annabelle gazes at Camden longingly as the melody echoes through the halls.

To her surprise, he asks, "Do you remember this song?"

She smiles. "I could never forget. It is the song that played at the Midwinter Ball when you first approached me and asked me to dance."

Camden looks down at the floor. Annabelle closes the locket, and the night sky fades around her. The melody ends suddenly.

"The night I gave you that, I made you a vow," says Camden. "Do you remember what I said?"

Annabelle answers, "You vowed that you would be the rock beneath my feet. You would raise me high enough to reach the stars. You vowed to bring me joy each day of our lives together."

Camden nods. "That I did."

Then Camden does something he had not intended on doing when he came here. He kneels at the gate that cages Annabelle and hoists it up with all his might. His face turns red, and his muscles protrude from his shirt. He holds it a foot or so off the stone floor and urges her to slide underneath. He frees her.

Just as Annabelle thanks him for his kindness, he interrupts her, "I have kept my promises to you. I ask only one thing. Leave this place and never return."

He can't face her now. He knows the sorrow in her eyes will only cause him more grief.

"You don't have long," he adds.

He walks away. She watches his every step.

CHAPTER 31

Kala takes a seat at the table and motions for Greon to sit across from her. There is an open glass jar in the center of the table, the lid beside it.

"Place the pendants in the center of the table," she directs. "Do you wish to send a message to Ianna and Mary?"

"Yes."

"They will know you're dead if they hear your wandering voice."

Greon pauses. "Oh, I don't want them to know. Can I send them a written message?"

Kala nods. With a wave of her hand, a pen and paper float through the room to Greon. As Greon writes, streaks of his hair turn white. Kala watches as wrinkles form under his eyes.

"Quickly! You're aging by the moment," she says.

Greon places his letters in the center of the table, and Kala extends her arms.

"Will it hurt?" Greon asks.

Kala shakes her head solemnly. "You will feel no pain. You will accompany me to the Extraordinary Division, and we will deliver the objects together in spirit. When the task is complete, my side of the bargain will be fulfilled. Then you will belong to me. The moment we pass through the worlds, your soul will emerge from your body. After the Welcoming Moon, your vessel will catch up with your actual age, and you will be nothing but ash."

Greon looks at the jar, then at Kala. "This is where you will put my soul?" he asks.

Kala looks at him blankly.

Greon swallows and says, "We have an agreement."

"Take my hands," Kala says.

Greon takes hold of her hands, and she shudders at the touch of his ice-cold skin. Kala begins to chant. Her grip is steadfast, and he can feel a surge rush through her and into his body. Kala's eyes roll back as she falls into a trance. Her chanting continues at an even pace.

Greon drifts off into an enchanted daydream of Ianna. Her golden, sun-kissed image caresses his face lovingly with a gentle smile. This memory is the last thing he recalls before slipping away; before his torso falls forward on the table and his eyes flutter shut; before his hair turns completely white, and before the objects in the center of the table vanish except for the jar.

Wherever Greon is now, it is a dark place. But he can still hear the crackling of the fireplace beside the table and Kala's chanting. Slowly, the sound of her chanting fades, and the crackling of the fireplace with it. Yet, he can still feel her hold on him.

Suddenly, her airy laugh echoes. "Why are your eyes closed?" she asks. Greon is confused. He didn't know his eyes were closed. He didn't know he still had eyes. "Look. We've arrived at the gate."

Though Greon feels as if he is in some strange, foggy dream, he heeds Kala's words and opens his eyes. He is surrounded by color and light. Everything here is alive, shapeless, and free. He looks down at himself in wonder, and he looks the same. He turns to Kala, and she too looks the same.

"Since I am alive, I resemble my vessel. You are bound to me, which is why your spirit resembles your vessel," she explains. "Are you ready to pass through the gate?"

Greon nods. Kala turns around, and Greon does the same. Before their eyes, a wondrous tree, larger than life, stands in the middle of the colorful lights.

"Your nymphs were right. The ancient peoples of the extraordinary created the boundary between the realms using the oldest tree in Malphora as the gateway. If you look closely enough, you can see the ground and the sky. The tree lives by a river, mountains in the distance. Do you see it?"

Greon finds it difficult at first, for nothing appears to him. Then moments later, he sees it all. The colorful lights surrounding them become opaque, and the world he was once familiar with comes into view. "Yes," he answers finally.

"Good. You will need to see clearly when we deliver your pendants."

They glide toward the tree while colorful lights float in and out as if the tree is breathing.

"Where do spirits go?" Greon asks.

"A free spirit fresh from their vessel is usually pulled from here and taken away in a wave. There are some who fight the wave and stay to roam these parallel planes, perhaps even travel through this gateway."

"Where does the wave lead?"

"It depends on who you were," Kala answers.

"Do you mean if you are human or beast or a Griffin?" Greon asks.

Kala shakes her head and laughs. "No. *Who* you were, not what you were." She doesn't elaborate, and though Greon is still in a haze, he knows what she means.

Many of the colorful lights touch Greon's skin as they pass through. Each, he notices, carries its own energy. Some are sad; some are angry, and some are confused. He wants to stop one and speak to it, but Kala pulls him along.

"You won't be able to help them," she explains. "What causes them distress is of their own making." They approach the tree, "Think of your destination. It will take you there."

They touch the tree, and at once, they are pulled into it.

Suddenly, they are someplace else—a place where there are no colorful lights of the spirits, only darkness. The Elders' Dome.

"We must be here," she says, noticing the complete darkness that surrounds them. "Since Bayo stole The Eyes, he has used them to block out all creatures from the Griffin Clan, including spirits."

"Yes," Greon answers foggily. "I remember. But how are we able to be here, then?"

"I am not dead, and you are bound to me," she says.

Greon stares into this dark abyss until shapes come into view. One by one, trees appear around them, and blades of grass become visible under their feet. The midnight blue sky is dotted with twinkling stars. Past the trees to their left is a golden dome that shines in the light of the growing full moon.

At the sight of the moon, Greon's internal fog clears. "The Welcoming Moon celebration is near," he notes. He watches the moon expand by the moment, moving slowly upward into the sky. "That means my time will soon come to an end."

"Yes," Kala says.

He turns to her. "I know it is not what we agreed, but I would very much like to see it one last time."

They walk hand-in-hand until they near the field where all the Griffins have gathered, speaking of old times and laughing at silly memories.

Then Kala says, "I always wondered what it feels like to be connected to the moon the way the Griffins are."

Greon nods. "It is a wonderful feeling. Indescribable. But it is not just the moon you feel a connection to. It is everything in the universe, all at once."

"Hmm. I remember when Bayo would not let me attend—my first year of living here."

"Yes, he feared the moon would be able to bless non-Griffins as well," Greon recalls.

Kala smiles. "Either he was wrong, or the moon passed me over that night—since I did attend, despite his orders. I snuck out from the dome. I was so curious to see what all the extraordinary nations so desperately envied."

"Maybe because you'd already been blessed with divine powers and gifted with magic?" Greon suggests.

"The magic I stole. As you recall, I did not know such tricks while here, only potions and incantations from my tribe . . . as well as my natural ability to speak with spirits. The Human Division has many secrets they don't easily share. Everything I knew about potions I taught you and Ianna."

Greon says, "Lot of good your teachings did me. I wish you never showed me. After you left, Bayo was on my tail for eleven years, pushing me to retrieve his brother! He didn't even bother with Ianna's help."

Kala smirks. "Because Ianna wasn't as interested as you. She lacked your drive and enthusiasm. Not to mention, she was sloppy."

Greon gives her a look, though he knows Kala is right. "Did you teach Felix as well?" Greon asks.

Kala laughs. "Felix knew more things in terms of magic than me. He was well learned."

"So he created the pendants himself?"

"Yes, he did, but I perfected them. Felix knew much, but there were still some things I knew better than he," she says proudly.

"In what way did you perfect them?" Greon asks.

Kala does not answer.

A moment later he catches on. "It was *your* doing that allowed them to live without the Welcoming Moon, wasn't it? When Hale was taken, we assumed Felix and Naomi died the following Welcoming Moon, and Carly was alone to fend for Hale. But when I finally found a trace of Hale, we saw Felix and Naomi were still alive."

Kala admits, "Yes. I cursed both Felix's and Naomi's pendants to relinquish them of the powers the Welcoming Moon bestowed them. The longer they wore them, the more they dulled their gifts. However, the immortality that the Welcoming Moon bestowed on them for returning to it every year was reversed, and they began to age as normal."

Greon understands now that Kala has the capability to save his life the way she saved Felix and Naomi. Now that the bargain was made, there was no reason to lie about it.

Kala continues, "Carly did not need this curse on her pendant—she never had immortality to begin with. She only attended the Welcoming Moon once. She didn't crave power like the others. It was her own decision to live and grow old. She would have been how old by now? Twenty-five?"

Greon nods. "Yes. I believe so."

"I wanted so badly for them to win. Carly was such a beautiful girl. I envied her wisdom. I wanted to see her have a life of her own, away from this place."

Greon adds, "As a child, she refused to transform. She said once, the longer you stay in the form of a beast, the longer you would act like a beast. Even as an adult, she said the same." He laughs. "She was so very different from us. Bayo mocked her often, then took to ignoring her altogether. She was not obedient like Mary, would not fulfill his commands. Mary desperately craved Bayo's attention. She would do anything for him, no matter the price." *Despite his cruelty, she adores him,* he thinks sadly.

Kala scoffs. "Mary takes after you and her mother. It is not love she feels for Bayo but intimidation of his great power. Yes, Carly was different, and so were her parents. Fearless. Smart. Passionate. It's a wonder they were Griffins at all." Just as Greon begins to interject, Kala says, "Tell me, what was it like to be the reason for your friend's death?"

Greon's face drops at once, and he suddenly finds himself tongue-tied.

Kala muses, "Do you think the wave whisked them away, or do you think they lingered as a shapeless color in this parallel world?"

Moments of silence pass until Kala asks another question. "Is Mary still the same?"

"She is the same and different all at once. Though she is not my child, I loved her instantly, as though she were my own. Once, Bayo sent her on a quest to venture into the Human Division. She voyaged out to sea during an era when women were not meant to have power. It was then she fell in love. With both a man and the sea."

"What happened to this man?" Kala asks.

"He had an untimely death," Greon answers gravely. "Though this happened centuries ago, she confided in me only recently. His face plagues her dreams suddenly. Since I've left her, I deeply regretted every moment that I could not be with her. Perhaps the promise of freedom could bring back what she's lost."

"Is that the only thing you regret?" Kala asks.

Greon looks up to the sky. "No, Kala. I regret most of this life. I am a coward—there is no reason to deny it. I've caused harm to the people I cared for and for the sole purpose of self-preservation." *Ianna would have left long ago . . . if it weren't for my fear of Bayo.*

"What would you have done differently if you could?"

"I would have said no to Bayo the moment we met."

"Then you would not have met Ianna or Mary."

"And all of that is still better than the chaos I helped Bayo achieve."

They come to the edge of the field and watch the Griffins standing motionless under the full moon. There is a rumbling throughout the ground, and a platform rises where the Elders stand. The spaces meant for Felix and Greon are vacant.

The young Griffins cheer. Greon and Kala watch as Bayo lifts his hand to silence the crowd.

Kala cannot help but laugh. "He doesn't change, does he? He's still the same old pretentious, pompous, arrogant, little Griffin anyone did see." Kala mimics Bayo's hand gesture. "Who does he think he is? The king?"

Greon gives her a puzzled look. "Well—"

"All right. But he's still an old, pretentious, pompous, arrogant, little Griffin man. And very old . . . have I said that already? How in Malphora did I ever fall for this guy?"

They continue to watch as illusions of six other moons appear over the heads of the Elders, then as the young Griffins experience the magic for the first time.

Greon sighs, remembering his first Welcoming Moon. They watch the young Griffins glow with color from within and the Elders leave the field.

"That was nice. You are officially dead. How are you managing?" Kala asks.

Greon responds coolly, "I'm at peace with it. Let's go."

●●●●●

Greon and Kala return to the Elders' Dome and are surprised to see Hale approaching it.

"Everything they worked so hard to keep him from is happening before our eyes," Kala says. "He looks like Bayo, don't you think?"

Greon shakes his head. "There is no resemblance whatsoever."

Hale raises his arm to knock on the front door, and Ianna opens it. Kala sighs. "Look at him. So innocent. So confused."

Greon melts at Ianna's smile. "She looks beautiful."

"Come, let's go inside," Kala declares, pulling Greon through the door. "How long do you think it will be before Bayo completely turns this innocent boy into a malevolent monster like him?"

Greon shakes his head. "This boy is too strong-willed. Felix and Naomi made sure of that."

Kala smiles. "There is hope then."

They lurk in the doorway of the parlor room while Ianna fetches a meal for Hale. "Let's place the objects on her when she is alone."

Greon agrees.

Suddenly, Bayo walks through their spirits unknowingly.

Kala squirms. "I would rather die than have him near me again!"

Greon chuckles. They curiously follow Bayo into the parlor, sit beside Hale, and watch Bayo spew his lies.

Kala rages. "I wish I could smack you!" she roars at Bayo, though he is ignorant of her presence. "Do his deceits ever cease?"

Greon tries to keep a calm mind. "The boy will see through it."

Kala spat at him, "You should hope so. You are the reason Hale's here to begin with!"

They wait for Ianna in her room. Finally, Ianna retires for the night. Greon watches as she removes her gown and slips into her sleepwear. His jaw drops at the sight of her bare skin. She is bruised and burned everywhere. No doubt the burns came from Rioma, but the bruises—those were always a favorite pastime of Deor's.

Kala cannot stand the sight of her. "How is it possible she continues to smile?"

Greon reaches out to touch Ianna longingly, but he cannot feel her skin. "She smiles because she is not a coward, as you labeled her."

Once Ianna slumps in bed, Kala hands Greon the pendant and note. He walks over to the side of Ianna's bed and places the objects delicately on her stomach. As soon as he lets go of them, they materialize in the physical world. Ianna notices them at once and nearly jumps.

She gasps noticing her name is written in Greon's hand and hastily opens the note. The first line reads, *Quickly, wear this pendant, then take your protective potion, then remove the pendant.*

Ianna always called the potion that dulled Deor's mind from reading hers her "protective potion." It was the only way Greon knew how to describe it to her in case Deor read her mind.

Ianna pulls the pendant over her head and makes her way to her wardrobe. She opens a secret compartment with hundreds of vials of potions.

She pulls out a vial and drinks its sparkling turquoise contents. She lets the potion digest; then, a few moments later, she removes the pendant and continues reading.

> *Dearest Ianna,*
>
> *The pendant I give you now is freedom. No form of magic can detect you while you wear it. Mary has its twin. Take her, and leave the Griffin Clan when the timing is right. Though I cannot be by your side now, know you are in my heart for all of eternity.*

Tears rush down Ianna's face. They waited so long to share a life together, and now it seems they never will. She reads the note over and over while Greon's spirit strokes the side of her face gently, imagining what it would be like to actually feel her skin.

Kala pulls his hand. "Come, let us deliver the other."

Greon has no choice but to follow Kala out of the door. He etches this last image of Ianna into his mind, clutching the pendant with one hand and his note in the other. He hopes he will never forget it as he is pulled through the door and out of the dome completely.

"Where is Mary?" Kala asks. "Is she in the dome as well?"

"No, she was likely ordered to pose as one of the young Griffins. She could be anywhere in the Clan."

Kala huffs. "Ugh. We don't have time for this!" She begins to chant. At once, she and Greon float through the air as if a magnet pulls them toward Mary.

They see her in her Griffin form, landing in a field, then making her way toward a devastated young man. Her eyes shine purple in the night.

"There she is," Greon says.

Mary is speaking to a young man. His features hardly visible in the dark.

Greon takes in the look on Mary's face. "She loves him," he manages, his mouth gaping open. Then Greon jumps. "This must be him. The boy she once loved, returning as a Griffin!"

Kala's brows furrow. "How would you know?"

They watch Mary leave. As she takes to the air, Greon and Kala fly after her.

Mary lands on a beach and cries heavily. Greon wishes he could wrap his arms around her and tell her it will be all right. But all he can do is place the pendant over her head and the note between her fingers.

She notices the weight around her neck at once, and she looks to see the pendant. Then the note, written in Greon's hand. Her eyes light up, and her tears ebb.

She opens the folded paper quickly, like a child unwrapping a wonderful gift. Then she reads it.

Mary doesn't know how to feel about this note or the pendant. Why couldn't Greon be here? Why wasn't he here for the Welcoming Moon? Then she thinks about a life free from Bayo and his demands, and it scares her. Being here is all she knows. Winning his love and attention is all she knows. Then she rereads the last line of Greon's note: "I am always with you, and you are always loved."

She takes in a deep breath and stares into the ocean, lost in thought, and whispers, "Thank you, Greon."

Greon smiles as Kala pulls him from this place and back toward the great tree. Before they step through the gateway, Kala pauses. "It was a pleasure seeing you again."

"I wish I could say the same," he says.

"Seems almost a pity that I will be consuming your essence shortly."

Greon nods. "From a jar, no less."

Kala shrugs, and off they go through the gateway, into a parallel world full of colorful spirits trying to find their way, then back to her apartment once more.

The fireplace crackles as if Greon never left and Kala's chanting comes to a halt. He tries to move but a smooth barrier prevents him from escaping. He is in the jar.

Kala wakes from her daze and stares across the table in disbelief.

"How?" she manages breathlessly.

Greon's body is still intact. Dead but intact. His hair is back to blond, and the wrinkles on his face are gone. He is replenished and young again instead of the ash he was meant to become.

Then Kala realizes—Greon *did* attend the Welcoming Moon. Even though he was not in his vessel, his vessel had received the gift of youthful immortality for yet another year. However, Greon had died all the same since she had placed his soul in the jar. Kala smirks as his soul bounces angrily in the glass. She lets go of Greon's cold, dead hands, and his body slides from the table and onto the carpet with a thump.

As she drums her fingers rhythmically on the table, she ponders aloud, "I wonder what an immortal soul tastes like."

◦●●●◦

"'aven't you 'ad enooegh fahr one night?" the bartender barks at Garet, who drunkenly asks for another pint.

With great strength and precision, Garet lifts his head and mutters with wet lips, "I'm suppos't to be mee-in' someone."

"Well, you've been waitin' two hours then."

Garet looks up at him bleary-eyed. "I've waa?"

"You 'eard me. Two hours," the bartender says. "I'm sorry, but I'm cuttin' ya off."

"Now look 'ere!" Garet interjects, "I've been payin' ya! How can you stand to turn business away? Look at this mank dump!" His tongue is so loose that he manages to spit directly in the bartender's face as he speaks.

The bartender slams the glass down on the bar and wipes his face. "You're droehnk. Now, ooehtta de kindness o' me 'eart, I'm goin' to give you tel de cooehnt o' three to crack on!"

"All right, all right! No need fahr all dat!" Garet raises his hands in surrender and stumbles across the floor. "Sorry 'bout the erm—" He points to the man's face and watches as it reddens.

"One!" the bartender snaps.

"I'm goin', I'm goin'. Geez!" As he walks out of the bar, another man walks in. Directly behind the stranger, a shadow is lurking.

Garet curses. The stranger turns. But Garet is too drunk to care and leaves, rambling, "What does a person 'ave to do fahr a 'alf-decent dose o' potion so dey won't 'ave to see death 'anging around?"

He storms back toward Kala's apartment, zigzagging along the sidewalk. "All the souls she's collected, danks to me. All of 'em, and I'm still seeing dese wretched things!" He continues, "And where the 'ell is dat *green* man? Whatever da 'ell 'is name was!"

It was a deathly hour to be roaming about, but thankfully, the rain has subsided. Once at Kala's apartment door, he bangs hard. "Wetch! Ahpen oehp!"

The door opens suddenly. Garet makes his way upstairs, tripping and fumbling and cursing the whole way. "Where de 'ell is dat green fellow?" Garet roars. "I need me payment!"

Garet reaches for the knob of the door but is stopped at once.

Kala's voice sounds from behind him, "Here is your payment."

He turns to see her outstretched hand, holding a vial.

Hardly surprised by her magic trick, Garet grabs the vial and places it safely in his pocket. "Where is de green fellow?" he asks once more.

Kala shrugs. "He left."

Garet cocks a brow. "So you took 'im back 'ome. To dat ahther place 'e was talkin' abooeht."

Kala nods.

"So what did you take frahm *'im*, then? You dedn't take 'is sooehl?"

Kala looks at him blankly for a moment. "You look so tired. Don't you need to go rest?" She makes her way between Garet and her door.

Ignorantly, Garet asks, "Why 'aven't you tahld me abooeht this place 'e came frahm, a place fahr people like oehs?"

"That place is far from what you think it is. Life is better here."

Garet nods and turns to make his leave. "Goodnight, den."

"Goodnight."

Just when she turns her back to him, Garet jumps in front of her, opens the door, and walks inside. Greon is dead on the carpet. His soul dances around in a glass jar on the table. "I knew it! You gaht what you wanted frahm 'im after all. You dedn't 'elp 'im. You joehst take yooehr souls. Screw everythin' else!"

Kala glares as she closes the door in haste. "Would you keep your voice down?"

Garet shrugs. "Me apahlogies," he says as he takes a seat beside Greon's dead body. "I 'ave sahme questions I'd like answered."

Kala huffs. "Why don't you ask me when you're sober?"

Garet smiles. "I wooehld like to. Boeht it seems I wahn't ever be sahber as lahng as I see dahse dang shadows walkin' in people's footsteps, and I keep seein' dem because yooehr pahtions are naht permanent sahlutions fahr me prahblem."

"Do your job, and you'll get what you need from me."

"Ah, boeht you see, I've been doin' my jahb. Boeht yooehr pahtions are lahsin' their pahtency. Dey've been wearin' ahff faster and faster each time."

Kala sneers, "Give me more souls, and the potions will last longer."

"Why dedn you tell me dere was a place where people like oehs are free to be who dey are?"

"Because," she exclaims, "you still won't be free! Yes, the people there have supernatural abilities, but they will find ways to bind you, judge you, and break you. It is better to live hidden."

Garet laughs. "All me life I tried to sahppress me sight. You give me tempahrary pahtions dat dull all me senses. Ahnly a 'eavy drink can make me feel nahrmal anymore. All dis time, dere was a place fahr people like me. A place where I cooehld do sahme good in the wahrld, instead o' feedin' you innahcent sooehls!"

"Innocent?" She laughs eerily. "Have you forgotten the lives we helped in exchange for the souls I consume? It is a *bargain*. I do not just take from others. I give them whatever they desire. And you bring these people to me in exchange for something for yourself. It is simply good business."

Garet takes a moment to digest her words; then he looks down at Greon's dead body. "I moehsta been desper ate to 'elp you. Boeht I dink I'm ahkay wet me sight now." He fumbles over to the fireplace, pulls the potion from his pocket, and tosses it in. As the glass shatters, the fire turns white for a moment.

Kala is wide-eyed.

Garet walks right past her and reaches for the door. She grabs his arm. "Stop. What do you want?"

"I want to know abooeht dat ahther place."

Kala looks up at him with fear in her eyes.

Garet squints. "What are you 'idin' from? Aren' you tired o' sittin' 'ere, alone and in de dark?"

"Here I am safe."

"When are you goin' to face what gives you fear?"

She doesn't answer, and Garet turns to leave.

Horrified, she exclaims, "If you leave me, I will die!"

"You're already dead."

"I will make it so you will not see the shadows anymore. I will make you a permanent potion," she pleads.

Garet shakes his head. "I dahn't want it anymahre."

"I'll give you anything you want."

"I want to go to de ahther world," Garet states. "I want you to stahp dis business—and I want you to comb wit me."

"I will not go back. I swear, you will meet your end there! It is not what you think."

Garet turns back to the table and opens the jar that contains Greon's soul.

Kala screams, "What did you do?"

With a chair in hand, he dashes to the other room Kala always keeps closed. The room is alight with hundreds of souls in jars on countless shelves. Garet smashes the chair against the shelves, breaking the jars.

"How could you do this to me? I'll die!" she screams.

Garet looks down at her and sees a shadow appear behind her. "Like I said, lahve. You're already dead. And I've just comb to me senses."

Kala attempts to collect the freed souls with any salvageable jars, but they are escaping. Greon's soul dances around the room, searching for its vessel. Finally, it rushes right back into his chest.

At that moment, while Kala is distracted, salvaging her souls, sucking them into her mouth, and ingesting as many as she can while they are still in reach, Garet readies himself to strike her with the back of the chair. But she waves her hand, and Garet flies into a wall.

That is when he sees it—an old book. Garet takes the book in hand and runs to the fireplace.

"Stop, ahr I'll tahss it into de fire!" Garet threatens.

Kala sees what he is doing and pauses. "I'll kill you," she hisses.

"Try it, and yooehr preciooehs wetch's book'll be lahst fahrever, alahng wet yooehr sooehl seeker."

She glares at him and raises her hand high into the air. Garet feels himself being lifted by his throat. He is suddenly floating, his head inches away from the ceiling. He chokes and drops the book.

Kala's laugh echoes throughout the apartment. "Oh, darling! I was fine before you, and I'll be more than fine *long* after you've gone. Pity. You and I could have been *lovely* together."

Just as she is about to twist his neck with the wave of her hand, she hesitates at the sound of Garet's chuckle.

He points behind her. "Shadow."

At that exact moment, the free spirits swarm around Kala, whirling around her body like a cyclone. Kala desperately chants a spell to keep them at bay, but her voice weakens by the moment, and she seems to be gasping for breath.

With her power weakening, Garet falls to his knees with a grunt.

Her contracted spirits suddenly disperse, revealing Kala's lifeless body on the cool floor.

The shadow of death Garet saw is gone as well. He takes her into his arms, neither startled nor sad. "You should have comb wit me."

Greon regains consciousness and looks around the mess of the room. He stops at Kala's half-opened eyes and swallows. At once, he understands that Kala's wrongdoings have caught up to her, even though she acted this way to survive.

Shivers rush up his spine as he comes to the sudden realization that he will be met with the same fate for all he's done in his long life.

Breaking his morbid train of thought, Garet mutters snidely, "I see you've made a miraculous recovery." He slams Kala's book onto the table and flips through its contents. "Seems you dedn't get to go back 'ahme as you wanted. Perhaps your answer is 'ere. Do you know dis language?"

Greon rises and peers over his shoulder. "Yes."

Garet continues to flip the pages. "See anythin'?"

Greon looks over each page. "There! Stop!" Greon nearly pushes him over, trying to get closer to the book. "I can't believe it!" Greon mumbles. "Here it is: 'Creating a Portal to the Extraordinary Division.'"

Garet shakes his head. "I told you, she's 'ad it all alahng. Dis is 'er game—I've ahnly learned recently. She will stahp at nahthin' to get 'er souls. Can you make de pahrtal?"

Greon nods. "I think so."

They enter the other room in search of ingredients and return with several vials and jars. Greon spills the contents over the table and rereads the instructions. While Greon works on creating the portal, Garet watches in awe. His eyes are strangely wide, and his brows are contorting every which way as he reads some of the labels on the vials.

"You must be drunk," Greon mumbles as he works.

Garet takes a seat, nearly missing it completely. "I moehst be—"

Greon looks up at him. "Are you sure you want to come with me? There's no going back, and you might regret it, considering."

"Oh, pesh-pahsh," Garet spits as he flips his hand in Greon's direction. "Dis isn't de first life-alterin' decision I've made while 'ammered."

Greon shrugs. "Suit yourself."

An hour later, Garet is knocked out, his head resting on the table, and Greon exclaims, "I did it! I finally did it!"

Garet jumps up, drool dripping from the corner of his lip. His eyes are tired, but he's sobered up a bit. He looks over the table to see Greon looking down at the floor beside the fireplace. What he sees now is very odd, like a mirror lying face down on the floor. Or perhaps a reflective puddle. At this point he can't tell.

"Come," Greon says, poking the portal with a single finger. His finger goes right through. "Are you ready?"

Garet swallows. "'ow do you know if it wahrks?"

Greon shrugs. "We won't know until we jump."

Garet grunts.

Then Greon remembers the book. "Ah, best I take this, just in case. It is most informative." He snatches the book from beside his feet. "We must be quick. The portal only stays in this state for ten minutes. Afterward, it turns to water." He takes a deep breath. "I'll see you on the other side." He jumps and disappears into the portal.

Garet stands there, thinking everything over. Then he stops himself. "No. Dinking makes everythin' wahrse," he declares, though he knows of many circumstances in his life that have taught him otherwise. He wonders about the new life he could have, one where he is celebrated for his gifts and helps others with them. With that thought—and only that thought—Garet jumps through.

CHAPTER 32

Sunlight creeps through the closed drapes. Hale wakes up in brilliant comfort in his king-sized bed, covered with warm throws and surrounded by pillows.

There is a knock at the door. "Hale, breakfast will be served in a few moments. Please meet us in the dining room," says Ianna through the door.

Hale opens his door and rushes through the hallway to the stairs. The savory aroma of food fills his nostrils.

"Whoa, slow down," says Bayo, chuckling from behind him. He had just come out from his own bedroom.

Hale stops and turns back to share Bayo's smile.

"Are you ready for our big day?" Bayo asks.

Hale nods.

"Wonderful. You know, if you're going to descend the steps with haste, you must do it in style." With that, Bayo leaps onto the top of the railing and slides down. He jumps off before the railing ends. "Come on," Bayo calls from below.

"Oh, I can't do that," Hale says.

Bayo laughs. "I'll catch you."

Hale is more startled by the comment than the idea of sliding down the railing. Still, he is unsure.

"Don't worry," Bayo assures him. "It's perfectly fine."

Hale climbs up the railing, closes his eyes, and slides down on his two feet. The railing ends quicker than he expected, and he flies into the air, bracing for impact on the hardwood floor when Bayo catches him.

Bayo's arms are around his body, and his chuckle resonates in Hale's chest. "Told you I would catch you!" They walk through the hallway and into the dining room.

In the center is an extravagant, long wooden table, with many chairs placed around it. The table is covered at each end with breakfast. Each plate is steaming.

"Hale, come sit beside me," Bayo calls from the head of the table.

Just then, Rioma waltzes through the door with a wide grin. "Good morning, Bayo!" she says as she takes the seat to his left. She extends an arm out to greet her guest.

Hale immediately rises to shake her hand.

"Hale, I presume?" Rioma says. "Ianna told me we had a guest this morning. Pleasure." After taking her seat she asks, "Are you enjoying your stay?"

Hale nods. "Yes, I am."

"Delightful." Rioma pours herself a cup of coffee from a pot beside her. Bayo shoots her a look that she does not seem to notice. When she reaches out for a waffle, Bayo objects.

"Rioma, dear. We must wait for the others."

Rioma's cheeks redden. "Oh, how silly of me. I apologize, Bayo. I've must have misplaced my manners."

Deor walks in. He does not greet anyone, and so Bayo introduces him instead.

"Hale, this is Elder Deor," says Bayo.

"Hello," Hale manages, quite intimidated.

Deor glances over at Hale as Ianna rushes through the door.

"Oh, I am so sorry to have kept you all waiting," she says, hastily making her way next to Hale. "My apologies, Bayo," she says again. "I lost track of time."

He winks at her, and she blushes. Once she sits down, Bayo unfolds his napkin and places it on his lap. "Dig in, everyone."

Observing Bayo, Hale takes the napkin on the side of his plate, unfolds it, and places it on his lap.

Deor says to Bayo telepathically, *He is already copying your gestures. He thinks highly of you.*

Bayo looks at his younger brother and smiles. "Hale, after breakfast, how about you join the young Griffins while the others and I make preparations for this afternoon?"

Rioma looks up quizzically. "What are we meant to be doing this afternoon?"

"Hale has informed me the young Griffins do not use the living quarters we have arranged for them. They have no idea it exists."

Rioma's eyes widen. "Then where have they been living?"

Bayo answers, "Outside."

Rioma brings a hand to her chest. "Oh my."

Bayo continues, "There are other issues that need to be resolved with the young Griffins. It has become evident to me—thanks to Hale—that we need to be more present in their lives. Lead them by example, train them in the ways of their gifts, and provide a more loving, nurturing environment. They are only children, after all."

Rioma looks dazed with Bayo's words. "Oh, how right you are, Bayo. Marvelous idea!"

"The only problem I have is that there is no one to train the Griffins of the Light, since Greon is gone."

Ianna looks down at her plate. All the Elders think Greon has died. It is a secret she must keep, no matter the cost. She has been taking a dulling potion against the powers of the Dark. It isn't new behavior, and Deor can obviously sense the potion clouding his entry. But he has merely not cared recently about what Ianna does or does not do. As long as she does her work and Bayo is pleased with her, Deor couldn't care less.

Bayo continues, "Does anybody have any suggestions?"

The Elders sit silently.

"Ianna?" Bayo says catching her attention. She looks up at once. "You knew Greon better than anybody here. Do you know how his powers worked?"

Ianna stutters. "N—no, Bayo. All I know is that he simply imagined things he wanted to bring out into the physical world, and there they were . . . as if they were real."

Bayo grunts. "Wonderful. I would say that is good enough, wouldn't you all?"

Rioma nods while Deor simply takes no part in the vote.

"It is settled, then. Ianna will coach the young Griffins of the Light as well as those of Shielding," declares Bayo.

Hale watches as Ianna begins clearing the table still filled with food. He turns to Bayo, though he is embarrassed to ask, and whispers, "Is it okay if I bring some leftovers to a friend of mine? He always helped me get food."

Bayo leans in to hear Hale's whisper and then whispers back, "Of course. There is no need to ask, Hale. You can take whatever you want, anytime you want."

Hale leaves, carrying a cloth full of food. As Bayo closes the door behind him, Hale stops and asks, "Bayo?"

"Yes?"

"Why don't you tell the Griffins what happened to their parents? I think it would help them understand why they are here and who they are."

Bayo is silent for a moment. "I, too, have been thinking about it. But I thought it better left alone. I think . . . not everybody needs all the answers, though they do need proper guidance."

Hale nods, though he is a bit differed. He scurries off through the field and back to the Griffins with everything that has happened running endlessly through his mind. Bayo watches him from the doorway.

• ● ● ● ● •

The field filled with young Griffins is bustling, noisy, and most of all, dangerous. Powers explode left and right and fights break out everywhere. Hale has his food hidden under his shirt as he searches around for River. He goes to the cliffs where River took him the day that he lost the tree dome, and sitting on the very edge, watching the rushing waterfalls in the distance, is River.

Hale approaches him slowly and calls his name. "Hey. I brought you some food," Hale offers it with an extended hand. "It was a waffle and some eggs, but it got sort of smushed."

River takes it and thanks him.

Hale takes a seat beside him, and River offers him some of the waffle. Hale shakes his head. "I already ate. And I have a lot to tell you."

River nods with a full mouth. "Me too."

Simultaneously, they spit out their stories. "I went to the Elders' Dome, and I met all the Elders!" says Hale, while River says, "I got attacked last night by Leon's goons and—"

They both laugh.

"You first," they both say, then laugh again.

River lets Hale go first.

"Umm, last night after the Welcoming Moon, I went to the Elders' Dome, and I met all the Elders. They let me spend the night."

River's eyes widen and his mouth hangs open, the food he had yet to swallow is visible. "I thought you looked different!" River exclaims. "They gave you new clothes? You're not wearing that ironic 'I'd flex but I like this shirt' shirt anymore! And, wow"—he sniffs Hale—"you're *clean*, aren't you?" Then he pokes Hale's belly with an index finger. "And you're nicely plump and well-fed!"

"Ow—come on." Hale laughs, pushing River's hand away. "Yes. I am squeaky clean and well-fed. Anyways, not the point—you won't believe what I found out!"

⋅•●●●•⋅

A few hours later, a voice speaks in the minds of every young Griffin in the Clan. *Attention, Griffins. I, Elder Deor, am informing you of a mandatory gathering.* Suddenly, all the minds of the Griffins flood with a single image of the stage. *Meet us here, in your human form, in half an hour.*

It is clear to Hale how powerful Deor is if he is able to penetrate the minds of all the Griffins in the Clan at once. He and River share a look.

Then River proclaims, "And I thought Mary was powerful. Come on, let's go."

Hundreds of Griffins approach the stage, murmuring excitedly as they walk. The Elders are there and waiting. On top of the stage is a small desk and seat. Sitting in the seat is Bayo, wearing his reading glasses, an open book in front of him, and a pen in hand. The other Elders stand behind him silently.

Deor enters their minds once more and says a single word: *Silence.* When River's jaw instinctively tightens, he looks to Hale, a worried expression on his face.

Bayo rises from his seat. "Griffins! There will be no more death or punishment between the individuals of this Clan. All people within the Clan will be checked every day and every night. No person shall go missing or die. You have my word that you are protected under my rule. Form a line and, on my command, approach the stage, where I will take down your information."

As the Griffins form a line, Bayo adds, "Ianna will collect all gold coins in your possession. To those who wish to keep them hidden, be mindful that Deor knows which of you conceal the truth, and Rioma is ordered to punish you if that should happen."

One by one, each individual approaches the stage. Bayo takes down their name, age, and power while Ianna places the collected gold coins into large sack. One boy does not heed Bayo's warning and tries to hide his coins. Like a whip, a gust of fire erupts from Rioma's finger and licks the skin of his forearm. The boy shrieks in pain and hands over his coins at once. No one else makes the same mistake.

All of a sudden, River exclaims, "Grace!"

Hale looks up and sees Grace jump on the stage in front of Bayo. Hale looks at River and smiles.

•●●●●•

Long wavy locks of auburn hair whoosh from the corner of Bayo's eyes. The pen drops from his hands. *No*, he thinks in disbelief. It is that girl he ordered Mary to kill. Grace. Hadn't Rioma watched her demise from The Eyes? Hadn't Mary done as she was asked? How is she still alive?

Grace approaches his desk and speaks her name. Bayo forces himself to write her name in his book. He could kill her here and now. It would only take one moment. As he ponders his options, Deor hastily invades his mind, "Your brother is watching you intently."

With piercing eyes, Bayo stares as Grace leaves the stage.

●·●●●●·●

Hours later, after all the Griffins met with Bayo, he looks to the crowd, removes his glasses, and closes the book. "Thank you all for your patience. I understand the Elders and I have not been very involved, but that is going to change. We will teach you how to use your powers. Among yourselves, you will live in peace. If you think your actions will be secret, guess again."

At that moment, Deor's voice enters everyone's minds, causing unsuspecting people to jump in fright. *I see everything.*

Bayo laughs as he paces the stage. He continues, his broad voice projecting out into the crowd, "Food is free. Clothes are free. Water is free. Essentials are free. Medicine is free. You need only ask of us if you are in need. There are sleeping quarters on the outskirts of the field. A group of three will live together in each dome. Their names will be marked on the stone outside their domes. Every morning and evening, each dome will be checked for all three Griffins."

There is a great murmur as the young Griffins grumble against the strict rules. Bayo clenches his jaw, and at once, all the young Griffins feel an electrifying surge course through their bodies. Some people scream. Many fall to the ground. Hale simply stands there watching as everybody else winces in pain. He rushes to lift River to his feet.

"As Griffins, there are rules to live by!" Bayo shouts. "If you all had acted in peace, such rules would be unnecessary.

"Now, Rioma will escort the female Griffins to their living quarters, and I will escort the male Griffins to theirs. But I will say one more thing before you all leave. I will give you the privilege to choose whom you live with. There will be no switching, no complaints, no additions, and no less than three people per dome. The people you choose in your group are considered family. You will refer to one another as members of your pack—your pack brothers or pack sisters.

These are the people who will vouch for you, protect you, and support you. As I have the other Elders beside me, you, too, will know such support. I suggest you choose wisely."

With that said, Bayo signals Rioma, and she transforms on the stage and leaps into the air. As a Griffin, her shining red fur and feathers glisten in the light of the sun. Even in her Griffin form, she is stunning. The female Griffins follow and skyrocket into the sky, flying after her.

Bayo transforms. His flowing brown mane shines with flints of gold. His eyes have the same distinguished look so recognizable in his human form. He stands tall and strong, dominating the crowd.

• ● ● ● ● •

Bayo descends toward several domes in the distance. All the domes are made of stone, unlike the Elders' Dome. River and Hale quickly rush for the nearest dome. Bayo observes Hale from afar and smiles at the sight of pure happiness in his brother's eyes.

The inside of each dome is the same. The floor is made of cherry hardwood, and the walls are stone. In the center of the dome is a raised fire pit, which is enclosed by a glass cylinder. Directly above it is an opening that allows the smoke to escape. The opening could be closed, if necessary, by pulling a lever on the wall. To the left of the door are triple bunk beds, all with their own blankets and pillows. On either side of the bed are drawers filled with sets of sleepwear, daywear, coats, and undergarments. Directly across from the front door is an arched window that ends a foot above the floor. To the right of the door are a small, circular wooden table and three wooden chairs with grey-cushioned seats. On the wall opposite the beds is another door leading to the bathroom.

River runs toward the bed and belly flops right on it. With his head buried in the covers, he mutters, "I'm in heaven!" Then he springs up and shouts, "I call the bottom bunk!"

Hale smiles. There is a knock on their door, and Hale answers it.

"Evan!"

Meeting Hale's eyes, he smiles. "Hey."

"I saw you both coming in, just wondered if I could—"

"You're more than welcome to stay here," Hale says, inviting him in.

"Whoa, whoa, whoa. Hold on! You didn't even discuss it with me," River says.

Suddenly, Hale is caught in a strange position. He walks over to River. They turn their backs to Evan and begin whispering.

"He needs a place to stay," Hale argues in a hushed whisper.

River looks over his shoulder to see Evan standing there, playing with his thumbs and looking around. He cuts in, "I understand why you wouldn't want me here. It's not a big deal. I'll find someplace else." Evan turns to leave.

River curses under his breath, and Hale slaps him on the back.

"We decided," Hale states. Evan turns. "You can stay."

River groans. "I'm going to regret this, aren't I?"

"The top bunk is yours," Hale says. "We have one condition if you're going to stay here, though."

Evan raises his brow, waiting for the blow.

"You have to be civil toward River," Hale says.

Evan bites his lip and huffs. He sticks out his hand for River to shake. River jumps at the sudden gesture and is hesitant to take his hand. He looks to Hale for help, but Hale only stares.

So River sticks out his open hand warily.

Climbing the ladder and jumping giddily on his bed, Hale declares, "I guess we're pack brothers now."

River winces.

◦●●●●◦

That evening, Hale, River, and Evan carve their names on separate stones beside the front door of their dome. When they walk into the dome reserved for food, they nearly stumble. There is food everywhere they look. Clean white plates are stacked high and silverware, as well. Everyone is free to take as much food as they want.

A bit overzealous, the three of them grab two plates each, take everything back to their dome, and dig in. But once they sit down, they realize they forgot the drinks.

"Not it!" River calls out.

"Not it!" says Evan.

Hale is a split-second too late, so he rushes out of the dome and comes back with their drinks. By the time Hale returns, much of the food is gone.

"I don't remember the last time I had something this good!" River moans.

"Me neither," Evan says, shoving a big bite into his mouth.

The following day, they get ready to begin their training with full bellies. As Hale leaves his dome, he feels a warmth in his heart that he hasn't felt in a long while. It's the same kind of warmth as coming home to a loved one. The last time he felt this way was with Carly, and though he knows it isn't the same thing, he is happy he is able to have a fresh start.

• ● ● ● • •

"Griffins of Endurance!" Bayo shouts into the crowd. Young Griffins are still approaching in the distance, jogging because Bayo has already begun his lesson. "You are all late!" he shouts as he paces back and forth in front of them all. "There are many aspects to the power of Endurance. We are most famous for causing our victims' physical anguish. However, we also have the capability of enduring physical pain unlike any other. This does not mean you do not feel pain. It means that you are able to recover more quickly." He meets Hale's eyes, then turns away and continues. "I will teach you to master these aspects of yourself and train you in physical combat.

"I assume you might think such skills are unnecessary. But, the nation of Griffins is small compared to the other nations in this strange part of the world. We must learn to defend ourselves if the need arises. Take a seat," Bayo commands.

"I want you to lose yourselves in your breathing. When you are completely still, your power will kick in. You will see the bodies that surround you as forms of light in the darkness of your mind."

There is a long moment of silence as the Griffins in the field concentrate. Then, to Bayo's right, three Griffins start screaming in great agony.

Bayo shouts, "Stop!"

One boy sits in a meditative trance while the Griffins around him wince in agony, gripping the grass and turning red.

Bayo commands once more, "Stop this at once!"

Hale peers through the bodies in front of him to get a look at who is causing all the trouble in the distance. He recognizes the light brown hair at once. *Leon.*

As a result of Bayo's deathly glare, Leon awakens from his trance with a mighty yelp.

"You have not impressed me by showing me you're advanced. Stand!"

Leon struggles to get on his feet and fumbles onto his knees instead.

Bayo releases his grasp on him. "Stand. If you mean to show me your talents, then, by all means, show me your talents," says Bayo, his arms extended wide, inviting Leon to attack.

Leon does not hesitate. His eyes narrow as he throws his hands at Bayo. The field is silent and everybody watches.

Bayo starts to chuckle. "Is that all you've got?" he asks. "Come on, you must try harder than *that.*"

Leon concentrates with all his might, and Bayo seems to grow bored. Suddenly, Leon shrieks in pain. He falls forward on his face and whines in agony.

"I am the High Elder of the Griffin Clan. I am your superior. You will not make a mockery of this class again. You will not unleash your pathetic, low-grade talent without my permission. Is that understood?"

Leon is incapable of answering through the pain.

"Is that understood?" Bayo repeats.

Leon turns red with embarrassment, his eyes daggering at Bayo. "Yes!" he bellows.

* * * * *

A flock of Griffins flies to the southern beach to meet Ianna. River is one of them. While he flies, he glimpses an elegant Griffin many yards away, flying in the same direction, with auburn-colored fur. He dives toward her, bumping into anyone in his way just to get closer.

The Griffin has not noticed River and descends to the beach. He follows her and watches her transform. Grace. River transforms midair and lands on his feet behind her. An overwhelming joy fills him. They had yet to meet again since the incident.

His heart pounds as he marches up to her. She turns, and her long locks of hair whip around. Suddenly, his world moves in slow motion.

The pupils of her big doe eyes dilate. Instantly, her arms are around him, pulling him in an embrace. He feels the tears well up in his eyes as he wraps his arms around her.

"Grace," he chokes out, squeezing her tight. "I'm so happy you're okay."

She doesn't let him go, and her head nestles deep into his chest.

CHAPTER 33

The jungle comes alive at night. From the small crevices in the bark to the fungus growing on the ground, everything is alight in neon colors. Such wonders did not exist in the woodlands of the Arketcha tribe.

There is a peaceful humming that has occurred every night for the past few days. This particular humming is so inviting, and Ellionna often wonders what creature makes such a noise. As she tries to doze off, she hears it again.

She whispers to Robin, "Do you hear it?"

Robin whispers back, "Yes."

There is a rustling beyond the fire, and Robin and Ellionna look up to see Atomi tossing in his sleep. This is the last night of the full moon's phase, the last night he'll be stuck in the form of a wolf. He rolls over onto his back, his paws bent and relaxed.

Ellionna says, "Doesn't it sound so lovely? What creature do you think makes such a sound?"

Already drifting into sleep, Robin mutters, "Not sure."

Ellionna closes her eyes once more and listens to the wonderful humming. The song of this mysterious beast lulls Ellionna into a peaceful sleep. As she drifts, she feels more content now than she has this whole journey.

Hours later, sometime in the dead of night, the humming fades away. Ellionna tosses and turns uncomfortably without the peaceful music. She scratches at her irritated throat, and suddenly, her eyes burst open. She springs up and dashes away. But it is too late—the voice of the siren unleashes itself. The immense satisfaction of freeing her voice causes her to smile in relief.

A wolf yelps in the distance. With a pounding heart, Ellionna runs until she doesn't know where she is, until she is surrounded by the strange, glowing lights of critters in the middle of a great, wide darkness. Her voice spews from her mouth as though she has held it in for days. As she sings now, the other noises of the jungle quiet, and the neon lights of the critters around her fade to black. She stands there alone until the last of it pours out of her.

She turns to find her way back to their campsite, but she sees nothing. She remains there, frightened, until she hears Robin calling her name.

Ellionna looks around. "I'm here!"

Robin emerges, holding a torch she made from firewood to guide her way. When Ellionna sees the small light, she rushes toward it.

Robin is crying, and at once Ellionna knows what she has done. They walk back toward the fire in silence. That is when Ellionna sees Atomi. He lies there in his wolf form, lifeless, his eyes open, his tongue hanging out from his snout. He looks so much smaller than he did when he was alive. So helpless and frail.

Robin comes to his side and sobs over his body. Looking down at Robin, Ellionna feels the corners of her mouth stretching into a wide grin.

Ellionna's eyes flutter open, and she gasps.

It was just a dream.

She looks at Robin, who is still asleep, then at Atomi, who is also asleep and alive. She exhales and tends to the smoldering fire, noticing the humming of that strange creature has vanished, just as in her dream. Ellionna does not dare go back to sleep. Instead, she stares into the flames until the sun rises and watches Atomi's transformation begin.

The transformation of a werewolf is much different from that of a Griffin. Griffins transform peacefully in light whenever they please, without physical turmoil. But the werewolves mutate physically. Their bones break, reform, and then reshape themselves.

As dawn approaches, Atomi shrieks and squeals in pain. Ellionna jumps at the sudden sounds. Atomi runs from the girls and into the bountiful flora. Several cracks and screams follow. Even the buzzing critters are startled.

Robin wakes, too, and several painful minutes later, Atomi's human voice sounds from beyond.

"Could one of you bring me my clothes?" he asks.

Robin stands, grabbing her pouch, which holds everything she usually carries on her back. She pulls out a pair of trousers and a shirt and walks over to the bush.

"Thank you," Atomi says.

Atomi returns to the fire, dressed and exhausted, and lies down where he had been sleeping. Robin looks at Ellionna.

"You stayed up again, didn't you?" she asks.

"I had a bad dream."

"You can't keep doing that. We won't ever make it to Bimmorus."

She turns to Robin and says flatly, "I don't think I should go to Bimmorus."

"There is no other place to go, Ellionna."

Ellionna says, "You've both sacrificed everything for me. It is not safe for me to be around. Imagine how it will be in Bimmorus."

Robin says, "We knew the battles we would face. This was our decision."

Ellionna shakes her head. "You don't understand. I can *feel* her. She tells me she wants to come out, but I swallow her down. Once a day is not enough."

"Then sing twice a day!" Robin suggests.

"Robin, heed her words," Atomi says from beside the fire. "She is frightened."

Robin looks to her father. "I am trying to make her less frightened!"

"Try to understand," Atomi suggests again. "This is an ancient being living within her. Do you think it's easy to contain such a beast?"

Robin's eyebrows furrow. "It wasn't that difficult for our grandmother."

Ellionna snaps, "How would you know what was or wasn't difficult for our grandmother? You were off gallivanting in a temple, learning how to be a warrior while I was there, with her every single day. You act as if you know her." Ellionna's eyes dagger through Robin's soul.

But Ellionna's was not the only spirit made of fire. Robin shoots back, "I went to that temple, not because I wanted to—I was forced to do so by law because the siren was in need of a guard, as it always needs a guard. Your gift is a power that is envied as a weapon throughout all of Malphora. It is my duty to protect you. It was not my duty to befriend our grandmother as if she were some sort of playmate of mine. And if I had a choice of what kind of life I would have lived, I would have known more about grandmother than you."

"I suggest you both tie your mouths before you cause a war," Atomi declares. "You both have said more than your piece." He is interrupted by his daughter walking away. "Where are you going?" Atomi calls after her.

"I'm collecting more firewood."

While Robin is gone, Atomi invites Ellionna to come to sit beside him. She walks over slowly. "Uncle, this is not a good idea."

"Come, Ellionna. Don't be frightened. I know what the voice wants," he says. "It is the same thing the wolf wants. Robin, thankfully, does not have such a burden placed on her shoulders. She thinks she is burdened because of her past and the role she must play in life. She is angry at both you and me—you for forcing this life upon her and me for not protecting our family the way she thinks I could have."

He sighs. "You must know you are not alone. If you don't feel safe going to Bimmorus, I understand. In truth, I don't believe they would take in Arketchians, to begin with." He shrugs. "But who knows. Livia is sending you there so you can have a chance at finding your happiness."

Ellionna shakes her head. "I will never be happy as long as this is a part of me. And it will never be happy until it kills everything in its path."

Atomi says, "You speak of the siren as if she is a thinking entity."

Ellionna nods. "She is. She tries to control me. She makes me dream cruel things. I just dreamt that I murdered you, and in my dream, I could feel myself smiling while Robin cried. I felt satisfaction in your death, and it is the same for all others."

Atomi understands. "She thinks you're weak. She tries to take advantage of you. But don't you see?" Atomi continues, "You are so much stronger than that. You don't give in to her demands."

Then Ellionna whispers gravely, "I think she knew that boy was following me that day. And when his brother appeared in my room, she couldn't wait to get out." Ellionna wipes the tears from her face. "When I try to fight her—and I try, Uncle, I really do—she is no match for me. She must have their souls. She must see her victims in anguish. All the while, she uses me as a means to get what she wants."

Atomi looks at his niece gravely. "You shouldn't be able to feel such a connection to her. The binding spell that was used to place her in a human vessel all those years ago was designed to suppress her spirit. But you are speaking as if she is no longer suppressed."

Ellionna continues, "She loves the ocean. When I sing by the water, she is happy. But she always wants me to sing inside the water, and grandmother has told me many times to do no such thing, no matter the urge. She is very unhappy with me now because there is no ocean to sing beside. I think the dreams are meant to threaten me."

Atomi begins to pack their belongings.

"What are you doing, Uncle?" Ellionna asks.

Atomi replies, "We are not going to Bimmorus. I believe the siren is taunting you, and we need to help you before it gets out of hand."

Robin has been listening to their conversation all along, though she had pretended she was gone. When she hears her father say this, she returns to question him. "Father, there is nothing besides Bimmorus. There is nowhere else to go."

He looks at her sternly. "I may not have had the opportunity to be your father for many years, but my opportunity has come. Your cousin is in great need of help, and I am going to help her. Since we are not in the Arketcha tribe anymore, we are not bound to their rules and laws. Therefore, you are not obligated to be her guard." He continues gathering their belongings, then tosses Robin her pouch. "Here you are. You may leave."

Robin looks at her father in fury. Her deep olive skin reddens, but she says nothing.

Ellionna asks, "Where are you taking me, Uncle?"

"I'm taking you to the Temple of Priestesses. They were once a part of the Arketcha tribe but have since cut their ties. They are skilled in the ways of the old magic. It is rumored that is the place Palla and Kala were born."

"Who is Kala?" Ellionna asks, trying to catch up to her uncle, who is now ten steps ahead of her.

Atomi shakes his head in disbelief. "Do they not teach you your history anymore?" He turns around to see if Robin is following them, but she still stands where she was when he had handed her the satchel.

He calls, "Well, daughter, are you coming, or are you changing your profession to a small tree?"

Ellionna giggles, and even more when Robin marches angrily toward them. She can see Robin's nostrils flare from where she stands.

Atomi elbows his niece playfully and continues walking on. "As I was saying. I believe they will be able to help you, Ellionna. When the siren was moved from Livia's body and into your body, something must have gone wrong. These priestesses are very skilled in the old ways. I'm sure they will be able to help you."

CHAPTER 34

Hale knocks on the Elders' front door, but Ianna does not come to open it. As he waits outside, he hears screaming from within.

"You've made a mockery of me in front of the Griffins!" Bayo yells. "I gave you a great opportunity to be my apprentice, and this is how you repay me? By going against my orders!"

Hale hears Leon shout back, "I chose to be an apprentice to the Elder who allowed the Griffins to live without rules."

Bayo's voice rises. "I never allowed anyone to live without rules!"

Leon fires back, "What game are you playing? Why choose me, then?"

"I chose a boy with an outstanding reputation among the others. A boy whose name was quickly feared and respected within a matter of a few weeks. I did not choose someone who goes against my authority. My authority is the law! Is that understood? Mark my words: you are easily replaceable."

Leon sneers, "By who?"

"You'll see very soon."

"You need me. Otherwise, you wouldn't have brought me here after what I did today. You're pretending to be someone you're not. At least I know who I am," Leon declares.

Bayo's jaw clenches. "Everybody is moldable."

Leon storms out of the Elders' Dome. He hits Hale with the door as it swings open. When Leon has transformed and left, Bayo approaches to close the door and sees Hale standing just behind it, rubbing his head.

"Oh, Hale," he says in a calmer, exhausted tone. "I didn't know you were there."

Hale adds, "I knocked."

Bayo waves his hand as he walks back into the parlor. "We hardly hear the knocks on this door; it is so thick. We usually rely on Deor to tell us, but he is still mentoring his group." He turns to see Hale still standing in the doorway. "Come in, Hale."

Hale does as he is told and enters the parlor. Bayo sits slumped on the sofa, then rubs his face with his hands, staring off into space. Hale takes a seat across from him.

"How are you?" Bayo asks.

"I'm good," he answers reluctantly. Then he blurts, "You wanted *Leon* to be your apprentice?"

"You know him?"

"He's an awful, terrible person. He's a murderer. He enjoys hurting people for fun."

"He is also very influential. He has many followers. It is his demeanor and confidence they follow. Not his actions."

"What does confidence matter if the actions are harmful toward others?"

Bayo sighs. "People are weak-minded, Hale. They can be molded at any given moment. What I am giving this boy is a chance at change. In exchange, I gain a powerful assistant who will help me gain allegiance and acceptance with the young Griffins."

Hale doesn't understand. "You have our allegiance."

Bayo leans closer to Hale. "No, I don't. The Griffins don't know anything about me. I am a mystery to them. Leon, on the other hand, makes a great impression on them."

"Do you think you can change him?"

Bayo lets out a deep sigh. "No. But he wants his freedom, and he knows I'm the only person who can give him that luxury. And to get something from me, you have to do something for me first."

•●●●•

Robin and Atomi are several feet ahead of Ellionna. The lack of sleep is finally catching up to her. She tries to quicken her stride when Atomi calls her name.

"Ellionna, make haste!" he says.

Then she feels the itch. Her hand grabs her throat, and she turns in the other direction.

Robin quickly takes notice. "Father," Robin says. "Run!"

Atomi speeds away, covering his ears just in time.

Suddenly, the whole jungle is engulfed in the song of the siren.

As Ellionna sings, she knows the siren will expose herself every time she is weak. It craves Atomi's death. It wants to watch him quiver and squeal with pain. Once Ellionna finishes the siren's song, Robin is beside her.

"Is Atomi—"

Before she can finish her question, Robin answers, "He is fine." Robin holds out a leaf toward her. "In my temple, they taught us about different plants. This one will cause you to sleep for several days. Perhaps it will be easier and tame the outbursts if you can sleep until we get to the temple."

"How will we get to our destination if I am asleep?" Ellionna asks.

"We will carry you."

Ellionna turns from her and begins walking again. "That is absurd. How will you face dangers in the jungle while carrying me?"

She meets Atomi a few yards away. With a grave tone, he says, "Ellionna, take what Robin is giving you."

Ellionna is baffled that Atomi has agreed to this ludicrous plan. "Uncle, I will only burden you both."

Atomi ignores her statement and repeats, "Ellionna. Take it."

Ellionna turns to Robin, who is still extending the leaf to her. Ellionna takes it warily to her lips. It is wildly potent, and its strange odor causes her to hesitate. But she opens her mouth and shoves the leaf inside.

Chewing, she feels its bitter juices running down her throat, and at once, she feels herself losing consciousness. The world around her becomes a blur, and suddenly, she is looking at treetops of the jungle—then nothing.

Robin opens Ellionna's mouth and pulls out the leaf she has not swallowed. Atomi and Robin place Ellionna in a blanket. They each take one side and pull her across the jungle floor.

An hour or so later, Robin declares, "This was a stupid idea."

Atomi ignores her.

Robin continues, "We wouldn't have needed to do this if you didn't join us."

"Then you would both be in Bimmorus, endlessly murdering their male population. She is sick, Robin. If we must pull her to the end of the earth to help her, that is what we will do."

Robin shouts, "Why should we?"

Atomi scowls. "This is not the time for your anger. When we come across more Shigbis, that will be a more appropriate time."

• ● ● ● ● •

Ellionna opens her eyes three days later. She is in a dim, cool place, resting on a cushioned mat with many colorful pillows. The armor her grandmother gave her is now gone. Instead, she wears a dark purple leather top that was cut off at the belly and a white throw around her shoulders, which is attached to her breast by a large aqua quartz crystal. The crystal is dazzling. She has never had such expensive jewelry. Stroking it in wonder, she swears it glows at her touch. A long, flowing white skirt drapes from her hips. There are golden flats on her feet.

Standing up to face a long mirror, she gets a better look and is in awe of the clothes. She twirls gleefully and notices the pretty perfume in her hair and the new golden tint of her skin. And when she touches the crystal once more, it does, in fact, glow as she thought it might. Simultaneously, her eyes flash a turquoise color, and Ellionna jumps.

A woman enters the room through the open archway. Her head is wrapped in a colorful scarf, and at the base of her crown is an orange crystal. She has a dark complexion, and she is stunning and tall—taller than most Arketchian women Ellionna has ever seen. She walks elegantly and without sound, and she stands erect and confident.

"Ellionna, I am a priestess of the old magic. You may call me Calliope. Your family is waiting for you outside. Come, I will escort you."

Ellionna follows this woman out into the hallway. Some women pass, and Calliope greets them with a light head nod in their direction. When the girls pass Ellionna, they nod to her as well, so Ellionna greets them in the same fashion. The temple has an open architecture. The right side of the hallway is open so she can see the treetops of the jungle. The sky is cloudy on this day, and the air is humid. The tropical birds chirp and flutter in and out of the temple, and none of the women seem to pay any mind.

They come to a stone patio. At its edge sit Atomi and Robin, both dressed in equal luxury. They greet one another and joke about the journey.

"When did we arrive?" Ellionna asks.

"Last night. You were a lump!" Atomi says, rubbing his sore upper arms.

"Ellionna," Calliope says, "you were indeed gravely ill, as your uncle suspected. The crystal at your breast is a healing crystal. It is meant to tame the siren within you. It provides the wearer with serenity and clarity. That is why you feel as though you have more control over your vessel. The problem did not reside in the ritual that gave you the siren. It resides in you, Ellionna. The siren assumes you are a weak vessel, and she is right. You lack faith in yourself, and that leaves you open for her."

"You are all priestesses of the old magic. Do you know how to destroy her?" asks Ellionna.

Another priestess answers. "The siren exists for a reason, as do all other things. Therefore, we will not do as you ask. Instead, we will help you in any way we can. We can teach you to control it, and if you are still unsure, we can offer you a home here with us. There are no men in our temple, and therefore, the siren cannot hurt anyone."

Calliope adds, "But I do not advise you to stay here, Ellionna. This will only hinder you from growth."

Ellionna touches her throat as she thinks everything through. "There is no reason for the siren to exist but for destruction. There is no good that comes from it. It would be best for the world if it is destroyed."

Calliope says sternly, "There are reasons for everything. Just because you do not know a good reason does not mean one does not exist. Perhaps, when you learn the reason for its existence, that would help you control it."

Ellionna has no words.

"What do you choose, Ellionna?" asks Calliope.

She looks to Atomi and Robin, but neither give her an answer.

Ellionna looks to Calliope and the other priestesses. "I wish for you to teach me to control it."

Calliope smiles. "Then we shall begin now. Follow me."

Five priestesses walk with Ellionna to a large room within the temple. The room is small, and there are mirrors everywhere. In the center of the room is a stone fountain. The priestesses work over the colorful bubbling liquid inside while chanting. A pungent aroma fills the room along with a deep smoke. Ellionna feels her head dizzying and makes for the door.

"Look to the mirrors, Ellionna," Calliope instructs while holding her steadfast.

"I don't want to," she confesses.

"Trust us," Calliope says.

The priestesses stand in front of the mirrors and chant. Their reflections are masked by the thick smoke emerging from their potion.

"Look at yourself, Ellionna," Calliope says.

Ellionna looks up and jumps. There is an awful shadow creature staring back at her through the mirror. Its long black hair floats in a nonexistent wind. Its eyes are as black as squid ink, and it smiles menacingly at Ellionna. Ellionna swears she can hear it laugh, and when the being reaches out for her, she feels as if the mirrored walls have vanished. She rushes from the room, but Calliope catches her in time.

"Do not be frightened. Look, we all share the same monster," she says.

Ellionna dares to gaze at the others' reflections, and in them are similar monsters as her own—but monsters that resemble the priestesses.

"They cannot hurt you," Calliope says, urging her back to the mirror. "They are called Haloks, our shadow selves. They are a part of you, and when not balanced with their counterparts, they take over."

Ellionna resumes her post beside Calliope but stares at her feet, unable to face the demon before her. "Is my Halok the siren within me?"

"No," Calliope says. "Your Halok is your darkness. Distinct of the siren entirely. Priestesses," Calliope calls, "speak of the beauty you see within yourselves!"

"I see my kind eyes and my joking smile," says one. And at once, her Halok's face shatters as if it is made of glass. Its black eyes and mouth are replaced with human eyes and lips, shining as bright as the sun.

"I see my elegant hands that I love to dance with," says another priestess as she lifts her hands and moves them around rhythmically. Her Halok's hands shatter and are replaced with golden hands.

"I see my nicely fed belly," says another, causing all the other girls to laugh. Her Halok's midsection breaks, revealing her true form.

"I see my strong arms," says another as she flexes in the mirror. The room is alight with their individual shine, and the smoke of the potion recedes. The foul odor turns sweeter by the moment.

"I see my long legs. They can outrun even the fastest gazelles!"

Calliope gazes sternly at her reflection. "I see the strength of my personality. I see a woman who cannot be broken." Her Halok ruptures in whole, revealing a divine sparkling and smiling image of her human form.

They all turn to Ellionna for her statement. Ellionna lifts her head to face the monster and finds herself tongue tied. As her fear grows, the monster approaches. With a raspy voice, like that from the underworld, it taunts, "There is no goodness in you, Ellionna! You are ugly and weak. You are a murderer!"

"Do not listen to it!" Calliope shouts. Ellionna desperately wants to look away from the being but is paralyzed. The monster reaches out for her, its arms emerging from the mirror, but Ellionna cannot scream or move.

The priestesses are frantic. "Should we intervene, Calliope?" one asks.

"No. She can do it. Ellionna, force yourself to speak." Calliope says.

Pulling her shut lips apart feels like peeling a scab from an unhealed wound. Tears flow from her eyes, "I see . . . I see only a scared girl. I see nothing else," while she speaks, the monster's mouth moves in sync with hers as if it's controlling her words. Calliope gasps. Ellionna's Holok is inches away from grabbing her and pulling her into the mirror with it. She grabs onto Ellionna and pulls her away. But the Holok has already snatched Ellionna's hand.

"Do you know what I see?" Calliope says while wrestling with the Holok. The priestesses rush to Ellionna's aid and begin a powerful chant. "I see a beautiful young woman. She is scared, yes, but only because her heart is so big. She is a caring, soft, and loving soul. She does not wish to inflict harm on any person."

Ellionna's Holok begins to shatter, and Ellionna regains her ability to move. She pulls violently from the Holok's cold grasp.

The priestesses join in.

"She is strong!"

"She is humble!"

"She is selfless!"

With every sentence, the Holok rips apart, revealing rays of light beneath its surface.

"She is more than she knows."

The Holok explodes, finally, leaving Ellionna's true glistening reflection behind the glass.

Ellionna blubbers and Calliope pulls her in an embrace. The other girls approach and wrap their arms around her, as well.

"Look at your true form," she says. "That is who you are. Never think otherwise."

In the warm and loving arms of the priestesses, Ellionna has never felt freer.

⁕⁕⁕⁕⁕

Ellionna, Atomi, and Robin are invited to dine with the priestesses. The trio walks together to the dining room. It is bare and lit with several candles along the hardwood floor. There is a single thin red rug running the length of the room. Placed on this rug are wooden plates of food of different types: rice dishes, dumplings filled with meat and vegetables, and a whole roasted fish. There are also different meat dishes, salads, fruits, and wooden pitchers of water. The room smells of great spices. Ellionna feels as though she has suddenly been transported back into the Arketcha tribe with the familiar smells. There are small wooden bowls stacked in the middle of this spread. On either side of the rug are colorful cushions.

The great room is filled with nearly a hundred priestesses, young and old alike. The bowls are passed to everyone. Ellionna, Robin, and Atomi feast as if they have never eaten such a meal. They savor every bite, and Ellionna nearly cries when she tastes the roasted fish.

The priestesses eat in silence. When Ellionna speaks, the priestesses look over at her as though she is breaking a sacred rule. "This fish is just like my grandmother makes!"

Calliope, who sits directly across from Ellionna, quickly leans in and whispers, "We do not talk while we eat. We consider eating an intimate experience here. It is very sacred. As we eat, we concentrate on our gratefulness for the bountiful food."

Ellionna nods and continues to eat from her bowl in silence while attempting such mindfulness.

After their meal, the sun has set, and Calliope asks Ellionna to join her for a walk. She and Calliope stroll along a large balcony that circles the temple. The sky darkens by the moment, and the pair watch the jungle come alive with bright lights.

"Are you satisfied with the person you are?" Calliope asks. "Or do you wish you were someone else?"

Ellionna does not know how to answer such a forward question and looks out into the jungle in deep thought. "I am not happy with who I am," she finally admits.

"That is good," Calliope says. "A seed that is unsatisfied with its height takes the water given and uses it to grow. Perhaps into a tree."

Ellionna takes in this wise analogy and counters, "But trees do eventually stop growing."

"The seed wished to be a tree and has become one," says Calliope. "Even so, it grows wider and taller, though you might not take notice."

"When does it stop growing?" Ellionna asks.

"When it is satisfied with who it has become. Who do you wish to become?"

"I wish to be a strong woman who can fend for herself," Ellionna says, thinking of Atomi's and Robin's sacrifice for her. "I want to be stronger than the siren. I want to give life rather than take it away."

Calliope listens, and when Ellionna is done speaking, she thinks for a long moment. "Your first wish for yourself is filled with anger and resentment toward your situation. I got these scars when I was a young girl, no older than yourself," Calliope says, showing her midsection to Ellionna. "Afterward, I vowed I would run away and find my independence so that no one could do such a thing to me again. I wanted to be like a tree and stand alone. Do you think the trees stand alone?"

Ellionna nods. "Yes. Of course, they do."

Calliope shakes her head. "You are wrong. Beneath the soil, the roots of trees grow so wide that they get tangled with one another. They do not stand alone. When I came here, I learned that although I grew to be my own person, I was still not alone." She searches Ellionna's eyes to see if she understands. Calliope places a hand on her shoulder and says, "I know you will become a strong woman, and I am happy you see where you want your life to lead. You are very lucky your roots are deeply embedded."

Ellionna nods. "If I stay here, I would be safe and loved, and I could grow."

Calliope smiles and leans on the railing, staring out into the jungle. "Yes, you would, and we would be happy to have you. But could you grow to the person you want to be if you stay here? Could you give life the way you intended?"

"No," Ellionna admits.

The next morning, the three set out to leave the temple. The priestesses visit each of their personal chambers to provide them with provisions for their journey, along with healing totems. Ellionna keeps her blue crystal at her chest, while Robin is gifted with purple amethysts that are embedded into her armor. Atomi is given a large moonstone ring that is placed on his right ring finger.

"The moonstone has been a natural balancing agent for wolves since ancient times. It will help you during your phases and protect you against harm," Calliope says.

Atomi laughs. "I didn't tell you I am a wolf."

Calliope smiles. "We are priestesses of the old magic. We can tell a wolf from a human. An animal's heartbeat is usually faster than a human's. A man-wolf is usually somewhere in-between." She places a hand on his chest. "However, at this moment, I would say otherwise . . ."

Atomi blushes. "You know, we wolves have great abilities, as well. Our eyes can recognize the marks other wolves leave behind."

Calliope blushes, looking down at her midsection. "Yes, that was a long time ago."

He leans in and whispers, "I know your story, Calliope. And I know what you did to escape."

Her heart skips a beat.

"We also have impeccable hearing," Atomi adds. "If I did not know better, I would assume you to be a wolf as well."

"Do you judge me for what I did?" she asks.

He shakes his head. "I applaud you."

CHAPTER 35

Large rain clouds appear and roll in with haste. Starlight quickly fades, and Hale suddenly finds himself flying against the wind and rain. The fur of his Griffin body is now soaking wet, and he strains to flap his wings through the current.

As he swerves in the sky, trying to escape the heavy fog, a flash of lightning bolts so near his body that he feels the heat of it on his skin. But when the bolt extends an arm, engulfing Hale, a surge courses through his veins. At this excruciating moment, Hale can feel the bolt impact the ground below as if he, too, is connected to it. His eyes grow wide as the pain overtakes him, but he makes no sound.

Somehow, he transforms into his human form at the touch of the bolt. The lights flicker on and off in the sky, and suddenly, Hale loses consciousness. He somersaults in the air, free-falling toward the wet ground.

A second Griffin, large and magnificent in build, had been flying right behind him above the clouds. His soaking brown fur flakes off the excess water as he dives in search of Hale. His deep brown eyes scan the skies frantically, but he cannot see anything in the night.

Using his power of Endurance, all it takes is a simple blink to see what the naked eye cannot. In the blackness of his mind, Bayo spots a human figure engulfed in red light plummeting below him.

He tilts his body and narrows his wings until he, too, descends at a rapid pace. He senses the lightning, though the bolt has yet to strike. He swerves left when the bolt means to strike him, then he swerves right. Large bolts cut through the air, each missing Bayo.

Finally, Hale is near his grasp. Bayo reaches out his front paw, nearly grabbing the back of Hale's shirt. He strains, but Hale is too far away.

While Hale flips unconscious in the air, smoke radiates off of his body. The ground gains on them. The center of a spiral vein design is directly below them, created by the lighting.

Bayo unfurls his wings and pulls them back in. This speed against gravity causes great friction on his skin, and he can feel it tearing. He does not stop. Gaining speed, he is inches away from Hale. But the ground is gaining on them.

Reaching his claws toward Hale, reaching until they unhinge from his shoulders to get to him, Bayo catches Hale's burning torso. He shrieks and spreads his wings wide, fighting the pull of gravity, and lands roughly on his hind legs. He places Hale down gently in front of him. His human body now seems so small and frail beside Bayo's Griffin form.

Bayo quickly transforms. The scrapes and tears from falling so quickly adapt to his human shape, and Bayo's limbs and face bleed. Though Hale's skin is burning hot, Bayo shakes him. Hale's bruised and blistered figure remains motionless. Splintering veinlike designs scar his skin.

Bayo sees a pool of water nearby. He lifts Hale's sizzling body into his arms and rushes to the pond. Bayo nearly tumbles in. The cold water provides instant relief. Hale steams in his arms, and though Bayo is in great pain, he does not let go.

He shakes Hale and begs, "Hale! Wake up! Wake up!" He moves a single hand from underneath and washes the water over Hale's face and arms. "Hale," he cries. "I should have never let you come out tonight. How could I be so foolish?" The sight of Hale causes Bayo to go pale.

•●●●●•

Many years ago, Felix had an awful vision. To explain what he saw to Bayo, he drew the image of Hale engulfed with dark, veinlike markings all over his body. He warned Bayo, "When this happens to your brother, the war between you will begin, and it will prevent your plans from taking place."

Bayo countered, "You said there was a possibility he would stand by my side."

Felix nodded. "Yes. This is a sign that pushes the odds against your favor. If this should happen to him, then the chances are slim . . . and it will be your decision to turn away from him, not his from you."

Bayo looked over his shoulder to the young boy asleep on a white bed. This same boy who was stunted since his fifth year, alive but in an enchanted sleep. "I will never turn from him, and such markings will never befall his skin. He is under a sleeping spell, and here he is protected. Once my plans are complete, I will break the spell, and Hale and I will be the family we once were."

Felix looked toward the young boy and said, "Be the family you were always meant to be now. Are your plans so important that you would dull such ties?"

Bayo grew cold. "It is a sacrifice I made to give our people the power we don't have in this world. We are beneath all the nations in Malphora, especially the extraordinary nations. If I had not taken measures into my own hands, the Arketchians would have found the means to sever our ability to transform between human and Griffin. We would have been domesticated by the Bimmorians and used as a means of transportation when they first invaded hundreds of years ago. If I had not protected us, one or the other would have stolen our Welcoming Moon, our only chance of survival."

Felix looked down at the floor gravely. "Yes. I know."

"It is because you and I and the rest of the Elders put a stop to all such happenings. It was never my plan to live this long and curse you all with me. I chose this fate because I knew I was able to do what was necessary to protect us. Now, that is simply not enough. It is time we fight back. Finally, we have the technology and ability to do so. If I must wait to be reunited with Hale for several hundred years more, then that is what I will do."

"But, Bayo. Your plan will only bring destruction to Malphora. I've seen it—"

"You're wrong. You will see."

⁌ ● ● ● ● ⁍

The dark clouds overhead disperse as quickly and as eerily as they came. Bayo looks up and curses his fate. "I should have known the moment I saw the clouds . . ."

Hale stirs in his arms. Bayo looks down to see Hale's chest rising and falling. He chuckles. "You are a true Endurance Griffin," he whispers gently, moving the hair away from Hale's face.

While walking out of the pond with Hale in his arms, he declares, "This moment does not become us. We will defy the odds. I will have my empire, and you will be by my side."

CHAPTER 36

"Well, I think it's time you get to your living quarters—school begins first thing in the morning," says Lady Meir.

Marcus grabs his belongings, and Lady Meir leads him to his room through the dark, winding hall. She stops at a door on the right and hands him the key.

"This is your room. The school uniform and nightwear are in the drawers. The facilities are a few doors down and are shared by all the students. If you have any trouble, come to me—at any reasonable hour.

"Goodnight, Marcus. It was a delight to meet you." She extends one hand to him and adjusts her glasses with the other.

He shakes her small, dry hand, and she walks away. The clicks of her heels pitter-patter through the halls and back to her chambers. Marcus drops his things and closes the door behind him. He sits on the bed, feeling the lavish covers, and he sighs. His bed back home isn't nearly this comfortable, and he never had a desk before.

All this, and he still misses his home. He undresses from his fancy clothes that pinch and chafe his body and searches the drawers for the nightwear. He puts on only the pants—the shirt is too stiff—and he sits in this bed, facing the window, and imagines himself lying outside under the stars, the grass prickling his bare back, the sound of crickets chirping, perhaps even hopping onto his body.

Marcus finds himself too distressed to sleep. He wonders if he'll be accepted among the Bimmorian students. When the sun finally begins to rise, Marcus has just fallen asleep. At the sound of a horn echoing throughout the academy, he jolts up and falls off the bed. His eyes are crusted and swollen. He rubs his face and gets himself dressed. In no more than a minute, he is out the door, rushing up the steps along with his peers.

Fifty elite students wait in front of a large golden door at the foot of the stairs. Marcus hears snickering and turns to see a group of students pointing at the color of his skin. Marcus's fair complexion stands out among the sea of blue.

There are a few other exceptions, however. Off in the opposite corner stand two dazzling centaurs. The girl doesn't seem to mind the attention she and the centaur boy beside her are getting. Casually, she looks about the room and leans in to whisper in her companion's ear. Every so often, she whirls her long, curly golden-blonde hair and proceeds to adjust the silver wreath wrapped around her head.

Her friend is a handsome boy who likewise has a silver wreath atop his disheveled hair. His tan chest is bare, and his black back is covered with a deep blue garment. He doesn't seem to like it very much and tugs at it now and then while nodding through her whispering, carelessly.

Somewhere behind them is a lone faun who scratches his long slender horns nervously. The snow-white skin of his face is just as striking as Marcus's. They lock eyes and Marcus quickly turns away, hoping he didn't offend him by staring. And wonders briefly if he could find some way to befriend this faun who seems to feel just as out of place as he does.

Catching most of the attention in the crowd is a harpy. When Marcus sees her in the distance, his jaw drops at her radiant beauty. The feathers of her wings are white with tints of pink and purple. They are so large that their tips drag behind her on the floor, even though they are tied to her back with leather straps around her shoulders. Her hair is straight and black. She has a long face with elegant features and wears a sleeveless light blue dress. Marcus has never seen someone so striking. As a matter of fact, he's never met a non-Bimmorian in his life. Such creatures he's only ever heard exist from the many stories of his parents. In this one moment, the world seems bigger and brighter than ever.

Coming up the steps after everybody else arrived are five imperial guards who conceal someone between them. Everybody gazes and whispers, moving around to see who is hiding in the guards' care. The guards disperse as soon as they escort their subject up the steps, revealing Princess Evangeline Belflore. Her blonde hair is tied in a long, intricate braid, ending at the small of her back. Her lips are a dark plum, which matches her long, flowing dress. As she moves, her dress changes color in the light, radiating pink and blue hues.

The golden door in front of them opens wide, uncovering the breathtaking space that is their classroom. The rectangular room is open on all sides, showing off gushing waterfalls pouring out from mountains in the distance. Numerous white columns hold up the ceiling. Individual desks are evenly positioned along the white marble floors, two of which are specifically designed for the centaurs. Each desk is furnished with several books and pens. Birds chirp and flutter freely throughout the classroom and out again.

Standing behind the professor's desk, waiting for the students to take their seats, is a Bimmorian woman. After one glance at her narrow eyes and pursed lips, Marcus feels intimidated.

Once all of the students are seated, the professor doesn't bother to introduce herself. She simply begins her lecture. "We will be using the first book placed on your desks, *The Complete Works of Bimmorian History*. Chapter 1, the Foundation of Bimmorus."

Marcus fumbles to open the pages of the book and looks over to the other students, who take notes as the professor speaks. He grabs the pen on his desk and glances over to his neighbor for a clue of how to use it. The Bimmorian girl quickly catches on to his wandering eye and grimaces. At once, Marcus's pen falls out of his hands and onto the floor. The girl laughs, drawing the professor's attention.

"You there! What is your name?" the professor barks, making direct eye contact with Marcus.

Marcus is already on the floor, trying to find the pen he's lost. The class laughs, and he turns red. Standing up to face the professor, he answers, "Marcus."

"Do you know how to write, Marcus?" asks the professor.

Marcus stutters, "A little."

The professor is wide-eyed. "Pardon?"

"A little. My mother taught me, but I haven't written for some time."

"Can you read?"

Marcus nods, though the last time he's actually read anything is more than a year ago. The professor purses her lips. "Have you had any previous schooling?"

Marcus shakes his head.

The professor looks horrified. "How on Malphora did they allow an uneducated minor into this academy," she mutters. "I advise you to meet with the headmaster this instant and explain this class will be too advanced for you."

Marcus fumes. Who is this woman to say something is too advanced for him? She didn't even know him! Still, he takes his books in hand and turns to the door.

"Leave them!" the professor commands.

Marcus reddens again, and the class laughs. Just before he is through the double doors, a classmate ridicules, "Good riddance, flying vermin!"

Marcus pauses for a moment to see if the professor would stop the boy from making such a comment or even speak against his laughing peers, but the professor says nothing.

Marcus rushes down the steps and stops outside Lady Meir's door. He wonders if he should tell her what happened, or if he should just leave this academy and go back home where he was safe and comfortable.

He knocks on the door. Just like the previous night, clanks and thumps come from the other side as Lady Meir rushes to open it. "Marcus!" she exclaims. "What on Malphora is wrong?"

Before he can stop them, tears well in his eyes, and Lady Meir urges him inside.

Back in the classroom, the professor continues her lecture. The centaurs, faun, and harpy refuse to open the books or take notes. She stops her class once more. "I assume you all are also illiterate? There is no room for illiterate folk in this classroom. Please leave."

The golden double doors burst open, and behind them is a fuming Lady Meir, marching toward the front of the class.

"Marcus, take your seat," she directs. Marcus follows her orders, though he is fearful and embarrassed to be returning to this classroom after he'd been kicked out.

Lady Meir continues, "These students will *not* be leaving, Lady Ena."

The professor's face flushes at the sight of the headmaster. "Lady Meir, this class is too advanced for illiterates," she explains.

"I advise you to hold your tongue. These students were hand-selected to join the academy. Perhaps this class is too advanced for the likes of you."

The professor does not know what to say, so she watches as Lady Meir piles up the contents of her desk and hands them to her. "You may leave, Lady Ena. I will be taking over this class."

Lady Ena has no words. Her eyes nearly bulge from their sockets. Lady Meir stands steadfast as though the woman is not in front of her. When Lady Ena begins to make her exit, Lady Meir starts the class.

"In this class, there will be no embarrassing another student. There will be no such thing as one being above the other. There will be no laughter at another's expense, no physical or verbal assault. The talents of each individual will be celebrated, and whatever an individual lacks, they will learn. I will not stand for anybody who shows disrespect and superiority to any being."

Lady Ena departs silently.

Lady Meir continues. "If you prefer to write your notes, write them. If you prefer to underline the text in your textbook, do so. If you prefer to memorize my words, do so. If you have not used these tools on your desk before, I will be more than happy to show you. Knowing how to hold a stick in your hand and wave it around on a surface does not make you smarter than a person who has not done it before."

At the end of the day, Marcus leaves the classroom and rushes down the steps to his room. He is holding all of his books in his arms, and the pile is so high it blocks his vision. Suddenly, he bumps into somebody running up the stairs. The textbooks go flying, and Marcus falls on his bum. As he rubs his backside, the stranger apologizes. Marcus turns to meet the familiar voice.

"Camden!" he exclaims.

"Marcus! I was just looking for you. I've come to ask for your help."

CHAPTER 37

Bayo storms through the front door of the Elders' Dome and rushes up the stairs. "Ianna! Rioma!" he shouts.

A door from above flies open, and Rioma descends the steps to see Hale unconscious in Bayo's arms. Ianna is just behind Bayo, and they rush to bring him to the guest room.

Bayo is frantic as the women hurry to his aid. Ianna speedily gathers her medicines. They rub his burned skin with creams while Bayo watches in horror. *How could I let this happen?* The sight of Hale's body is unbearable to behold.

Deor enters Bayo's mind from wherever he is in the Dome and assures him, *His head is unharmed.*

Bayo watches as Ianna pulls a teal potion from her pocket and stops her before she can pull at its cork. "What is that?"

"It should speed up his recovery."

Knowing how Ianna's potions are never consistent and more experimental than they ought to be, Bayo holds out his hand so she'll hand it over. He drinks half its contents and feels the viscous substance coat his throat, then proceed to spread throughout his body. Looking down, he watches his open skin heal and scab. He hands the remainder of the potion back to Ianna and says, "Give it to him."

She slides her hand under Hale's neck and raises his head a few inches. She places the vial to his lips and pours the contents in. After several moments of waiting, the potion takes effect. Hale's skin begins to heal, and suddenly, his eyes flutter open.

Bayo kneels beside the bed and calls Hale's name.

Hale looks in the direction the voice comes from but cannot see who is speaking. "Bayo?" he calls out in fright.

"It's me. I'm right here," Bayo assures him, caressing his head.

"I—I can't see you. Where are we?"

"We are in the Elders' Dome, in your room."

Hale's voice quavers. "Why can't I move? I'm trying to move, but I can't move. My body is tingling everywhere."

"Listen to me," Bayo asserts. "You will be okay, and Ianna has given you a potion to heal you. It's going to take some time, but after you rest, you will be as good as new, you'll see."

"Is she here?" Hale asks, a tear falling down his face.

Ianna steps forward and takes Hale's hand. "I'm here."

Bayo strokes Hale's head and says, "Try to sleep."

Hale dozes off shortly after. Bayo stays by his side the whole night until there is a knocking at the door.

It is his pack brothers, Deor says. *They've come to see why Hale hasn't returned for the night.*

Bayo leaves Hale's side to answer the door himself. Behind it stand two young boys, and he quickly recognizes them both. The first was Mary's pet, and the second was meant to be Mary's victim.

"Good evening, Elder Bayo," River begins politely. "Is Hale here? He didn't come home today."

Bayo nods. "He was hurt."

The color drains from River's face, and Evan furrows his brows.

"Is he okay?" River asks.

"Yes, he is sleeping upstairs."

"What happened?" asks the other.

Bayo coldly says, "He's okay. You will see him soon."

⁘ ⦿⦿⦿ ⁘

Marcus rests on his stomach on a lavish bed with one of his schoolbooks in front of him, trying to recall how to read and make sense of the words before him. But his night of sleeplessness has caught up with him, and he finds himself drooling on the book instead.

Camden walks in with two plates of food and notices Marcus dozing. He put the plates down on one of the tables in his room, pulls the book slowly from under Marcus's face, and replaces it with a pillow. Marcus is so exhausted that he doesn't notice. Camden looks at the book, reads a few sentences, and tosses it onto the table behind him.

"I don't miss those days," he mutters. He slumps over the desk while the sun sets and scribbles his many plans on numerous papers.

It is the middle of the night when Marcus rouses. Camden looks over his shoulder. "How did you sleep?"

"What time is it?"

Camden shrugs. "Middle of the night. Here, I brought you some food. It's cold by now."

Marcus rubs his eyes, walks over to the plate, and digs in. "When are we going to—"

Camden interrupts him, "As soon as you're done eating." Marcus gobbles down his food and belches.

Camden chuckles. "There was no rush," he says.

Then he blows out the candles and opens the door to his chambers slowly. He exits, and Marcus follows him through the dim, empty palace. They walk with soundless steps up the stairs and through dark corridors. Camden approaches the lone door at the end of this hall then takes a set of keys from his pocket.

Marcus pokes him in the back. "Don't do that," he warns.

"Why?"

"I just know you shouldn't."

"How are we to open it, then?" Camden asks.

Marcus shrugs. Camden lets out a deep sigh and lifts his hand to grasp the doorknob in front of him.

Marcus stops him at once. "Don't do that."

"Why?"

"There's something wrong in there" is all Marcus is able to say.

Camden doesn't doubt Marcus's abilities, but he needs to get that book. "All right. Is it life-threatening?" he asks.

Marcus shakes his head. "No."

"Then we're just going to have to be brave, aren't we? Perhaps you should stay here."

Marcus stops him again. "It will be safer if I go and get it."

Camden raises his brows. "How on Malphora will that be safer?"

But Marcus doesn't listen. He takes the keys from Camden's hands and unlocks the door, shuddering at the touch of the knob. He pushes Camden away then enters slowly with his eyes closed. "Don't come in," he says, closing the door behind him.

Marcus knows something else is in this room, and he knows that if he opens his eyes, he will see it and be very afraid. A gust of wind whooshes past his face, and with a light whimper, he steps forward.

Not truly understanding how, Marcus is able to sense the book is hidden somewhere in a trapdoor in this room. As he takes another step, that same eerie wind approaches his ear. He feels its chill standing beside his body, and he swallows hard.

"Please. I'm not here to hurt you," Marcus says to it. "I'm just here to take something. I'll go quickly, I promise."

Then an eerie voice comes beside his ear. "What are you here to take?"

"A book."

The wind rushes to the far corner. "Who is the person beyond the door? His presence is familiar to me."

Marcus swallows again and takes another step forward. His arms reach out in front of him, searching for the trapdoor that conceals the book. "You know who he is."

"Why don't you open your eyes, child?"

Marcus shakes his head. "No, thank you."

Camden knocks on the door lightly and calls Marcus's name. "Marcus, are you all right?" he asks.

The wind rushes to the door and presses itself up against it.

"Yes, I am fine," Marcus says.

Then the wind rushes in front of Marcus again. "I want to see him. Let him in!"

Marcus ignores the voice.

"Let him in, and I'll give you the book you seek."

"Give me the book first," Marcus says.

There is a clanking somewhere nearby. Marcus holds out his hands, and a book is placed on them.

"Let me see him now, child."

Marcus counters, "You're going to scare him."

The wind circles him. "Are you scared of me?"

"Yes."

"Why?"

"Because you shouldn't be here."

Camden knocks on the door once more, and the eerie being beside Marcus shouts, causing him to jump and the book to fly from his hands, "Let him in! We had a bargain."

Marcus scrambles to the floor, desperately trying to keep his eyes closed while searching for the book. He pats the cool surface but cannot find it. *Just a little peek*, he thinks.

Then he sees it. An opaque figure, neither white nor black, just there in the dark, wearing a dress. Marcus jumps in horror, finds the book, and runs to the door. He pulls it open and rushes through, his heart pounding.

Camden grabs onto his shoulders and asks, "What happened? Who were you talking to?"

Marcus finally opens his eyes and shakes his head in fear. "She wants to see you."

"Who does?"

Marcus can't answer this question, and Camden is already growing impatient with curiosity. He asks Marcus to step aside as he grabs the knob.

"No! Stop! Don't go in there."

"Why?"

Marcus didn't know the true answer, so he said all he knew. "It will hurt you."

"Will I die?" Camden asks seriously.

"No."

He smiles at the young boy and says, "Then we have nothing to be afraid of. I'll be out in a minute."

Camden enters the room and closes the door behind him. The study is just as he remembered it as a child. It was the study for all the queens of Bimmorus, and now it is just an empty room filled with dust shining in the moonlight.

Camden stands there, remembering how his mother always sat by the window while she worked on her stitching. He looks around, recalling small bits of memories here and there, but he does not see anyone.

"Show yourself to me," he declares.

He waits a moment, yet nothing reveals itself.

"You've asked me to come, and now I am here. Who are you?" he asks into the void.

A voice comes from the darkness in the far corner. "You will be afraid."

Camden holds his breath at the sound of this familiar voice. "Come closer."

Emerging from the corner of the room is a woman's figure. Her hair is long and down, and her dress is old and ragged. Camden can see through her body.

Camden's face drops, and his skin goes pale. "Adene?"

"Yes, I was once called that . . . And you were once my nephew."

The being steps closer to Camden and strokes the side of his face. Her touch on his skin is uncomfortable and cold.

"Why are you here?" Camden asks. "Is my mother here, too?"

The spirit shakes its head. "I am alone, bound to these four walls for eternity as punishment for my crimes."

"We thought you died of sickness," Camden says.

Adene laughs, and she spins around without warning. Her face is horrifying and misshapen. "I died like this! The sickness of fire at the hands of the new king!"

Camden is in shock. "What did you do?" he asks.

"Your father is too, the father of my child."

"You and my father . . . Evangeline?" Camden asks in a cold whisper.

The ghost frowns deeply. "When William found out, he and your father dueled over the right to my life. Owen lost the battle and was struck by a blade in the chest. He survived for many months before the injury took him completely."

Finally, Camden understands. "Evangeline is the rightful heir to the throne."

The ghost of Adene looks up at him and nods. "William claimed her as his own to spare the family from scandal—and so she would not steal the crown from him after Owen's death. Will you promise to keep your half-sister safe?"

Camden nods.

"Then I am finally free."

The ghost is engulfed in blinding white light and suddenly vanishes from the room.

Camden remains there for a long moment, trying to come to terms with what Adene told him. He turns to the door and opens it. Marcus is standing there, waiting with the book.

"What happened?" Marcus asks.

"She's gone. And I am unhurt. Your intuition was wrong," Camden explains.

Marcus looks Camden deep in his eyes and says, "No, it wasn't."

As they walk back, Camden's thoughts consume him. *Was this who my father truly was? A deceitful man who would take his brother's wife then hand over the kingdom as a means of apologizing?*

Marcus whispers, "The past is a guide for the future."

Camden breaks from his daze. "What did you say?"

"King Owen Belflore always said, 'The past is a guide for the future.' I read it in my history book."

Camden recalls his father's moments of wisdom. "Yes."

　　　·●●●●·

Resting beside a single burning candle is *The Book of Peace*. It is unlike any book any ordinary or extraordinary creature would be accustomed to. The leather-bound book is kept closed with silver clasps on three sides. It emits a purple light, and its pages on all sides are yellow and frail with old age. The front cover is smooth to the touch and is engraved with three circles, representing The Eyes. Each outline of the orbs is aglow.

"This wasn't what I expected," admits Camden.

"Why is it glowing?" Marcus asks.

Camden shrugs while continuing to observe it.

"What are you waiting for?" Marcus asks, fed up with just staring at it. "Open it!"

Camden reaches for the clasps. He unlocks the first, and the book radiates more light through the cracks of the pages. A whooshing noise comes from within. He and Marcus exchange a glance. The sound increases as he continues unclasping the book.

The book starts to vibrate on the desk. The whooshing noise grows louder and louder by the moment. Marcus and Camden cover their ears and wince.

"Open it!" Marcus urges. "Or the whole palace will wake up!"

Camden opens the book, and at once, the noise and the rumbling on the desk cease. The air around the book is illuminated. Starlike particles emit from the pages and dance about the room.

Marcus reaches out to catch a tiny floating particle, and when it lands ever so gently in his hands, he feels their warm, inviting light cool and fade completely.

The first pages of the book are blank. Then before their eyes, the table of contents appears, one line at a time. Marcus hovers over Camden's shoulders and tries to sound out the words.

When the words *Creating Organic Portals* appear in the table of contents, Camden flips through the pages of the book.

Somewhere in the middle of *The Book of Peace*, the same title reveals itself, then disappears completely.

"I've never seen such technology before. This must be how advanced Bimmorus was when King Lorain found The Eyes," Camden thinks aloud.

The pages themselves project an image of a woman a few inches above the book itself. Suddenly, the woman moves. She is strikingly beautiful, and Camden recognizes her right away.

"Dear Reader," she says. "I am Queen Norelle."

Marcus pats Camden's shoulder with enthusiasm. "It's her! It's really her!"

"This section once included instructions on how to create natural portals to the other worlds. However, I have learned and mastered such portals. You need only flip to the next page for Orcura, then the following page for Thurana. A portal will appear for an interval of ten seconds. Both portals are designed to take you to the palaces of these other worlds. A portal for return will appear in the same place an hour after travel. Caution to all travelers: The customs and nature of these worlds are not like the ones you know."

The image of Queen Norelle disappears, and the pages are once again blank.

Camden urges Marcus to move back. "I need you to keep watch. Do not let anyone into my room, under any circumstances. Try not to fall asleep while I am gone. If I am not back within the hour, you might have to come and get me."

"Me?" asks Marcus.

"Yes, you. You're my closest friend now, the only person here I can trust."

Marcus swallows at the thought of this newfound pressure. "Maybe you're rushing into things. Maybe you should wait—"

Camden shakes his head. "I cannot. I have to reverse the deal my uncle made with the Orcuran empress before it is too late. You must speak of this to nobody."

Marcus nods.

"Will you help me?"

Marcus nods again.

Camden places both hands on Marcus's shoulders. "Thank you." He flips the page.

Before their eyes, a blue whirlwind emerges. Camden quickly places *The Book of Peace* on the floor so he can easily step into the portal. Before he steps in, he notices Marcus's pale face.

"I'll be back. Don't worry." He winks and jumps into the portal. The whirlwind vanishes and is replaced with a hovering window showing Camden on the other side in real-time.

Marcus pokes the hovering glass, but his hand cannot go through. Likewise, Camden cannot hear Marcus call out for him.

Marcus pulls up a chair and sits in front of it, waiting for the hour to pass.

●●●●●●

Camden finds himself standing at the edge of a cliff. In front of him are wonders he never imagined could exist. The air feels moist and warm. Tropical flora surrounds him. There is a colossal diamond-shaped crystal hovering in the sky several miles away. Its shining azure color gives light to half of this wonderful world. As it turns slowly, at its own speed, Camden can see its other half is pitch black.

Camden peers to the part of the world where the teal light does not emit its color. He can see the tiny lights of cities in the distance. Though that part of the world is enclosed in blackness, he spots balls of light that resemble the stars of Malphora. As the strange crystal at the center of Orcura turns ever so slightly with each passing moment, the stars at the dark end move along with it.

He is under an ocean sky and watches as large tides leap thousands of miles above his head. Yet, they look like small waves from where he stands. In this massive bubble world, thousands of rock surfaces levitate. Gushing waterfalls spew out from their sides, and cities rest on their surfaces. Natives are walking the bridge between two islands just above his head.

The world is buzzing, chirping, and humming with sounds he has never heard before. Magnificent horse-like creatures roam the skies, flying through mists of clouds, used as transportation between far-off islands.

Camden feels a cool blade at the base of his neck. He raises his hands in surrender as an Orcuran officer shouts at him in a language he doesn't understand. He is poked with the blade and attempts to go on his knees so they do not think he is a threat. Once his knees meet the ground, his hands are seized and tied together behind his back. Camden doesn't fight their authority. "I am royalty from Bimmorus. I wish to speak to your empress."

He is thrust into the air by a strange force he has never experienced. There is a company of twenty Orcuran soldiers behind him, armed and ready. A single soldier from the group keeps his arm raised above his head, and Camden understands this man is the reason he is floating off the ground.

The soldiers march. Camden follows with the wave of the lone soldier's hand. Past the thicket is a vast, glittering lake. On the other side is what Camden can only assume is the palace.

This palace makes the Bimmorian palace seem meager. It could have easily been the size of the whole Bimmorian kingdom. The ivory towers of the palace boast pink and purple tints from the distant reflecting light of the crystal so very far away.

Camden watches as the soldiers step over the ocean. Their feet never actually touch the water. What makes Bimmorus an extraordinary nation has always resided in their knowledge and magical technology, which no other nation possesses. Even that seems insufficient to Camden as he experiences this strange new world.

They escort him straight into the palace. The interior has many floors but no stairs. Orcurans within create small tornadoes beneath their feet, which allow them to fly to the floors above.

The soldiers enter a mighty throne room decorated in red. In the distance, a woman sits on a large golden throne.

The soldiers toss Camden on the floor in front of her and launch into what Camden assumes is an explanation. She listens intently and then waves her hand to signal them to leave. They follow her order.

Camden rolls over onto his knees, taking in the physical image of this breathtaking woman. Her Prussian blue skin glistens with golden makeup. She has long, narrow, violet eyes. Her lips are plump; her cheekbones are high, and her eyebrows stretch to her temples. Her head is wrapped in colorful scarves, and she wears a matching sleeveless gown that exposes her long neck and collarbone. On her neck are priceless jewels unlike any Camden has ever seen. As Camden turns his head, the jewels around her neck change color.

At the sight of Camden making eye contact with her, she crosses her legs and leans back as though indifferent. Then, in a thick Orcuran accent, she speaks the Malphoran tongue. "Why do you come, Camden Belflore?"

"How do you know who I am?"

The empress gestures above her head where three orbs levitate horizontally. The Eyes. "Each world has Eyes, as you know," she says. "Why do you come?"

"I've come to ask you to break the contract you made with my uncle."

The empress uncrosses her long legs and rises from the throne. "Why would I do this?"

"There is nothing for you in Malphora. Bimmorus is a small kingdom compared to your world."

"I know."

"Then why do you take interest in our world?"

The empress steps closer. "You see the large rock in our sky? It is the Loom. Much like your sun, yes? It is dying. This is its last phase of life. My people have nowhere to go but Malphora. Thurana is a deserted wasteland." She waves her hand in frustration and sits back on her throne.

"Why does my uncle give you money?" Camden asks.

She laughs. "Do you know how your nation was born? It is but an Orcuran colony, providing for the motherland."

"Do you wish to rule over Bimmorus when you arrive?"

"It is my right."

"How many people are you bringing to our world? When will you come?"

The empress snaps, "You speak to rulers like they are your equals. Who are you to inquire of me?"

It seems that much of Camden's life is under this woman's control, and though that bothers him a great deal, he bows. "I apologize for offending you, Your Majesty. I only wish to find answers to better serve my kingdom. I must know when you are arriving and how many because I plan to create a barrier around my nation, preventing anyone from entering."

The empress huffs, "I am aware."

After a long moment of waiting for the empress to answer his question, he says, "Perhaps there is a way to heal your Loom."

The empress scoffs. "Can you make an old man young?"

"There are many wise people in my nation—very gifted in magic. I've seen them do wonders," Camden says.

The empress's eyes light up with hope. Camden continues, "If I find a way to heal your world before it dies, will you reconsider your contract with my uncle?"

The empress flashes her dazzling teeth. "I know you to be a man of your word, Camden. You have a deal."

"How much time do I have?" Camden asks.

"One year. And Camden," she looks up and waves her hand to reveal a fourth orb in the center of the trio. Camden's eyes widen. "I share with you a secret your ancestors have long forgotten. The Fourth Eye." She gestures as though pulling the air down, and the mysterious glowing orb lowers until it is in front of her. "Time. Hidden in your staff."

Camden's hands shake. There is a fourth Eye?

"It reveals only in presence of pure magic," she explains, confirming Eliath's theory. And yet, before Camden has the chance to ask, she answers, "Your world has chosen you to guard it, as my world chose me. Guard it well."

With a wave of her hand, a portal emerges from The Eyes of Orcura above her head. She sweeps Camden up with the might of a single finger and thrusts him into the portal. With another wave of her hand, the portal closes, and Camden finds himself standing right behind Marcus, who watches the empress through the window.

"Told you I'd be back," Camden says before the contents in his stomach rush to his throat, and he speeds to his lavatory to vomit.

CHAPTER 38

July 1, 2021

Robin, Ellionna, and Atomi sit in the treetops watching the sun set behind the mountains. As Robin and Atomi doze off, Ellionna pulls a pocket-sized book and a pen from her satchel. Ellionna opens the empty book and readies her pen over the page. After thinking of what to say, words appear on the page in black ink.

> *Dear Grandmother,*
> *We are safe. Atomi says we have reached the outskirts of the Griffin Clan, but we will not see any Griffins since they have enclosed their nation. I am very thankful for that. I wonder if any Arketchian people live in Bimmorus. I hope so. I really miss the food.*
> *Ellionna*

A moment after the letter is written, it fades away one line at a time. Ellionna looks up to the setting sun then back down at the book, hoping she will still see her grandmother's response before it becomes dark. Finally, words appear on the paper, one at a time.

Ellionna,

I am glad you are all safe. There aren't Arketchians in Bimmorus that I know of. But the Bimmorians consider themselves accepting of all extraordinary nations, and they are allies of the Arketcha tribe. I imagine you are nearly there, my sweet granddaughter. May the rest of your journey be safe. I miss you every day.

•●●●●•

In a chain reaction, one treetop after the next sways in a fashion that makes it seem as though they are whispering to one another. The winds are eerie, reflecting from their conversation. The trunks of the trees are hidden by fog. Pushing her bare toes into the soil, she stares out into the distance. The blankness of the scope matches that of her mind. There is no confusion, no drive to move, no thoughts at all.

A plop comes from behind. Perhaps it was a frog jumping into the nearby stream. She catches the sound and whips her head. She wants to see where the sound came from, but her legs do not move. Another plop. At this noise she looks up, dazed, forgetting her feet, and follows the sound, gliding over the ground as if she is one with the wind.

The noise of the stream grows louder. It all looks so familiar—she must have seen it before. Yes, and there had once been a boy, he was so sad ... why was he sad? He once sat on the rocks in the middle of the water, making a net. A force propels her to the rocks' surface. Turning to her left to gaze at the shore, she sees a small shelter, empty and rotting from the wind and rain.

Her heart thuds in her chest. *Where is he?* Her shaking hands pull at the base of her knotted hair. She bites her lip. *The boy—he used to be here, and now he is gone. Now everything is missing. Missing. The boy . . . the boy.*

She tries to remember more, but all she knows is that she needs to be beside him. She wraps her hands around her body. It is so cold. Her fingertips meet the sides of her ribs. She feels a tear in her clothes. Around the tear, the fabric is hard and stiff. She looks down and reaches the tip of her finger into the tear. She screams and jumps back, falling into the water.

Turning onto her side to pull herself back up, she allows herself to face her reflection. Her face is deformed and half-rotted. She screams at the top of her lungs with her eyes closed while banging at her head with her arms.

No. That's not me. Not me. No. No.

She wants to shout, but all that comes out are moans and howls. She takes the water and rubs her face with it. She has to wash it away. Again and again, her hands run across her face. She hesitates to open her eyes, afraid of the horror that awaits her.

Her hands shake as she forces them down at her sides. *Open.*

She stares into the water, waiting for it to steady itself, half expecting that terrible face once more. A moment later, she gasps. She cups her face in her hands in astonishment. Her essence is suddenly aglow in white light. Flashes of memories appear before her eyes. She once looked upon this face a thousand times in a mirror in a peach room, in the shine of silverware, glass, a reflection in windows—everywhere. She saw this face everywhere . . .

She lifts her head, recalling the life she's lost.

Her family, her mission. Her death. She touches the inside of the tear once more, then closes her eyes as she shudders, remembering the cool blade that had entered her body. *I died. He stabbed me right where I was standing a moment ago.*

She opens her eyes. The boy. "Hale."

All around, the trees begin to whoosh horrifically, though she does not notice. On the other side of a tree that faces away from the stream, a being emerges from the trunk so the girl does not see it. It is an opaque figure with nimble limbs, a forest green complexion, and an illuminating glow around it. The other nymphs within the trunk attempt to pull it back inside, but it tugs and escapes their grasp.

"Come back," call a thousand childlike voices in a whisper. "Come back!" But the little nymph walks around the trunk to where the stream flows.

"Don't do this!"

"Please, you're making a mistake!"

"Haven't you learned your lesson?"

"She's dangerous!" The trees howl and sway.

The being looks up at the trees and touches its finger to its lips. "I know."

But this nymph has to help. This particular spirit has been lost for a very long time, but this night is different from all the other nights it has wandered through the woods. *She remembers.*

The other nymphs are not happy about this—not one bit—especially since this very same nymph helped a Griffin Elder not too long ago in the very same woods. They poke their heads from the trees to watch their lone kin brave this daring adventure on its own.

The girl's head is bent down, and her chest heaves as she sobs. Her hair dangles over her face. The nymph approaches her slowly.

"Psst!" the nymph calls out. It waits for her to turn, but she did not hear. "Psst!" it says again. Not a single reaction. It lifts a pebble and tosses it at the girl's feet. *Plop.*

At once, the spirit whips her head around. Her face has turned back to its horrid, corroded form. The being on the other side of the stream gasps and jumps back. They share a daunting glance.

Arms stick out from the trees, calling the nymph back home.

"See. We told you," one says.

"We should not mingle with them. It is not our way," says another.

The nymph turns to them, then turns back with newfound courage. The girl is still in the water, her eyes still fixed on the nymph, never blinking. She glowers at it as though she might pounce at any moment.

Then the nymph calls to her with a single word. "Hale."

The girl's face becomes a vision of beauty and life before its eyes. "Where?" she asks in a whisper.

The being motions her to follow. "This way."

The girl rises from the water and walks toward the being. Its hands extend, pulling her from the stream. She places her hand on it gently. The nymph is cool to the touch, moist and nourishing. From this single touch, the fog in Carly's mind vanishes.

As they walk blankly into the woods, they too vanish.

•●●●●•

Griffins from all directions roam the clear black skies, flocking to a great arena in the middle of a wide field. Half the arena is fenced in by a stone wall. The field is alight with torches, illuminating the area where the Elders currently sit. They perch on lavish seats, waiting for their subjects to arrive.

Behind Bayo, on his left, stands Leon, and on his right is Hale. Both are dressed in shining black armor vests with swords at their hips.

The Griffins gather around the arena in their human forms, and Bayo stands. At once, everybody kneels before him. "Rise, Griffins!" he declares with an outstretched arm. "A year ago you were given a home, a family, and, most of all, you were given power. You have trained with great vigor, and you honor me as a nation. Tonight is the night we have long awaited! This will be the night I decide my heir. Who will we have?" Bayo asks with mischief in his eyes. "Leon the Merciless? Or Hale the Overpowering?"

The audience screams and roars. Bayo laughs.

Somewhere hiding in the crowd are River, Grace, and Evan, gazing up at the platform and searching Hale's eyes.

"Maybe if I step into the arena while he fights, I could talk to him," River suggests.

Grace looks up at River and counters, "He won't hesitate to hurt you. We need to let it go."

Evan steps between the two and agrees with Grace. "He's changed."

River turns back to Hale and says, "He just needs a stern talking-to."

Grace says, "River, if you go in that arena, so help me . . ."

Bayo shouts into the crowd, "Who will dare fight my successor?" The Griffins roar as Hale and Leon enter the arena. Leon and Hale share the same cold demeanor as they stare into the crowd, awaiting their opponents.

Two boys approach them. One makes his way toward Leon and the other to Hale. Hale and Leon exchange a hateful glance.

"May the best man win," Hale spits.

Leon smirks. "I intend to."

Hale spins around, sword in hand, trying to catch his opponent off guard. But the opponent uses the power of Shielding and blocks the blow with a bubble. Hale falls on his back at the impact.

Meanwhile, the other end of the arena echoes with the sound of forceful swords clashing.

Hale looks over to see Leon has already cut through his opponent's arm, and he growls at the sight. Hale pulls himself up while his opponent jumps into the air, preparing to cut through Hale's body.

With a raise of his hand, Hale causes the boy to fall on the ground, squealing in anguish. He watches as the boy contorts in the soil, the dirt chalking his pretty face. "Please!" the boy screams. "Stop!" He chokes on air.

Hale picks up his sword and approaches the boy slowly and without emotion. "Do you surrender?" he asks.

"Yes!" squelches the boy as the anguish heightens.

Hale releases his power, and the boy gasps, finally feeling relief, and stands.

"You see," says River from the sidelines, "he's still in there." He pushes his way through the crowd to get to the center of the arena. Suddenly, a bloodcurdling scream comes from the other direction. Leon has his first kill. Someone tugs at River's arm, and he turns to meet Grace's eyes.

"Are you crazy? Stop!" she shouts, but it is too late.

"It's going to be okay," he assures her, pulling away from her arm. River jumps into the arena and walks toward Hale. Just then, Hale takes the blunt end of his sword and hits it against his opponent's head. River stands motionless as the boy in front of him falls onto the ground.

Hale turns to face his next opponent, and his eyes widen in shock.

River holds his hands up in surrender. "Hale," he begins.

"River, get out of there!" screams Grace.

Evan pulls at his sister and argues, "Grace! Let him try!"

Hale spots River walking toward him, and his heart nearly stops. *What is he doing?* He swallows nervously. Under no circumstances could Bayo see Hale hesitate. He must fight whoever enters the arena.

"Hey," River says with a nervous smile. "Remember me? Your best friend? How's it going?"

At once, Hale charges forward with his bloody sword in hand. Just as Hale is about to slash his sword across River's chest, he is thrust several feet backward.

"I don't want to hurt you," River says, approaching him a second time. "I just want to talk."

Hale lifts his hand in front of him, trying to aim the power of Endurance at River, but it is no use. The barrier protects him. He is stronger than Hale's first opponent. Hale pushes harder until he can feel his power bleed through.

River winces in pain, and his strength begins to diminish. But he strains to keep his force field around him. Hale rises and grabs his sword. It won't be long before River wears out.

Hale runs to River and slashes at the force field like a madman. River feels every slash of the sword as a great impact on his body. He falls to his knees, and the force field collapses.

At that moment Grace bites Evan's hand and jumps in the arena.

Suddenly, Hale sees nothing but darkness. He grunts, striking thin air with his sword. In his mind's eye, using the power of Endurance, he sees the silhouette of a girl pulling River from the ground in front of him.

"I see you, Grace," he hisses, lifting his sword to attack her. But he misses, even though his vision tells him she is right there.

"No, you don't," comes her furious voice directly behind him. Before Hale can whip around, Grace kicks him in the head. Hale falls forward onto his palms and quickly turns around. His cheeks burn.

Suddenly, the whole arena, including the Elders, screams in pain. The only person left standing is Bayo, and even he struggles through it with a clenched jaw. "ENOUGH!" he booms.

Hale pauses his power.

"This fight is over!" Bayo hollers.

All the Griffins but the four Elders, Hale, and Leon transform and flee the arena. As they leave, Hale searches Bayo's eyes for any sign of satisfaction, but Bayo only gives him a cold look before he storms off the field. Hale turns to see Leon panting. His sword, hands, and clothes are bloody. He successfully defeated five opponents.

"I would have won!" Leon snarls in Hale's direction. "I should kill you."

Hale walks up to Leon until he feels his breath on his face. "You couldn't take me even if my body was tied."

Leon looks down at Hale and spits. "When Bayo gives the order, you're done."

Hale laughs and lets his power surge through him and into Leon's body. "What was that?" Hale mocks.

Leon's veins protrude from his neck and temples, and he growls through his clenched jaw. Hale's smile widens—he wasn't even trying yet.

"Come on, Griffin of Endurance. Show me what you've got," Hale taunts.

Hale waits for pain but feels only a minor headache. He laughs and lets Leon have all of it. The pain comes in a tidal wave, and Leon falls onto his back, his scream quaking the arena.

Suddenly Hale feels a presence from behind. He turns to see Bayo fuming. "I said enough!"

He looks up at Bayo in shock. Bayo has never raised his voice at him before.

"Leon. Leave," Bayo orders.

Leon transforms and dashes into the sky. Bayo gives the rest of the Elders the same order, and they, too, depart.

Once the arena is empty, Hale dares to growl, "How long do you still need to decide?" He raises his fist, but Bayo catches the blow as Hale rages. "I'm better than him in every way! I could kill this whole Clan in a minute!"

"You are not better than him," Bayo fumes.

Hale's heart drops.

"You are weak. He has no weakness. You are slow. He is fast. You're lacking in physical combat, and that is where Leon excels. Leon is bigger than you. He takes pleasure in the kill, you do not. The only thing that makes you better than Leon is that your power is greater. Greater than any power I've ever seen. But that isn't enough to command the nation."

Hale glowers. "I have no weakness."

Bayo cocks a brow. "Oh? Then who were that boy and girl you just fought?"

Hale pushes Bayo in the chest. "Did I hesitate with them?"

Bayo pushes Hale back then slaps him across the face. "Mind yourself, Hale," he states. Hale's nostrils flare. Bayo continues, "No, you did not hesitate. You were sloppy."

"Sloppy?" Hale barks.

"You are still letting your emotions get the best of you during a fight."

"I wasn't emotional at all!"

Bayo sucks on his lips. "Do you forget? Deor tells me everything. Are you saying the Elder of the Dark is a liar?"

Hale purses his lips then shouts, "That is not what I said!" He opens his mouth to counter Bayo once more, but Bayo holds out his hand to stop him.

"Hale, enough. I don't want to talk about it anymore. Come," he says, placing his hand on Hale's back. "Cheer up. You are improving. Let's go home."

Hale allows his anger to ebb. As they walk to the Elders' Dome, he asks Bayo, "Which of us do you want to win?"

Bayo stops walking and places both hands on Hale's shoulders. "I want you to win—never think otherwise." He puts his finger to his lips and whispers, "Don't tell Leon I said that."

Hale smiles.

Bayo says, "But you have to improve."

Hale nods. "I will."

°●●●●●°

Before Carly's eyes is a large tree in a vast spirit world. She wants desperately to join the spirits in their colorful flight, but the nymph holds her hand steadfast. "Don't forget."

She nods.

Hand-in-hand, she and the nymph approach the Great Tree, the gateway to the extraordinary world. The nymph urges Carly to touch it and visualize where she would like to go.

She places her hand on its smooth bark and envisions the Griffin Clan. But when she opens her eyes, she is still in front of the tree. She tries once more, but still, she is unable. That is when Carly remembers that Bayo has closed off the Griffin Clan from all creatures, living and dead alike.

She places her hand on the tree and pleads. "Please. I beg you. I must go there. I must help my brother."

This time, at the touch of her hand, she feels the spirit of the Great Tree reach out to her and enter her mind. It senses her sadness and urgency but looks deeper into the memories of her waking life.

As it searches, Carly explains, "He is very important. If he helps Bayo, the gateway between the Human Division and Extraordinary Division of Malphora will be severed. Malphora will perish under Bayo's rule. If I help him now, I will make sure that does not happen."

The tree senses the deep connection between Carly and Hale, and in return, Carly feels its sympathy.

She whispers, "Thank you."

Suddenly she and the nymph stand in the center of an arena, Hale directly in front of them. Carly gasps in awe. *It worked!* She reaches out to touch him, but she stops the moment he smashes the blunt end of his sword through her spirit, striking the boy behind her. She turns around to see the monstrosity Hale has committed and gasps in horror.

● ● ● ● ● ●

Once Bayo is ready for bed, Deor slips into his mind and taunts, *I know why you can't choose.*

Go to sleep, Deor, Bayo grumbles as he slumps into his sheets.

They are both so much like you, don't you think? Leon has the same monster in him that you do. And Hale has the same weakness. Not to mention the blood relation.

I said go to sleep, Deor!

But Deor only laughs. *You have chosen not to choose. You lied to the boy. You try to make one empathetic and the other into a monster. And yet neither of them is exactly like you.*

Bayo shoots up from his seat in fury with half a mind to break down Deor's door and shatter him to pieces. But instead, he sits back on his bed. *I don't know what you're getting at.* He brings his hand to his temple.

Yes, you do.

Bayo grips his mattress in his rage and lets his mind search for Deor's presence using his power of Endurance. He feels Deor clutch the walls in torment. *You forget to whom you speak so casually. I choose Hale. I have always chosen Hale.*

●●●●●

"Why can't he see me?" Carly barks from over Hale's bed.

The nymph shrugs.

"I need to talk to him!"

The nymph says, "When I want the living to see me, I just wish it to happen, and it happens. Try. See if it works."

Carly stands before Hale and wishes with all her might. "Come on, look at me! Look at me!" She calls Hale's name, but he does not stir from his sleep. She tries again and again.

The nymph curls up on the armchair and suggests, "Perhaps I can show myself to him, and you can speak through me."

"No!" Carly says. "It has to be me. No one else." She tries once more, but it is no use. She kneels over his bed and stares at his handsome face, noticing how it has matured and how much he looks like Bayo. "How could you become this person?" she whispers. She strokes his head and suddenly finds herself sucked into the depths of his subconscious.

The nymph jumps from the chair. "Find his dreams!" it declares.

Carly is lost in a sea of images and sounds. People she has not met. A boy with jet black hair and fair skin. Another boy, tall and big with short blond hair, and a smiling young girl with auburn hair. Then there are Ianna, Rioma, and Deor. Most of all, there is Bayo. Carly sees events that have already come to pass, and she screams at the horrors of Hale's mind. She watches as the boy with the black hair screams as well. Pleading with Hale to stop. But Hale is covered in blood.

"What have you done?" River asks in dread.

Though Hale looks up at him with cold eyes, he feels immense guilt. There is an unmoving boy at his feet. Though Carly does not know the boy, his name echoes in Hale's head.

"Norton," it says.

Suddenly, everything disappears. All that is left is darkness, and Hale is in the center of it. He is frightened and alone. Carly steps in front of him and calls his name.

"Can you see me?" she says. "Hale, it's me!"

Hale suddenly looks up into the void. "I know that voice."

"It's me," she repeats.

"Carly? Where are you?"

"I'm right here!"

Tears pour from Hale's eyes. "I can't see you. I can't see anything."

"I need you to follow the sound of my voice."

Hale takes a step forward eagerly, then the dark abyss fades away, and his eyes flutter open. The light of the sun peeks through his curtain. He jolts up in his bed with his head in his hands, trying to remember the far-off dream. It has been so long since he has thought of her. It has been so long since he has recalled the sound of her voice. He shakes it out of his head and proceeds to get ready.

Once he is dressed, he hears a whisper. "Hale."

He turns around, but no one is there.

"Hale. Follow me."

Hale is wide-eyed. He darts from the room and knocks on Deor's door. *He must be messing with my head.*

Ianna comes up the winding stairs. "Good morning, Hale. Deor stepped out for the day. He won't be back until evening."

"Oh," he says. "Thank you."

Hale shakes his head and returns to his room, closing the door behind him. "Hale. Follow me."

Hale jumps once more and whispers, "Carly?"

"Follow me," the voice says again, closer to the door. He steps out of his room. "Follow me." The voice is at the end of the hall where the second staircase in the dome sits. Hale is not allowed to go up these steps. The attic of the dome is Bayo's study.

"Follow me," Carly says again.

Hale looks over his shoulder to see if anyone is watching, but the dome is empty.

"Follow me."

He climbs the steps and comes to a thick, wooden door. Before Hale reaches out to grab its handle, the doorknob turns on its own, and the door opens a crack. "Go in," Carly whispers.

Hale's heart pounds as he wonders what Bayo might think. "Please," she says.

Hale grabs the doorknob and steps inside. He lifts his head and meets a set of familiar eyes. Hale gasps and falls to his knees. Those eyes do not belong to an actual person at all but a portrait. All along the walls are portraits, but the person before him is someone Hale knows from what seems like another life completely. It is the man who kidnapped Carly and him. Hale scans the wall. The first portrait, Bayo. The second, Rioma. The third, Deor. The fourth, his kidnapper. The fifth, Ianna. The sixth . . . his father.

Hale's jaw drops, and his heart thumps. He rises to his feet the moment he feels a pair of eyes watching him from behind. He whips around with his sword in hand, pointing it at Bayo's face.

"Hale," Bayo begins in a soft tone. "Let me explain."

"Who is the man on the wall?" Hale shouts.

Bayo swallows hard. "He is Elder Greon, of the Light."

"You had me kidnapped?" Hale shouts in rage. "You knew me all along! Didn't you?"

Bayo nods. "Yes, but—"

"You knew my father! There were many Felixes in the Griffin Clan, hmm?"

Bayo explains calmly, "Hale, he wasn't your father. He stole you! From me!" Bayo presses his hand to his chest. "You are my brother. Do you see the resemblance? Look, we have the same eyes, the same hair, even the same nose."

Hale panics. Tears overwhelm his eyes. "You lied to me this whole time. Why? You had me hurt and tortured for months. My sister—my sister died because of you. My parents died because of you."

Bayo shakes his head. "They weren't your family. They stole you from me. Felix was the elder prophet and my best friend. He was able to foresee the future. When you were a young boy, you had an accident. You were only five years old. To preserve your life until I found a cure, I placed you under a sleeping spell. Felix told me he saw two futures. One in which you stood by my side and helped me expand our empire, and the second, in which you turned against me and defied my plans.

"It was this news that made me decide not to wake you, even though I gave you the antidote, and you were already healed. I decided to wait until my plans were complete so you would neither join them nor wreck them. So you didn't have to make a decision. But Felix had another premonition. He begged me to wake you and give up the chase. He foresaw the world you would help me create. He saw a wasteland built by chaos and destruction—as a result of my influence on you.

"I chose to ignore him and make my own destiny apart from his premonitions. That was when he, his wife Naomi, and his daughter Carly found a way to steal you away and take you to the Human Division of Malphora. I was unable to find you, though I searched for eleven years.

"When we finally found you, we saw you were already a young man, and no matter what magic I tried to use, I could not transport you back home. You were protected, and we didn't know by what. I had Greon take you and Carly. It was his duty to find out what magic protected you and kept you from traveling here. To this day, I don't know what it was. But shortly after you escaped Greon, it wore off, and I found you and brought you here."

Hale weeps as he tries to come to terms with everything Bayo has said. "Why don't I remember being your brother?"

Bayo shakes his head. "That isn't my doing. When you arrived, I thought you would remember, but you didn't even know you were a Griffin. Felix must have given you something to keep you from remembering. He meant for you to live as a human."

"How did my parents die?" Hale asks, raising his sword higher. He could feel the blood rushing to his head and his heart pounding in his arms.

"Our parents died more than a thousand years ago—"

"No! My parents!"

"I don't know."

"He's lying," Carly whispers.

"You're lying!" Hale bellows. "Tell me!"

Bayo feels his tongue go numb. He doesn't understand why Hale is so upset with him after he explained he isn't at fault. "I found a trace of you once. You were younger. It led us to a small area of woods in the Human Division. We found Felix and Naomi but not you or Carly. They protected your location with their lives."

Hale swallows, "Did you come yourself that day?"

Bayo doesn't respond.

"Which one did you kill? Answer me!"

"Rioma took Naomi's life. I took Felix's."

Hale falls to the floor and wails. Bayo approaches him slowly and reaches down to touch his shoulder.

Hale flinches away. "You lied to me. Everything was a lie and a game. You tricked me." His voice breaks.

"Hale, you are my brother. I love you very much."

Hale wipes his tears. "That's why I was asleep for a thousand years." He raises his sword and steps forward, slashing it across the air. Bayo dodges the attack. Hale swings again, and Bayo jumps back.

"Stop!" Bayo cries.

"Pick up your sword," Hale says. Bayo does not listen. "Pick up your sword!" Bayo does not take his sword from his scabbard. He stands there, defenseless, looking into Hale's overflowing eyes.

"How could you kill your best friend?" Hale sobs.

Bayo's brows furrow. "If I hadn't stopped you, you would have done the same thing only yesterday."

Hale's eyes widen with the realization of what he's become.

"Everything I did, I did to get you back," Bayo says.

Hale slashes with his sword. Bayo whips his sword out just in time to defend himself against the blow. "Everything I did, I did for you!" Bayo repeats. "How can you go against me like this?"

"Everything you did, you did so you could get what you wanted without me getting in the way. Everything you did afterward"—Hale slashes his sword—"was so I would help you get your way."

"You're wrong!" Bayo declares.

"Why didn't you just leave us alone?" Hale cries, swinging his weapon. "Why didn't you let us live in the Human Division? Why didn't you tell me the truth when you met me a year ago?"

Bayo's eyes are filled with agony. "How could I tell you the life you lived was a lie?"

Hale drops his weapon and collides with Bayo. "It wasn't a lie!" he screams. "They loved me!"

Bayo tries to pull Hale's hands away from him, but they are too erratic. "No! I love you!"

Hale cries so hard, he can't see in front of him. "They would have never let me do the things you told me to do."

"I was making you strong!"

"I trusted you!" He pushes Bayo out the door and locks it behind him. Hale runs to the closed door on the opposite wall and opens it. Months ago, Bayo had taught him to use The Eyes in a different room, a reward for his improvement in combat—a reward Leon never received.

He runs through the door and waves his hands over and under the orbs. The orbs flicker, and suddenly, they glow in a bright white light. They haven't glowed like this since they were held in Bimmorus. The earth rumbles, and Bayo rages through the door.

"Hale! What are you doing?"

But Hale isn't listening. He opens the door and runs past Bayo. Bayo rushes into the room to check on the orbs. "What have you done!" he cries.

He quickly tries to remedy the situation, but it is too late. The barrier Bayo created around the Griffin Clan has been broken. It is then that Bayo realizes Hale's plan.

He's trying to leave.

• ● ● ● •

Mary feels the rumbling and runs to the Elders' Dome. She sees Hale racing out, and not a moment later, Bayo follows. She peers into their thoughts, and suddenly, her eyes are wide. *He knows. The barrier is open.*

Instantly, she pulls Greon's pendant from her pocket and over her head. She reaches Ianna's mind and urges her to come out. *We have to go now!*

Ianna rushes out of the Elders' Dome, Greon's pendant around her neck. They transform and take off.

As they fly, Ianna argues, *We will both die if we don't return for the next Welcoming Moon.*

We will return, and we will not be noticed, Mary says. *They will never find us.*

• ◦ ● ● ● ◦ •

Hale runs through groups of Griffins, still sobbing. Everybody turns to see Bayo's apprentice making a mockery of himself. Two of those people are River and Evan. As Hale rushes past them without realizing it, River catches the look in his eyes. It is the same look he had when he first met him. River jumps to his feet and runs after him. Evan follows.

A magnificent Griffin with great brown wings casts a shadow over the field. Everyone looks up to see Bayo. They cheer at the sight of him passing.

Hale comes to the cliffside and transforms.

Leon is sitting in a tree near the field as Hale passes by. He climbs down and transforms. *This is my chance,* he thinks.

His lion body breaks through the grass as he darts toward Hale. Just as Hale is about to fly off over the ocean, he catches sight of Leon. But it is too late. Leon's claws sink deep into Hale's skin, and his beak bites into Hale's neck. Hale shrieks as Leon pounces on him. Hale can feel the blood seeping from his body. His head is dangling off the edge of the cliff, and Leon tries to push him over. Hale kicks Leon's torso with his hind legs and watches as Leon flips over, loses his balance, and falls. But his claws are still sunk into Hale's skin. Hale plummets along with him.

Bayo flies over the scape and sees them falling. He grabs Hale by the skin of his back and pulls him up to the edge of the cliff. Bayo dives down once more to retrieve Leon, who is holding on to the cliffside.

Hale climbs the rock and transforms back to his human self. Another Griffin scoops up Hale and flies over the ocean and toward uncharted land.

Hale recognizes the beast's striking green eyes at once and bellows, "River! I'm so sorry!" A second Griffin, Evan, swoops nearby.

The sound of large wings cuts the air in the distance. Bayo is on their tail, and Leon is on his.

Bayo turns and squawks at Leon, but Leon does not listen. Bayo crushes Leon's body with the power of Endurance, but Leon fights it vigorously.

Bayo grabs onto Evan in the sky and sinks his claws into his backside. Anguish overcomes him, and with a shriek, Evan plummets into the ocean. River flaps harder. They are nearly at the uncharted land. River flies over the treetops, but Bayo is just about to catch him. River has no choice but to drop Hale into the trees.

Hale falls into the branches and hits his spine. He fights unconsciousness, and he sees a blur before him. Leon lands on a branch just in front of him. He leaps over to Hale with hungry eyes and grabs his throat.

Hale chokes and his vision fades to black.

Suddenly, there is a beautiful sound that echoes throughout the wood. Leon turns toward it. Before them is a girl, her brown hair flowing in the wind, her eyes shining a turquoise blue, the same color as the crystal at her chest. She pours out her song at the edge of the water. He has never heard anything so utterly beautiful.

Leon and Hale fall from the trees, unconscious, while the siren sings her song. Bayo pulls through the woods with his hands at his ears, fighting the voice, fighting unconsciousness, fighting the pull on his soul from his body with the great power of the High Elder of Endurance. In the distance, he spots Leon's and Hale's bodies. He knows he must be quick. There will only be enough time to save one before the siren finishes her song.

He dares to remove the hands covering his ears. The song penetrates his skull, he screams while crawling on the ground, reaching for someone, anyone. With closed eyes, he snatches the first body he feels, hoping it is Hale's. With all the might left in his body, he transforms and skyrockets. It is only when he is far from the voice of the siren and the anguish he feels subsides that he opens his eyes to see it is Leon he carries. Bayo shrieks in grief. It is done.

●●●●●

Bayo storms through the Elders' Dome with Leon in his arms. He places his body beside the door. Leon's breath grows faint. Rioma rushes down the steps.

"Where is Hale?" she asks urgently.

Bayo blubbers, "He's dead!" He falls to his knees and cries deeply. "Save him!" Rioma hurries to Leon's side. Deor enters the room, and they lift Leon from the floor and into the parlor.

"Ianna!" Rioma calls. "Ianna!" A moment later she shouts, "Where is she? His breath is weakening." Black bruises cover Leon's body.

Bayo walks into the parlor with whatever strength he has left.

Deor announces, "Ianna and Mary are gone."

Rioma's eyes are wide. "They what? Mary left?"

Bayo screams, "Rioma, do something—anything! Perhaps Ianna had a potion."

Rioma rushes upstairs and into Ianna's room. When she returns with a handful of vials, she sees Bayo kneeling beside a motionless, cold, pale body.

"It's too late," he says coolly. Tears seep from his red eyes. "It's done."

EPILOGUE

A great light illuminates the woods, blinding even the light of day and startling the voice of the siren to a standstill. Placing her hand over her eyes to see through the brightness, Ellionna jumps in fright. There is a massive Griffin rising into the sky before her. Its shimmering brown coat whooshes past, holding onto a lifeless young man in its front paws.

Robin dashes to her side when Ellionna spots what the Griffin left behind. She draws nearer toward the young man with strange veinlike markings all over his body. His every limb contorts violently as the effect of hearing her song.

Suddenly, the woods echo with his screeches. The places where his skin is bare, bruise before her eyes.

She gasps, rushing to his side. "Not again," she says.

Robin places her hand to her mouth, knowing how terrible Ellionna must be feeling. But the deed is done. "You have to finish your song, or he will suffer."

Ellionna takes Hale's face into her hands. "They usually die right away. Maybe . . . maybe he will live."

"Ellionna! He's in pain!"

Ellionna's hands shake, "He will live. He has to."

The ground rumbles and the trees sway. A large shadow looms over their heads, and the young girls look up to the sky. A jet-black Griffin with dazzling green eyes descends from the treetops, reaching out for the boy.

Robin grabs Ellionna straightaway, pulling her from the scene. The Griffin snatches Hale into his paws and flies away. Hale's heart-wrenching screams wane from afar like a dimming light.

About the Author

J.K. Noble grew up and resides in the Big Apple, where fantastical inspiration lives among the bright lights and colorful people. She envisions unique mythological creatures majestically roaming bustling streets and skimming the skies between skyscrapers. Absorbing fantasy stories in awe of the great magic each possesses, Noble soon learned that she, too, holds the same power as the mystic writers of old. Finally, Noble awakens in her debut novel, *Hale: The Rise of the Griffins*, but her imagination does not end there!

A free ebook edition is available with the purchase of this book.

To claim your free ebook edition:

Visit MorganJamesBOGO.com
Sign your name CLEARLY in the space
Complete the form and submit a photo of
the entire copyright page
You or your friend can download the ebook
to your preferred device

Morgan James BOGO™

A **FREE** ebook edition is available for you
or a friend with the purchase of this print book.

CLEARLY SIGN YOUR NAME ABOVE

Instructions to claim your free ebook edition:
1. Visit MorganJamesBOGO.com
2. Sign your name CLEARLY in the space above
3. Complete the form and submit a photo
   of this entire page
4. You or your friend can download the ebook
   to your preferred device

Print & Digital Together Forever.

Snap a photo   Free ebook   Read anywhere